STRANGE Academy
Bright Side

Bright Side

EMILY BRIGHT
DOYLE DORMAMMU
SHAYLEE MOONPEDDLE

ALVI BRORSON
IRIC BRORSON
DESSY

ZOE LAVEAU
TOTH
GUSLAUG

GERMÁN AGUILAR
CALVIN MORSE

STRANGE Academy

Skottie Young WRITER

Humberto Ramos ARTIST

Edgar Delgado COLOR ARTIST

VC's Clayton Cowles LETTERER

Humberto Ramos &
Edgar Delgado COVER ART

Jared K. Fletcher LOGO DESIGN

Danny Khazem &
Tom Groneman ASSISTANT EDITORS

Nick Lowe EDITOR

Doctor Strange
CREATED BY **STAN LEE** & **STEVE DITKO**

Jennifer Grünwald COLLECTION EDITOR

Daniel Kirchhoffer ASSISTANT EDITOR

Maia Loy ASSISTANT MANAGING EDITOR

Lisa Montalbano ASSISTANT MANAGING EDITOR

Jeff Youngquist VP PRODUCTION & SPECIAL PROJECTS

Jay Bowen BOOK DESIGNER

David Gabriel SVP PRINT, SALES & MARKETING

C.B. Cebulski EDITOR IN CHIEF

STRANGE ACADEMY: BRIGHT SIDE. Contains material originally published in magazine form as STRANGE ACADEMY (2020) #7-12. First printing 2021. ISBN 978-1-302-91951-1. Published by MARVEL WORLDWIDE, INC., a subsidiary of MARVEL ENTERTAINMENT, LLC. OFFICE OF PUBLICATION: 1290 Avenue of the Americas, New York, NY 10104. © 2021 MARVEL No similarity between any of the names, characters, persons, and/or institutions in this magazine with those of any living or dead person or institution is intended, and any such similarity which may exist is purely coincidental. **Printed in Canada.** KEVIN FEIGE, Chief Creative Officer; DAN BUCKLEY, President, Marvel Entertainment; JOE QUESADA, EVP & Creative Director; DAVID BOGART, Associate Publisher & SVP of Talent Affairs; TOM BREVOORT, VP, Executive Editor; NICK LOWE, Executive Editor, VP of Content, Digital Publishing; DAVID GABRIEL, VP of Print & Digital Publishing; JEFF YOUNGQUIST, VP of Production & Special Projects; ALEX MORALES, Director of Publishing Operations; DAN EDINGTON, Managing Editor; RICKEY PURDIN, Director of Talent Relations; JENNIFER GRÜNWALD, Senior Editor, Special Projects; SUSAN CRESPI, Production Manager; STAN LEE, Chairman Emeritus. For information regarding advertising in Marvel Comics or on Marvel.com, please contact Vit DeBellis, Custom Solutions & Integrated Advertising Manager, at vdebellis@marvel.com. For Marvel subscription inquiries, please call 888-511-5480. **Manufactured between 8/6/2021 and 9/7/2021 by SOLISCO PRINTERS, SCOTT, QC, CANADA.**

10 9 8 7 6 5 4 3 2 1

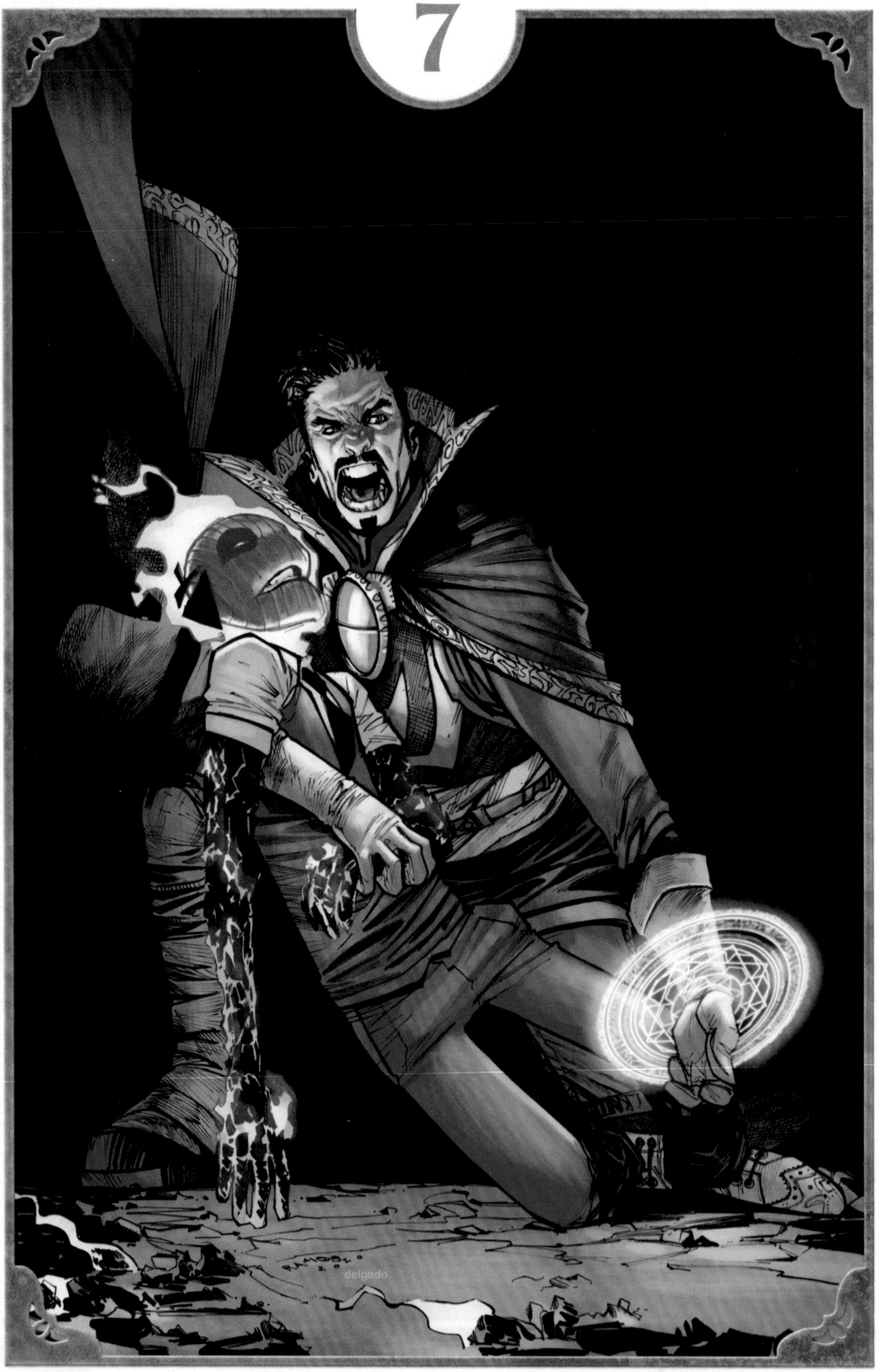
7

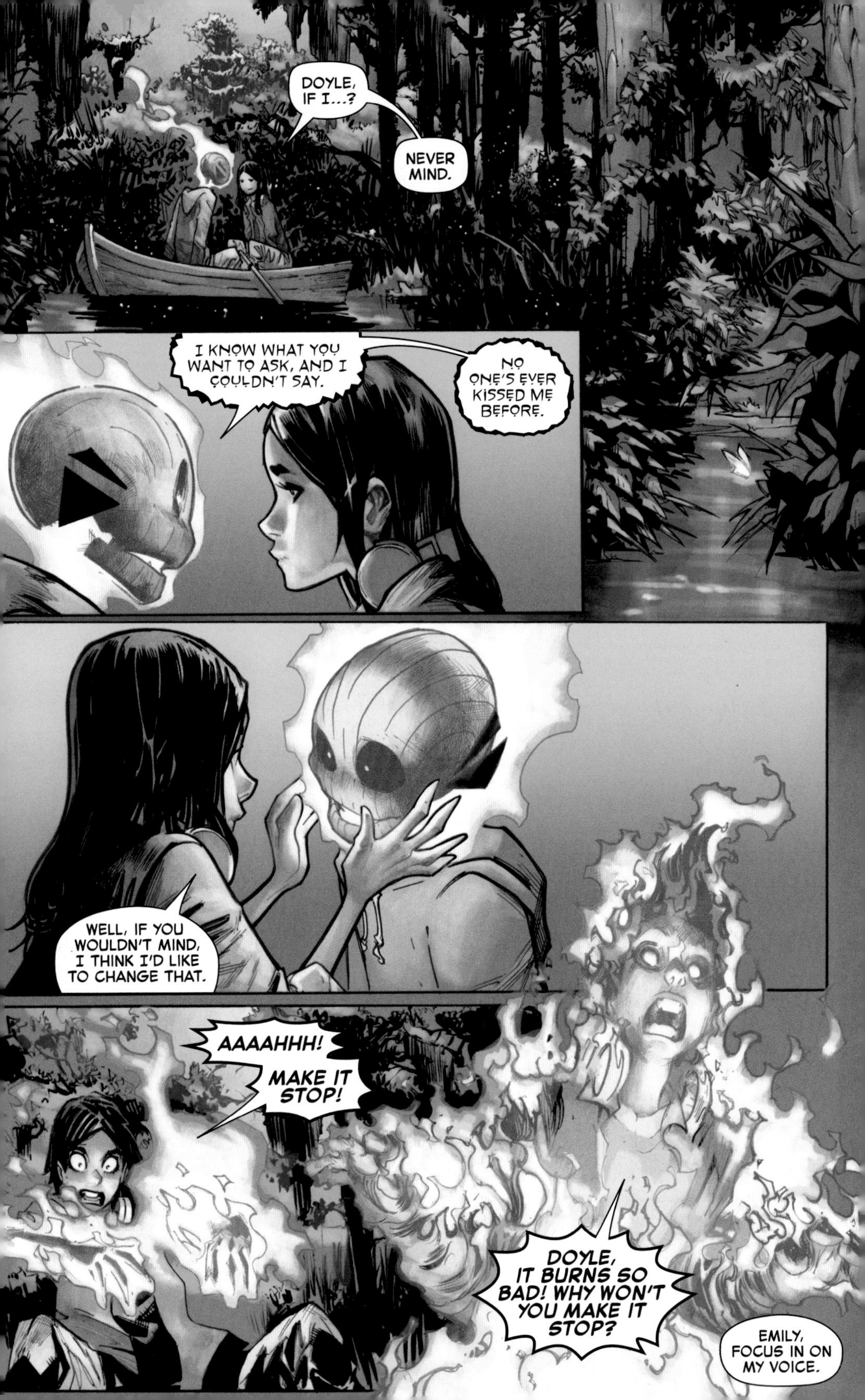
DOYLE, IF I...?
NEVER MIND.
I KNOW WHAT YOU WANT TO ASK, AND I COULDN'T SAY.
NO ONE'S EVER KISSED ME BEFORE.
WELL, IF YOU WOULDN'T MIND, I THINK I'D LIKE TO CHANGE THAT.
AAAAHHH!
MAKE IT STOP!
DOYLE, IT BURNS SO BAD! WHY WON'T YOU MAKE IT STOP?
EMILY, FOCUS IN ON MY VOICE.

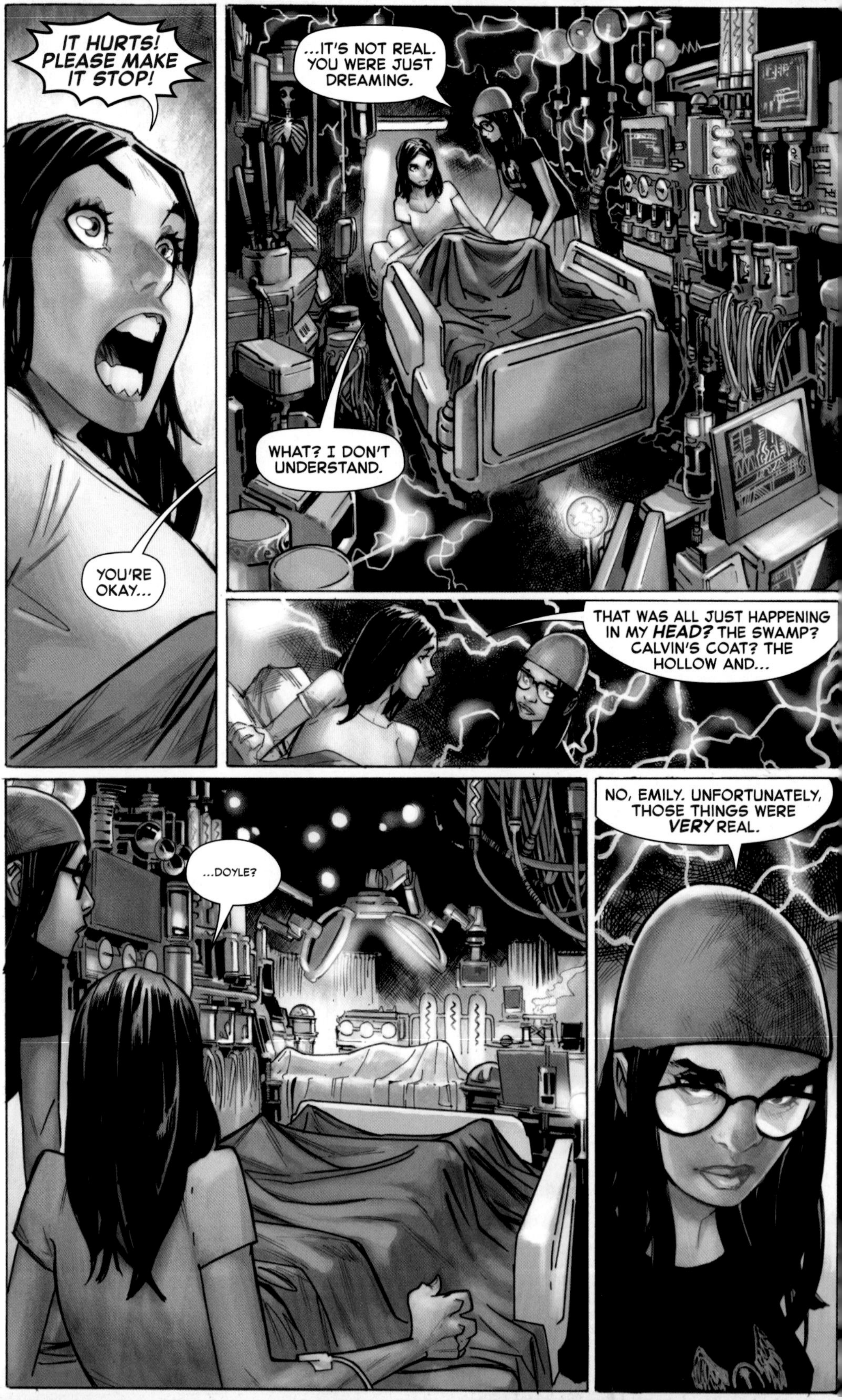
IT HURTS! PLEASE MAKE IT STOP!
YOU'RE OKAY...
...IT'S NOT REAL. YOU WERE JUST DREAMING.
WHAT? I DON'T UNDERSTAND.
THAT WAS ALL JUST HAPPENING IN MY HEAD? THE SWAMP? CALVIN'S COAT? THE HOLLOW AND...
...DOYLE?
NO, EMILY. UNFORTUNATELY, THOSE THINGS WERE VERY REAL.

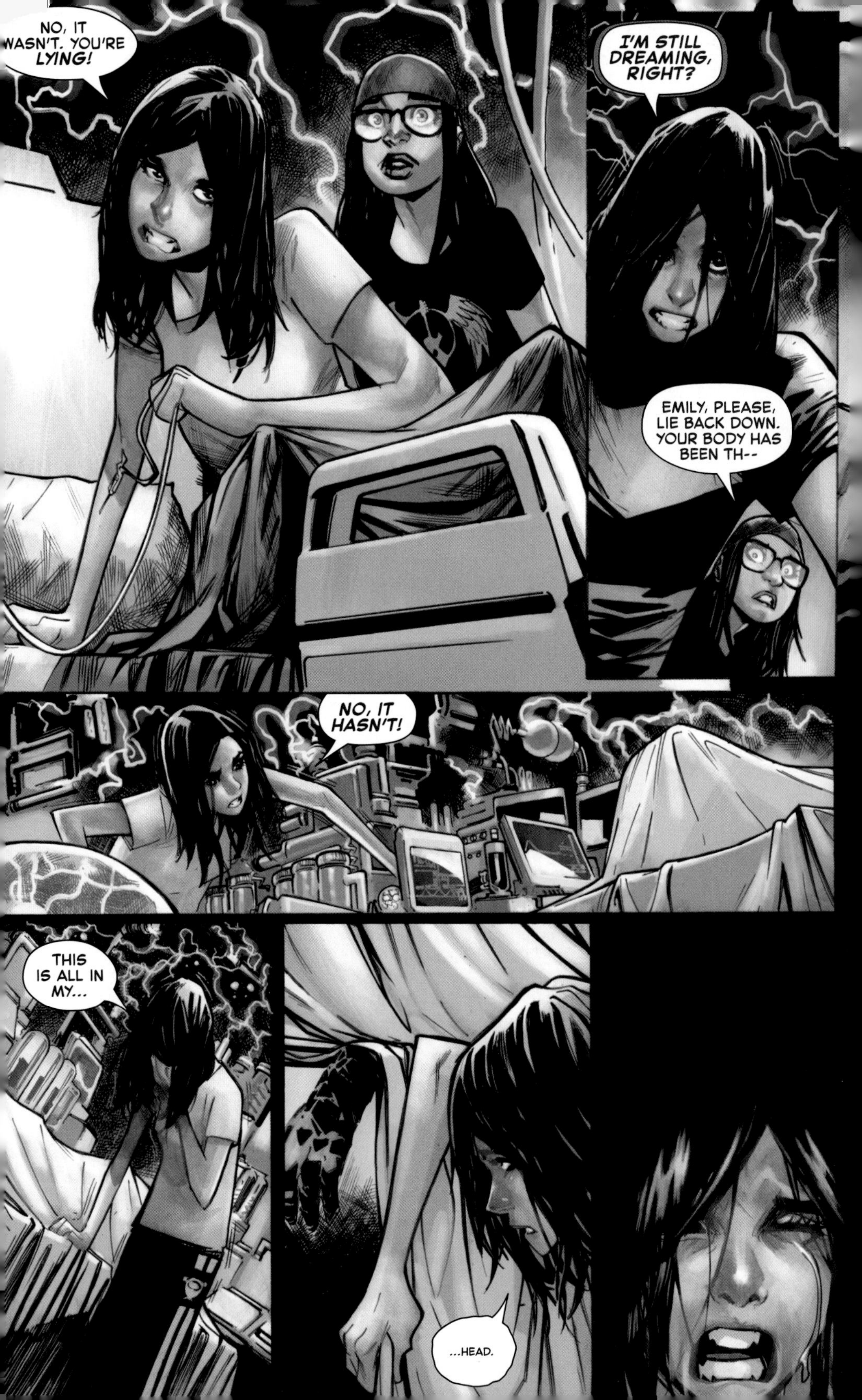
NO, IT WASN'T. YOU'RE LYING!
I'M STILL DREAMING, RIGHT?
EMILY, PLEASE, LIE BACK DOWN. YOUR BODY HAS BEEN TH--
NO, IT HASN'T!
THIS IS ALL IN MY...
...HEAD.

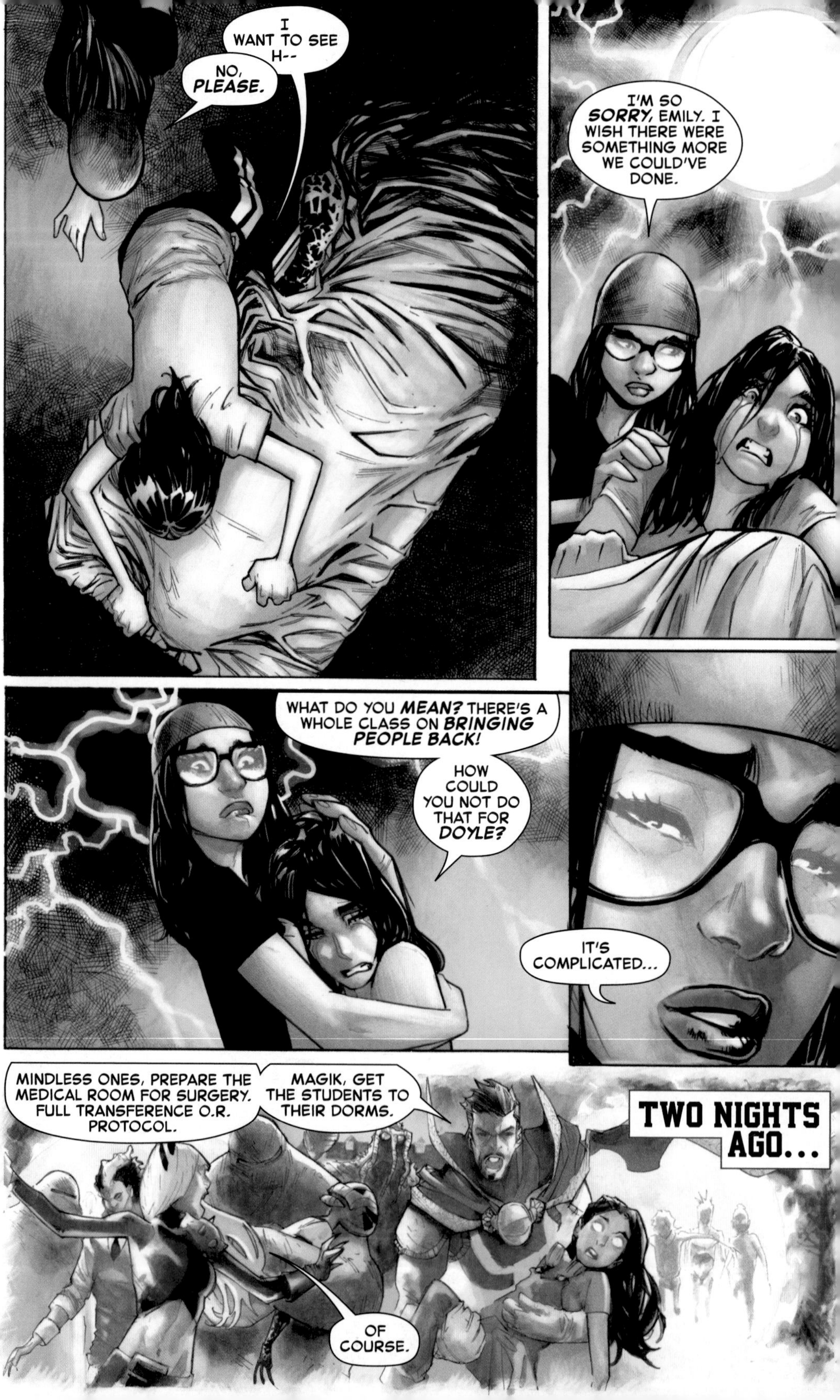
I WANT TO SEE H--
NO, PLEASE.
I'M SO SORRY, EMILY. I WISH THERE WERE SOMETHING MORE WE COULD'VE DONE.
WHAT DO YOU MEAN? THERE'S A WHOLE CLASS ON BRINGING PEOPLE BACK!
HOW COULD YOU NOT DO THAT FOR DOYLE?
IT'S COMPLICATED...
TWO NIGHTS AGO...
MINDLESS ONES, PREPARE THE MEDICAL ROOM FOR SURGERY. FULL TRANSFERENCE O.R. PROTOCOL.
MAGIK, GET THE STUDENTS TO THEIR DORMS.
OF COURSE.

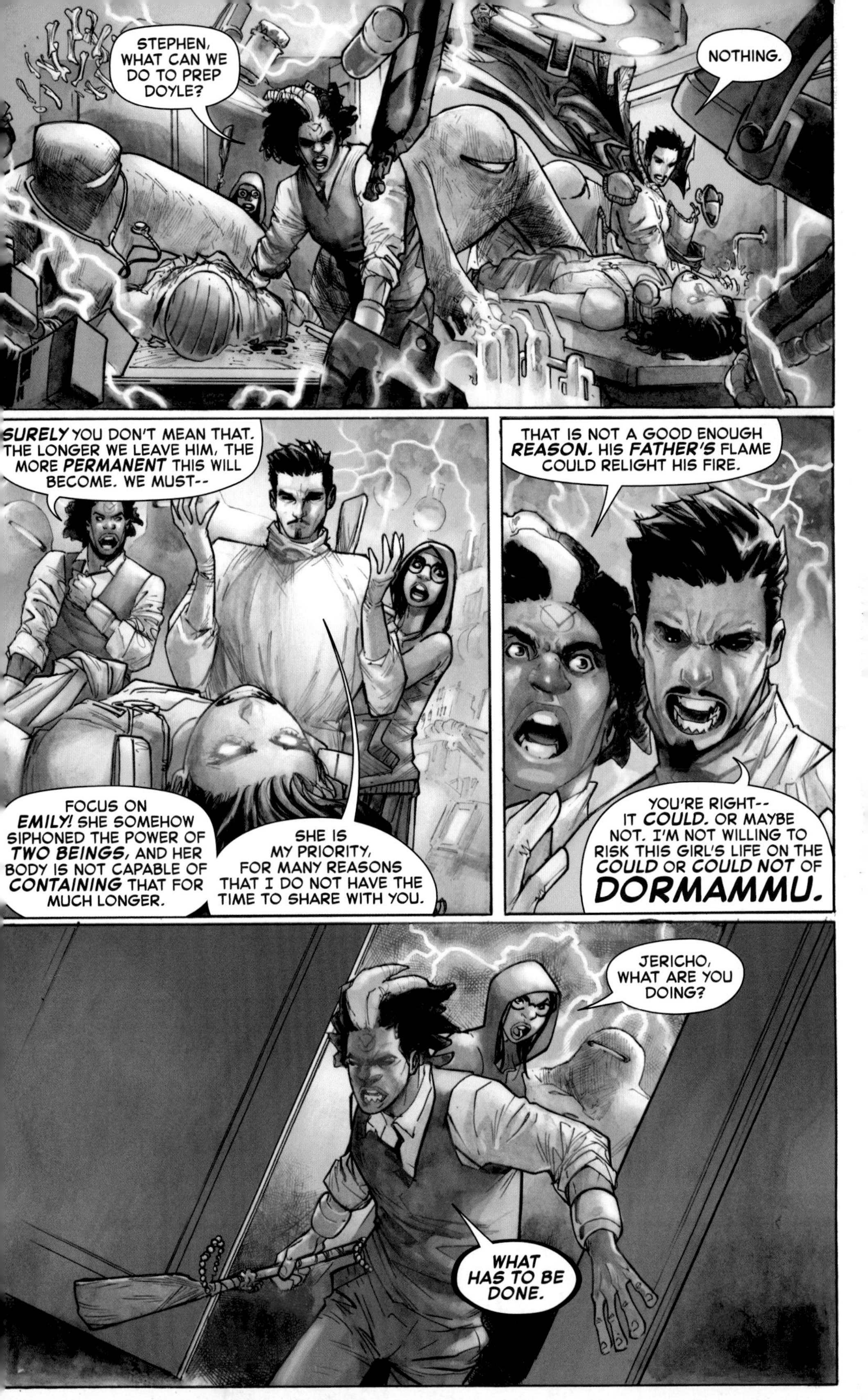

STEPHEN, WHAT CAN WE DO TO PREP DOYLE?
NOTHING.
SURELY YOU DON'T MEAN THAT. THE LONGER WE LEAVE HIM, THE MORE PERMANENT THIS WILL BECOME. WE MUST--
FOCUS ON EMILY! SHE SOMEHOW SIPHONED THE POWER OF TWO BEINGS, AND HER BODY IS NOT CAPABLE OF CONTAINING THAT FOR MUCH LONGER.
SHE IS MY PRIORITY, FOR MANY REASONS THAT I DO NOT HAVE THE TIME TO SHARE WITH YOU.
THAT IS NOT A GOOD ENOUGH REASON. HIS FATHER'S FLAME COULD RELIGHT HIS FIRE.
YOU'RE RIGHT-- IT COULD. OR MAYBE NOT. I'M NOT WILLING TO RISK THIS GIRL'S LIFE ON THE COULD OR COULD NOT OF DORMAMMU.
JERICHO, WHAT ARE YOU DOING?
WHAT HAS TO BE DONE.

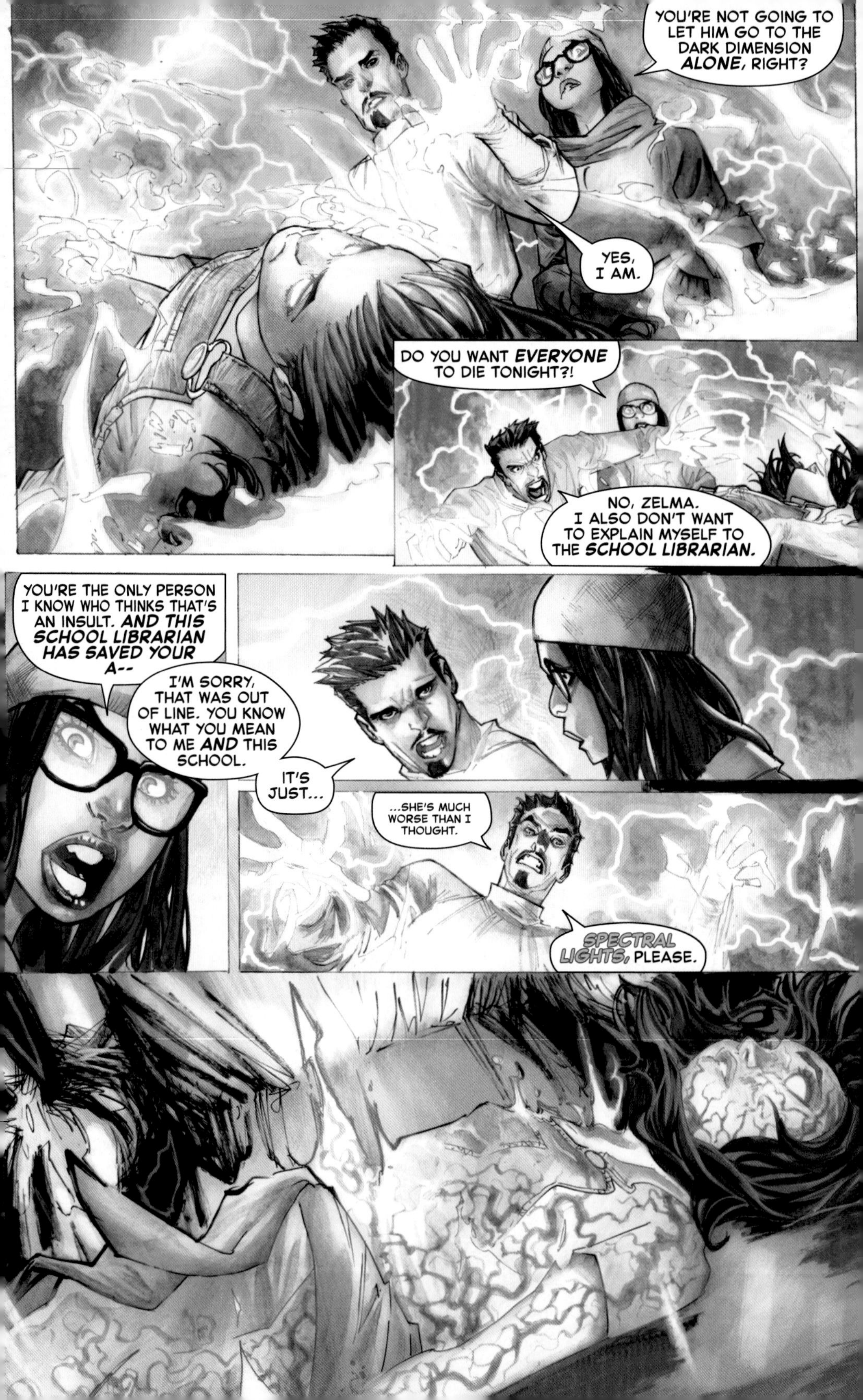

YOU'RE NOT GOING TO LET HIM GO TO THE DARK DIMENSION ALONE, RIGHT?
YES, I AM.
DO YOU WANT EVERYONE TO DIE TONIGHT?!
NO, ZELMA. I ALSO DON'T WANT TO EXPLAIN MYSELF TO THE SCHOOL LIBRARIAN.
YOU'RE THE ONLY PERSON I KNOW WHO THINKS THAT'S AN INSULT. AND THIS SCHOOL LIBRARIAN HAS SAVED YOUR A--
I'M SORRY, THAT WAS OUT OF LINE. YOU KNOW WHAT YOU MEAN TO ME AND THIS SCHOOL.
IT'S JUST...
...SHE'S MUCH WORSE THAN I THOUGHT.
SPECTRAL LIGHTS, PLEASE.

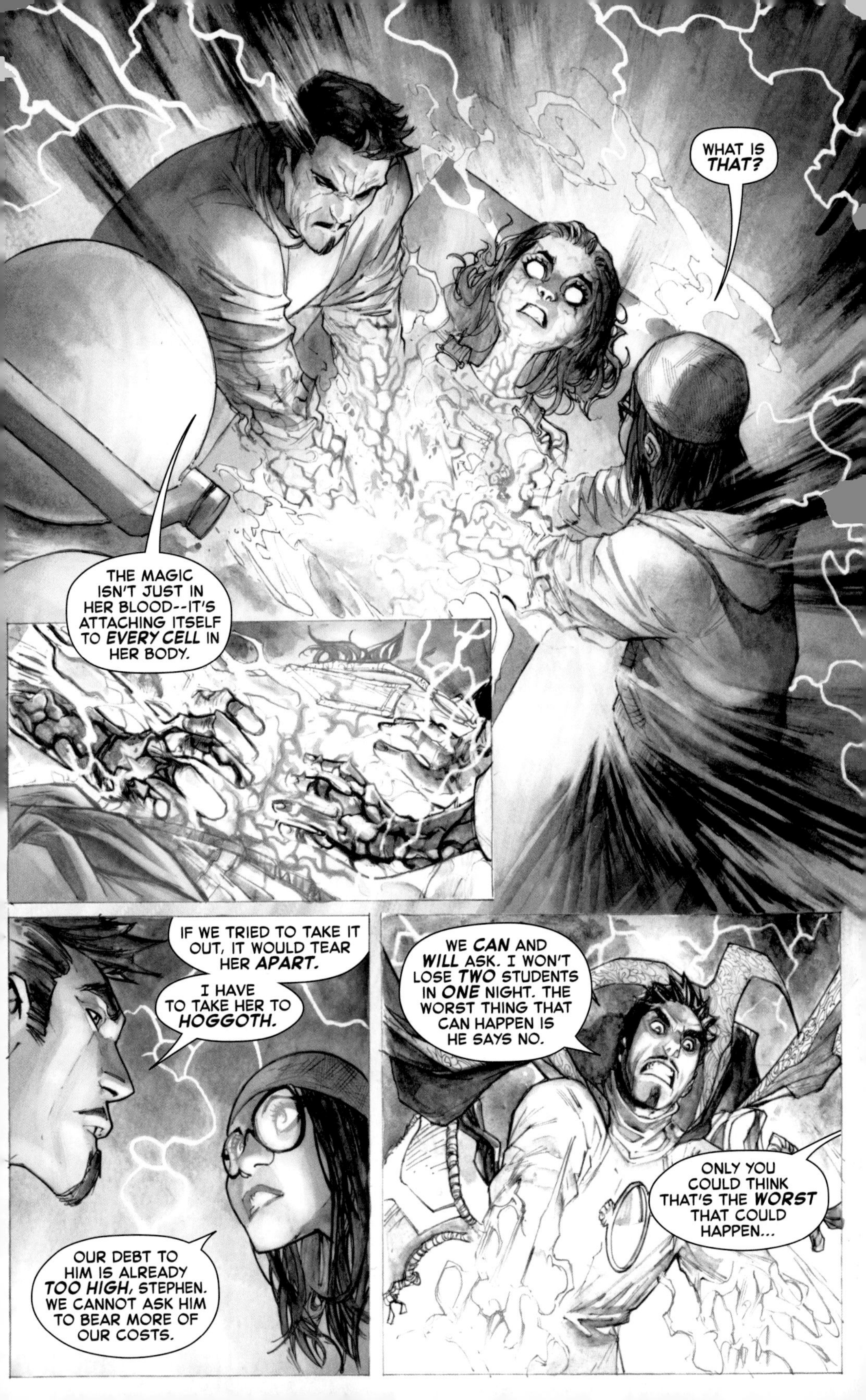
WHAT IS THAT?
THE MAGIC ISN'T JUST IN HER BLOOD--IT'S ATTACHING ITSELF TO EVERY CELL IN HER BODY.
IF WE TRIED TO TAKE IT OUT, IT WOULD TEAR HER APART.
I HAVE TO TAKE HER TO HOGGOTH.
OUR DEBT TO HIM IS ALREADY TOO HIGH, STEPHEN. WE CANNOT ASK HIM TO BEAR MORE OF OUR COSTS.
WE CAN AND WILL ASK. I WON'T LOSE TWO STUDENTS IN ONE NIGHT. THE WORST THING THAT CAN HAPPEN IS HE SAYS NO.
ONLY YOU COULD THINK THAT'S THE WORST THAT COULD HAPPEN...

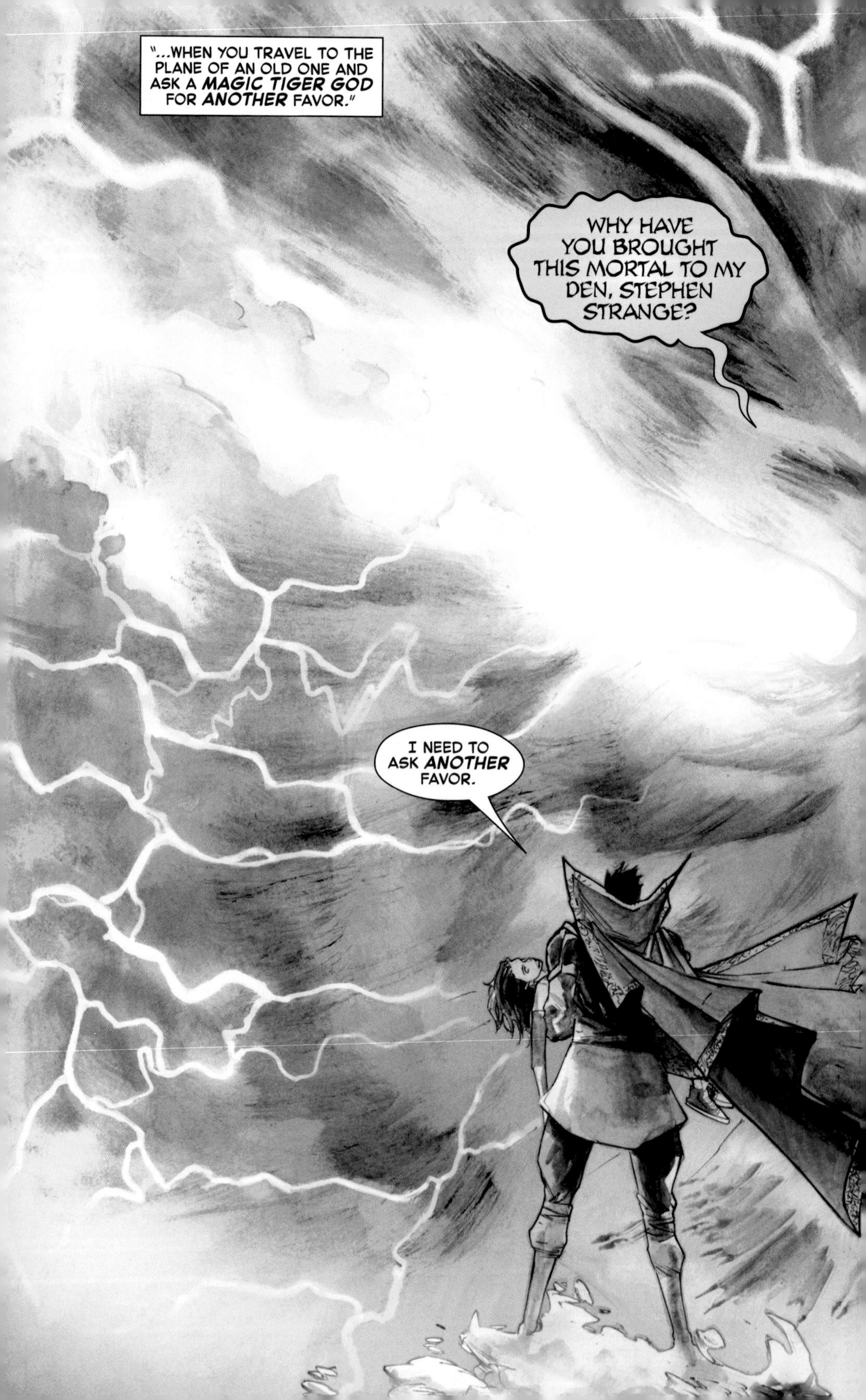
"...WHEN YOU TRAVEL TO THE PLANE OF AN OLD ONE AND ASK A *MAGIC TIGER GOD* FOR *ANOTHER* FAVOR."
WHY HAVE YOU BROUGHT THIS MORTAL TO MY DEN, STEPHEN STRANGE?
I NEED TO ASK *ANOTHER* FAVOR.

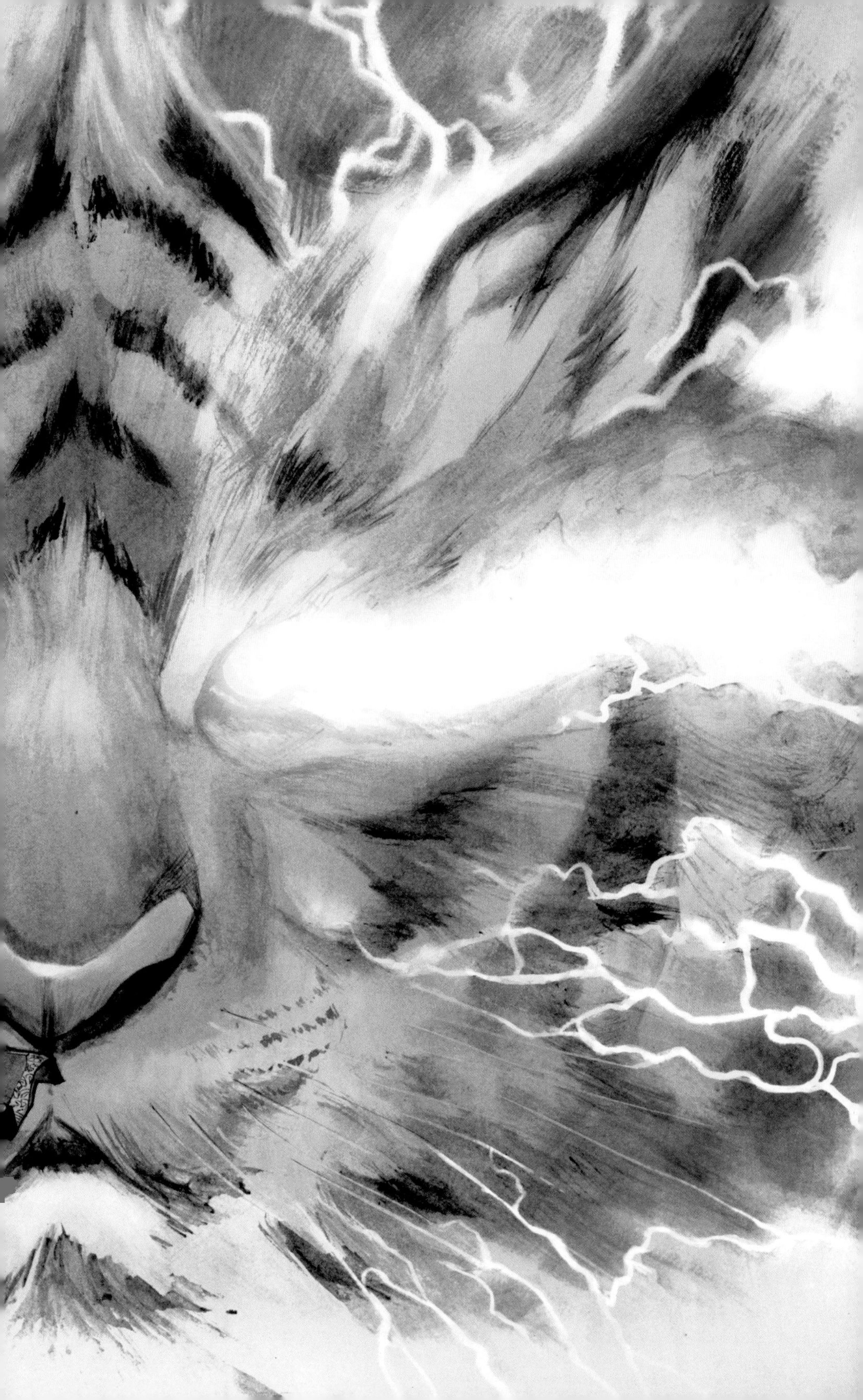

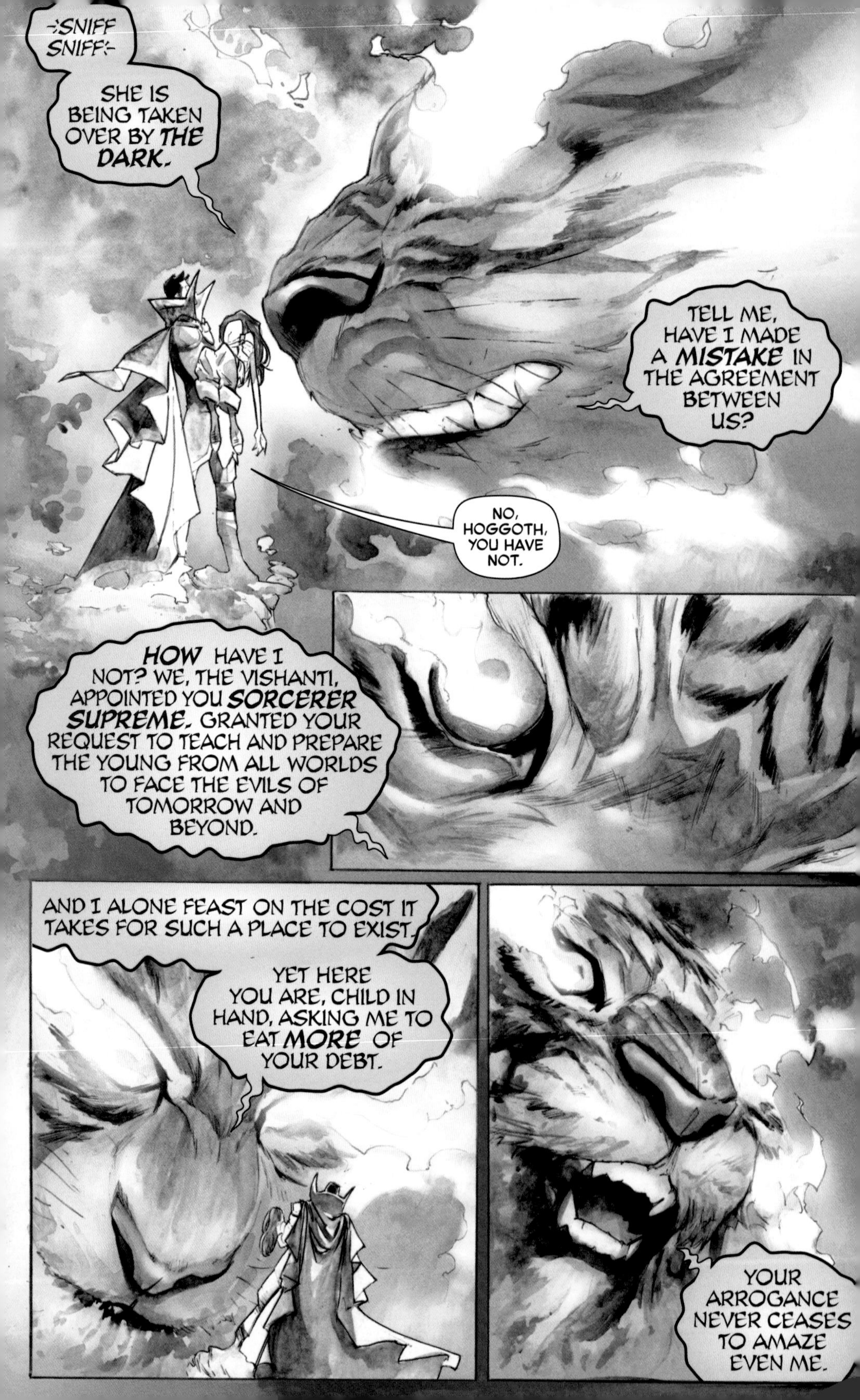
-SNIFF SNIFF-
SHE IS BEING TAKEN OVER BY THE DARK.
TELL ME, HAVE I MADE A MISTAKE IN THE AGREEMENT BETWEEN US?
NO, HOGGOTH, YOU HAVE NOT.
HOW HAVE I NOT? WE, THE VISHANTI, APPOINTED YOU SORCERER SUPREME. GRANTED YOUR REQUEST TO TEACH AND PREPARE THE YOUNG FROM ALL WORLDS TO FACE THE EVILS OF TOMORROW AND BEYOND.
AND I ALONE FEAST ON THE COST IT TAKES FOR SUCH A PLACE TO EXIST.
YET HERE YOU ARE, CHILD IN HAND, ASKING ME TO EAT MORE OF YOUR DEBT.
YOUR ARROGANCE NEVER CEASES TO AMAZE EVEN ME.

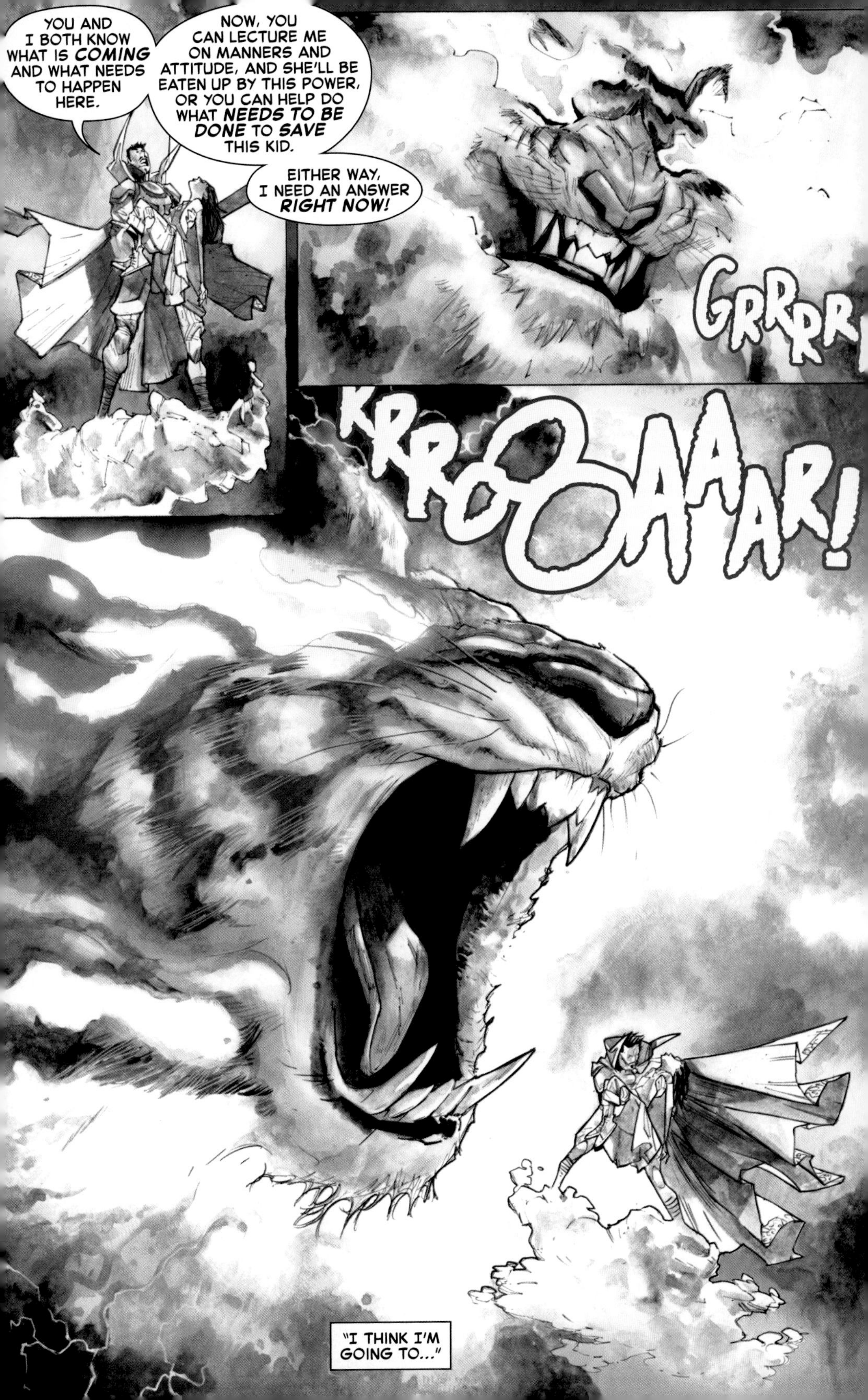
YOU AND I BOTH KNOW WHAT IS COMING AND WHAT NEEDS TO HAPPEN HERE.
NOW, YOU CAN LECTURE ME ON MANNERS AND ATTITUDE, AND SHE'LL BE EATEN UP BY THIS POWER, OR YOU CAN HELP DO WHAT NEEDS TO BE DONE TO SAVE THIS KID.
EITHER WAY, I NEED AN ANSWER RIGHT NOW!
GRRRR
KRROOOAAAAR!
"I THINK I'M GOING TO..."

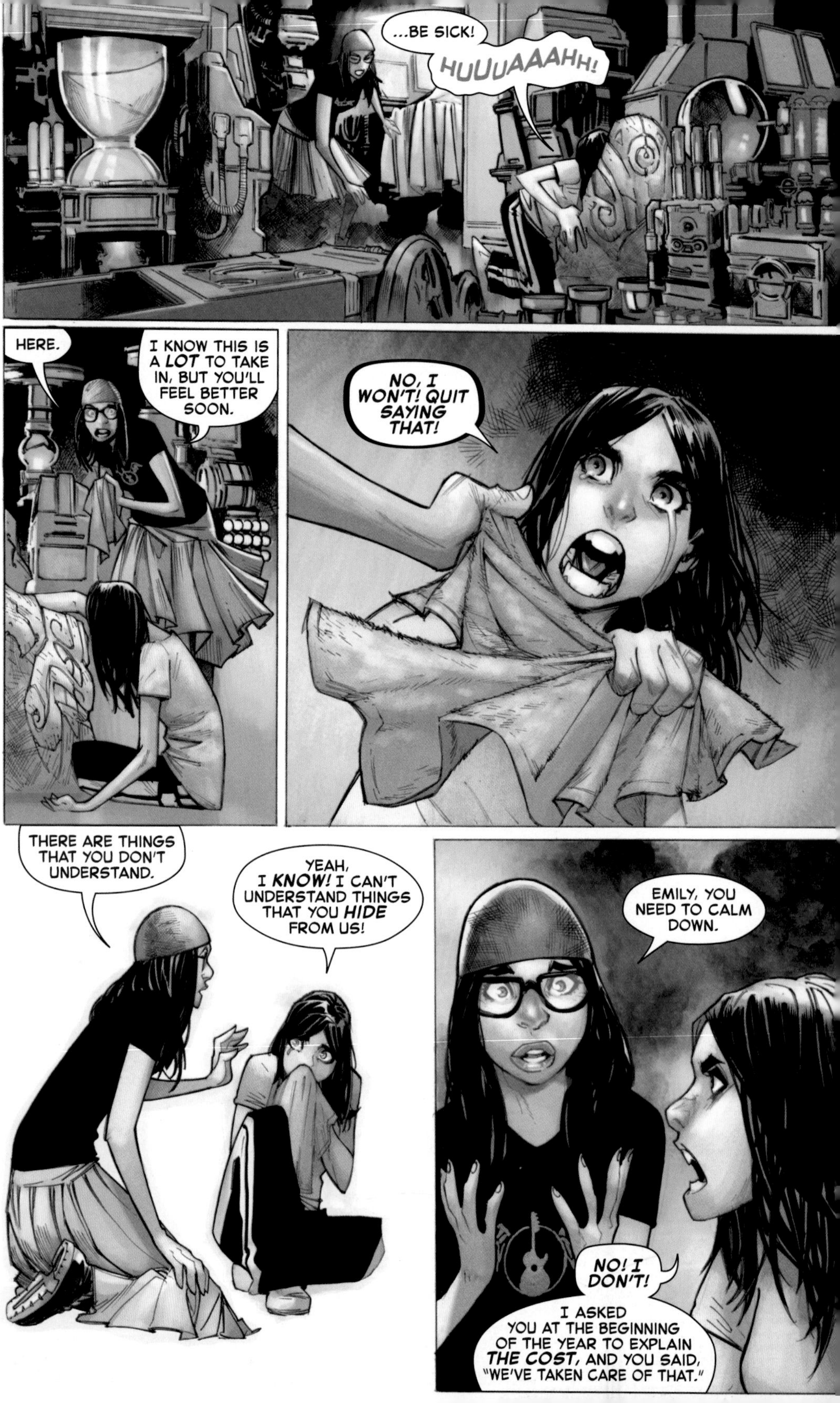

...BE SICK!
HUUUAAAHH!
HERE.
I KNOW THIS IS A LOT TO TAKE IN, BUT YOU'LL FEEL BETTER SOON.
NO, I WON'T! QUIT SAYING THAT!
THERE ARE THINGS THAT YOU DON'T UNDERSTAND.
YEAH, I KNOW! I CAN'T UNDERSTAND THINGS THAT YOU HIDE FROM US!
EMILY, YOU NEED TO CALM DOWN.
NO! I DON'T!
I ASKED YOU AT THE BEGINNING OF THE YEAR TO EXPLAIN THE COST, AND YOU SAID, "WE'VE TAKEN CARE OF THAT."

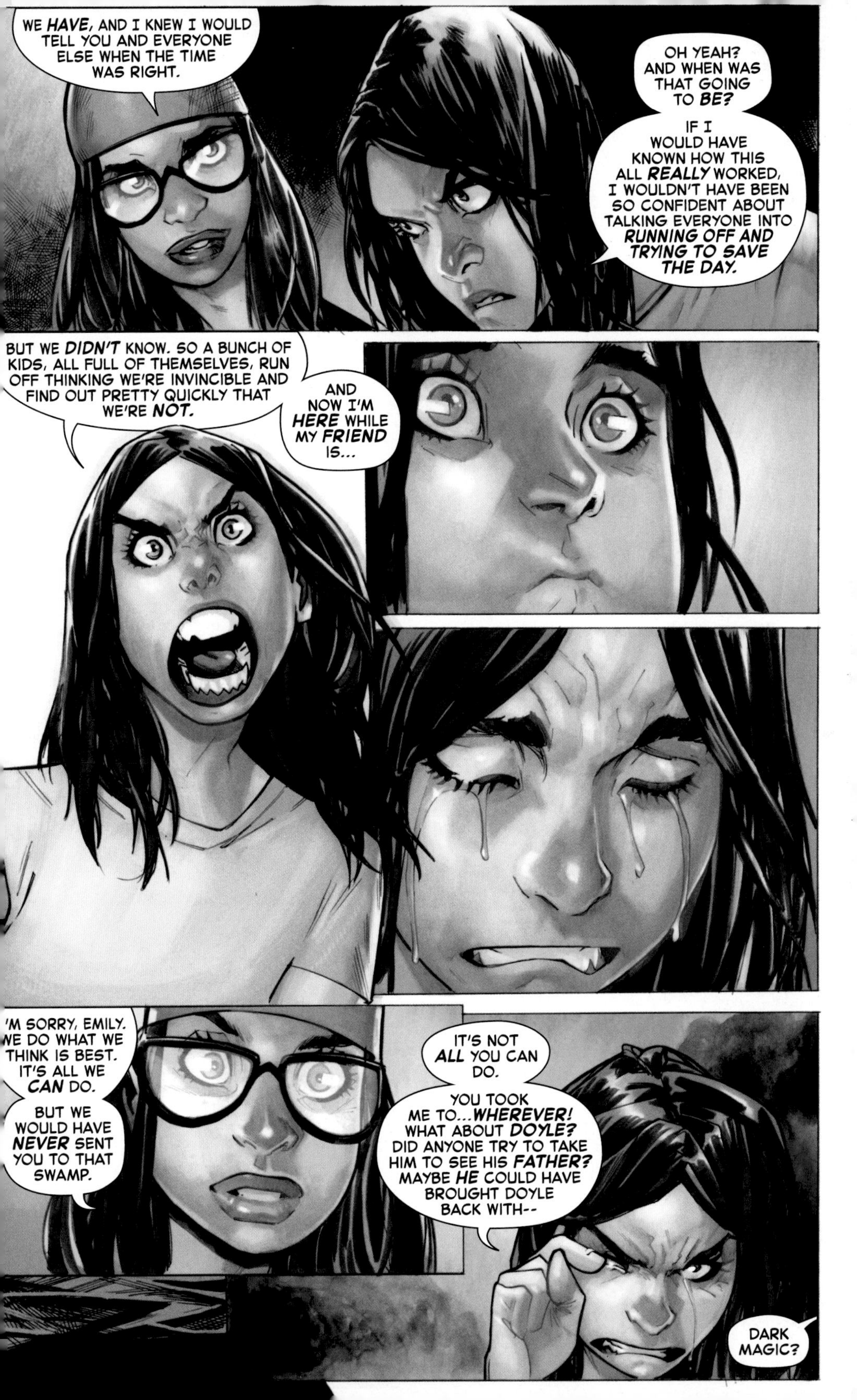
WE HAVE, AND I KNEW I WOULD TELL YOU AND EVERYONE ELSE WHEN THE TIME WAS RIGHT.
OH YEAH? AND WHEN WAS THAT GOING TO BE?
IF I WOULD HAVE KNOWN HOW THIS ALL REALLY WORKED, I WOULDN'T HAVE BEEN SO CONFIDENT ABOUT TALKING EVERYONE INTO RUNNING OFF AND TRYING TO SAVE THE DAY.
BUT WE DIDN'T KNOW. SO A BUNCH OF KIDS, ALL FULL OF THEMSELVES, RUN OFF THINKING WE'RE INVINCIBLE AND FIND OUT PRETTY QUICKLY THAT WE'RE NOT.
AND NOW I'M HERE WHILE MY FRIEND IS...
I'M SORRY, EMILY. WE DO WHAT WE THINK IS BEST. IT'S ALL WE CAN DO.
BUT WE WOULD HAVE NEVER SENT YOU TO THAT SWAMP.
IT'S NOT ALL YOU CAN DO.
YOU TOOK ME TO...WHEREVER! WHAT ABOUT DOYLE? DID ANYONE TRY TO TAKE HIM TO SEE HIS FATHER? MAYBE HE COULD HAVE BROUGHT DOYLE BACK WITH--
DARK MAGIC?

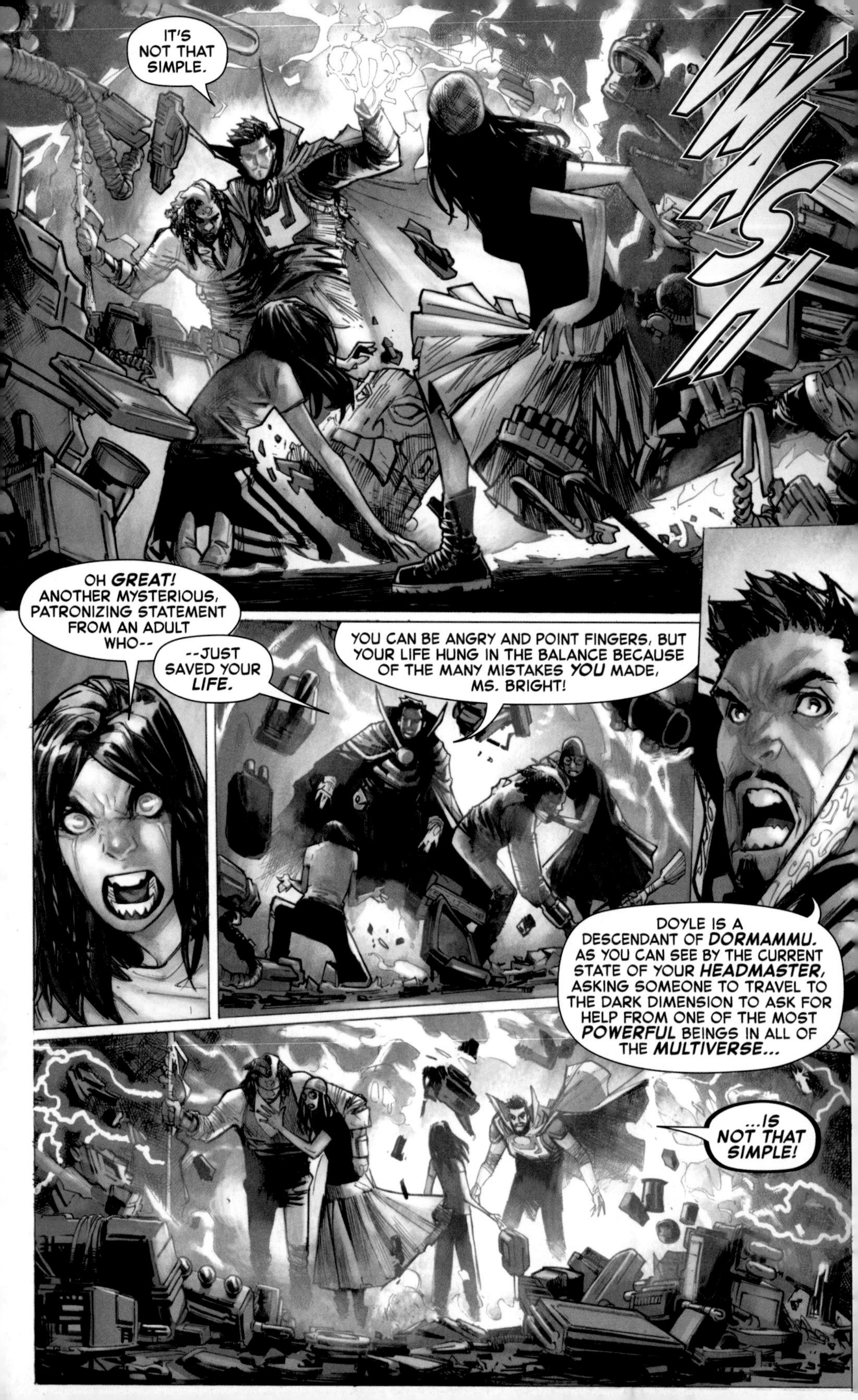
IT'S NOT THAT SIMPLE.
VWASH
OH GREAT! ANOTHER MYSTERIOUS, PATRONIZING STATEMENT FROM AN ADULT WHO--
--JUST SAVED YOUR LIFE.
YOU CAN BE ANGRY AND POINT FINGERS, BUT YOUR LIFE HUNG IN THE BALANCE BECAUSE OF THE MANY MISTAKES YOU MADE, MS. BRIGHT!
DOYLE IS A DESCENDANT OF DORMAMMU. AS YOU CAN SEE BY THE CURRENT STATE OF YOUR HEADMASTER, ASKING SOMEONE TO TRAVEL TO THE DARK DIMENSION TO ASK FOR HELP FROM ONE OF THE MOST POWERFUL BEINGS IN ALL OF THE MULTIVERSE...
...IS NOT THAT SIMPLE!

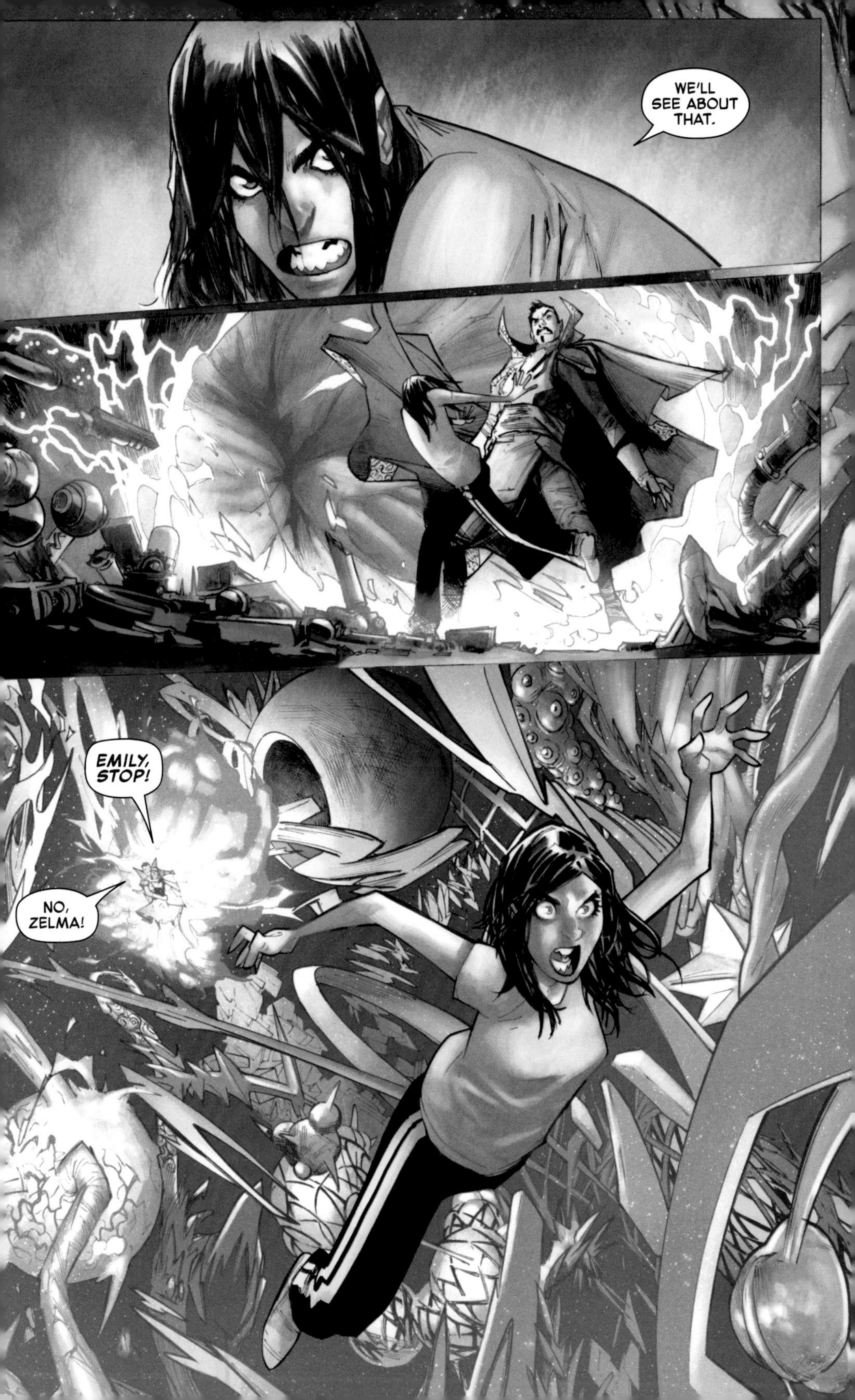
WE'LL SEE ABOUT THAT.
EMILY, STOP!
NO, ZELMA!

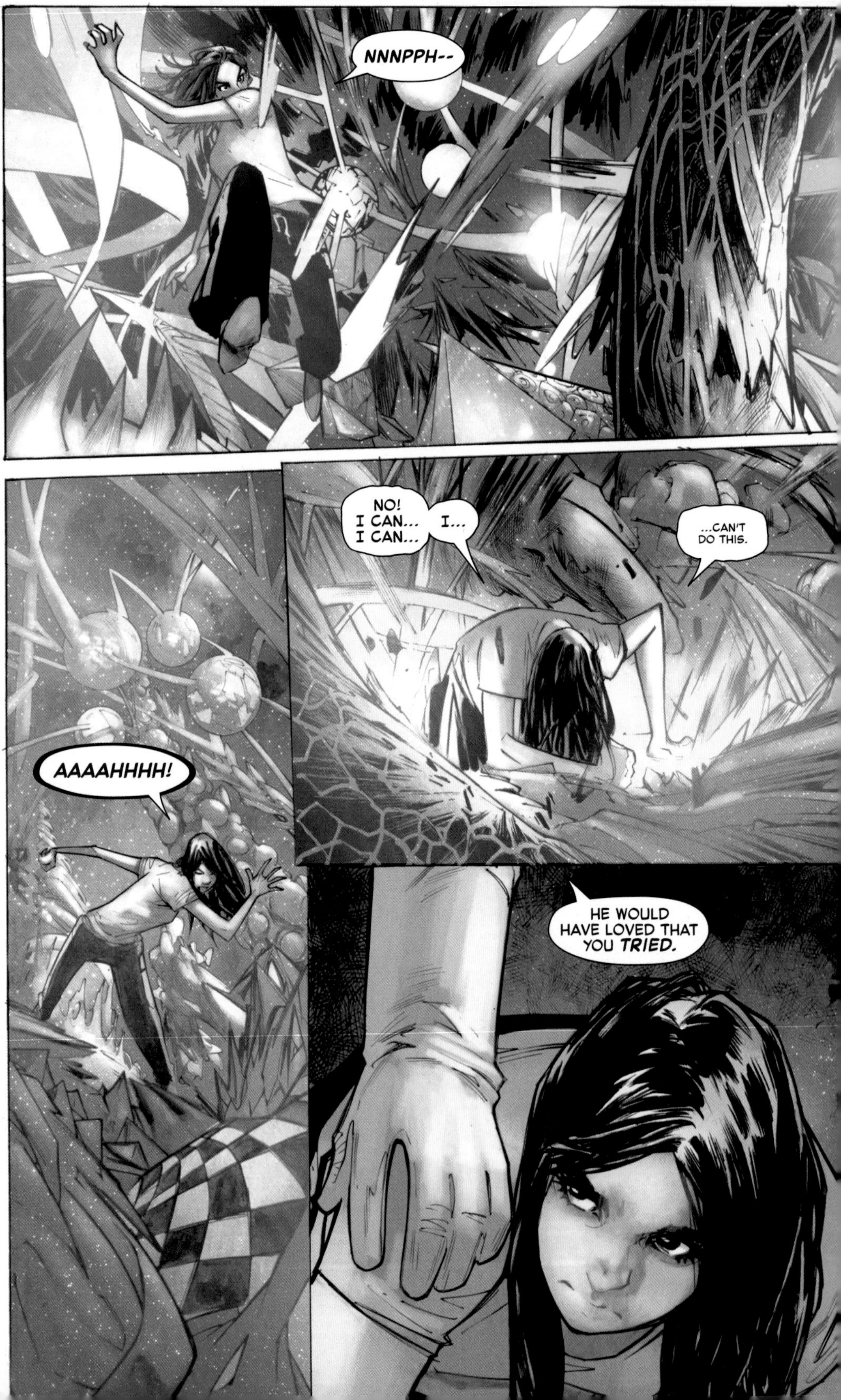
NNNPPH--
AAAAHHHH!
NO! I CAN... I CAN...
I...
...CAN'T DO THIS.
HE WOULD HAVE LOVED THAT YOU TRIED.

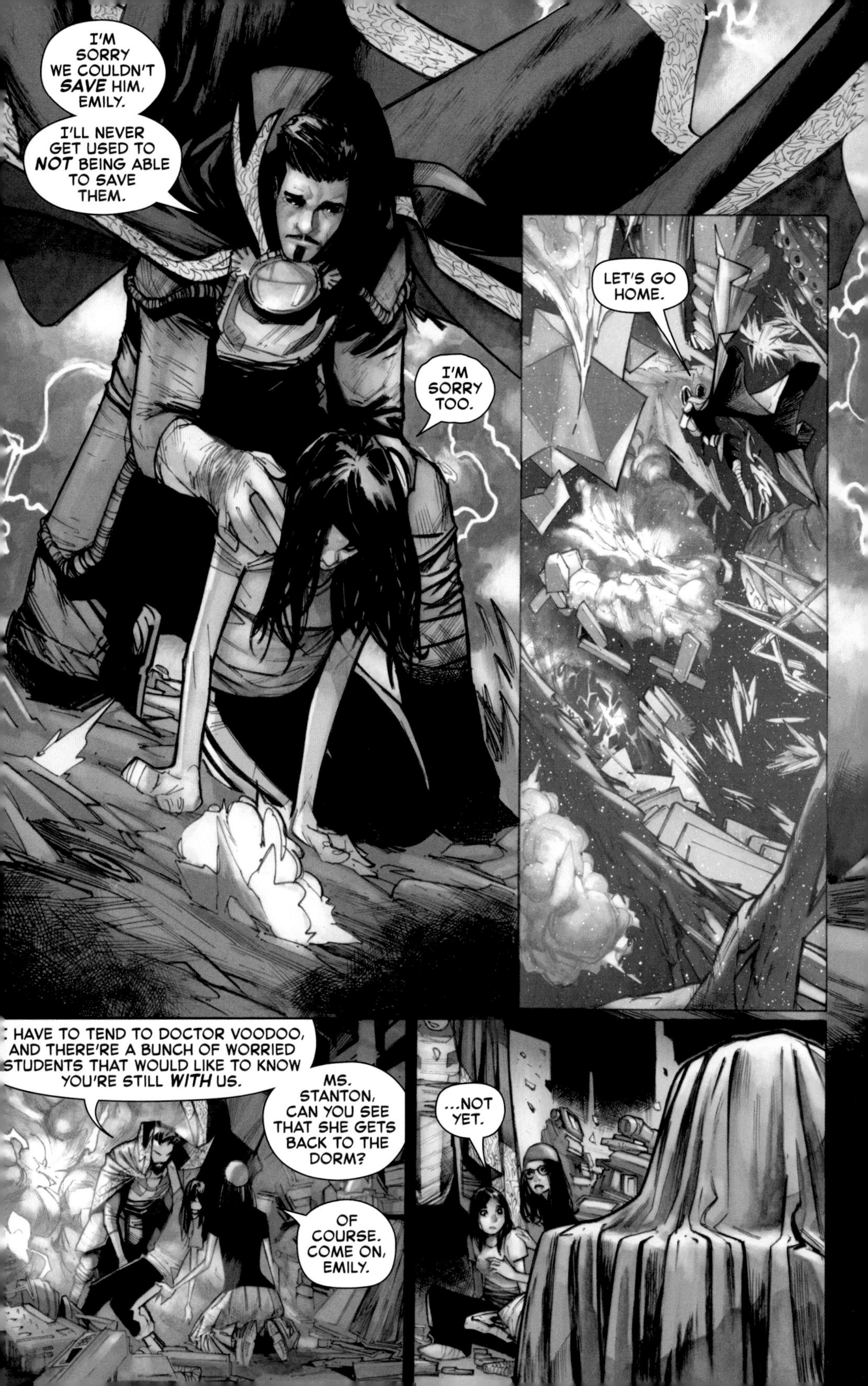
I'M SORRY WE COULDN'T *SAVE* HIM, EMILY.
I'LL NEVER GET USED TO *NOT* BEING ABLE TO SAVE THEM.
I'M SORRY TOO.
LET'S GO HOME.
I HAVE TO TEND TO DOCTOR VOODOO, AND THERE'RE A BUNCH OF WORRIED STUDENTS THAT WOULD LIKE TO KNOW YOU'RE STILL *WITH* US.
MS. STANTON, CAN YOU SEE THAT SHE GETS BACK TO THE DORM?
OF COURSE. COME ON, EMILY.
...NOT YET.

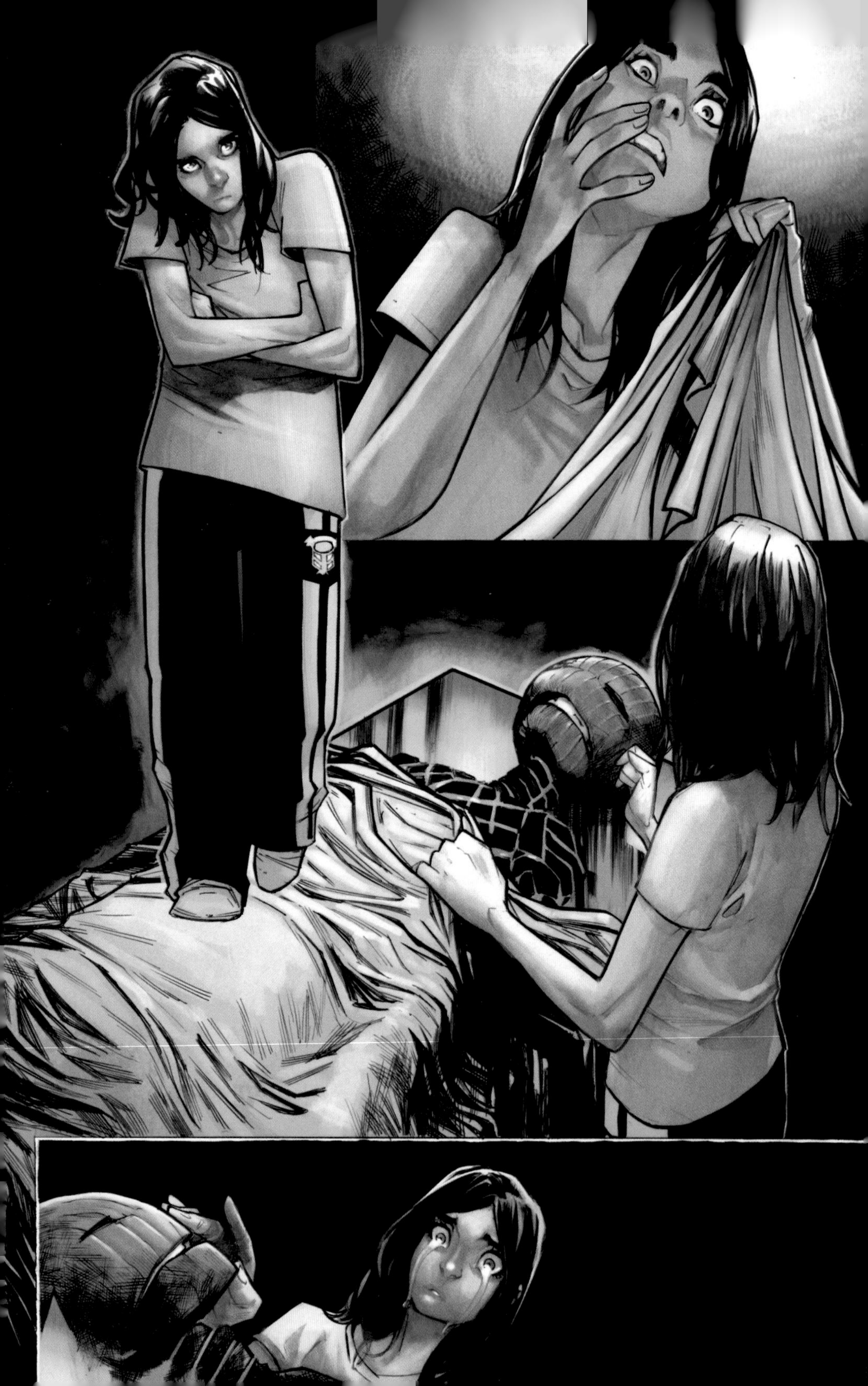

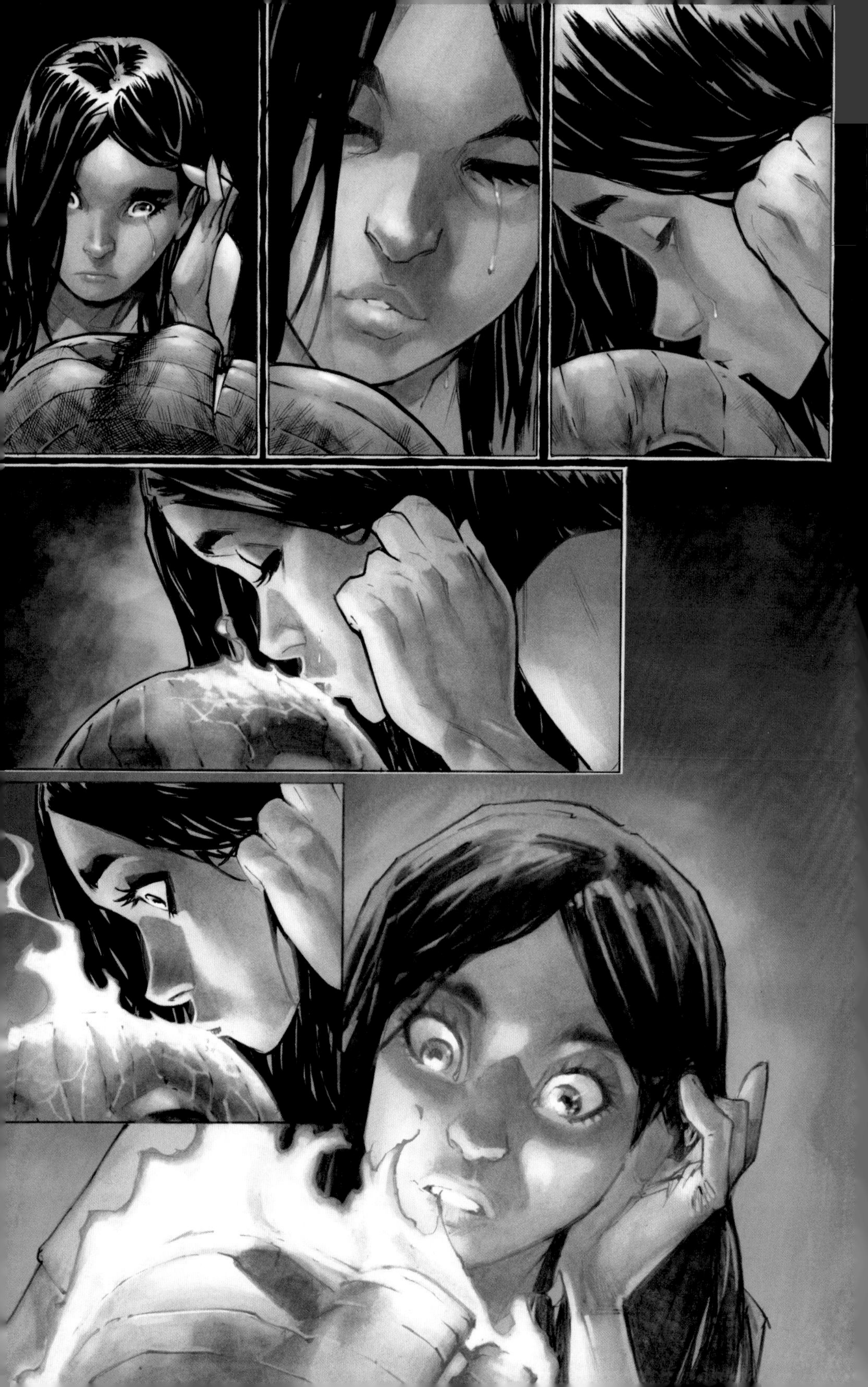

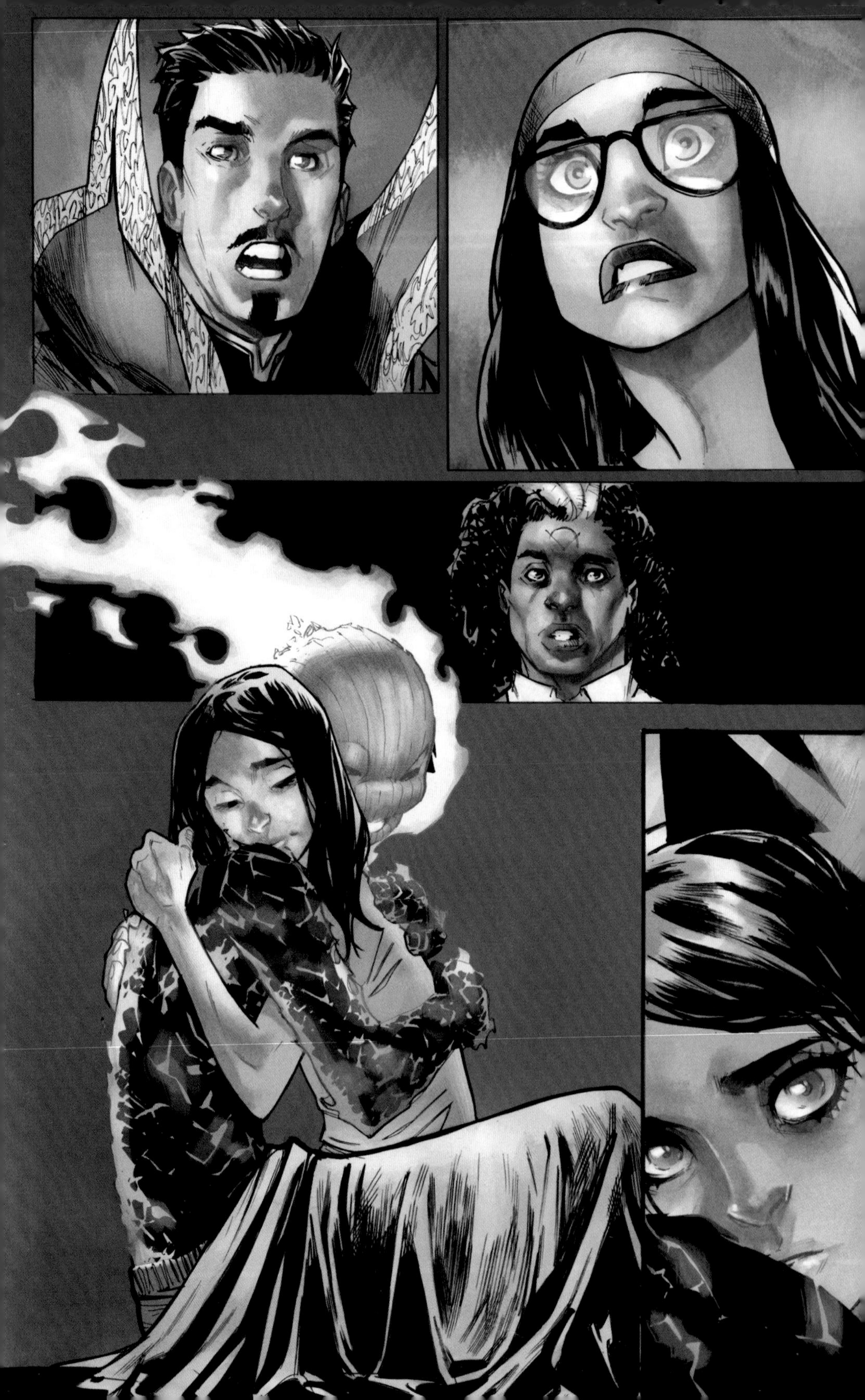

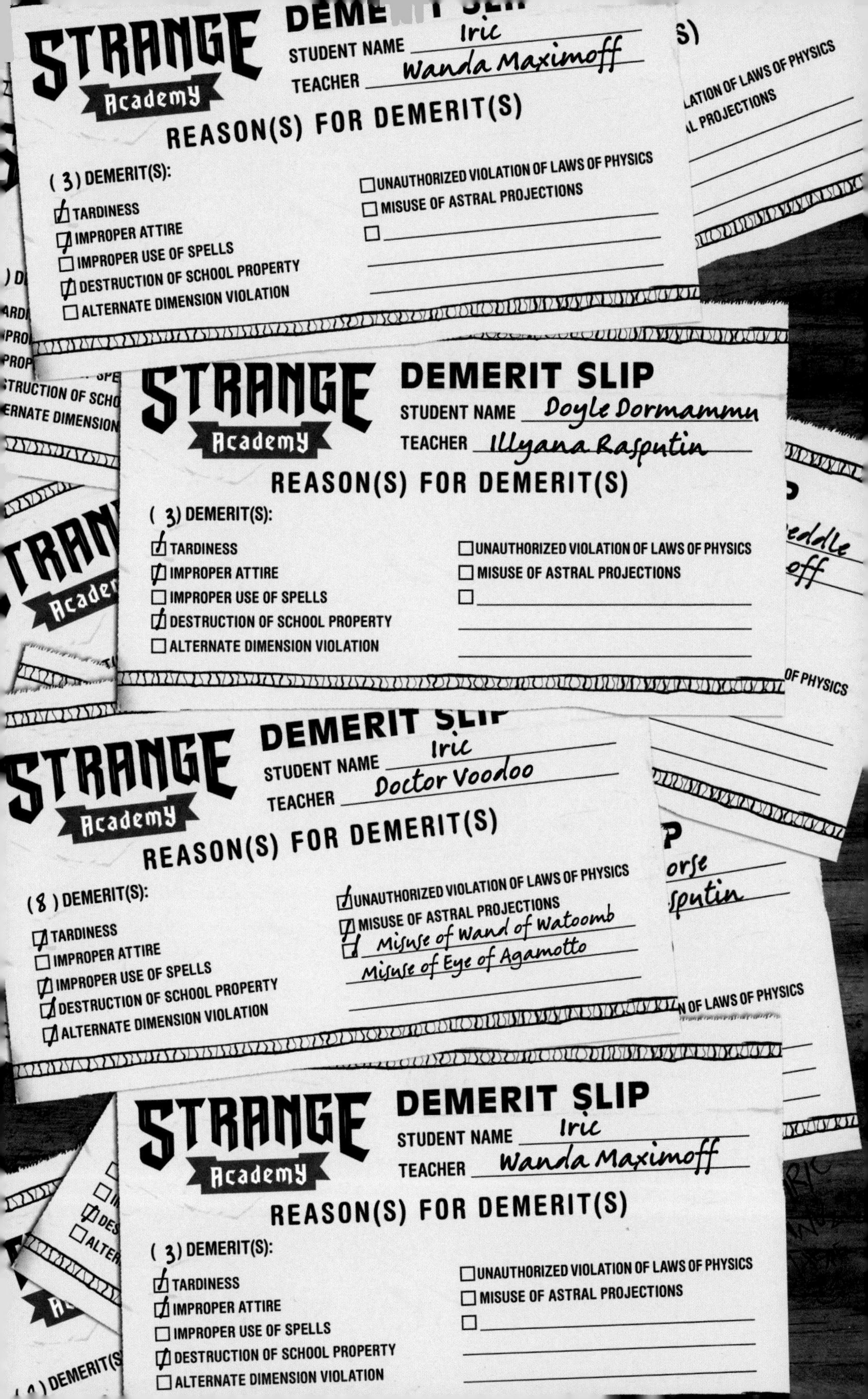
STRANGE Academy
STUDENT NAME Iric
TEACHER Wanda Maximoff
REASON(S) FOR DEMERIT(S)
(3) DEMERIT(S):
☑ TARDINESS
☑ IMPROPER ATTIRE
☐ IMPROPER USE OF SPELLS
☑ DESTRUCTION OF SCHOOL PROPERTY
☐ ALTERNATE DIMENSION VIOLATION
☐ UNAUTHORIZED VIOLATION OF LAWS OF PHYSICS
☐ MISUSE OF ASTRAL PROJECTIONS
☐
STRANGE Academy
DEMERIT SLIP
STUDENT NAME Doyle Dormammu
TEACHER Illyana Rasputin
REASON(S) FOR DEMERIT(S)
(3) DEMERIT(S):
☑ TARDINESS
☑ IMPROPER ATTIRE
☐ IMPROPER USE OF SPELLS
☑ DESTRUCTION OF SCHOOL PROPERTY
☐ ALTERNATE DIMENSION VIOLATION
☐ UNAUTHORIZED VIOLATION OF LAWS OF PHYSICS
☐ MISUSE OF ASTRAL PROJECTIONS
☐
STRANGE Academy
DEMERIT SLIP
STUDENT NAME Iric
TEACHER Doctor Voodoo
REASON(S) FOR DEMERIT(S)
(8) DEMERIT(S):
☑ TARDINESS
☐ IMPROPER ATTIRE
☑ IMPROPER USE OF SPELLS
☑ DESTRUCTION OF SCHOOL PROPERTY
☑ ALTERNATE DIMENSION VIOLATION
☑ UNAUTHORIZED VIOLATION OF LAWS OF PHYSICS
☑ MISUSE OF ASTRAL PROJECTIONS
☑ Misuse of Wand of Watoomb
Misuse of Eye of Agamotto
STRANGE Academy
DEMERIT SLIP
STUDENT NAME Iric
TEACHER Wanda Maximoff
REASON(S) FOR DEMERIT(S)
(3) DEMERIT(S):
☑ TARDINESS
☑ IMPROPER ATTIRE
☐ IMPROPER USE OF SPELLS
☑ DESTRUCTION OF SCHOOL PROPERTY
☐ ALTERNATE DIMENSION VIOLATION
☐ UNAUTHORIZED VIOLATION OF LAWS OF PHYSICS
☐ MISUSE OF ASTRAL PROJECTIONS
☐

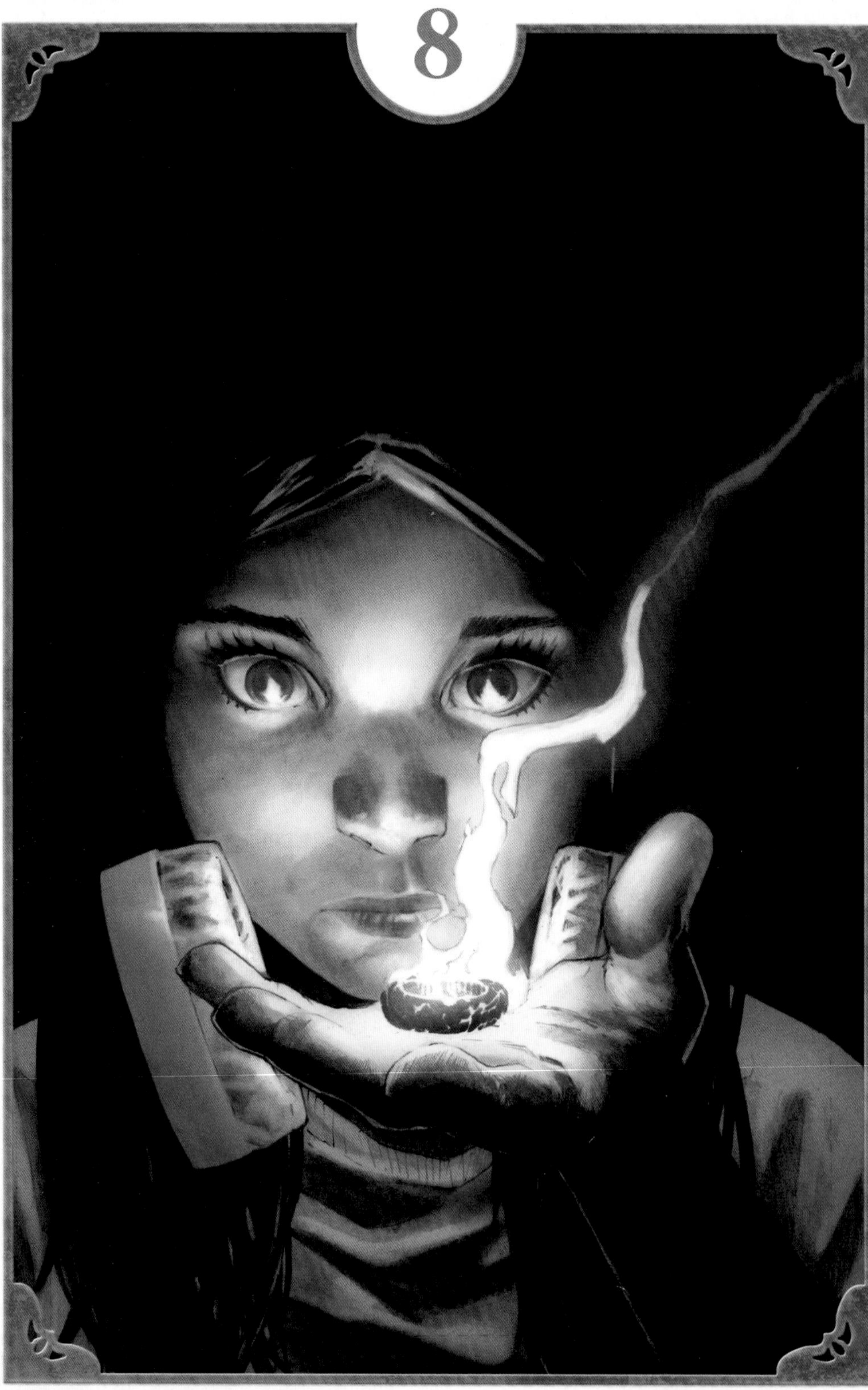
8

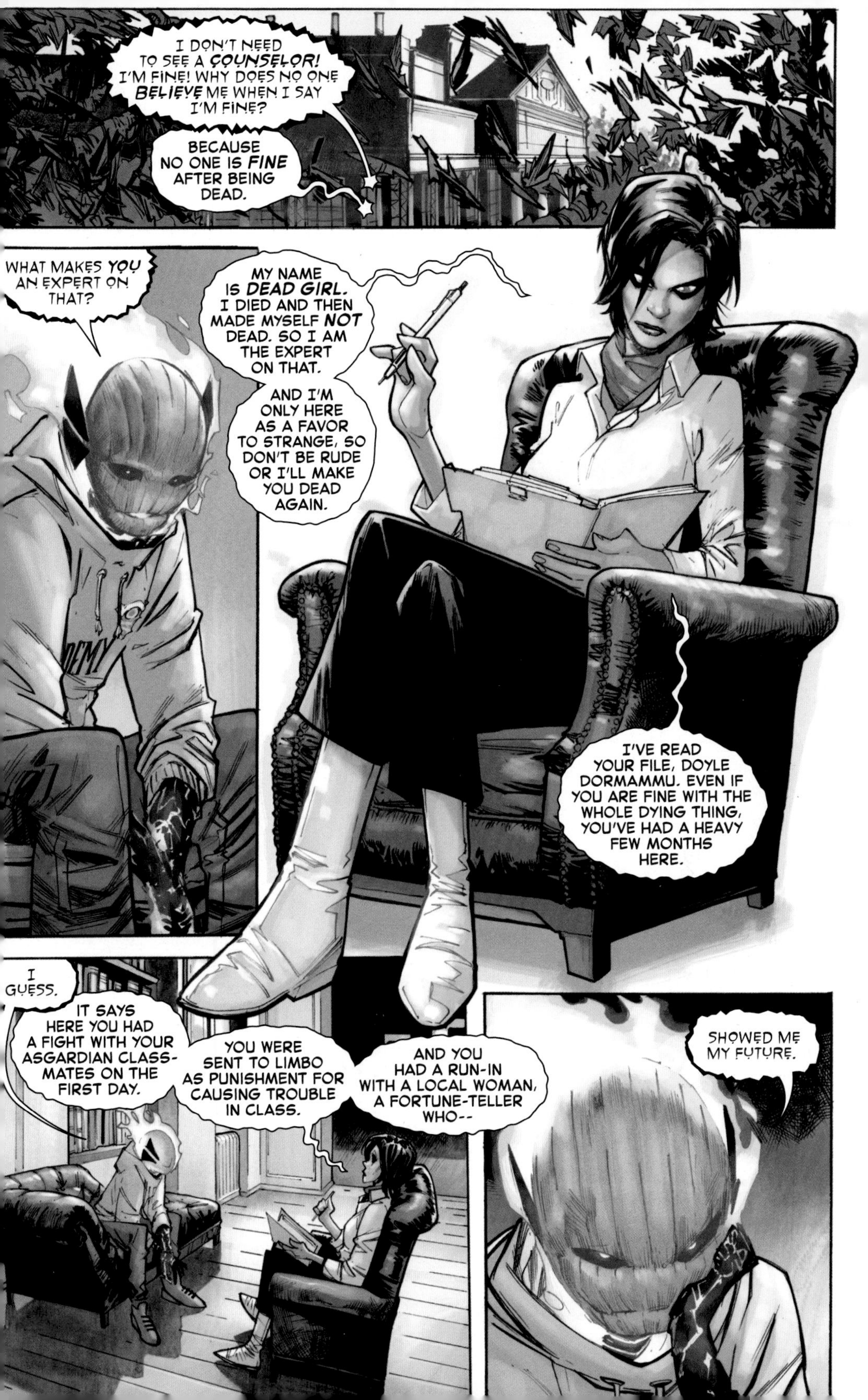
I DON'T NEED TO SEE A COUNSELOR! I'M FINE! WHY DOES NO ONE BELIEVE ME WHEN I SAY I'M FINE?
BECAUSE NO ONE IS FINE AFTER BEING DEAD.
WHAT MAKES YOU AN EXPERT ON THAT?
MY NAME IS DEAD GIRL. I DIED AND THEN MADE MYSELF NOT DEAD. SO I AM THE EXPERT ON THAT.
AND I'M ONLY HERE AS A FAVOR TO STRANGE, SO DON'T BE RUDE OR I'LL MAKE YOU DEAD AGAIN.
I'VE READ YOUR FILE, DOYLE DORMAMMU. EVEN IF YOU ARE FINE WITH THE WHOLE DYING THING, YOU'VE HAD A HEAVY FEW MONTHS HERE.
I GUESS.
IT SAYS HERE YOU HAD A FIGHT WITH YOUR ASGARDIAN CLASS-MATES ON THE FIRST DAY.
YOU WERE SENT TO LIMBO AS PUNISHMENT FOR CAUSING TROUBLE IN CLASS.
AND YOU HAD A RUN-IN WITH A LOCAL WOMAN, A FORTUNE-TELLER WHO--
SHOWED ME MY FUTURE.

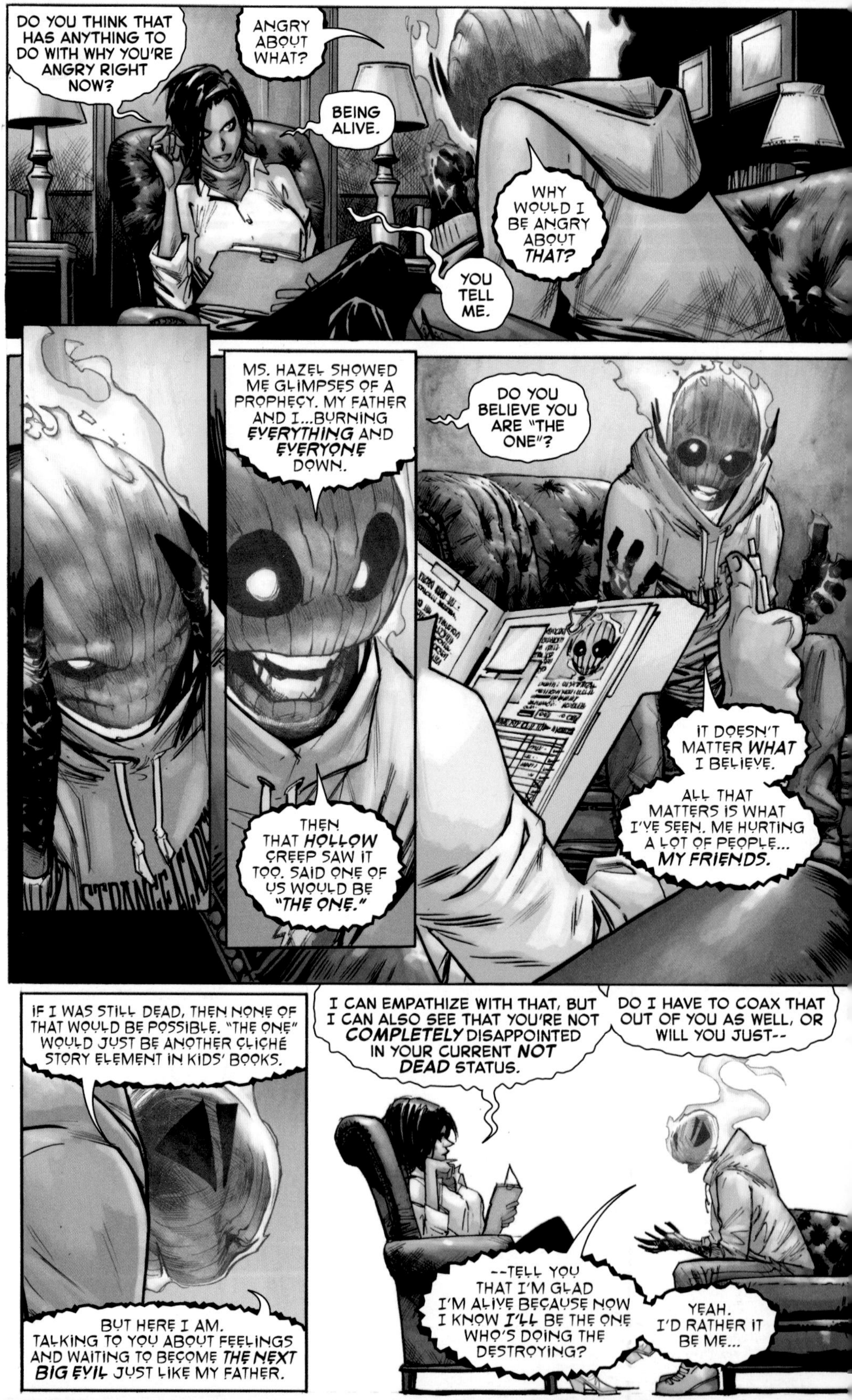
DO YOU THINK THAT HAS ANYTHING TO DO WITH WHY YOU'RE ANGRY RIGHT NOW?
ANGRY ABOUT WHAT?
BEING ALIVE.
WHY WOULD I BE ANGRY ABOUT THAT?
YOU TELL ME.
MS. HAZEL SHOWED ME GLIMPSES OF A PROPHECY. MY FATHER AND I...BURNING EVERYTHING AND EVERYONE DOWN.
THEN THAT HOLLOW CREEP SAW IT TOO. SAID ONE OF US WOULD BE "THE ONE."
DO YOU BELIEVE YOU ARE "THE ONE"?
IT DOESN'T MATTER WHAT I BELIEVE.
ALL THAT MATTERS IS WHAT I'VE SEEN. ME HURTING A LOT OF PEOPLE... MY FRIENDS.
IF I WAS STILL DEAD, THEN NONE OF THAT WOULD BE POSSIBLE. "THE ONE" WOULD JUST BE ANOTHER CLICHÉ STORY ELEMENT IN KIDS' BOOKS.
BUT HERE I AM. TALKING TO YOU ABOUT FEELINGS AND WAITING TO BECOME THE NEXT BIG EVIL JUST LIKE MY FATHER.
I CAN EMPATHIZE WITH THAT, BUT I CAN ALSO SEE THAT YOU'RE NOT COMPLETELY DISAPPOINTED IN YOUR CURRENT NOT DEAD STATUS.
DO I HAVE TO COAX THAT OUT OF YOU AS WELL, OR WILL YOU JUST--
--TELL YOU THAT I'M GLAD I'M ALIVE BECAUSE NOW I KNOW I'LL BE THE ONE WHO'S DOING THE DESTROYING?
YEAH. I'D RATHER IT BE ME...

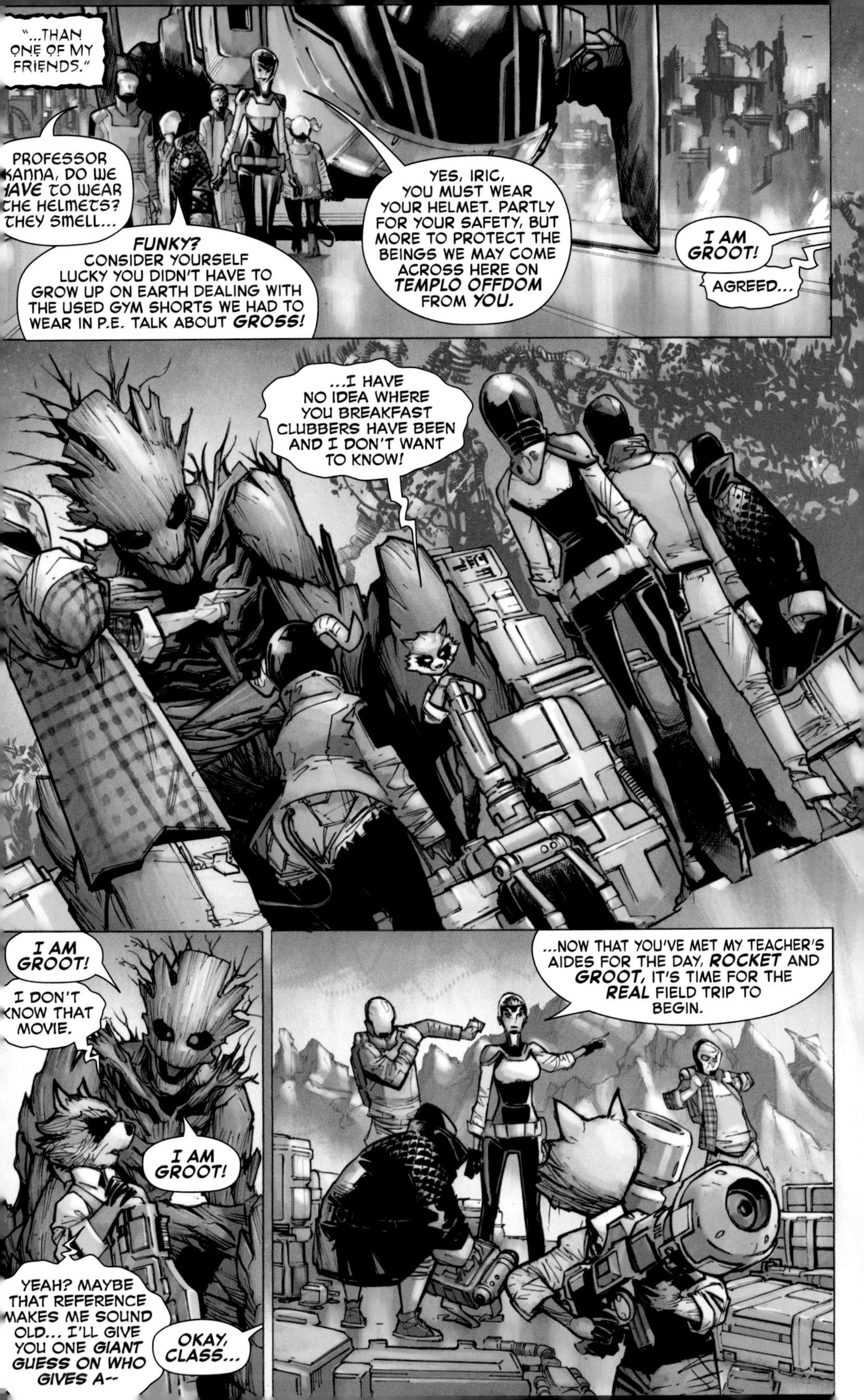
"...THAN ONE OF MY FRIENDS."
PROFESSOR KANNA, DO WE HAVE TO WEAR THE HELMETS? THEY SMELL...
FUNKY? CONSIDER YOURSELF LUCKY YOU DIDN'T HAVE TO GROW UP ON EARTH DEALING WITH THE USED GYM SHORTS WE HAD TO WEAR IN P.E. TALK ABOUT GROSS!
YES, IRIC, YOU MUST WEAR YOUR HELMET. PARTLY FOR YOUR SAFETY, BUT MORE TO PROTECT THE BEINGS WE MAY COME ACROSS HERE ON TEMPLO OFFDOM FROM YOU.
I AM GROOT!
AGREED...
...I HAVE NO IDEA WHERE YOU BREAKFAST CLUBBERS HAVE BEEN AND I DON'T WANT TO KNOW!
I AM GROOT!
I DON'T KNOW THAT MOVIE.
I AM GROOT!
YEAH? MAYBE THAT REFERENCE MAKES ME SOUND OLD... I'LL GIVE YOU ONE GIANT GUESS ON WHO GIVES A--
OKAY, CLASS...
...NOW THAT YOU'VE MET MY TEACHER'S AIDES FOR THE DAY, ROCKET AND GROOT, IT'S TIME FOR THE REAL FIELD TRIP TO BEGIN.

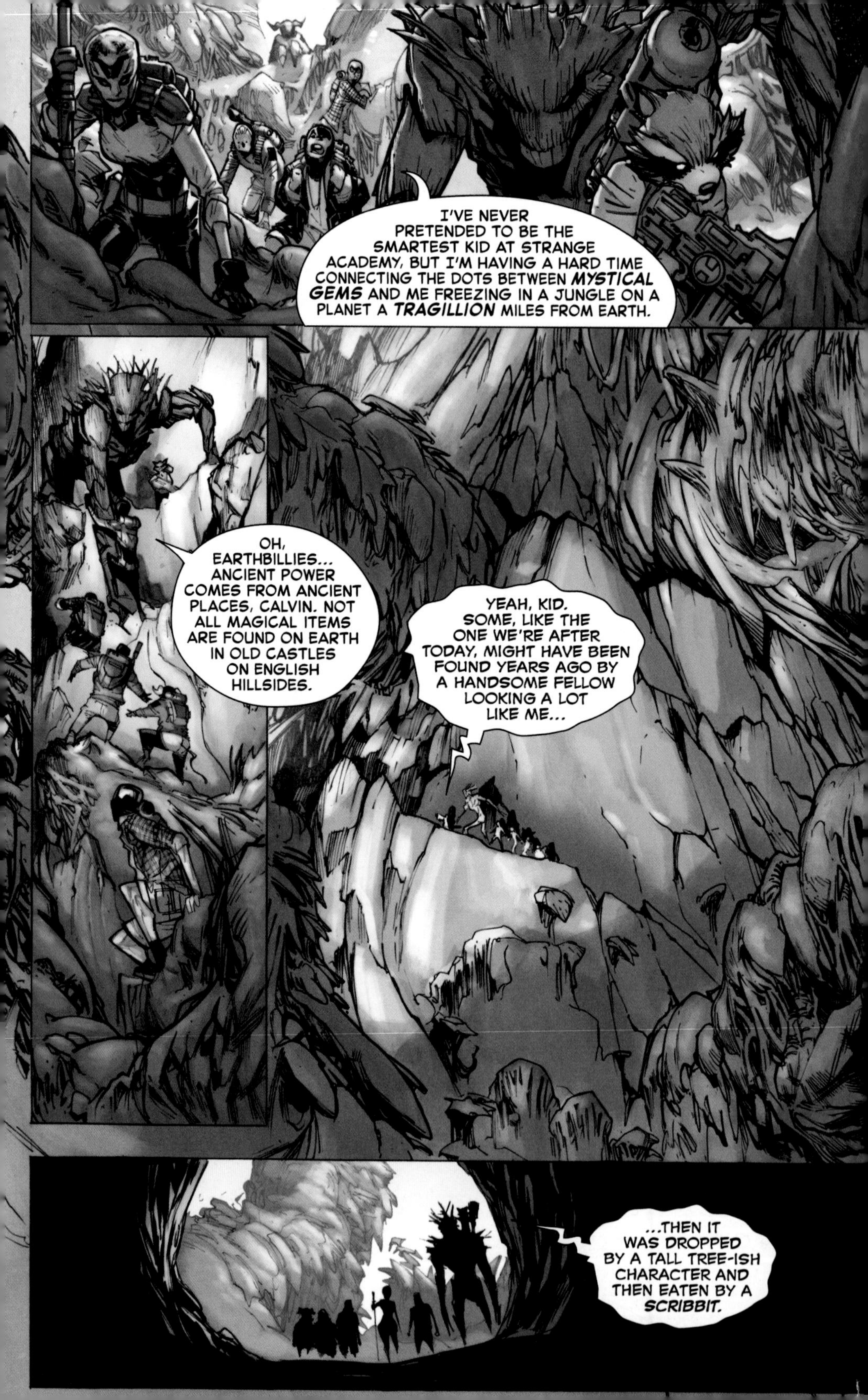
I'VE NEVER PRETENDED TO BE THE SMARTEST KID AT STRANGE ACADEMY, BUT I'M HAVING A HARD TIME CONNECTING THE DOTS BETWEEN MYSTICAL GEMS AND ME FREEZING IN A JUNGLE ON A PLANET A TRAGILLION MILES FROM EARTH.
OH, EARTHBILLIES... ANCIENT POWER COMES FROM ANCIENT PLACES, CALVIN. NOT ALL MAGICAL ITEMS ARE FOUND ON EARTH IN OLD CASTLES ON ENGLISH HILLSIDES.
YEAH, KID. SOME, LIKE THE ONE WE'RE AFTER TODAY, MIGHT HAVE BEEN FOUND YEARS AGO BY A HANDSOME FELLOW LOOKING A LOT LIKE ME...
...THEN IT WAS DROPPED BY A TALL TREE-ISH CHARACTER AND THEN EATEN BY A SCRIBBIT.

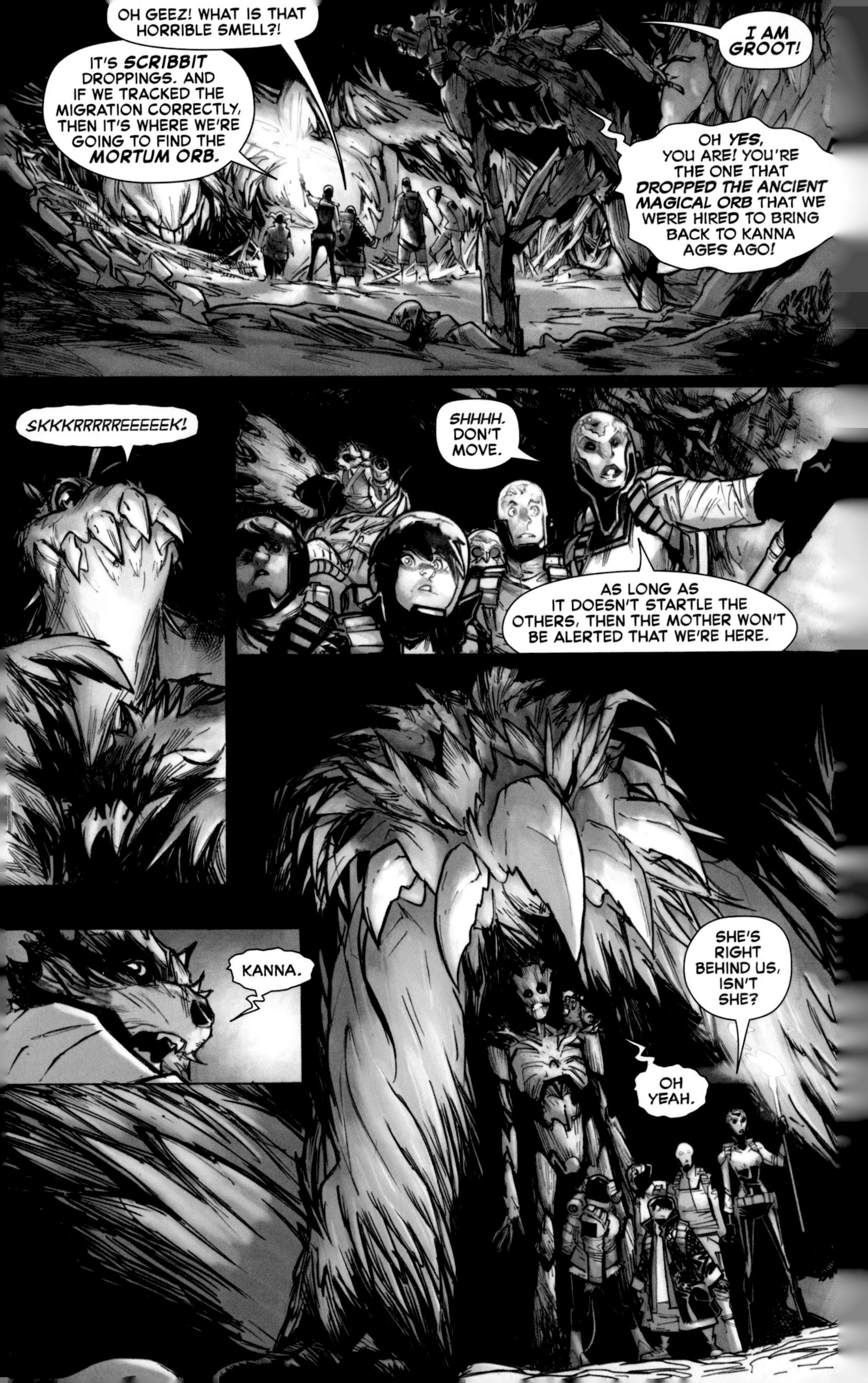
OH GEEZ! WHAT IS THAT HORRIBLE SMELL?!
IT'S SCRIBBIT DROPPINGS. AND IF WE TRACKED THE MIGRATION CORRECTLY, THEN IT'S WHERE WE'RE GOING TO FIND THE MORTUM ORB.
I AM GROOT!
OH YES, YOU ARE! YOU'RE THE ONE THAT DROPPED THE ANCIENT MAGICAL ORB THAT WE WERE HIRED TO BRING BACK TO KANNA AGES AGO!
SKKKRRRRREEEEEK!
SHHHH. DON'T MOVE.
AS LONG AS IT DOESN'T STARTLE THE OTHERS, THEN THE MOTHER WON'T BE ALERTED THAT WE'RE HERE.
KANNA.
SHE'S RIGHT BEHIND US, ISN'T SHE?
OH YEAH.

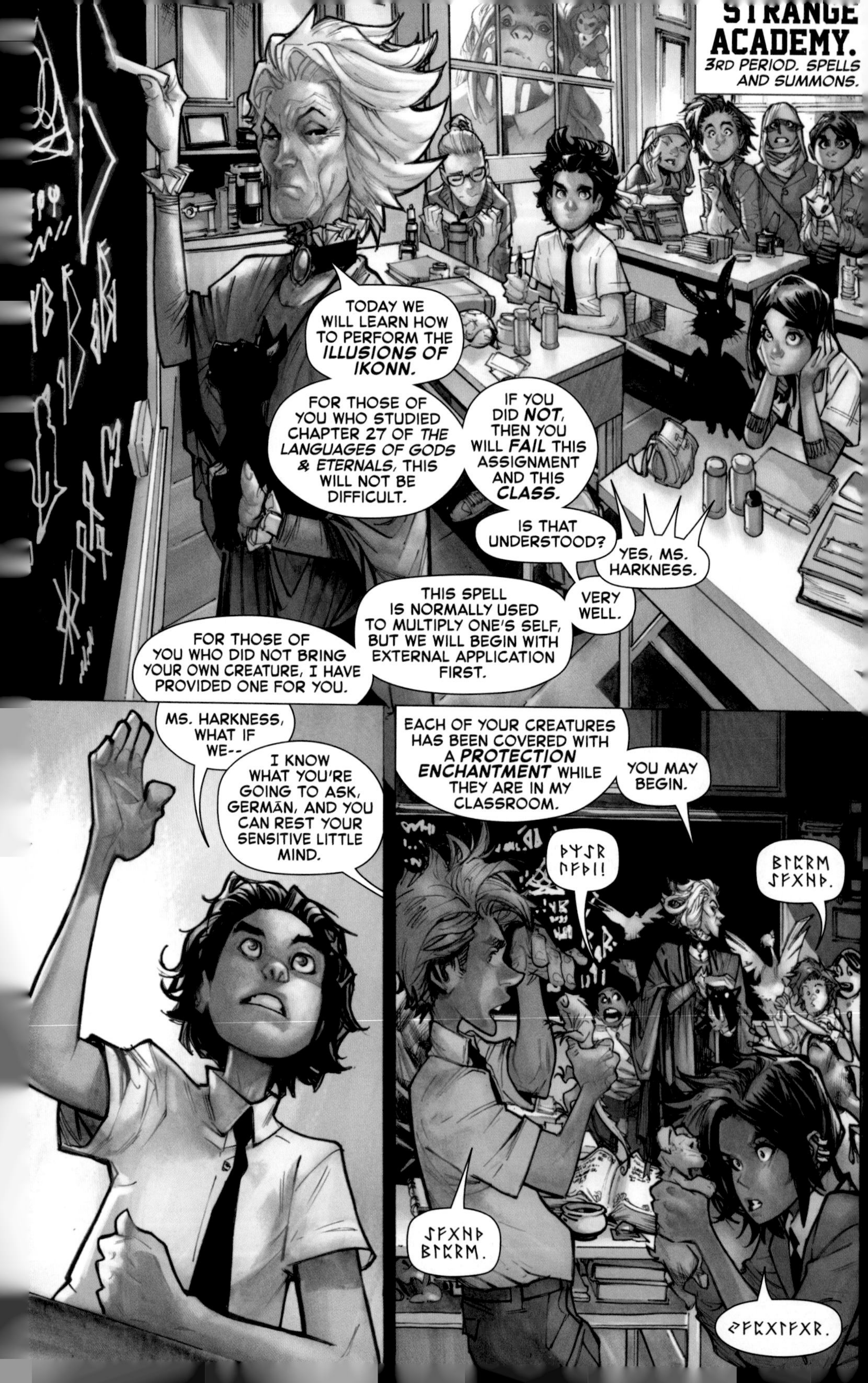
STRANGE ACADEMY.
3RD PERIOD. SPELLS AND SUMMONS.
TODAY WE WILL LEARN HOW TO PERFORM THE *ILLUSIONS OF IKONN.*
FOR THOSE OF YOU WHO STUDIED CHAPTER 27 OF *THE LANGUAGES OF GODS & ETERNALS,* THIS WILL NOT BE DIFFICULT.
IF YOU DID **NOT**, THEN YOU WILL **FAIL** THIS ASSIGNMENT AND THIS **CLASS.**
IS THAT UNDERSTOOD?
YES, MS. HARKNESS.
VERY WELL.
THIS SPELL IS NORMALLY USED TO MULTIPLY ONE'S SELF, BUT WE WILL BEGIN WITH EXTERNAL APPLICATION FIRST.
FOR THOSE OF YOU WHO DID NOT BRING YOUR OWN CREATURE, I HAVE PROVIDED ONE FOR YOU.
MS. HARKNESS, WHAT IF WE--
I KNOW WHAT YOU'RE GOING TO ASK, GERMĀN, AND YOU CAN REST YOUR SENSITIVE LITTLE MIND.
EACH OF YOUR CREATURES HAS BEEN COVERED WITH A ***PROTECTION ENCHANTMENT*** WHILE THEY ARE IN MY CLASSROOM.
YOU MAY BEGIN.

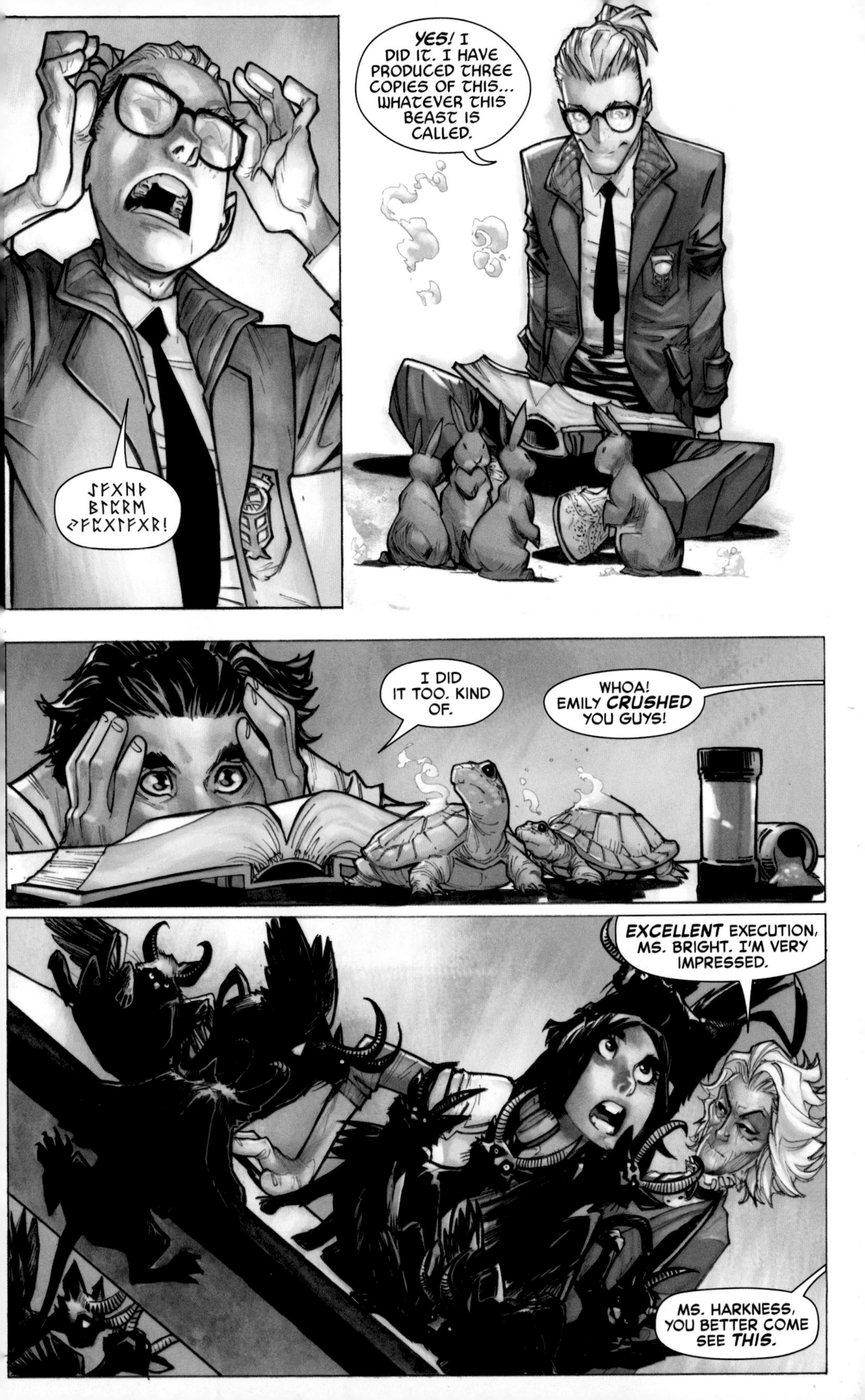
YES! I DID IT. I HAVE PRODUCED THREE COPIES OF THIS... WHATEVER THIS BEAST IS CALLED.
I DID IT TOO. KIND OF.
WHOA! EMILY CRUSHED YOU GUYS!
EXCELLENT EXECUTION, MS. BRIGHT. I'M VERY IMPRESSED.
MS. HARKNESS, YOU BETTER COME SEE THIS.

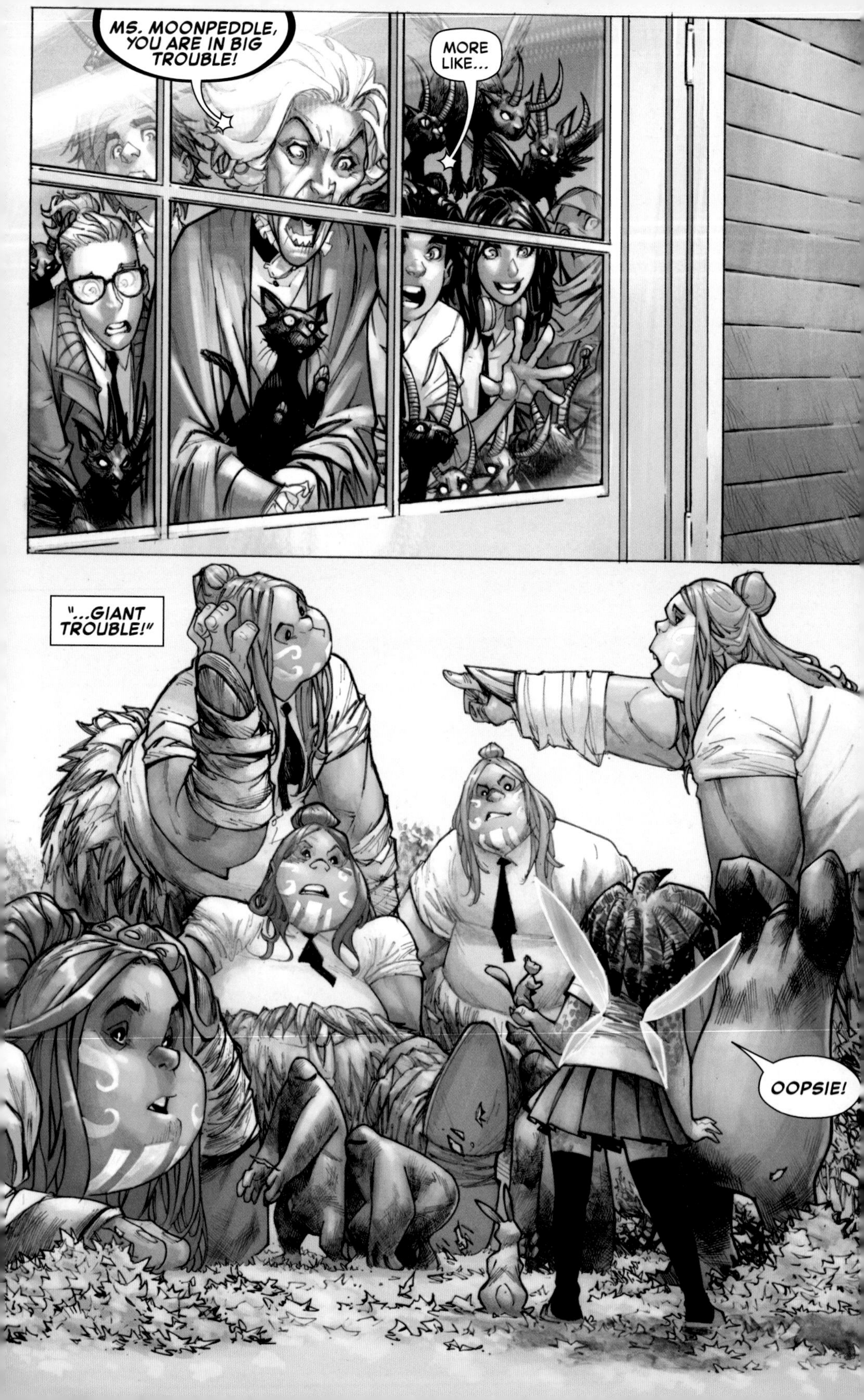
MS. MOONPEDDLE, YOU ARE IN BIG TROUBLE!
MORE LIKE...
"...GIANT TROUBLE!"
OOPSIE!

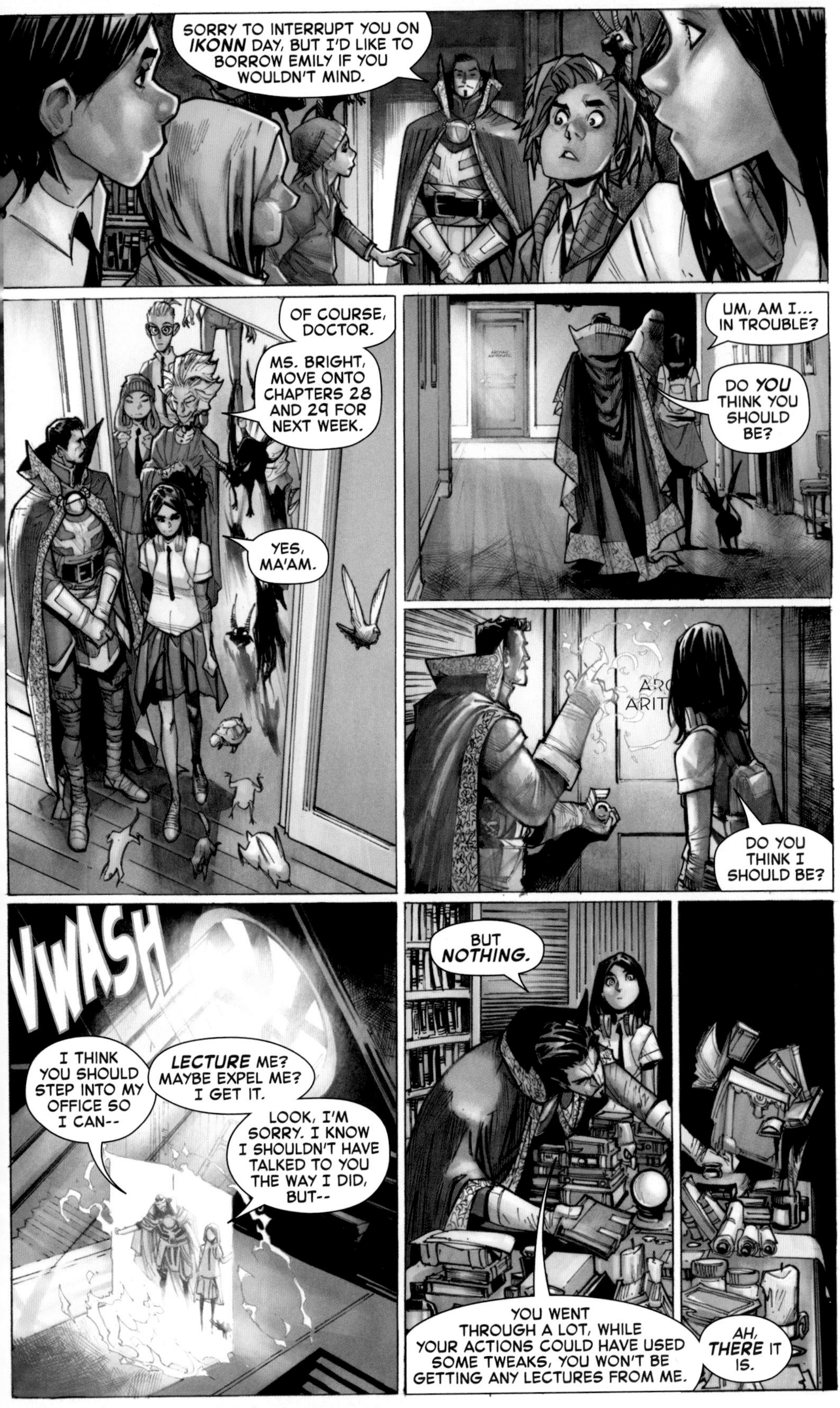
SORRY TO INTERRUPT YOU ON *IKONN* DAY, BUT I'D LIKE TO BORROW EMILY IF YOU WOULDN'T MIND.
OF COURSE, DOCTOR.
MS. BRIGHT, MOVE ONTO CHAPTERS 28 AND 29 FOR NEXT WEEK.
YES, MA'AM.
UM, AM I... IN TROUBLE?
DO *YOU* THINK YOU SHOULD BE?
DO YOU THINK I SHOULD BE?
VWASH
I THINK YOU SHOULD STEP INTO MY OFFICE SO I CAN--
LECTURE ME? MAYBE EXPEL ME? I GET IT.
LOOK, I'M SORRY. I KNOW I SHOULDN'T HAVE TALKED TO YOU THE WAY I DID, BUT--
BUT *NOTHING.*
YOU WENT THROUGH A LOT, WHILE YOUR ACTIONS COULD HAVE USED SOME TWEAKS, YOU WON'T BE GETTING ANY LECTURES FROM ME.
AH, *THERE* IT IS.

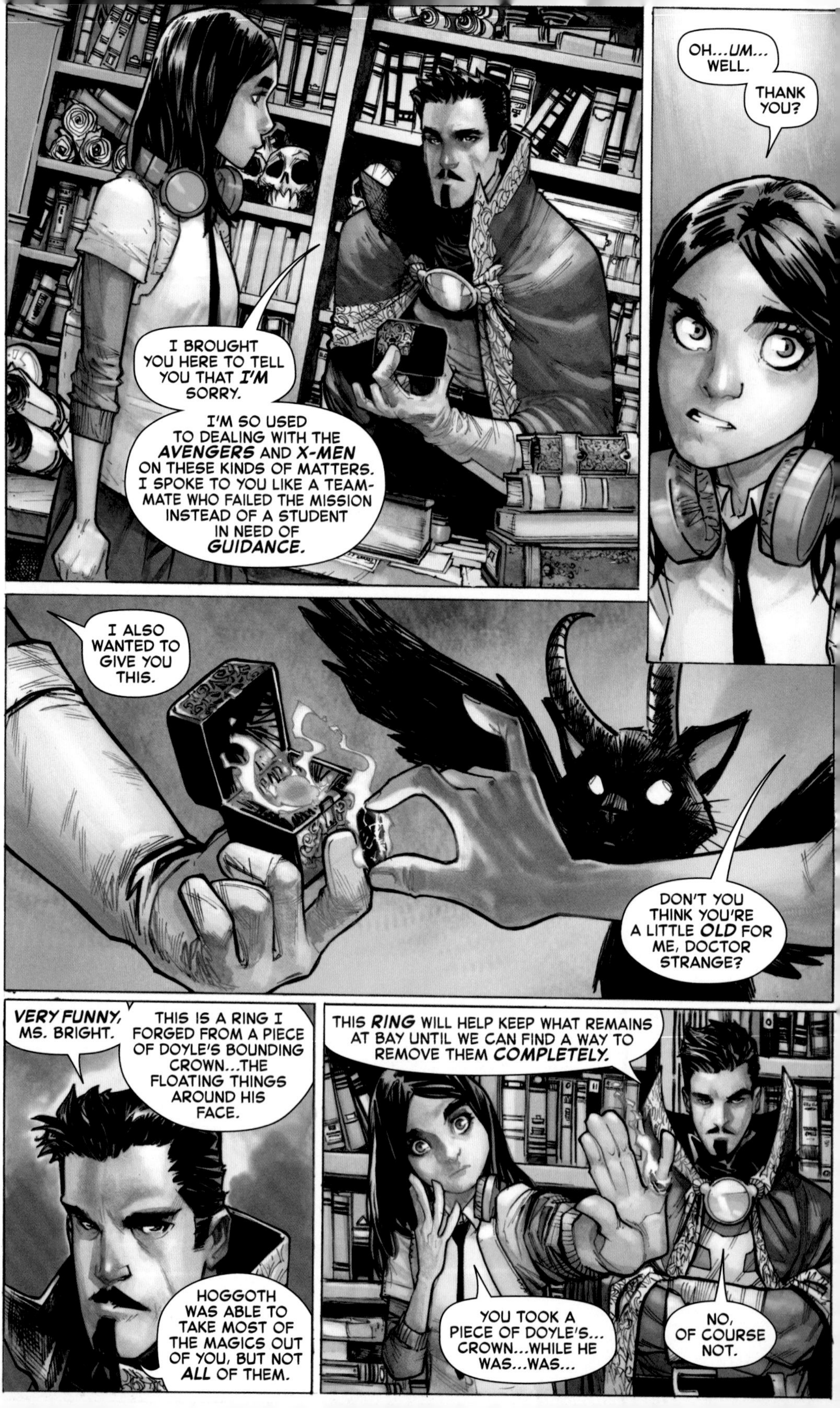
I BROUGHT YOU HERE TO TELL YOU THAT *I'M* SORRY.
I'M SO USED TO DEALING WITH THE *AVENGERS* AND *X-MEN* ON THESE KINDS OF MATTERS. I SPOKE TO YOU LIKE A TEAM-MATE WHO FAILED THE MISSION INSTEAD OF A STUDENT IN NEED OF *GUIDANCE.*
OH...*UM*... WELL.
THANK YOU?
I ALSO WANTED TO GIVE YOU THIS.
DON'T YOU THINK YOU'RE A LITTLE *OLD* FOR ME, DOCTOR STRANGE?
VERY FUNNY, MS. BRIGHT.
THIS IS A RING I FORGED FROM A PIECE OF DOYLE'S BOUNDING CROWN...THE FLOATING THINGS AROUND HIS FACE.
HOGGOTH WAS ABLE TO TAKE MOST OF THE MAGICS OUT OF YOU, BUT NOT *ALL* OF THEM.
THIS *RING* WILL HELP KEEP WHAT REMAINS AT BAY UNTIL WE CAN FIND A WAY TO REMOVE THEM *COMPLETELY.*
YOU TOOK A PIECE OF DOYLE'S... CROWN...WHILE HE WAS...WAS...
NO, OF COURSE NOT.

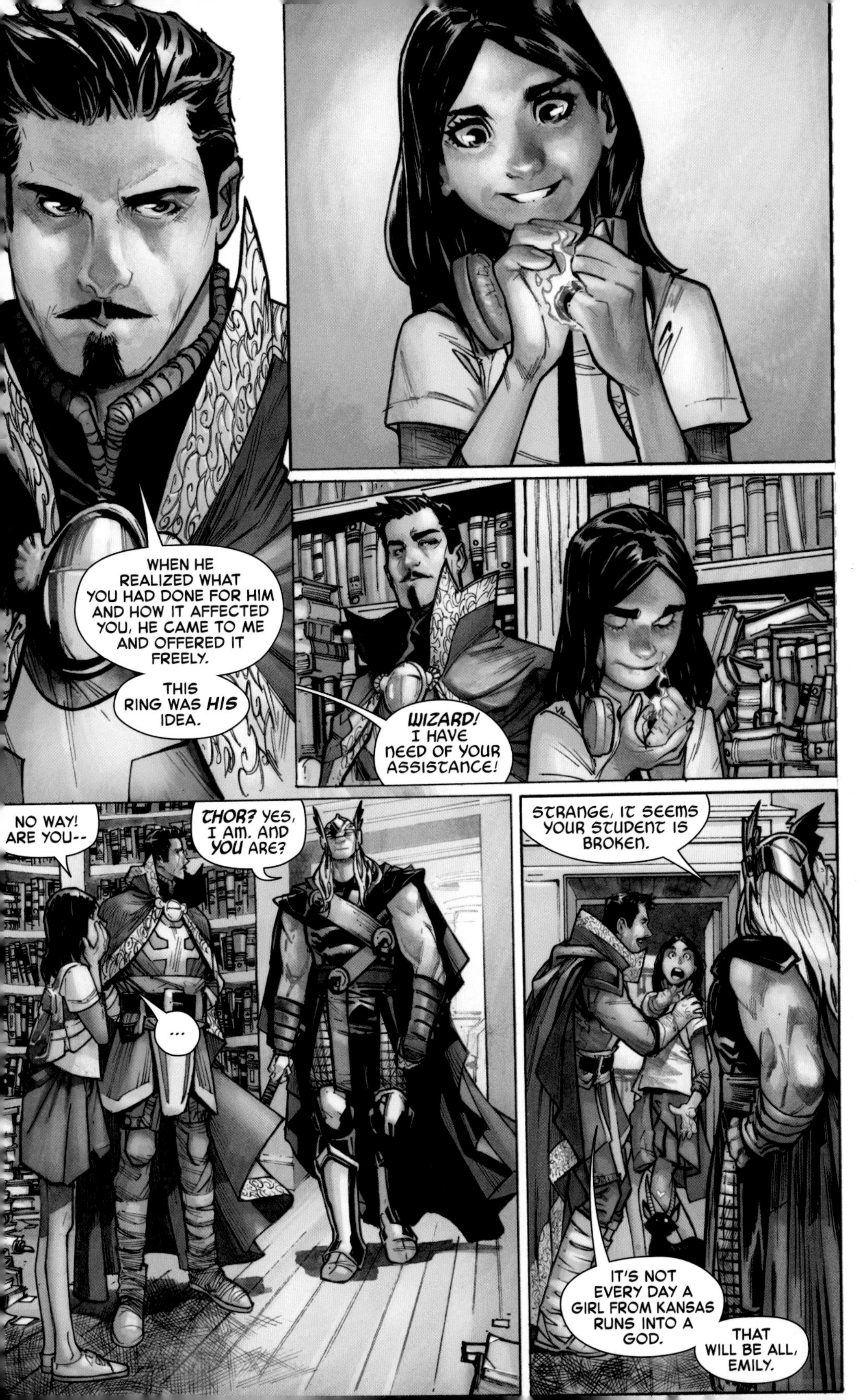
WHEN HE REALIZED WHAT YOU HAD DONE FOR HIM AND HOW IT AFFECTED YOU, HE CAME TO ME AND OFFERED IT FREELY.
THIS RING WAS *HIS* IDEA.
WIZARD! I HAVE NEED OF YOUR ASSISTANCE!
NO WAY! ARE YOU--
THOR? YES, I AM. AND *YOU* ARE?
...
STRANGE, IT SEEMS YOUR STUDENT IS BROKEN.
IT'S NOT EVERY DAY A GIRL FROM KANSAS RUNS INTO A GOD.
THAT WILL BE ALL, EMILY.

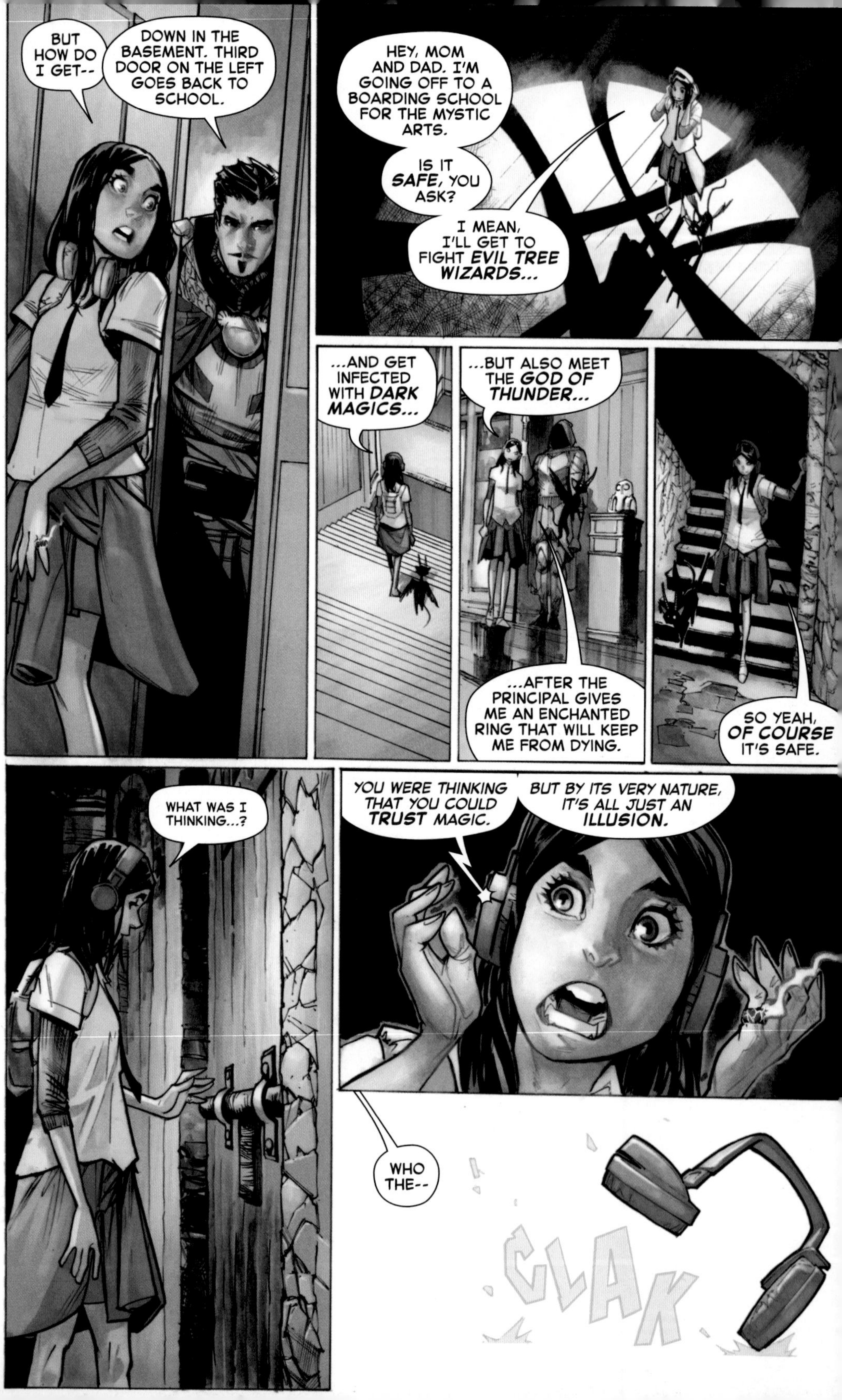

BUT HOW DO I GET--
DOWN IN THE BASEMENT. THIRD DOOR ON THE LEFT GOES BACK TO SCHOOL.
HEY, MOM AND DAD. I'M GOING OFF TO A BOARDING SCHOOL FOR THE MYSTIC ARTS.
IS IT SAFE, YOU ASK?
I MEAN, I'LL GET TO FIGHT EVIL TREE WIZARDS...
...AND GET INFECTED WITH DARK MAGICS...
...BUT ALSO MEET THE GOD OF THUNDER...
...AFTER THE PRINCIPAL GIVES ME AN ENCHANTED RING THAT WILL KEEP ME FROM DYING.
SO YEAH, OF COURSE IT'S SAFE.
WHAT WAS I THINKING...?
YOU WERE THINKING THAT YOU COULD TRUST MAGIC.
BUT BY ITS VERY NATURE, IT'S ALL JUST AN ILLUSION.
WHO THE--
CLAK

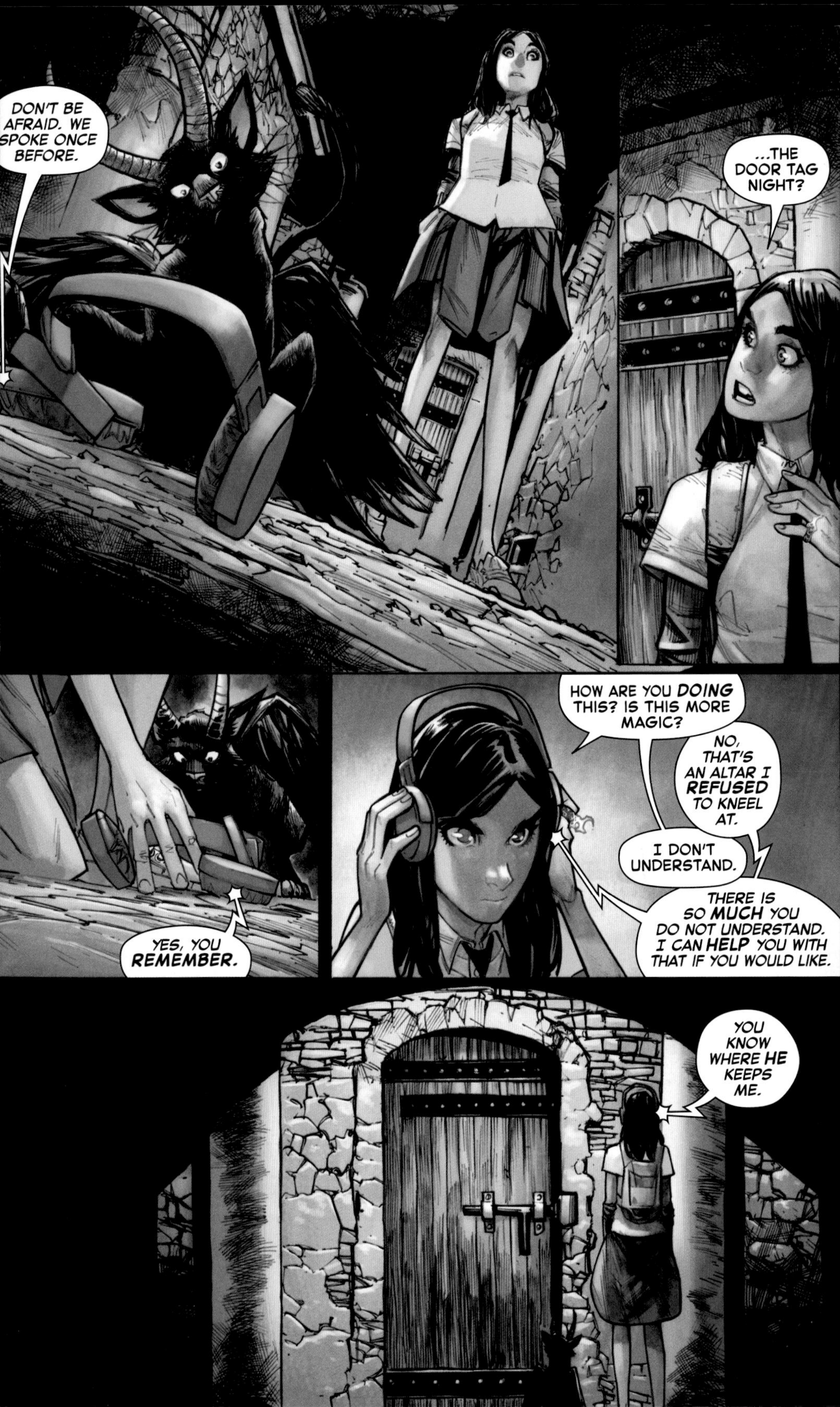
DON'T BE AFRAID. WE SPOKE ONCE BEFORE.
...THE DOOR TAG NIGHT?
YES, YOU REMEMBER.
HOW ARE YOU DOING THIS? IS THIS MORE MAGIC?
NO, THAT'S AN ALTAR I REFUSED TO KNEEL AT.
I DON'T UNDERSTAND.
THERE IS SO MUCH YOU DO NOT UNDERSTAND. I CAN HELP YOU WITH THAT IF YOU WOULD LIKE.
YOU KNOW WHERE HE KEEPS ME.

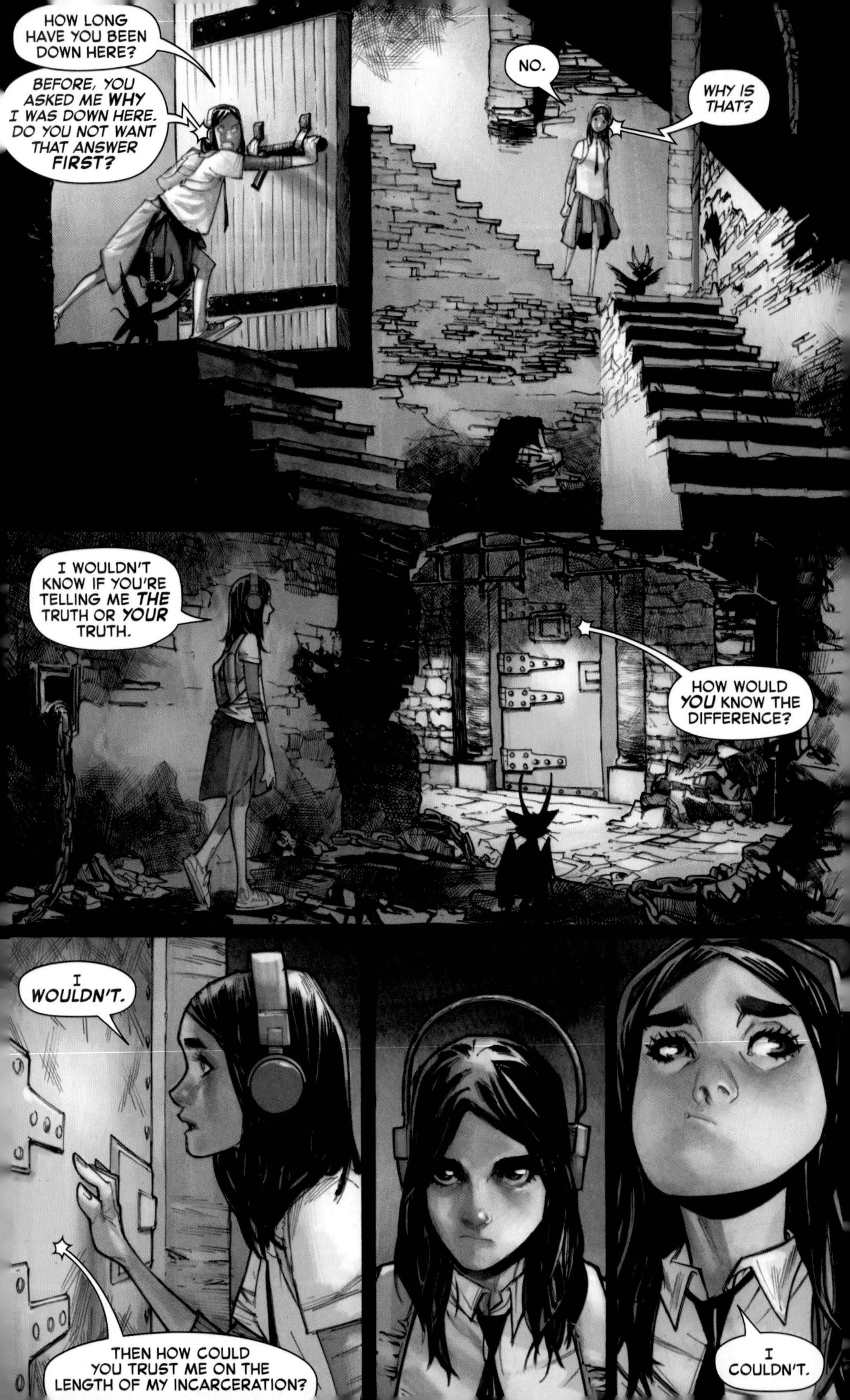
HOW LONG HAVE YOU BEEN DOWN HERE?
BEFORE, YOU ASKED ME WHY I WAS DOWN HERE. DO YOU NOT WANT THAT ANSWER FIRST?
NO.
WHY IS THAT?
I WOULDN'T KNOW IF YOU'RE TELLING ME THE TRUTH OR YOUR TRUTH.
HOW WOULD YOU KNOW THE DIFFERENCE?
I WOULDN'T.
THEN HOW COULD YOU TRUST ME ON THE LENGTH OF MY INCARCERATION?
I COULDN'T.

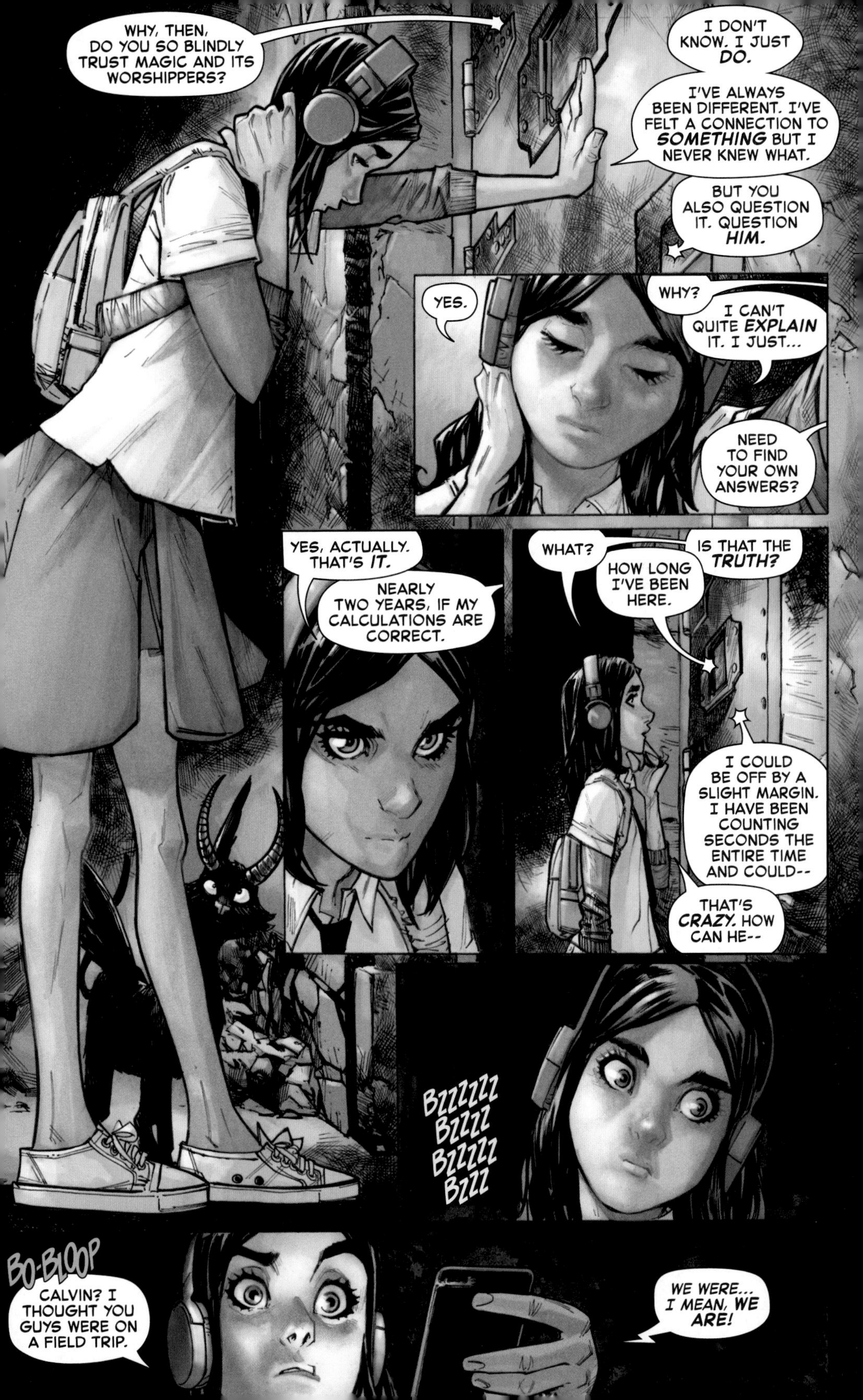
WHY, THEN, DO YOU SO BLINDLY TRUST MAGIC AND ITS WORSHIPPERS?
I DON'T KNOW. I JUST DO.
I'VE ALWAYS BEEN DIFFERENT. I'VE FELT A CONNECTION TO SOMETHING BUT I NEVER KNEW WHAT.
BUT YOU ALSO QUESTION IT. QUESTION HIM.
YES.
WHY?
I CAN'T QUITE EXPLAIN IT. I JUST...
NEED TO FIND YOUR OWN ANSWERS?
YES, ACTUALLY. THAT'S IT.
NEARLY TWO YEARS, IF MY CALCULATIONS ARE CORRECT.
WHAT?
IS THAT THE TRUTH?
HOW LONG I'VE BEEN HERE.
I COULD BE OFF BY A SLIGHT MARGIN. I HAVE BEEN COUNTING SECONDS THE ENTIRE TIME AND COULD--
THAT'S CRAZY. HOW CAN HE--
BZZZZZZ
BZZZZ
BZZZZZ
BZZZ
BO-BLOOP
CALVIN? I THOUGHT YOU GUYS WERE ON A FIELD TRIP.
WE WERE... I MEAN, WE ARE!

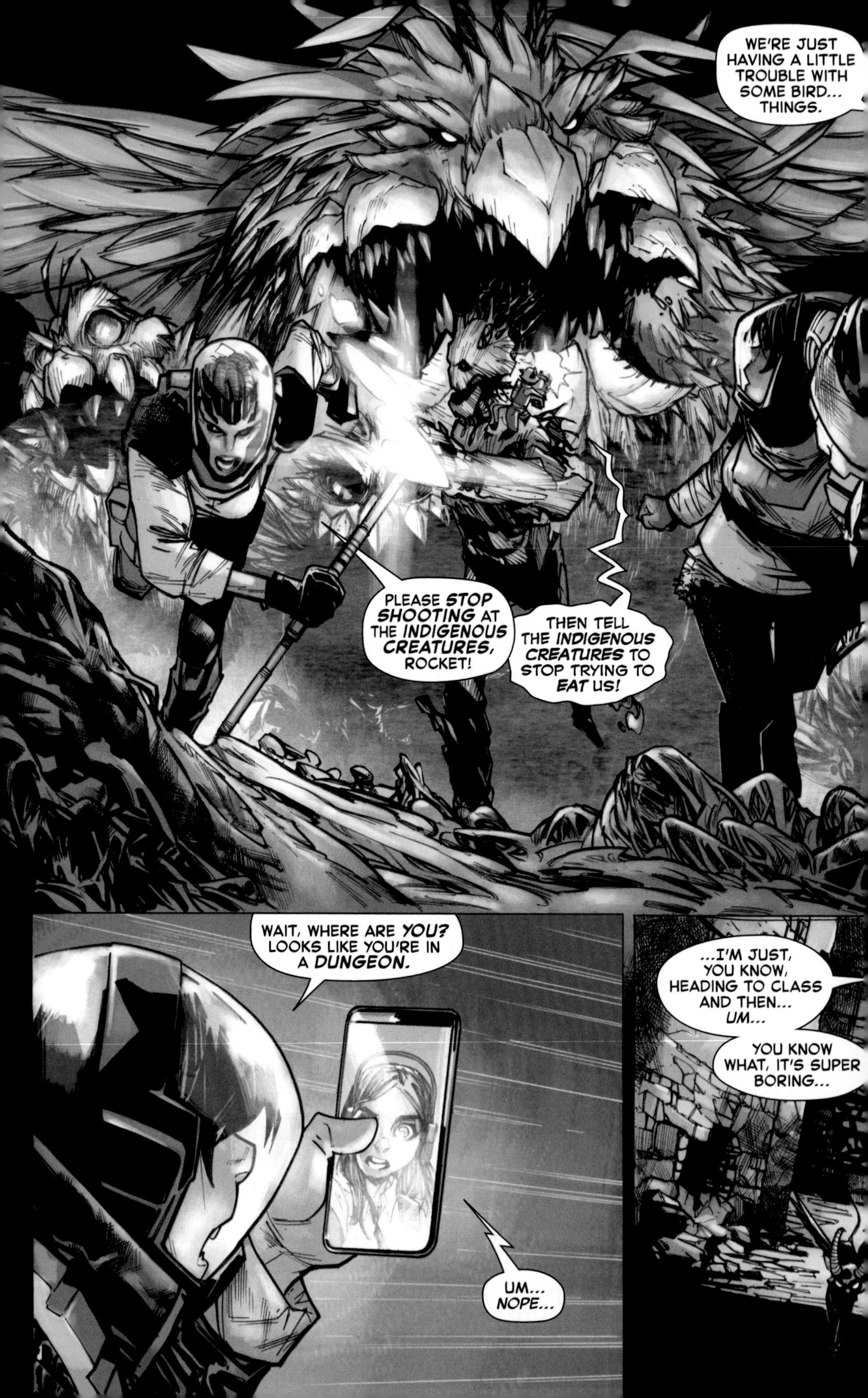
WE'RE JUST HAVING A LITTLE TROUBLE WITH SOME BIRD... THINGS.
PLEASE *STOP SHOOTING* AT THE *INDIGENOUS CREATURES,* ROCKET!
THEN TELL THE *INDIGENOUS CREATURES* TO STOP TRYING TO *EAT* US!
WAIT, WHERE ARE *YOU?* LOOKS LIKE YOU'RE IN A *DUNGEON.*
UM... *NOPE...*
...I'M JUST, YOU KNOW, HEADING TO CLASS AND THEN... *UM...*
YOU KNOW WHAT, IT'S SUPER BORING...

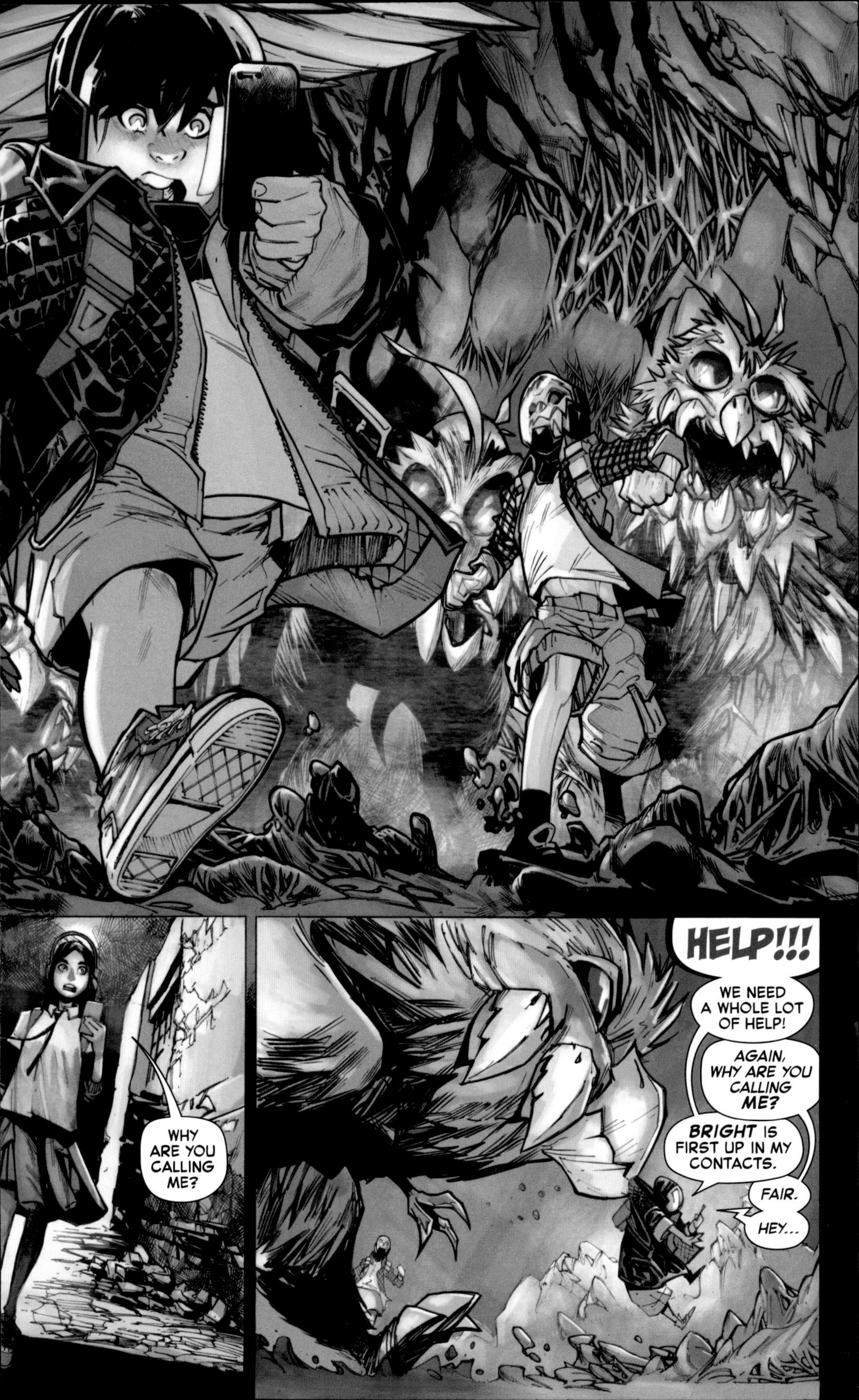
WHY ARE YOU CALLING ME?
HELP!!!
WE NEED A WHOLE LOT OF HELP!
AGAIN, WHY ARE YOU CALLING ME?
BRIGHT IS FIRST UP IN MY CONTACTS.
FAIR.
HEY...

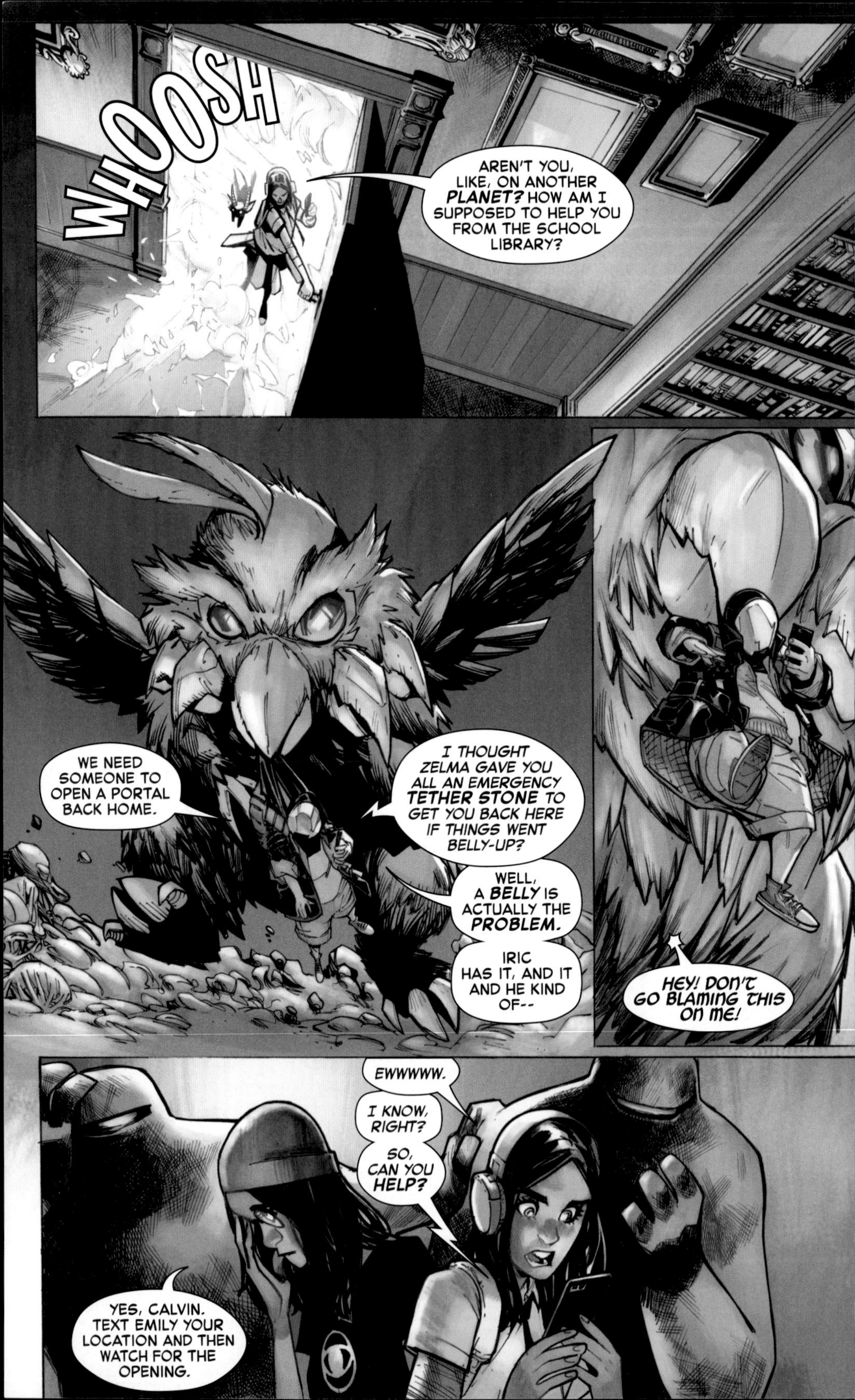
WHOOSH
AREN'T YOU, LIKE, ON ANOTHER PLANET? HOW AM I SUPPOSED TO HELP YOU FROM THE SCHOOL LIBRARY?
WE NEED SOMEONE TO OPEN A PORTAL BACK HOME.
I THOUGHT ZELMA GAVE YOU ALL AN EMERGENCY TETHER STONE TO GET YOU BACK HERE IF THINGS WENT BELLY-UP?
WELL, A BELLY IS ACTUALLY THE PROBLEM.
IRIC HAS IT, AND IT AND HE KIND OF--
HEY! DON'T GO BLAMING THIS ON ME!
EWWWWW.
I KNOW, RIGHT?
SO, CAN YOU HELP?
YES, CALVIN. TEXT EMILY YOUR LOCATION AND THEN WATCH FOR THE OPENING.

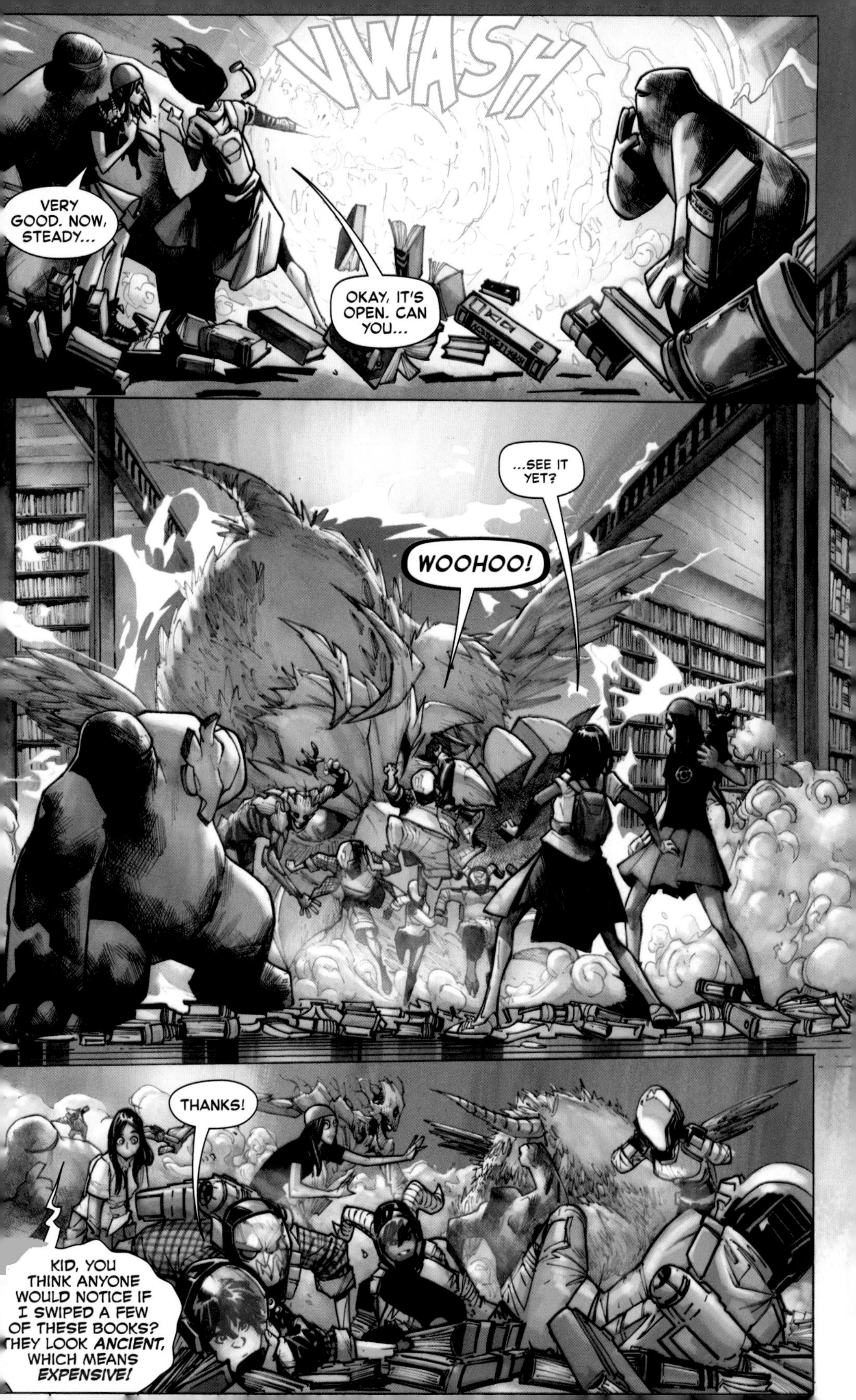
VWASH
VERY GOOD. NOW, STEADY...
OKAY, IT'S OPEN. CAN YOU...
...SEE IT YET?
WOOHOO!
THANKS!
KID, YOU THINK ANYONE WOULD NOTICE IF I SWIPED A FEW OF THESE BOOKS? THEY LOOK ANCIENT, WHICH MEANS EXPENSIVE!

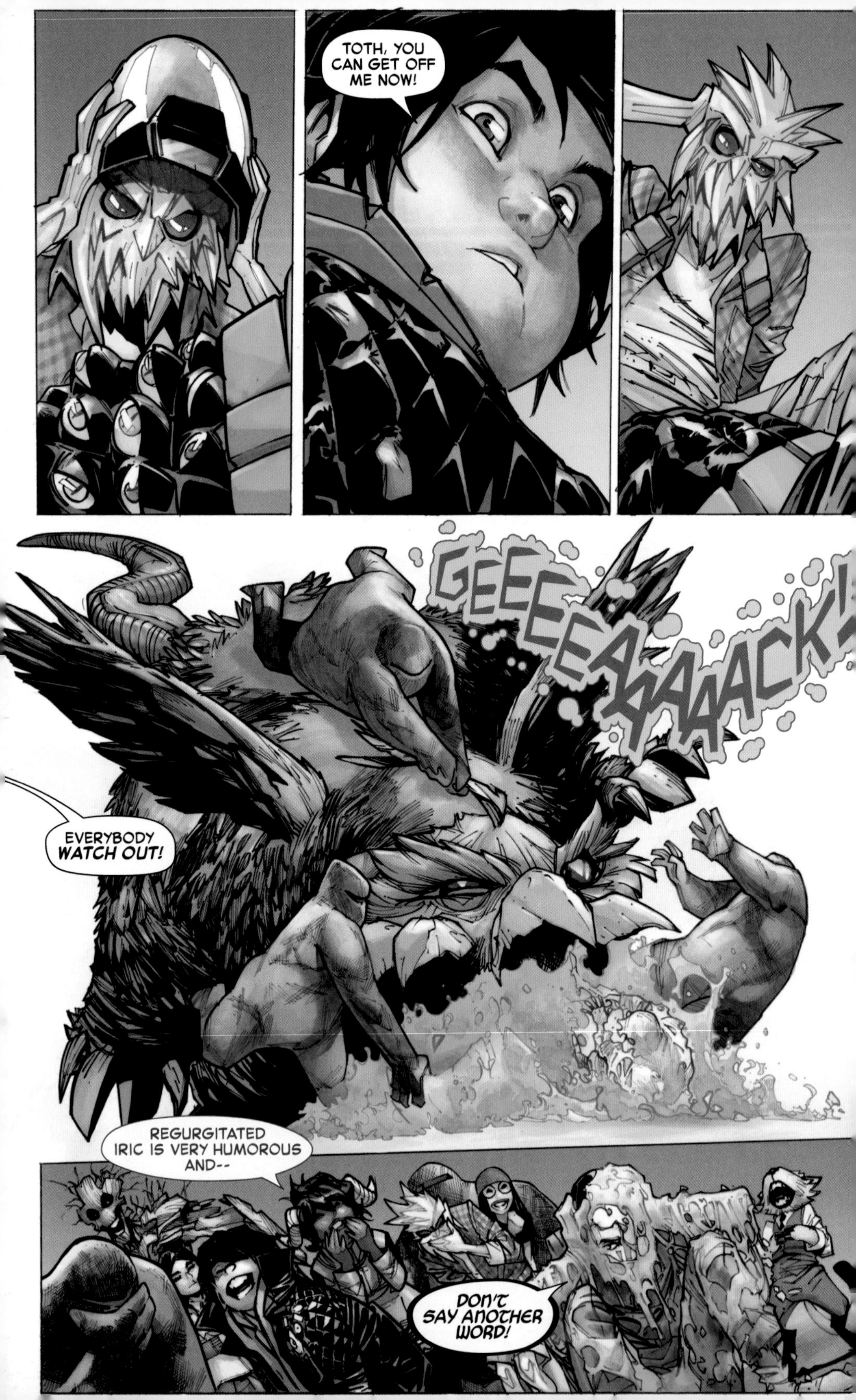
TOTH, YOU CAN GET OFF ME NOW!
GEEEEAAAAACK!!
EVERYBODY WATCH OUT!
REGURGITATED IRIC IS VERY HUMOROUS AND--
DON'T SAY ANOTHER WORD!

STRANGE
Academy

POST-DEATH AND RESSURRECTION ASSESSMENT SHEET

Appointment w/
Doyle 2/3
@ 1:00pm

Lunch w/
Strange 2/5
@ 12:30pm

Call Doop 2/11

Student: Doyle Dormammu

Death: Killed by the Hollow using magic.

Resurrection: A kiss from Emily Bright.

Initial Observation: Doyle, though the offspring of the leader of the Dark Dimension, Dormammu, seems to have a much softer touch than his father. He clearly cares for his fellow students and has deep-seated fears about following in his father's footsteps.

Notes: Doyle states he's happy to be alive so that the premonition of his being "the one" can be fulfilled; he states he'd rather end up the bad one instead of one of his friends. However, I believe there's more at play here. He's showing signs of relief at being alive again and no ill signs of negative impact from his death. Doyle should continue with sessions once a month for precautionary measures.

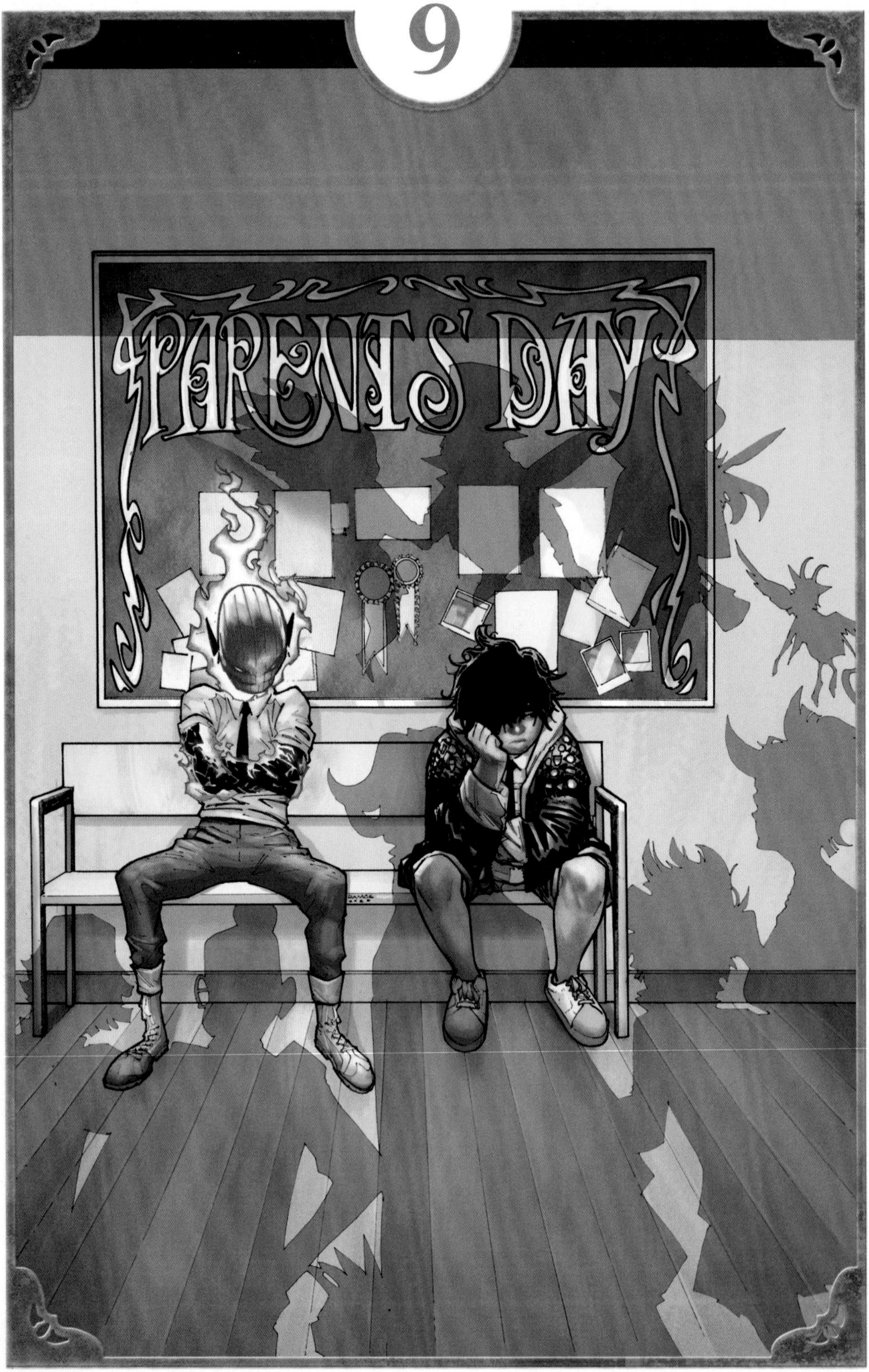
9
PARENTS' DAY

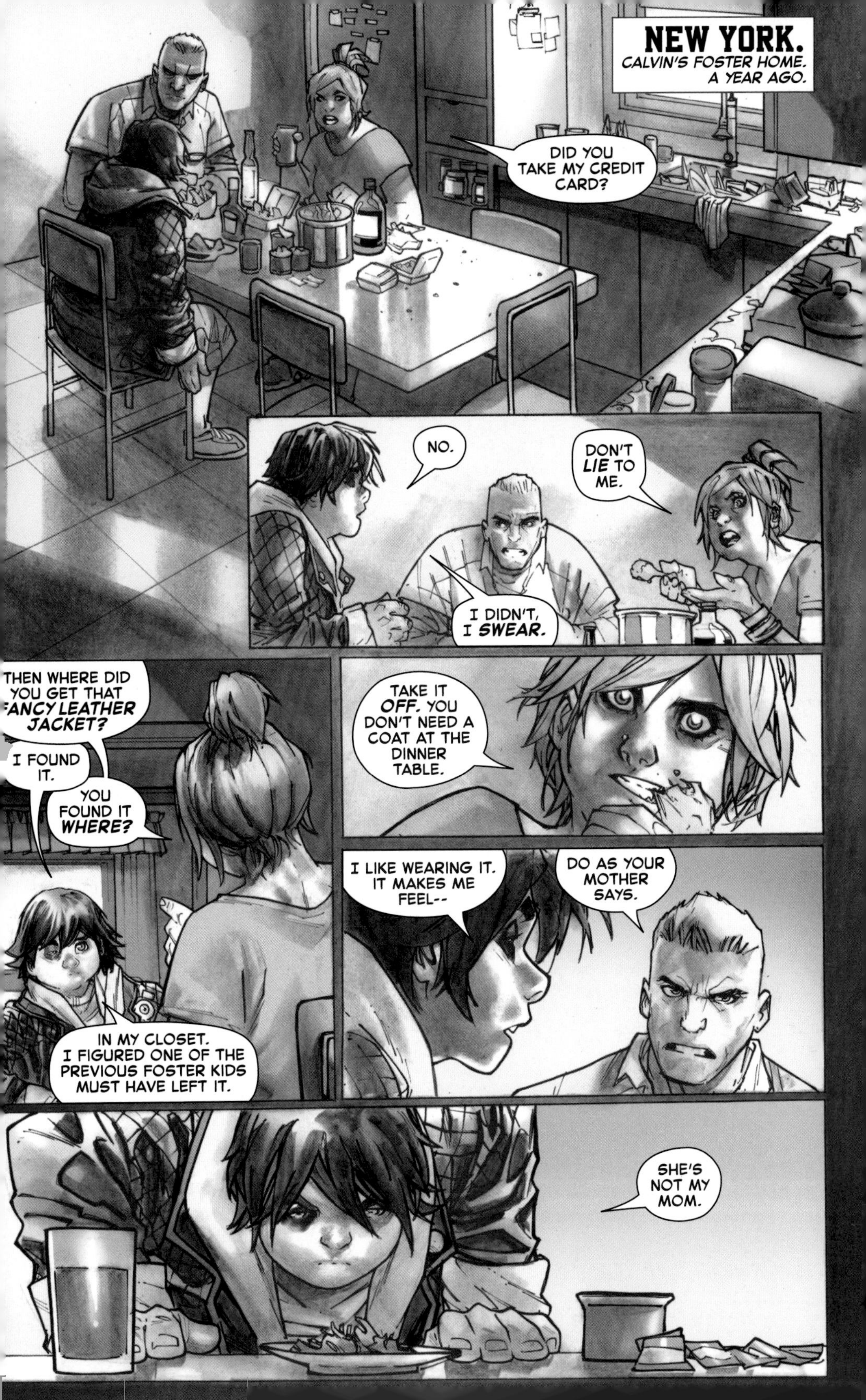
NEW YORK.
CALVIN'S FOSTER HOME. A YEAR AGO.
DID YOU TAKE MY CREDIT CARD?
NO.
DON'T LIE TO ME.
I DIDN'T, I SWEAR.
THEN WHERE DID YOU GET THAT FANCY LEATHER JACKET?
I FOUND IT.
YOU FOUND IT WHERE?
IN MY CLOSET. I FIGURED ONE OF THE PREVIOUS FOSTER KIDS MUST HAVE LEFT IT.
TAKE IT OFF. YOU DON'T NEED A COAT AT THE DINNER TABLE.
I LIKE WEARING IT. IT MAKES ME FEEL--
DO AS YOUR MOTHER SAYS.
SHE'S NOT MY MOM.

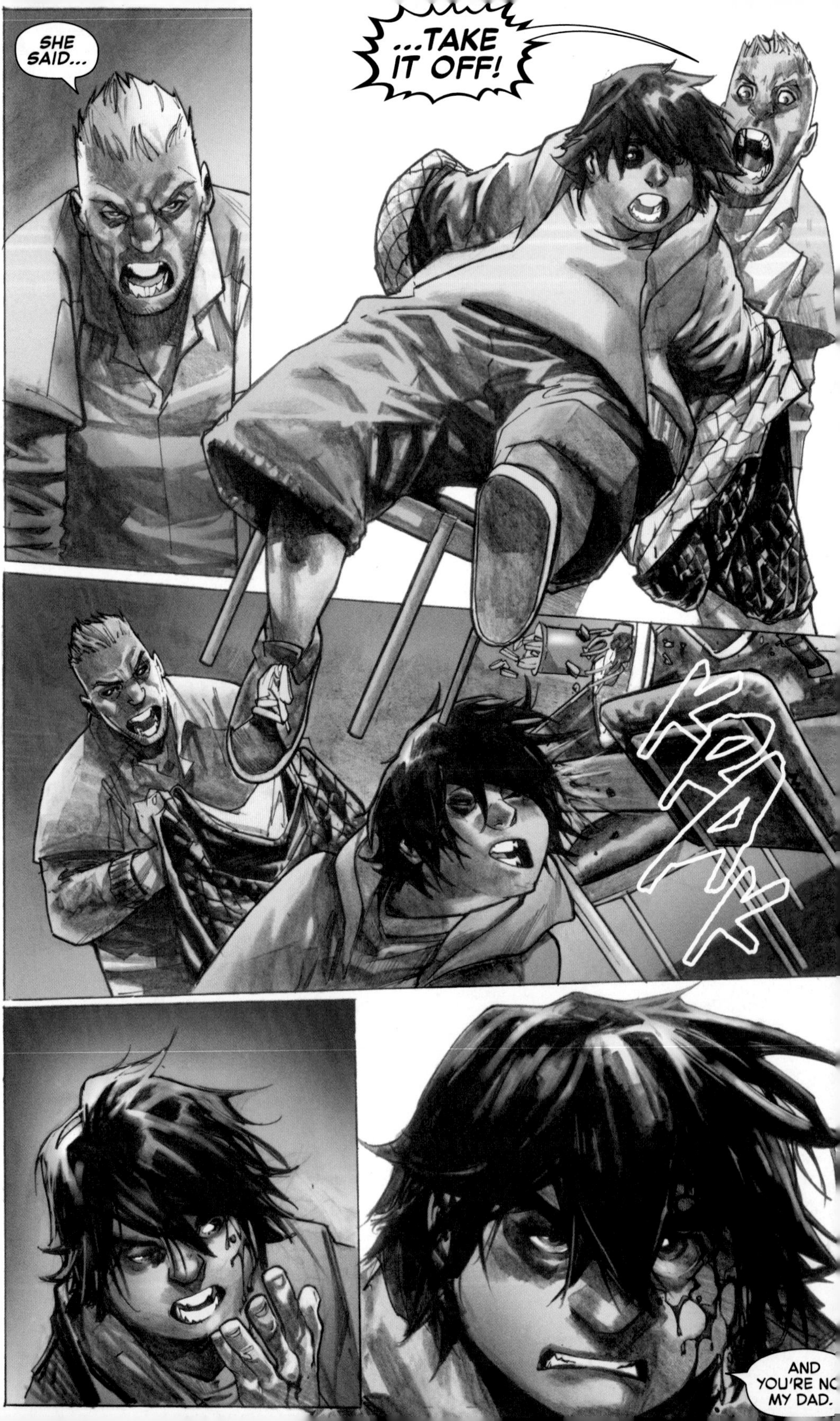
SHE SAID...
...TAKE IT OFF!
KRAK
AND YOU'RE NO MY DAD.

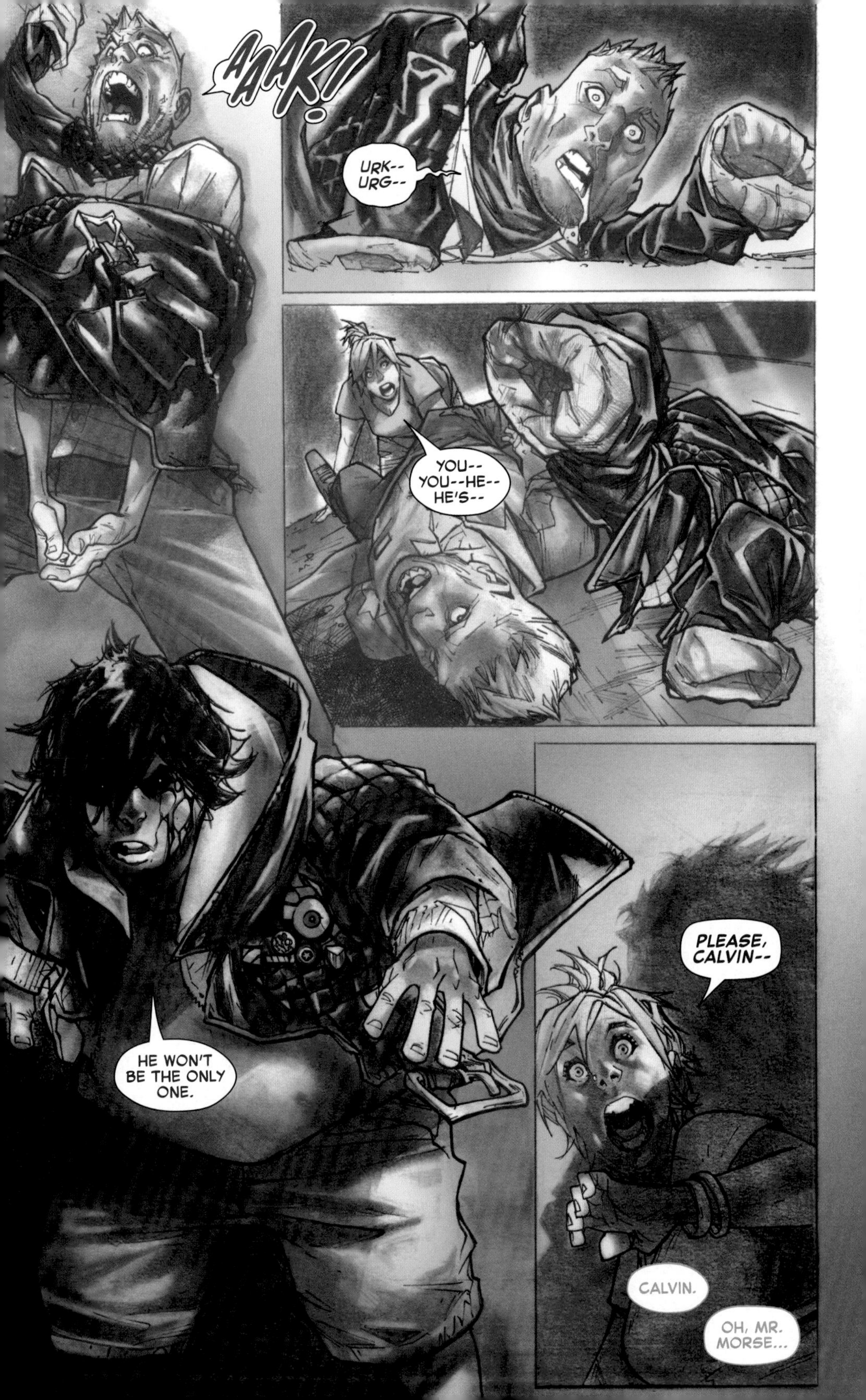
AAAK!
URK--
URG--
YOU--
YOU--HE--
HE'S--
HE WON'T
BE THE ONLY
ONE.
PLEASE,
CALVIN--
CALVIN.
OH, MR.
MORSE...

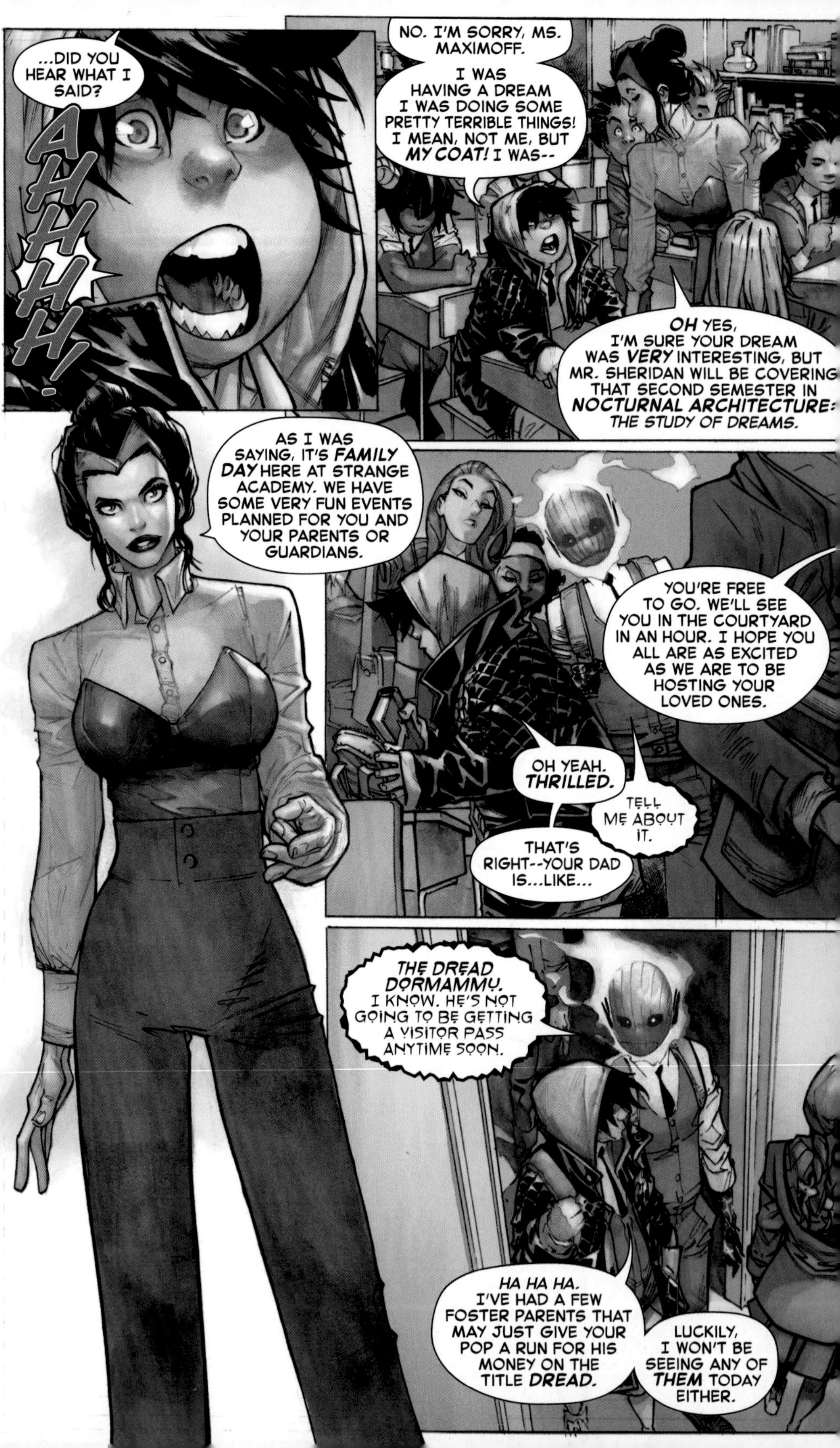
...DID YOU HEAR WHAT I SAID?
AHHHHH!
NO. I'M SORRY, MS. MAXIMOFF.
I WAS HAVING A DREAM I WAS DOING SOME PRETTY TERRIBLE THINGS! I MEAN, NOT ME, BUT MY COAT! I WAS--
OH YES, I'M SURE YOUR DREAM WAS VERY INTERESTING, BUT MR. SHERIDAN WILL BE COVERING THAT SECOND SEMESTER IN NOCTURNAL ARCHITECTURE: THE STUDY OF DREAMS.
AS I WAS SAYING, IT'S FAMILY DAY HERE AT STRANGE ACADEMY. WE HAVE SOME VERY FUN EVENTS PLANNED FOR YOU AND YOUR PARENTS OR GUARDIANS.
YOU'RE FREE TO GO. WE'LL SEE YOU IN THE COURTYARD IN AN HOUR. I HOPE YOU ALL ARE AS EXCITED AS WE ARE TO BE HOSTING YOUR LOVED ONES.
OH YEAH. THRILLED.
TELL ME ABOUT IT.
THAT'S RIGHT--YOUR DAD IS...LIKE...
THE DREAD DORMAMMU. I KNOW. HE'S NOT GOING TO BE GETTING A VISITOR PASS ANYTIME SOON.
HA HA HA. I'VE HAD A FEW FOSTER PARENTS THAT MAY JUST GIVE YOUR POP A RUN FOR HIS MONEY ON THE TITLE DREAD.
LUCKILY, I WON'T BE SEEING ANY OF THEM TODAY EITHER.

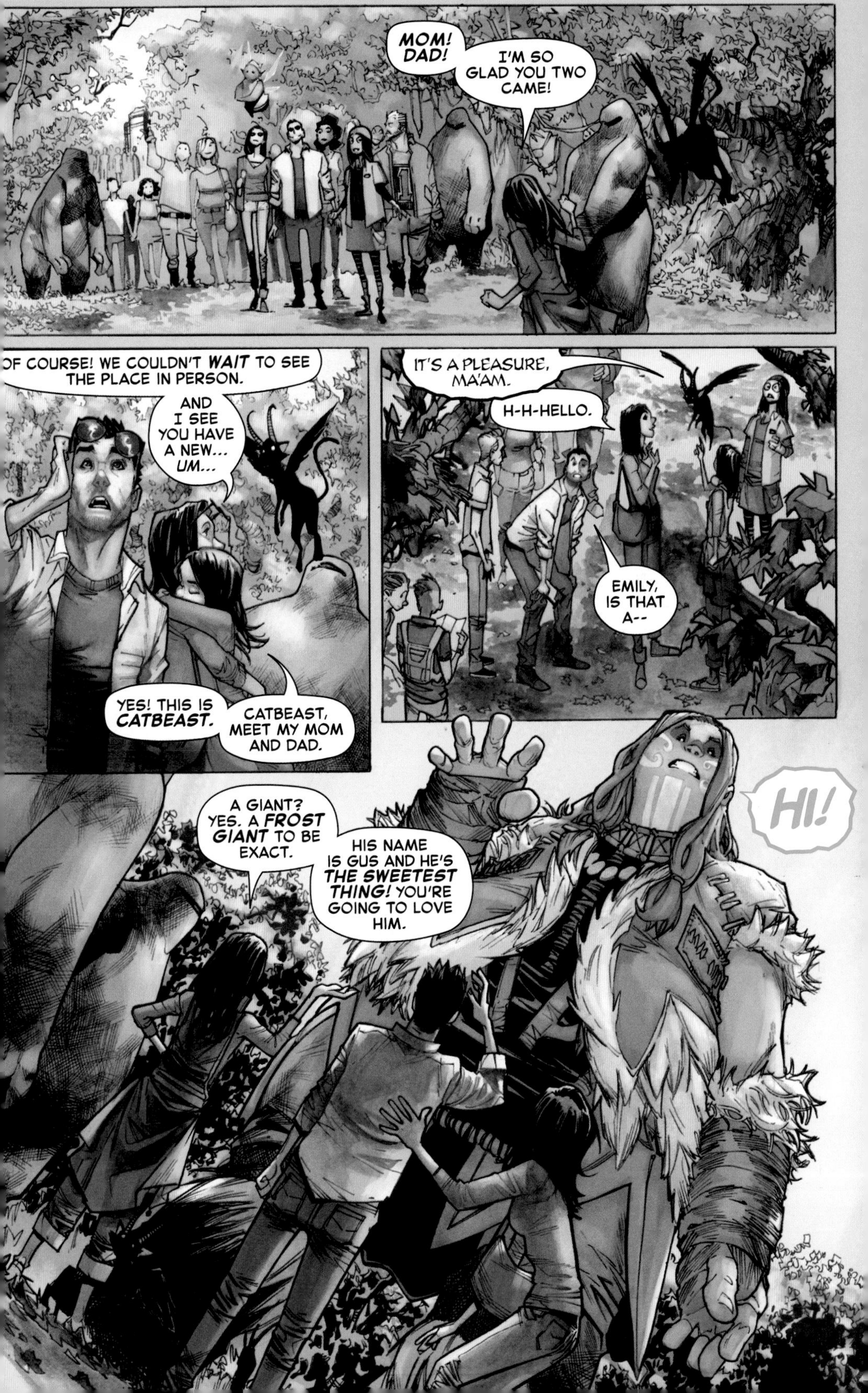
MOM! DAD!
I'M SO GLAD YOU TWO CAME!
OF COURSE! WE COULDN'T WAIT TO SEE THE PLACE IN PERSON.
AND I SEE YOU HAVE A NEW... UM...
YES! THIS IS CATBEAST.
CATBEAST, MEET MY MOM AND DAD.
IT'S A PLEASURE, MA'AM.
H-H-HELLO.
EMILY, IS THAT A--
A GIANT? YES. A FROST GIANT TO BE EXACT.
HIS NAME IS GUS AND HE'S THE SWEETEST THING! YOU'RE GOING TO LOVE HIM.
HI!

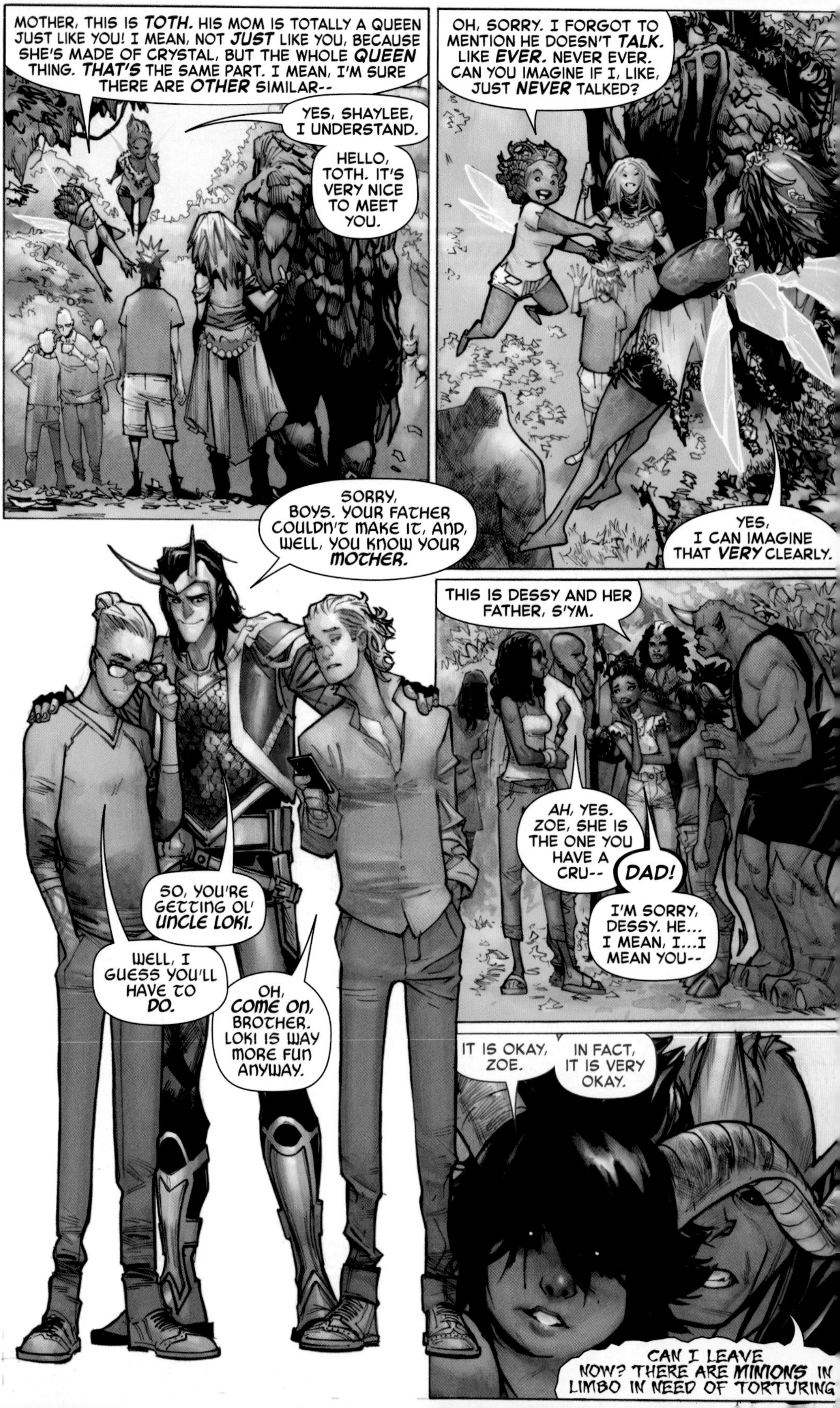
MOTHER, THIS IS TOTH. HIS MOM IS TOTALLY A QUEEN JUST LIKE YOU! I MEAN, NOT JUST LIKE YOU, BECAUSE SHE'S MADE OF CRYSTAL, BUT THE WHOLE QUEEN THING. THAT'S THE SAME PART. I MEAN, I'M SURE THERE ARE OTHER SIMILAR--
YES, SHAYLEE, I UNDERSTAND.
HELLO, TOTH. IT'S VERY NICE TO MEET YOU.
OH, SORRY. I FORGOT TO MENTION HE DOESN'T TALK. LIKE EVER. NEVER EVER. CAN YOU IMAGINE IF I, LIKE, JUST NEVER TALKED?
YES, I CAN IMAGINE THAT VERY CLEARLY.
SORRY, BOYS. YOUR FATHER COULDN'T MAKE IT, AND, WELL, YOU KNOW YOUR MOTHER.
SO, YOU'RE GETTING OL' UNCLE LOKI.
WELL, I GUESS YOU'LL HAVE TO DO.
OH, COME ON, BROTHER. LOKI IS WAY MORE FUN ANYWAY.
THIS IS DESSY AND HER FATHER, S'YM.
AH, YES. ZOE, SHE IS THE ONE YOU HAVE A CRU--
DAD!
I'M SORRY, DESSY. HE... I MEAN, I...I MEAN YOU--
IT IS OKAY, ZOE.
IN FACT, IT IS VERY OKAY.
CAN I LEAVE NOW? THERE ARE MINIONS IN LIMBO IN NEED OF TORTURING

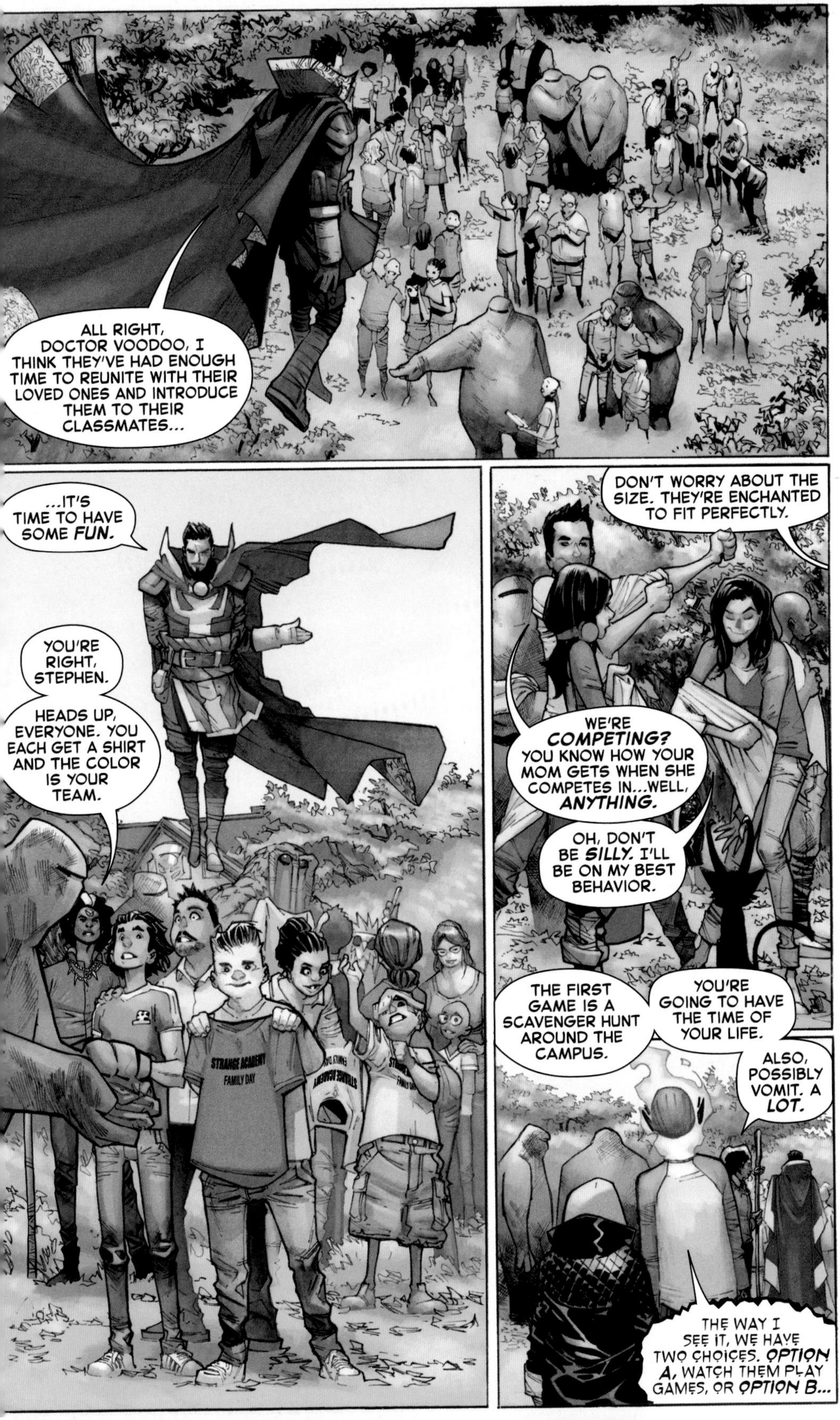
ALL RIGHT, DOCTOR VOODOO, I THINK THEY'VE HAD ENOUGH TIME TO REUNITE WITH THEIR LOVED ONES AND INTRODUCE THEM TO THEIR CLASSMATES...
...IT'S TIME TO HAVE SOME FUN.
YOU'RE RIGHT, STEPHEN.
HEADS UP, EVERYONE. YOU EACH GET A SHIRT AND THE COLOR IS YOUR TEAM.
STRANGE ACADEMY FAMILY DAY
DON'T WORRY ABOUT THE SIZE. THEY'RE ENCHANTED TO FIT PERFECTLY.
WE'RE COMPETING? YOU KNOW HOW YOUR MOM GETS WHEN SHE COMPETES IN...WELL, ANYTHING.
OH, DON'T BE SILLY. I'LL BE ON MY BEST BEHAVIOR.
THE FIRST GAME IS A SCAVENGER HUNT AROUND THE CAMPUS.
YOU'RE GOING TO HAVE THE TIME OF YOUR LIFE.
ALSO, POSSIBLY VOMIT. A LOT.
THE WAY I SEE IT, WE HAVE TWO CHOICES. OPTION A, WATCH THEM PLAY GAMES, OR OPTION B...

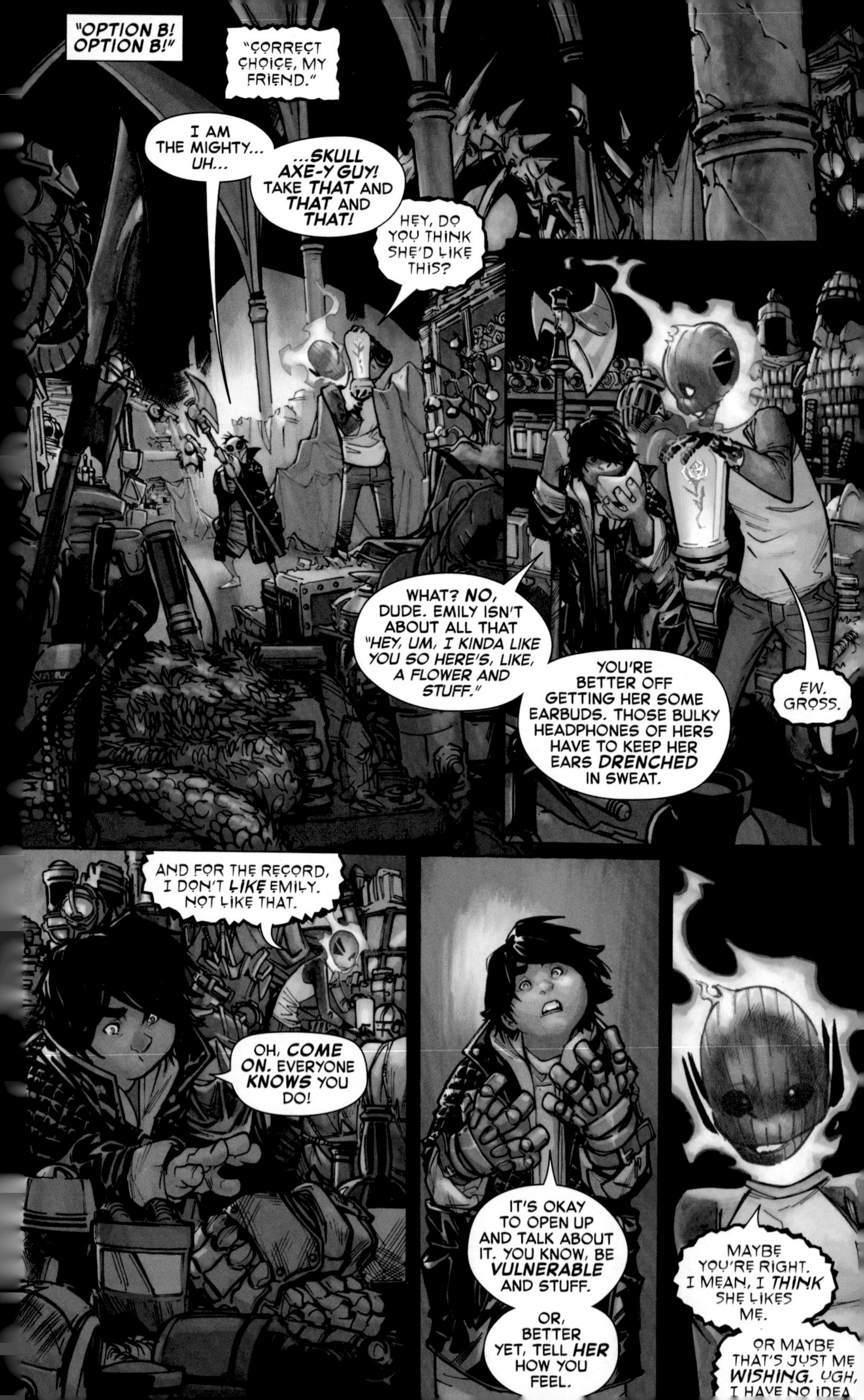
"OPTION B! OPTION B!"
"CORRECT CHOICE, MY FRIEND."
I AM THE MIGHTY... UH...
...SKULL AXE-Y GUY! TAKE THAT AND THAT AND THAT!
HEY, DO YOU THINK SHE'D LIKE THIS?
WHAT? NO, DUDE. EMILY ISN'T ABOUT ALL THAT "HEY, UM, I KINDA LIKE YOU SO HERE'S, LIKE, A FLOWER AND STUFF."
YOU'RE BETTER OFF GETTING HER SOME EARBUDS. THOSE BULKY HEADPHONES OF HERS HAVE TO KEEP HER EARS DRENCHED IN SWEAT.
EW. GROSS.
AND FOR THE RECORD, I DON'T LIKE EMILY. NOT LIKE THAT.
OH, COME ON. EVERYONE KNOWS YOU DO!
IT'S OKAY TO OPEN UP AND TALK ABOUT IT. YOU KNOW, BE VULNERABLE AND STUFF.
OR, BETTER YET, TELL HER HOW YOU FEEL.
MAYBE YOU'RE RIGHT. I MEAN, I THINK SHE LIKES ME.
OR MAYBE THAT'S JUST ME WISHING. UGH, I HAVE NO IDEA

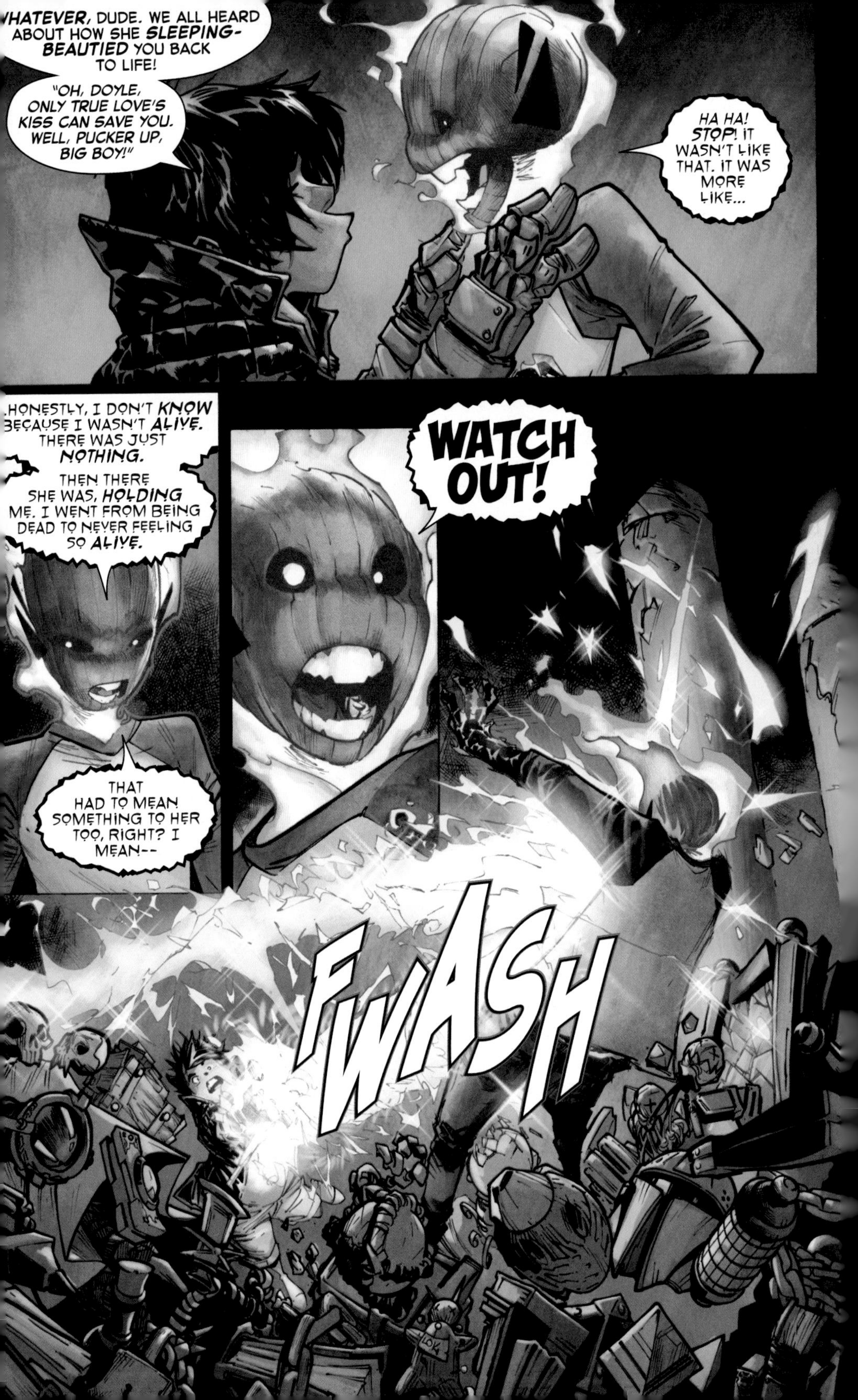
WHATEVER, DUDE. WE ALL HEARD ABOUT HOW SHE SLEEPING-BEAUTIED YOU BACK TO LIFE!
"OH, DOYLE, ONLY TRUE LOVE'S KISS CAN SAVE YOU. WELL, PUCKER UP, BIG BOY!"
HA HA! STOP! IT WASN'T LIKE THAT. IT WAS MORE LIKE...
...HONESTLY, I DON'T KNOW BECAUSE I WASN'T ALIVE. THERE WAS JUST NOTHING.
THEN THERE SHE WAS, HOLDING ME. I WENT FROM BEING DEAD TO NEVER FEELING SO ALIVE.
THAT HAD TO MEAN SOMETHING TO HER TOO, RIGHT? I MEAN--
WATCH OUT!
FWASH

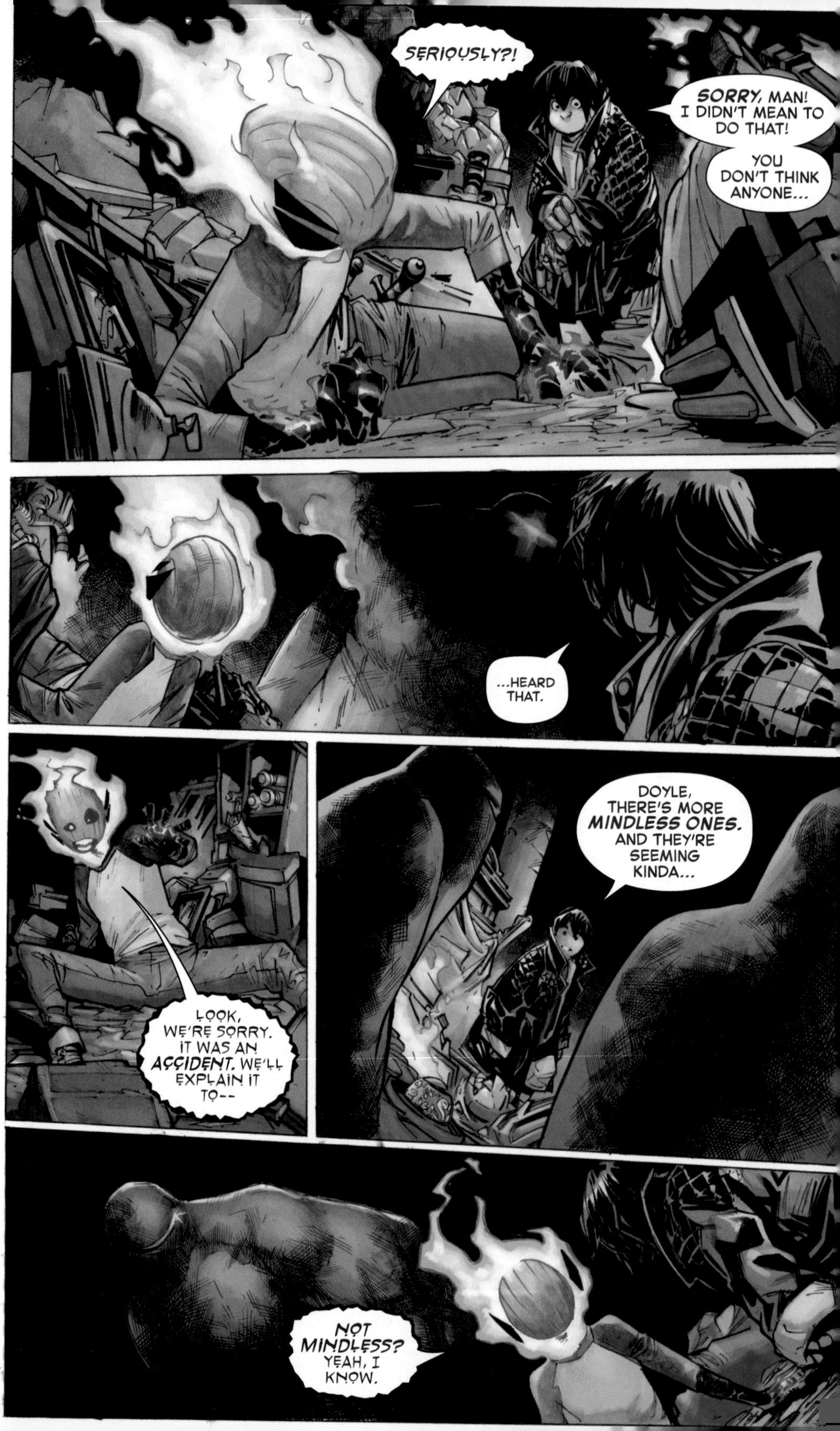
SERIOUSLY?!
SORRY, MAN! I DIDN'T MEAN TO DO THAT!
YOU DON'T THINK ANYONE...
...HEARD THAT.
LOOK, WE'RE SORRY. IT WAS AN ACCIDENT. WE'LL EXPLAIN IT TO--
DOYLE, THERE'S MORE MINDLESS ONES. AND THEY'RE SEEMING KINDA...
NOT MINDLESS? YEAH, I KNOW.

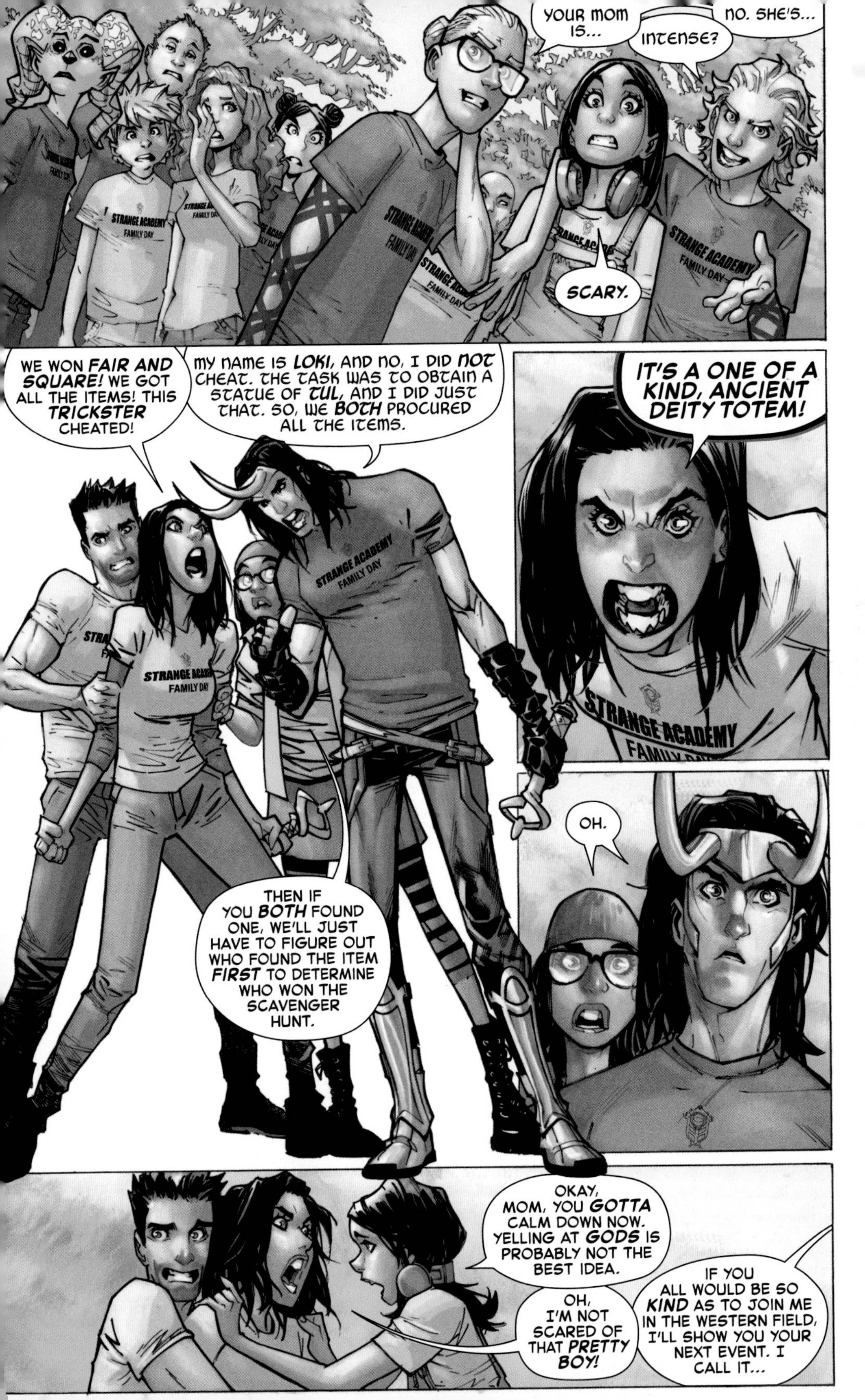
YOUR MOM IS...
INTENSE?
NO. SHE'S...
SCARY.
WE WON FAIR AND SQUARE! WE GOT ALL THE ITEMS! THIS TRICKSTER CHEATED!
MY NAME IS LOKI, AND NO, I DID NOT CHEAT. THE TASK WAS TO OBTAIN A STATUE OF TUL, AND I DID JUST THAT. SO, WE BOTH PROCURED ALL THE ITEMS.
IT'S A ONE OF A KIND, ANCIENT DEITY TOTEM!
OH.
THEN IF YOU BOTH FOUND ONE, WE'LL JUST HAVE TO FIGURE OUT WHO FOUND THE ITEM FIRST TO DETERMINE WHO WON THE SCAVENGER HUNT.
OKAY, MOM, YOU GOTTA CALM DOWN NOW. YELLING AT GODS IS PROBABLY NOT THE BEST IDEA.
OH, I'M NOT SCARED OF THAT PRETTY BOY!
IF YOU ALL WOULD BE SO KIND AS TO JOIN ME IN THE WESTERN FIELD, I'LL SHOW YOU YOUR NEXT EVENT. I CALL IT...

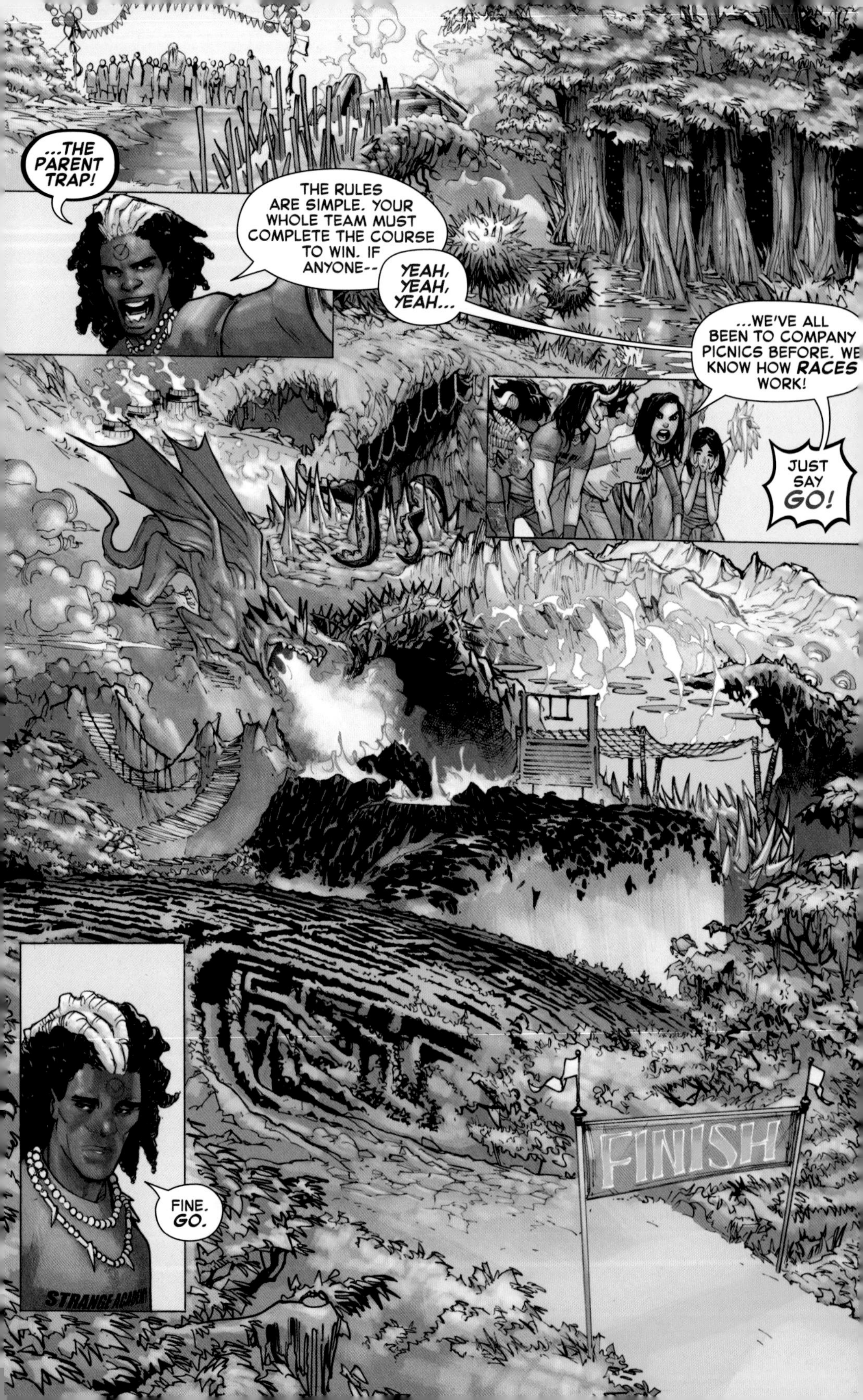
...THE PARENT TRAP!
THE RULES ARE SIMPLE. YOUR WHOLE TEAM MUST COMPLETE THE COURSE TO WIN. IF ANYONE--
YEAH, YEAH, YEAH...
...WE'VE ALL BEEN TO COMPANY PICNICS BEFORE. WE KNOW HOW RACES WORK!
JUST SAY GO!
FINE. GO.
FINISH
STRANGE ACADEMY

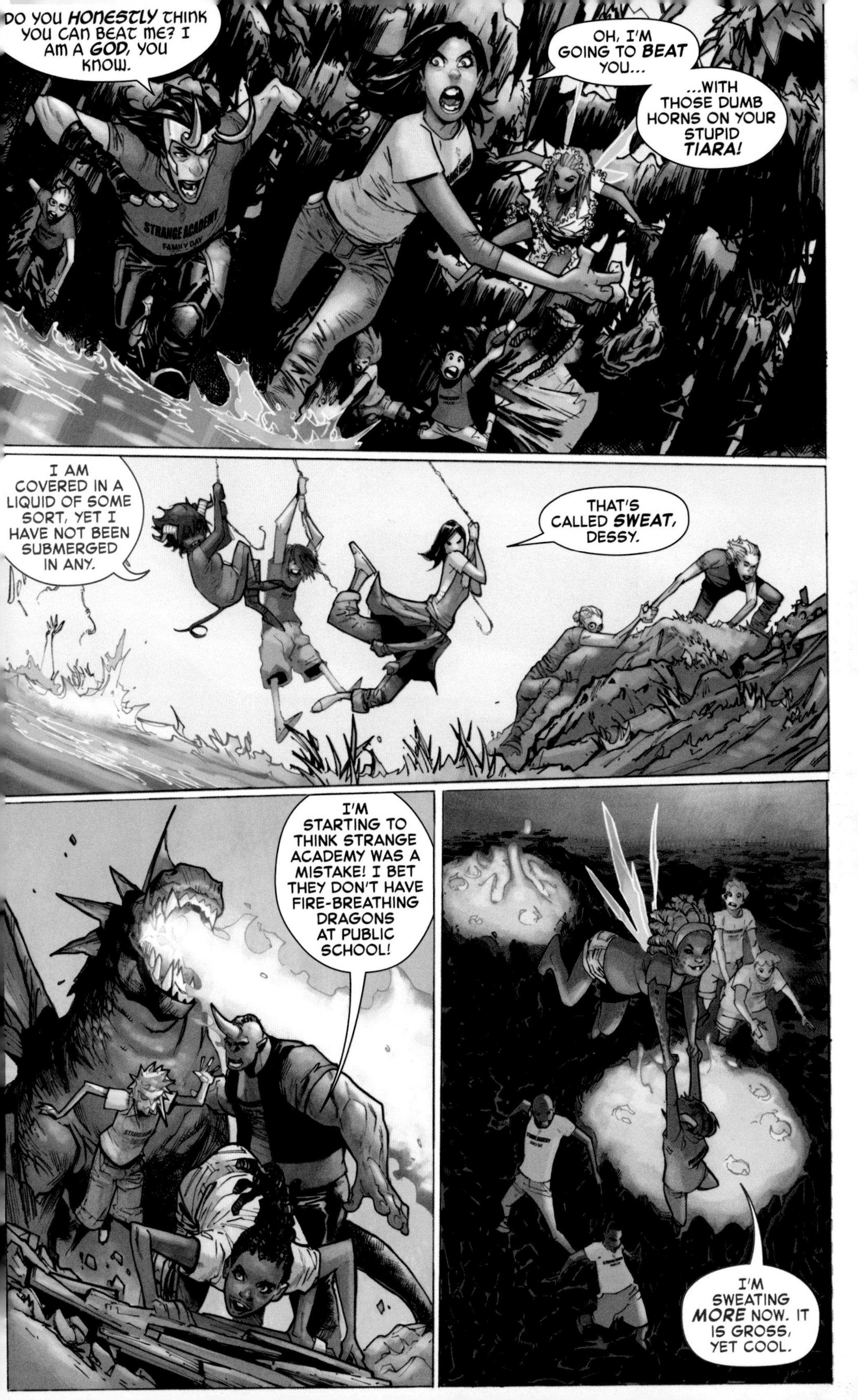
DO YOU HONESTLY THINK YOU CAN BEAT ME? I AM A GOD, YOU KNOW.
OH, I'M GOING TO BEAT YOU...
...WITH THOSE DUMB HORNS ON YOUR STUPID TIARA!
STRANGE ACADEMY FAMILY DAY
I AM COVERED IN A LIQUID OF SOME SORT, YET I HAVE NOT BEEN SUBMERGED IN ANY.
THAT'S CALLED SWEAT, DESSY.
I'M STARTING TO THINK STRANGE ACADEMY WAS A MISTAKE! I BET THEY DON'T HAVE FIRE-BREATHING DRAGONS AT PUBLIC SCHOOL!
I'M SWEATING MORE NOW. IT IS GROSS, YET COOL.

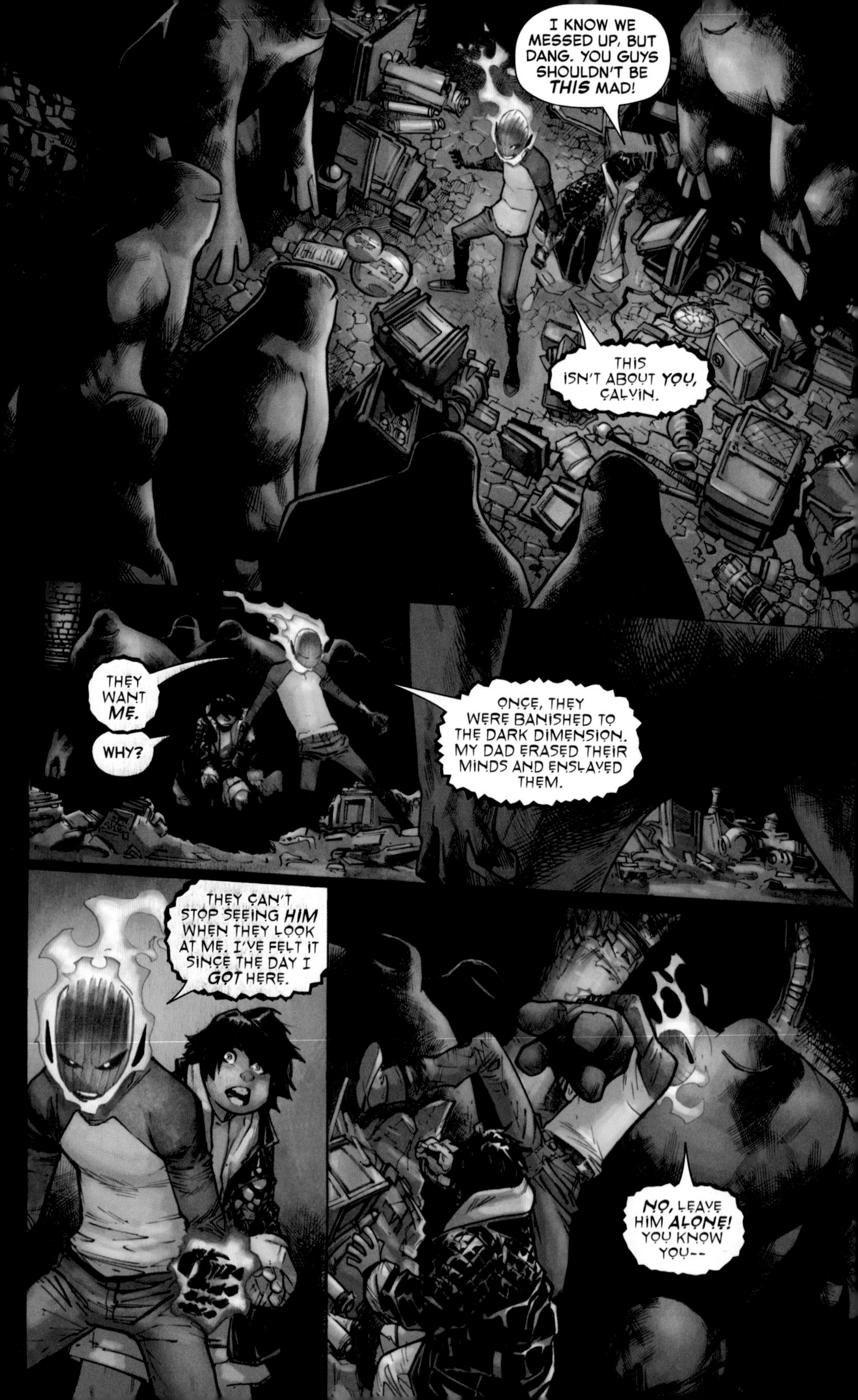
I KNOW WE MESSED UP, BUT DANG. YOU GUYS SHOULDN'T BE THIS MAD!
THIS ISN'T ABOUT YOU, CALVIN.
THEY WANT ME.
WHY?
ONCE, THEY WERE BANISHED TO THE DARK DIMENSION. MY DAD ERASED THEIR MINDS AND ENSLAVED THEM.
THEY CAN'T STOP SEEING HIM WHEN THEY LOOK AT ME. I'VE FELT IT SINCE THE DAY I GOT HERE.
NO, LEAVE HIM ALONE! YOU KNOW YOU--

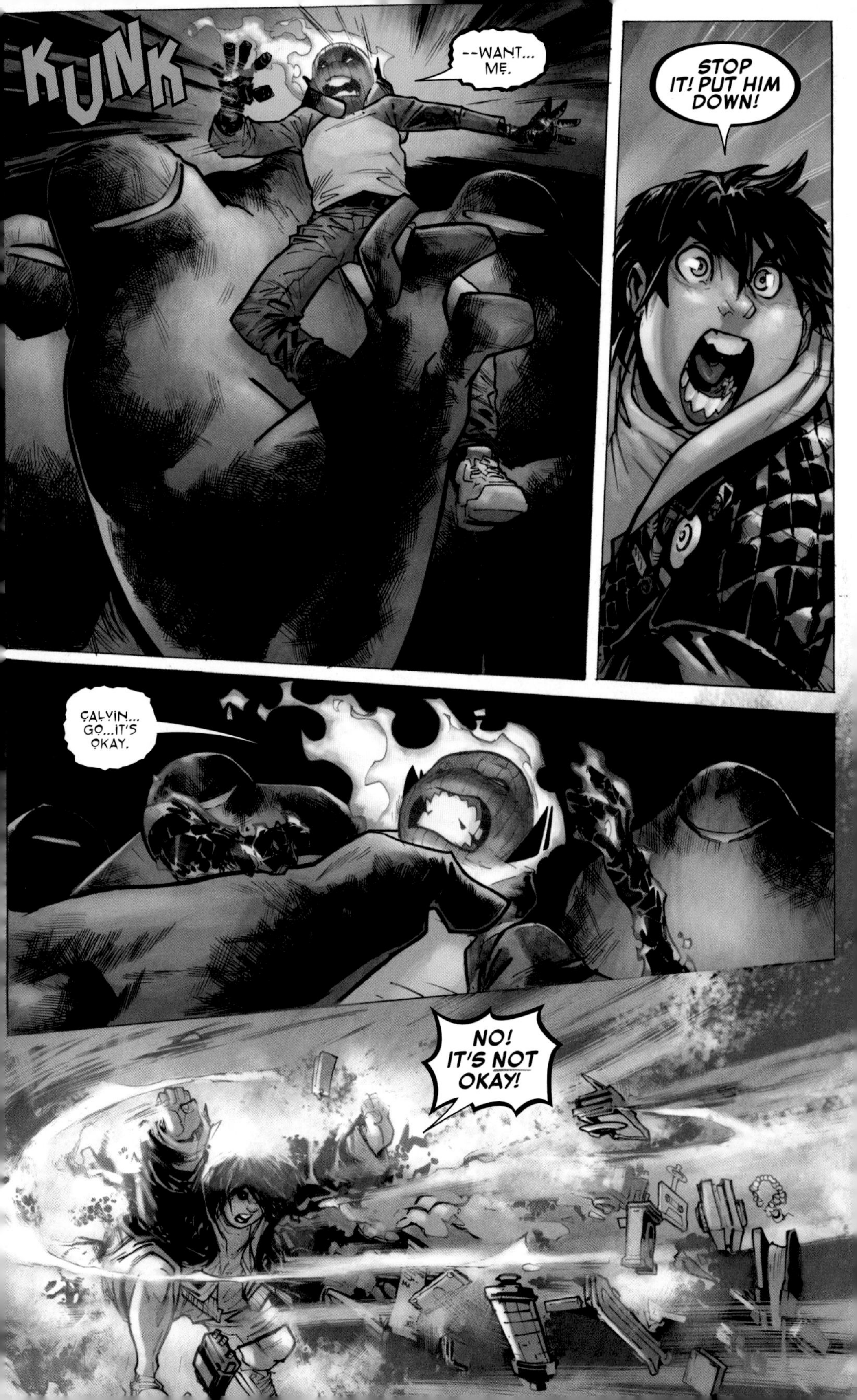
KUNK
--WANT... ME.
STOP IT! PUT HIM DOWN!
CALVIN... GO...IT'S OKAY.
NO! IT'S NOT OKAY!

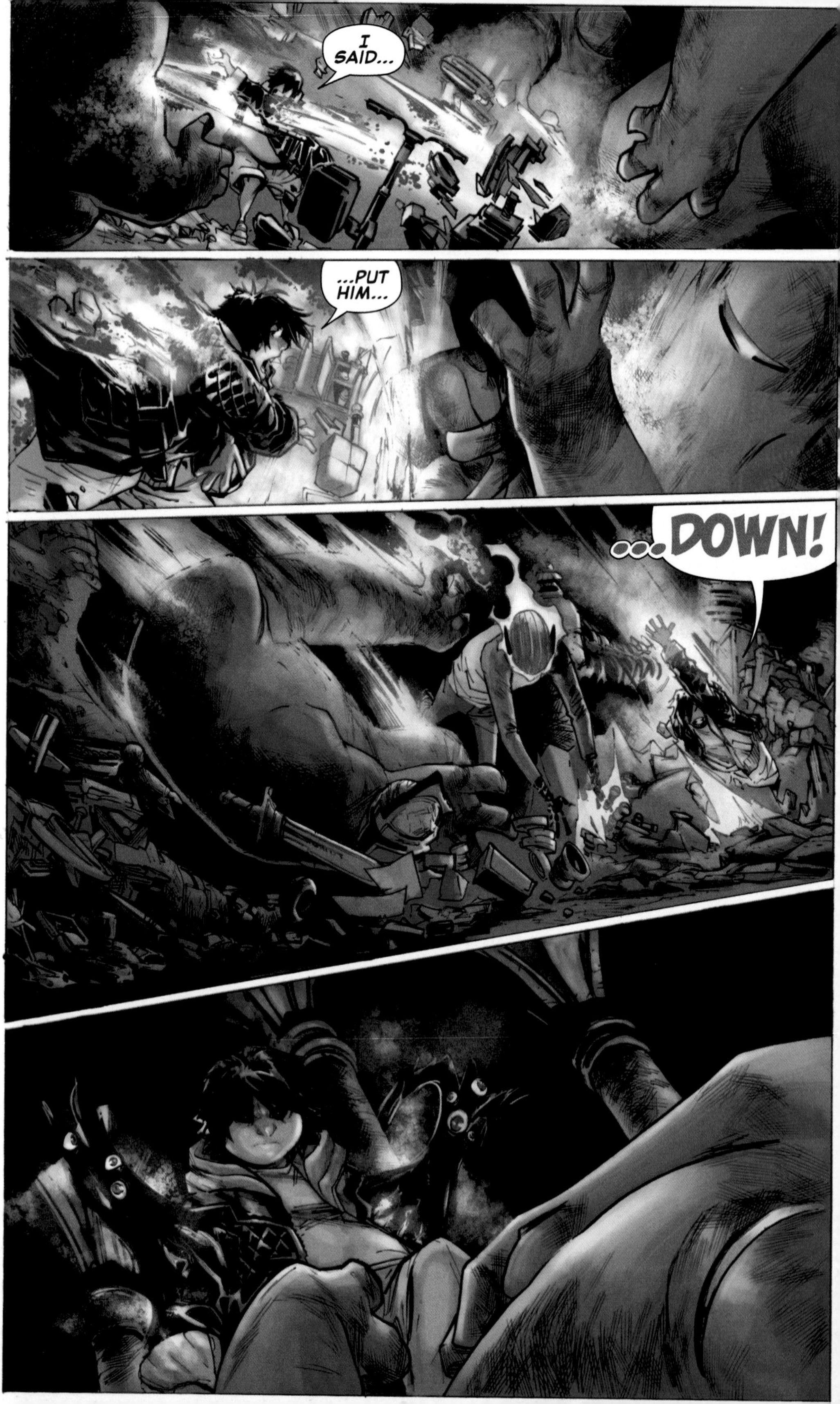

I SAID...
...PUT HIM...
...DOWN!

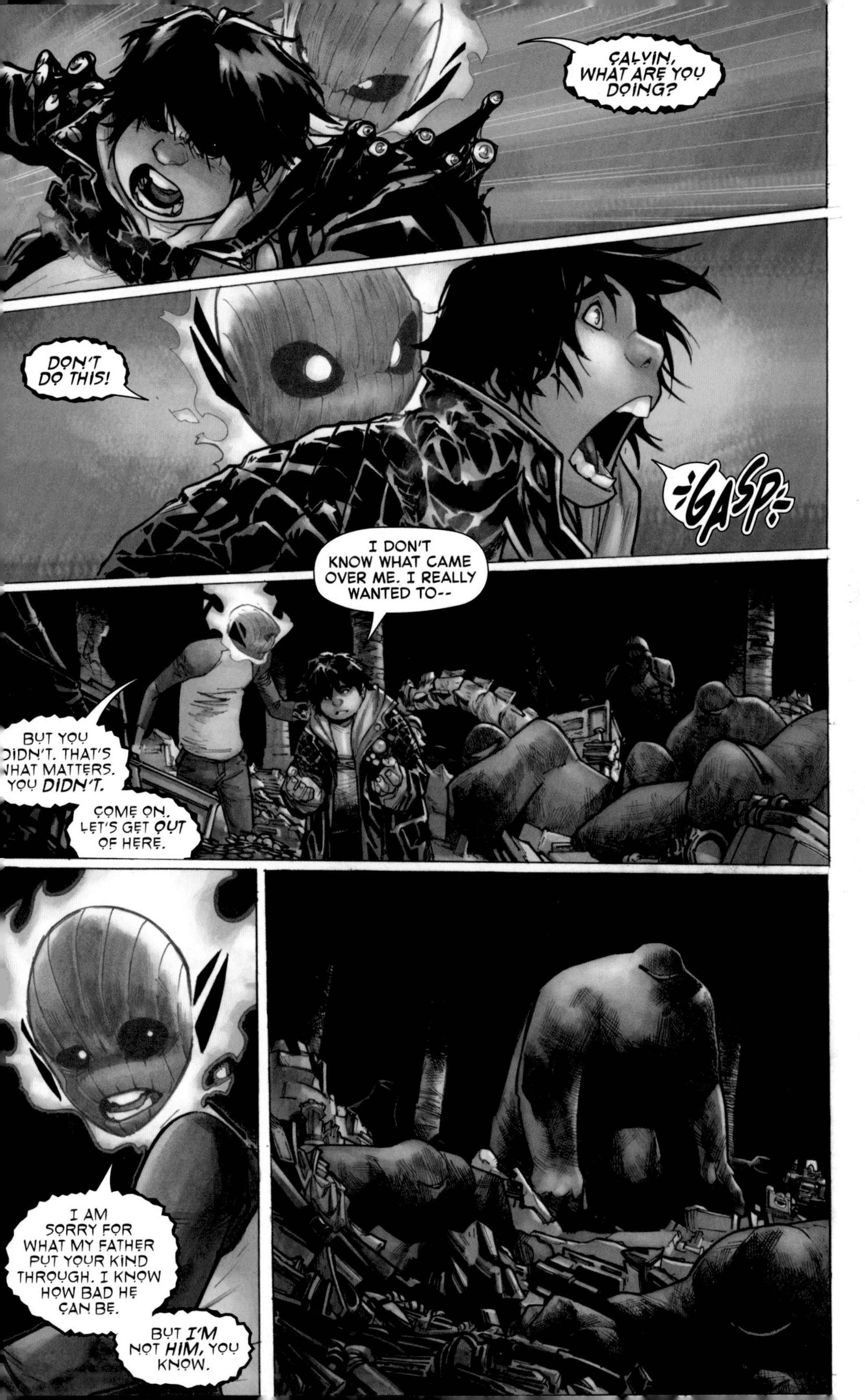

CALVIN, WHAT ARE YOU DOING?
DON'T DO THIS!
GASP
I DON'T KNOW WHAT CAME OVER ME. I REALLY WANTED TO--
BUT YOU DIDN'T. THAT'S WHAT MATTERS. YOU DIDN'T.
COME ON. LET'S GET OUT OF HERE.
I AM SORRY FOR WHAT MY FATHER PUT YOUR KIND THROUGH. I KNOW HOW BAD HE CAN BE.
BUT I'M NOT HIM, YOU KNOW.

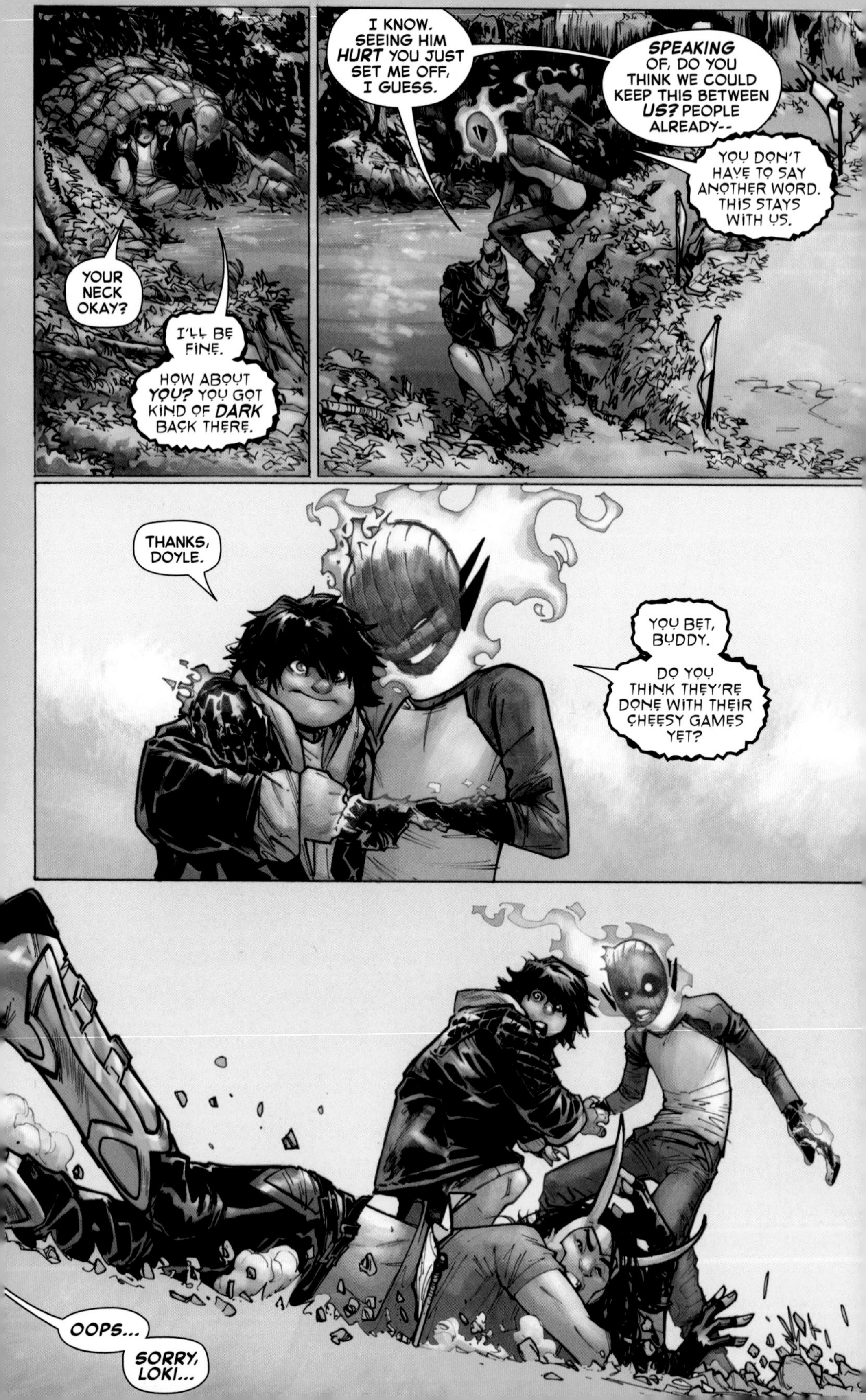
YOUR NECK OKAY?
I'LL BE FINE.
HOW ABOUT YOU? YOU GOT KIND OF DARK BACK THERE.
I KNOW. SEEING HIM HURT YOU JUST SET ME OFF, I GUESS.
SPEAKING OF, DO YOU THINK WE COULD KEEP THIS BETWEEN US? PEOPLE ALREADY--
YOU DON'T HAVE TO SAY ANOTHER WORD. THIS STAYS WITH US.
THANKS, DOYLE.
YOU BET, BUDDY.
DO YOU THINK THEY'RE DONE WITH THEIR CHEESY GAMES YET?
OOPS...
SORRY, LOKI...

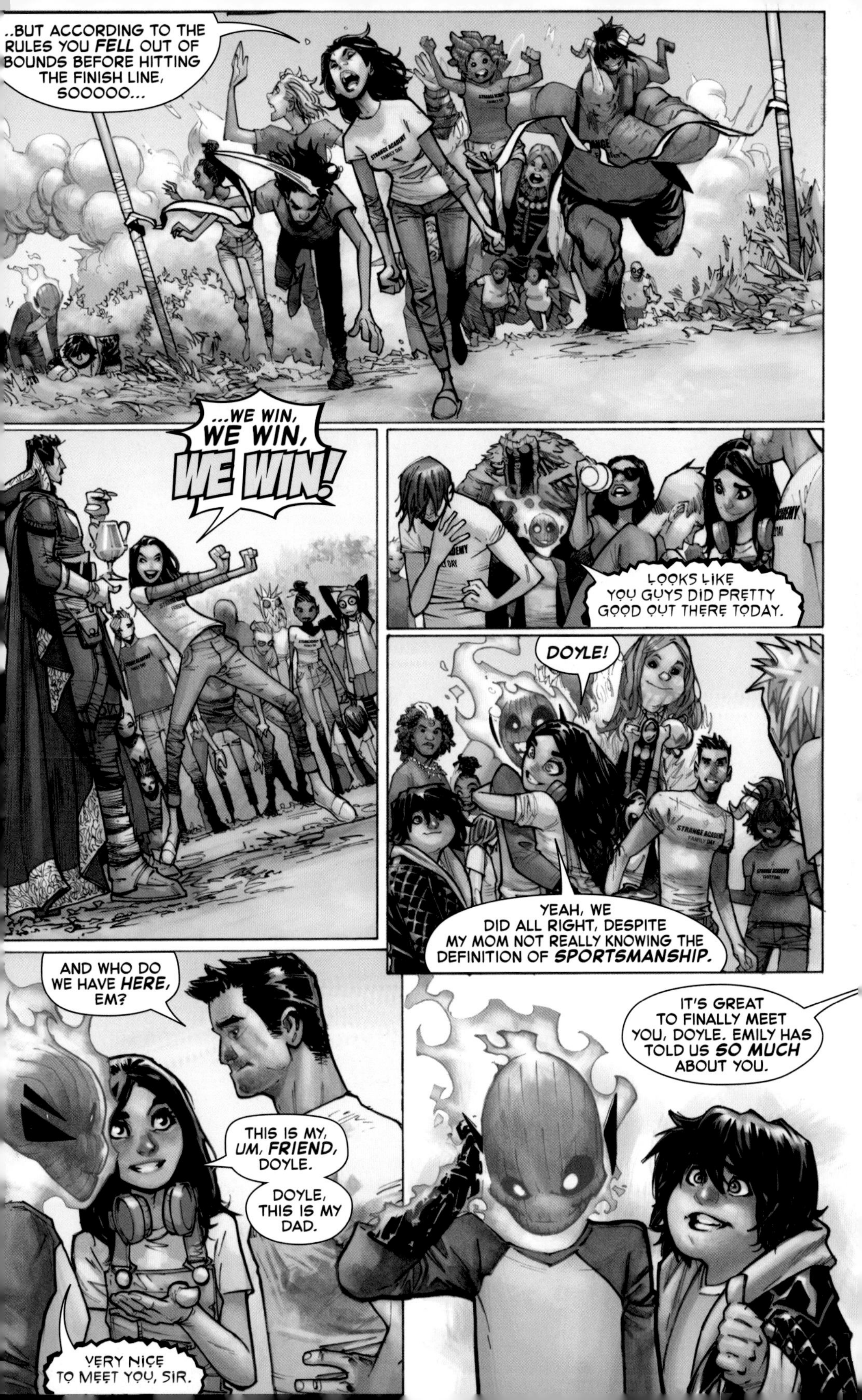
..BUT ACCORDING TO THE RULES YOU FELL OUT OF BOUNDS BEFORE HITTING THE FINISH LINE, SOOOOO...
...WE WIN, WE WIN, WE WIN!
LOOKS LIKE YOU GUYS DID PRETTY GOOD OUT THERE TODAY.
DOYLE!
YEAH, WE DID ALL RIGHT, DESPITE MY MOM NOT REALLY KNOWING THE DEFINITION OF SPORTSMANSHIP.
AND WHO DO WE HAVE HERE, EM?
THIS IS MY, UM, FRIEND, DOYLE.
DOYLE, THIS IS MY DAD.
VERY NICE TO MEET YOU, SIR.
IT'S GREAT TO FINALLY MEET YOU, DOYLE. EMILY HAS TOLD US SO MUCH ABOUT YOU.

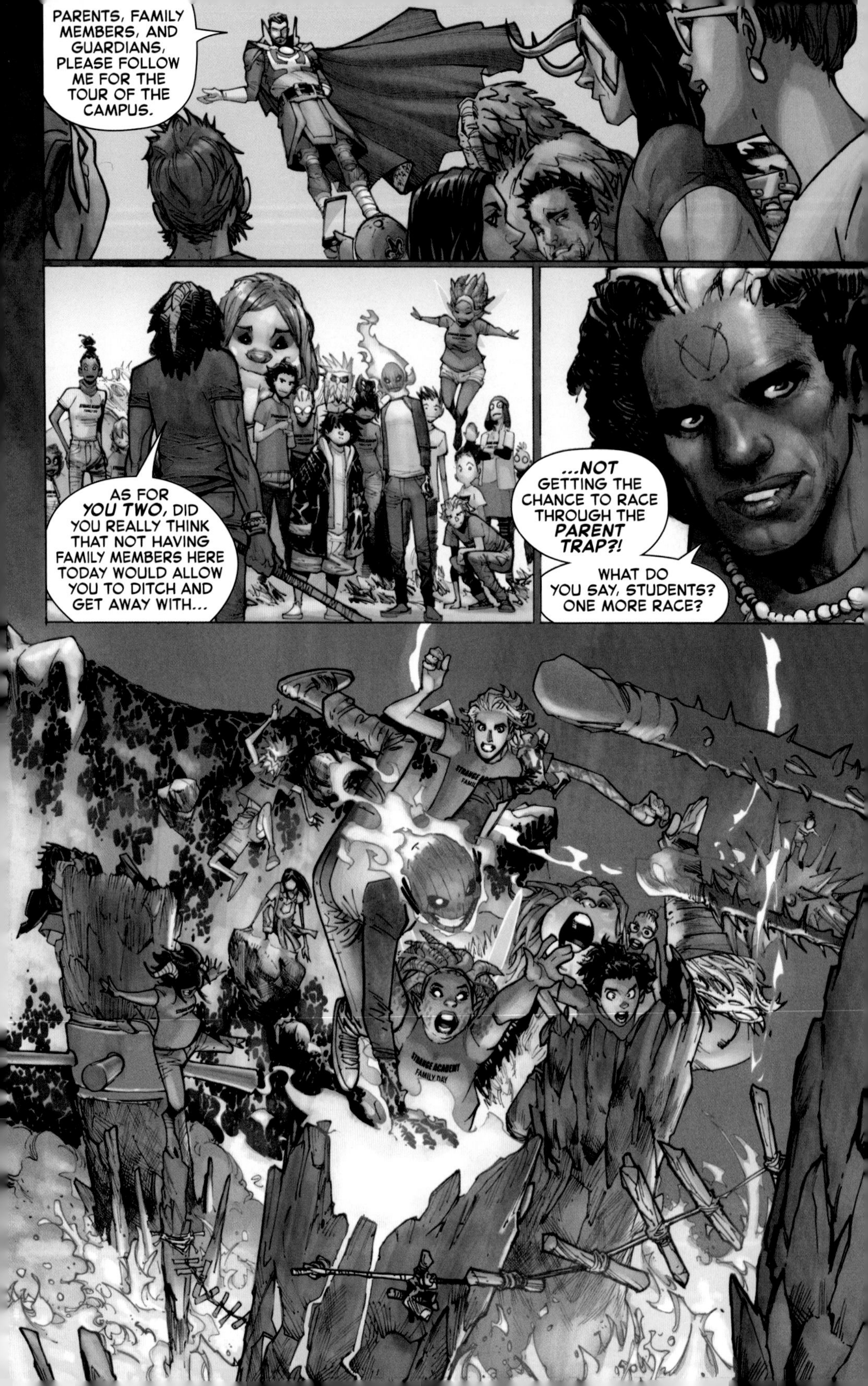
PARENTS, FAMILY MEMBERS, AND GUARDIANS, PLEASE FOLLOW ME FOR THE TOUR OF THE CAMPUS.
AS FOR YOU TWO, DID YOU REALLY THINK THAT NOT HAVING FAMILY MEMBERS HERE TODAY WOULD ALLOW YOU TO DITCH AND GET AWAY WITH...
...NOT GETTING THE CHANCE TO RACE THROUGH THE PARENT TRAP?!
WHAT DO YOU SAY, STUDENTS? ONE MORE RACE?

STRANGE Academy

PARENTS' DAY RACE RESULTS

1. MRS. BRIGHT – YELLOW TEAM – 18.5467

2. LOKI – ORANGE TEAM – 18.5466

3. GERMÁN AGUILAR – ORANGE TEAM – 18.89

4. IRIC BRORSON – ORANGE TEAM – 19.01

5. ZOE – YELLOW TEAM – 19.49

6. SHAYLEE MOONPEDDLE – ORANGE TEAM – 19.51

7. (TIE) DESSY & S'YM – ORANGE TEAM – 20.11

Something's up with Loki's time. Voodoo, please review.

STRANGE Academy

DAMAGE REPORT

LOCATION: Storage Facility
Notes:

- Rose of Despair: Glass encasement cracked; no deadly energies have escaped.

- Lightning Gauntlets: Discharged; missing left gauntlet's pinky finger.

- Asgardian Guard's Long Ax: Handle broken.

- Loki Voodoo Doll: Completely scorched.

- Ancient One's Hanging Perpetual Flame Lamp: Glass shattered; fire still lit.

- Mystic Visions Globe: Glass shattered; gas escaped. **HIGH PRIORITY.**

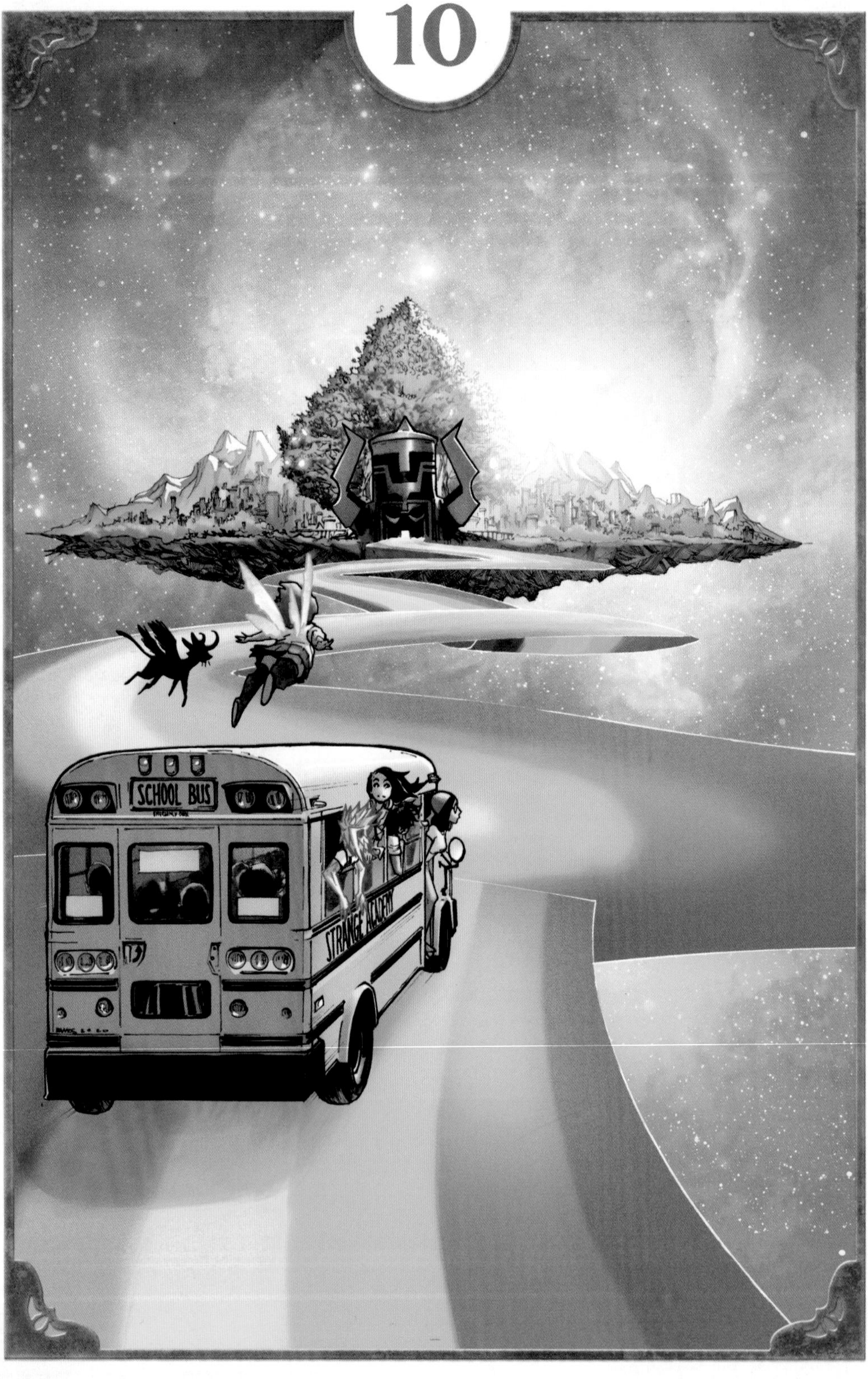
10
SCHOOL BUS
STRANGE ACADEMY

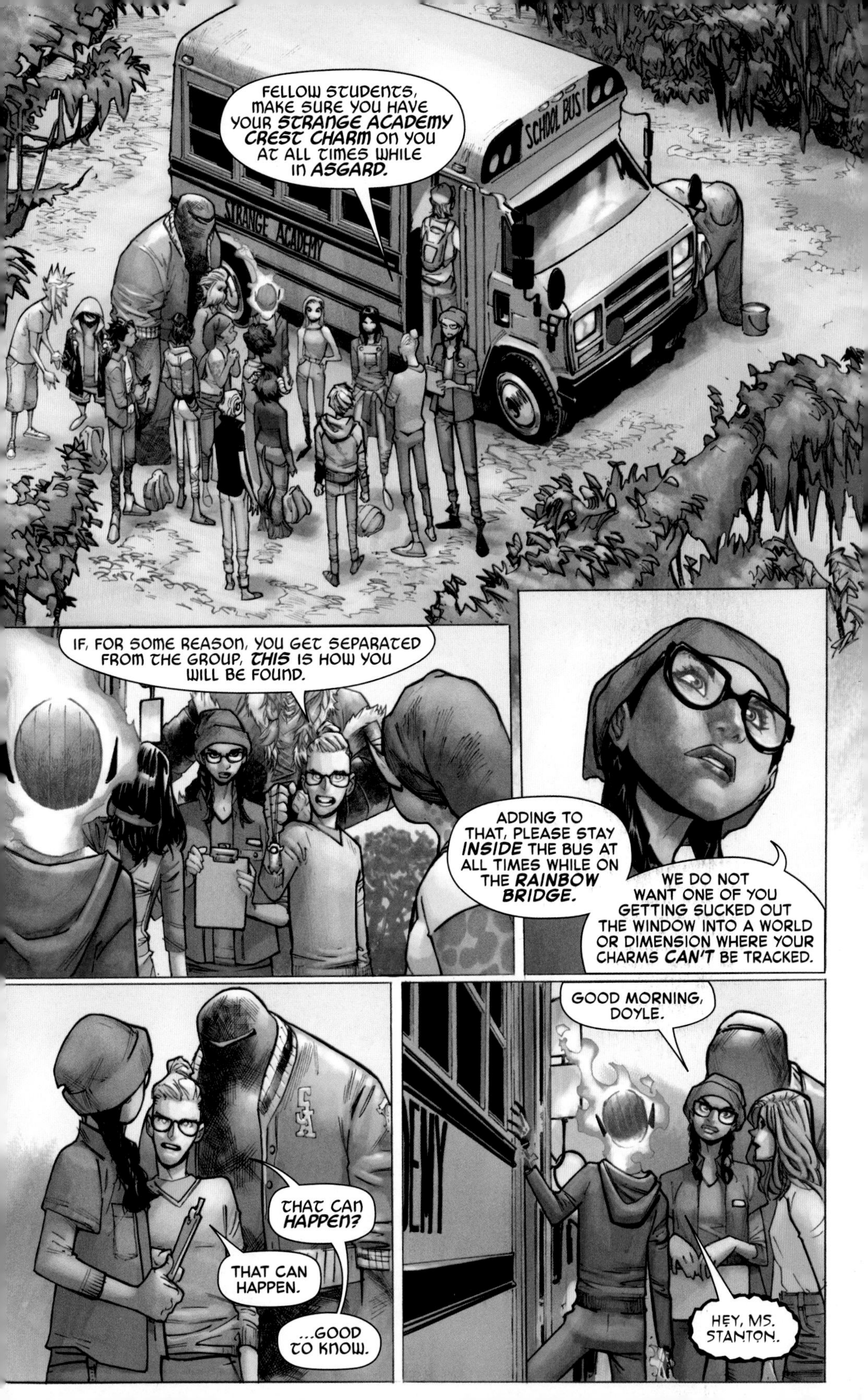
FELLOW STUDENTS, MAKE SURE YOU HAVE YOUR STRANGE ACADEMY CREST CHARM ON YOU AT ALL TIMES WHILE IN ASGARD.
SCHOOL BUS!
STRANGE ACADEMY
IF, FOR SOME REASON, YOU GET SEPARATED FROM THE GROUP, THIS IS HOW YOU WILL BE FOUND.
ADDING TO THAT, PLEASE STAY INSIDE THE BUS AT ALL TIMES WHILE ON THE RAINBOW BRIDGE.
WE DO NOT WANT ONE OF YOU GETTING SUCKED OUT THE WINDOW INTO A WORLD OR DIMENSION WHERE YOUR CHARMS CAN'T BE TRACKED.
THAT CAN HAPPEN?
THAT CAN HAPPEN.
...GOOD TO KNOW.
GOOD MORNING, DOYLE.
HEY, MS. STANTON.

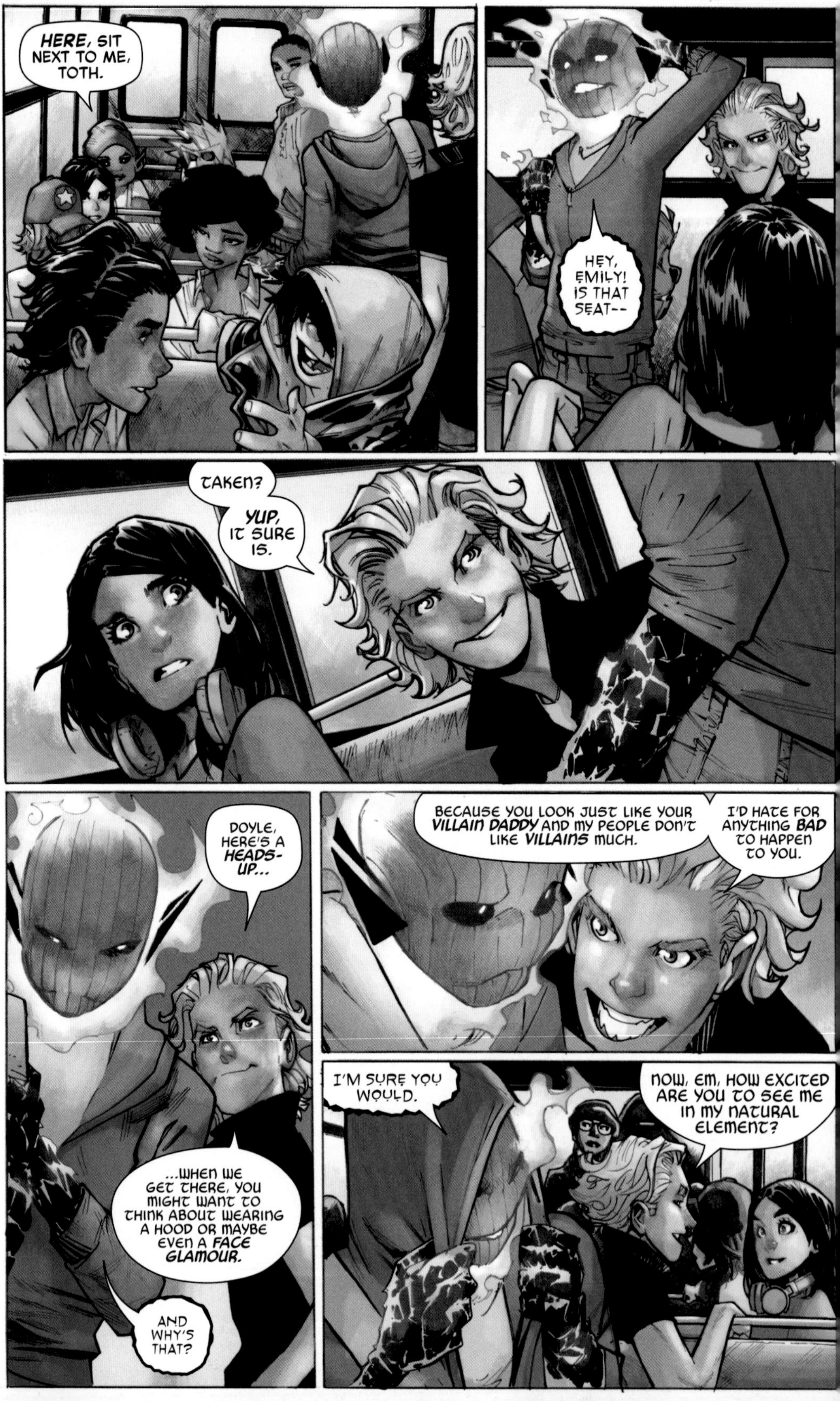
HERE, SIT NEXT TO ME, TOTH.
HEY, EMILY! IS THAT SEAT--
TAKEN?
YUP, IT SURE IS.
DOYLE, HERE'S A HEADS-UP...
...WHEN WE GET THERE, YOU MIGHT WANT TO THINK ABOUT WEARING A HOOD OR MAYBE EVEN A FACE GLAMOUR.
AND WHY'S THAT?
BECAUSE YOU LOOK JUST LIKE YOUR VILLAIN DADDY AND MY PEOPLE DON'T LIKE VILLAINS MUCH.
I'D HATE FOR ANYTHING BAD TO HAPPEN TO YOU.
I'M SURE YOU WOULD.
NOW, EM, HOW EXCITED ARE YOU TO SEE ME IN MY NATURAL ELEMENT?

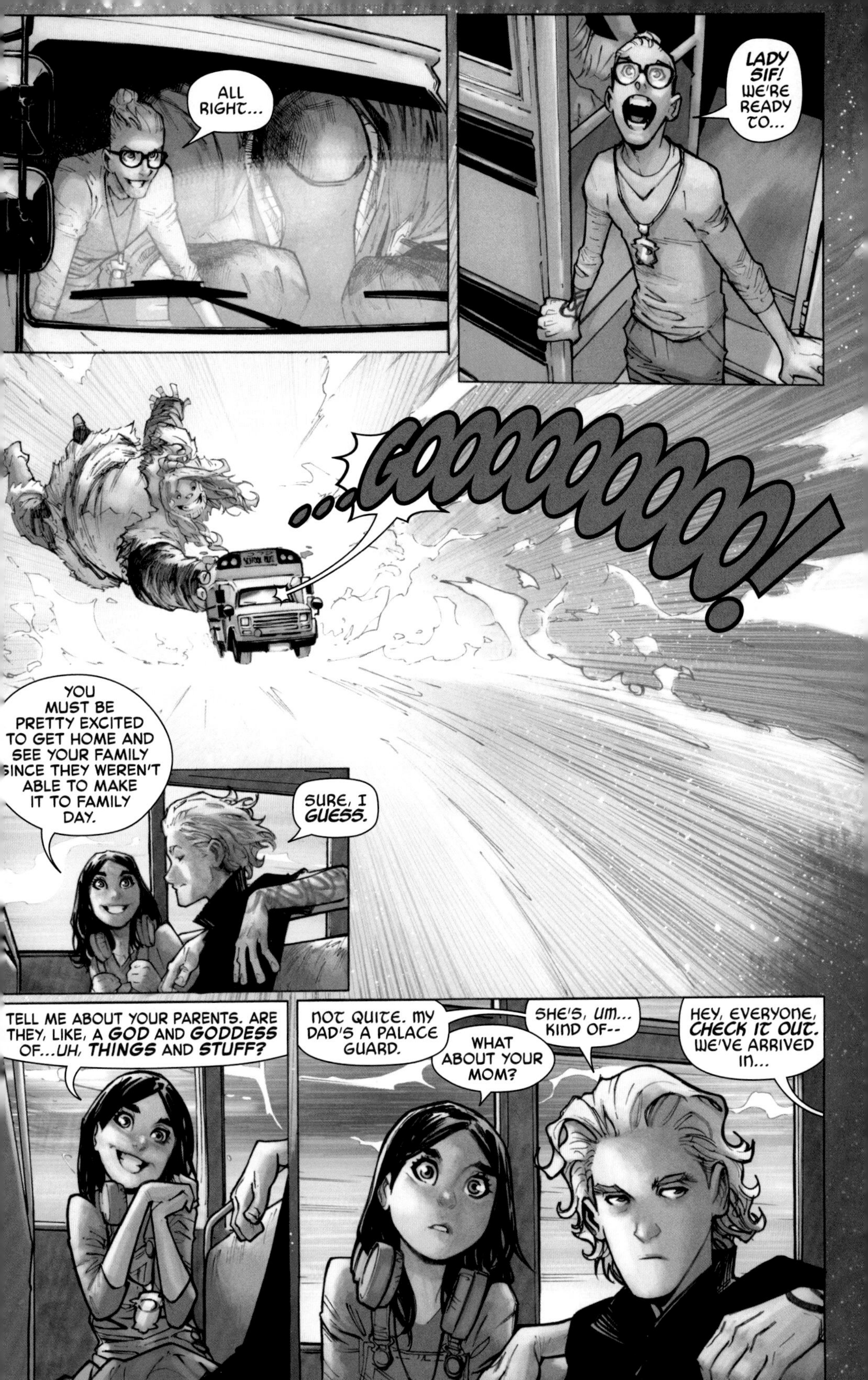

ALL RIGHT...
LADY SIF! WE'RE READY TO...
...GOOOOOOOOOO!
YOU MUST BE PRETTY EXCITED TO GET HOME AND SEE YOUR FAMILY SINCE THEY WEREN'T ABLE TO MAKE IT TO FAMILY DAY.
SURE, I GUESS.
TELL ME ABOUT YOUR PARENTS. ARE THEY, LIKE, A GOD AND GODDESS OF...UH, THINGS AND STUFF?
NOT QUITE. MY DAD'S A PALACE GUARD.
WHAT ABOUT YOUR MOM?
SHE'S, UM... KIND OF--
HEY, EVERYONE, CHECK IT OUT. WE'VE ARRIVED IN...

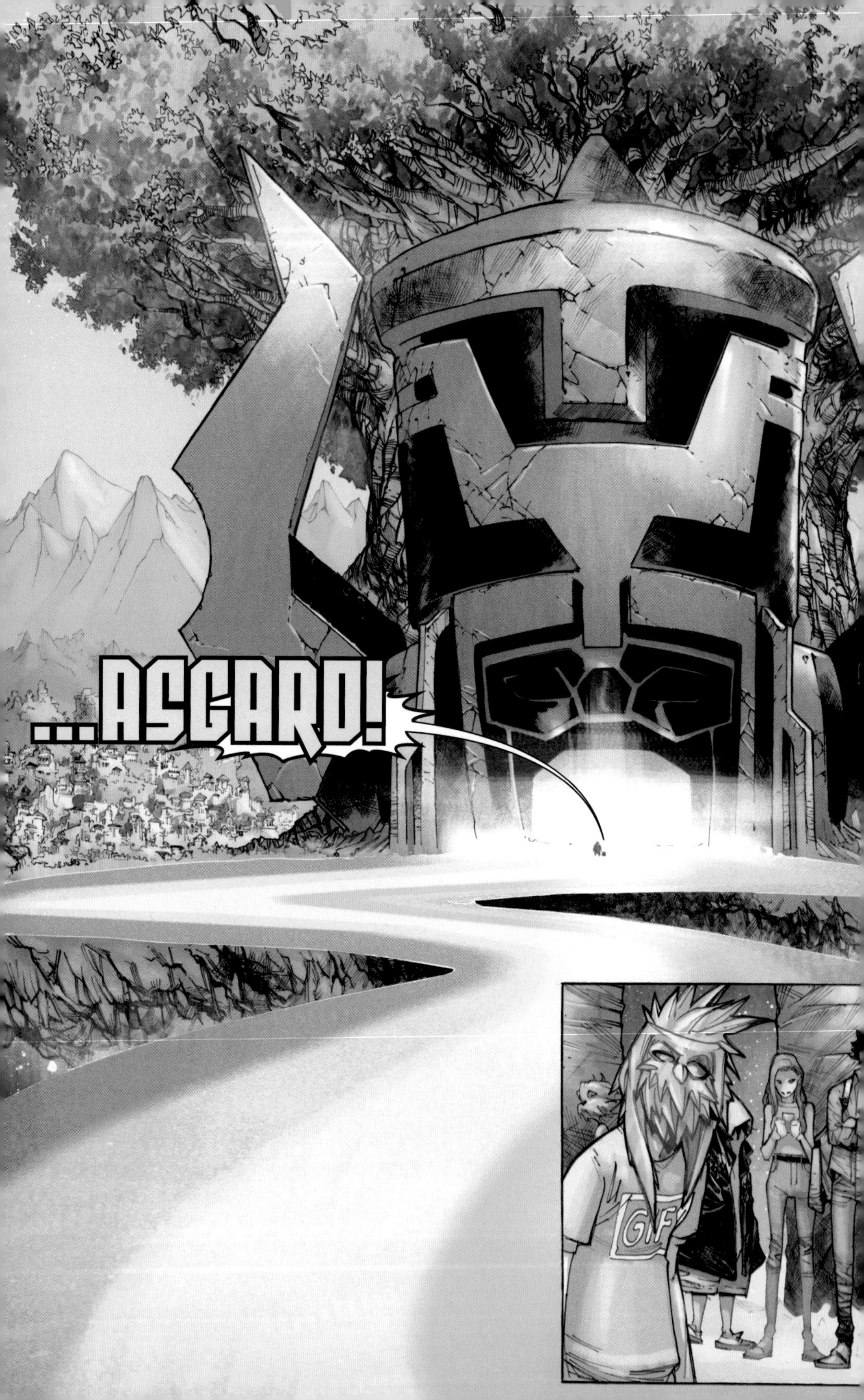
...ASGARD!

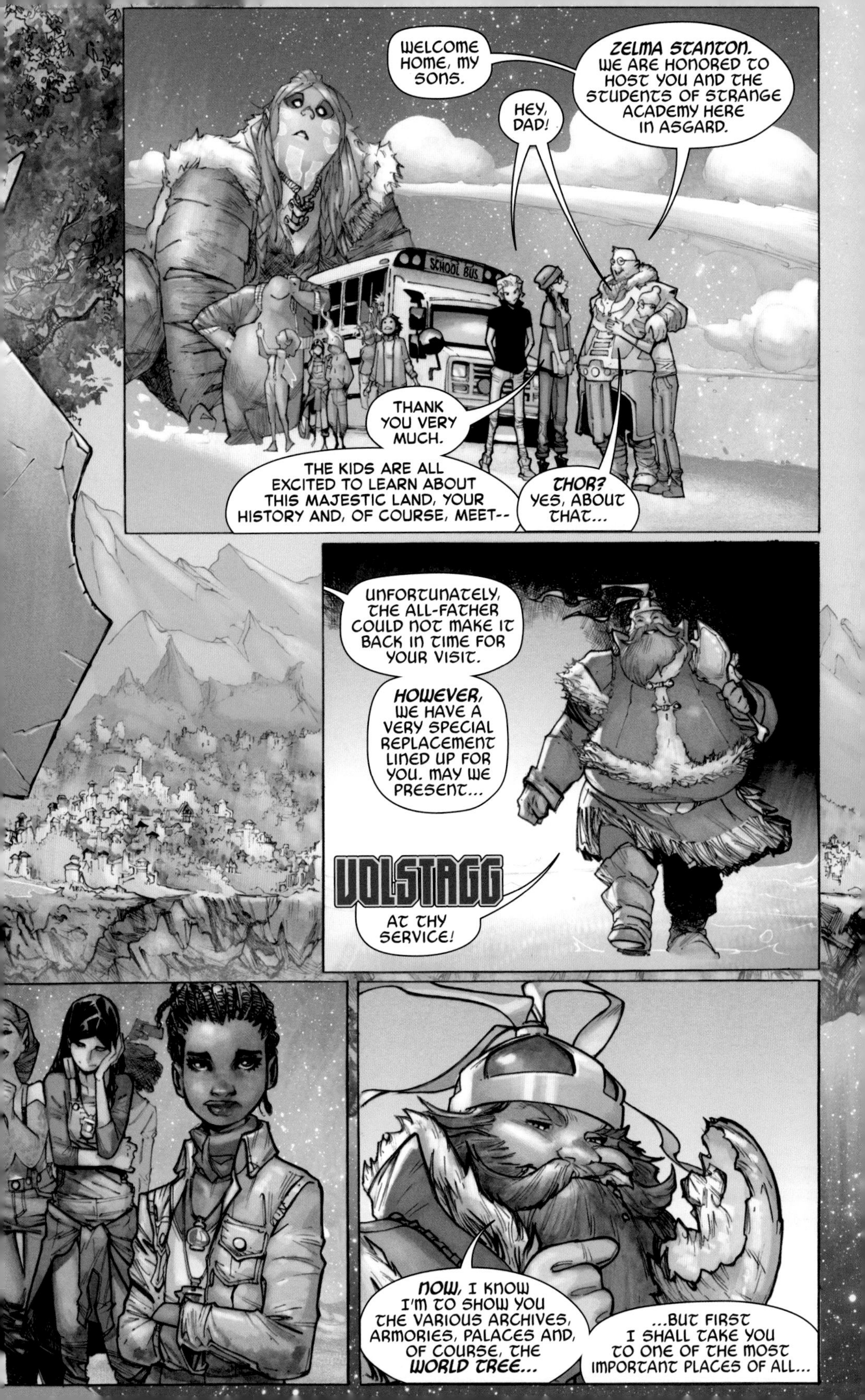
WELCOME HOME, MY SONS.
ZELMA STANTON. WE ARE HONORED TO HOST YOU AND THE STUDENTS OF STRANGE ACADEMY HERE IN ASGARD.
HEY, DAD!
SCHOOL BUS
THANK YOU VERY MUCH.
THE KIDS ARE ALL EXCITED TO LEARN ABOUT THIS MAJESTIC LAND, YOUR HISTORY AND, OF COURSE, MEET--
THOR? YES, ABOUT THAT...
UNFORTUNATELY, THE ALL-FATHER COULD NOT MAKE IT BACK IN TIME FOR YOUR VISIT.
HOWEVER, WE HAVE A VERY SPECIAL REPLACEMENT LINED UP FOR YOU. MAY WE PRESENT...
VOLSTAGG
AT THY SERVICE!
NOW, I KNOW I'M TO SHOW YOU THE VARIOUS ARCHIVES, ARMORIES, PALACES AND, OF COURSE, THE WORLD TREE...
...BUT FIRST I SHALL TAKE YOU TO ONE OF THE MOST IMPORTANT PLACES OF ALL...

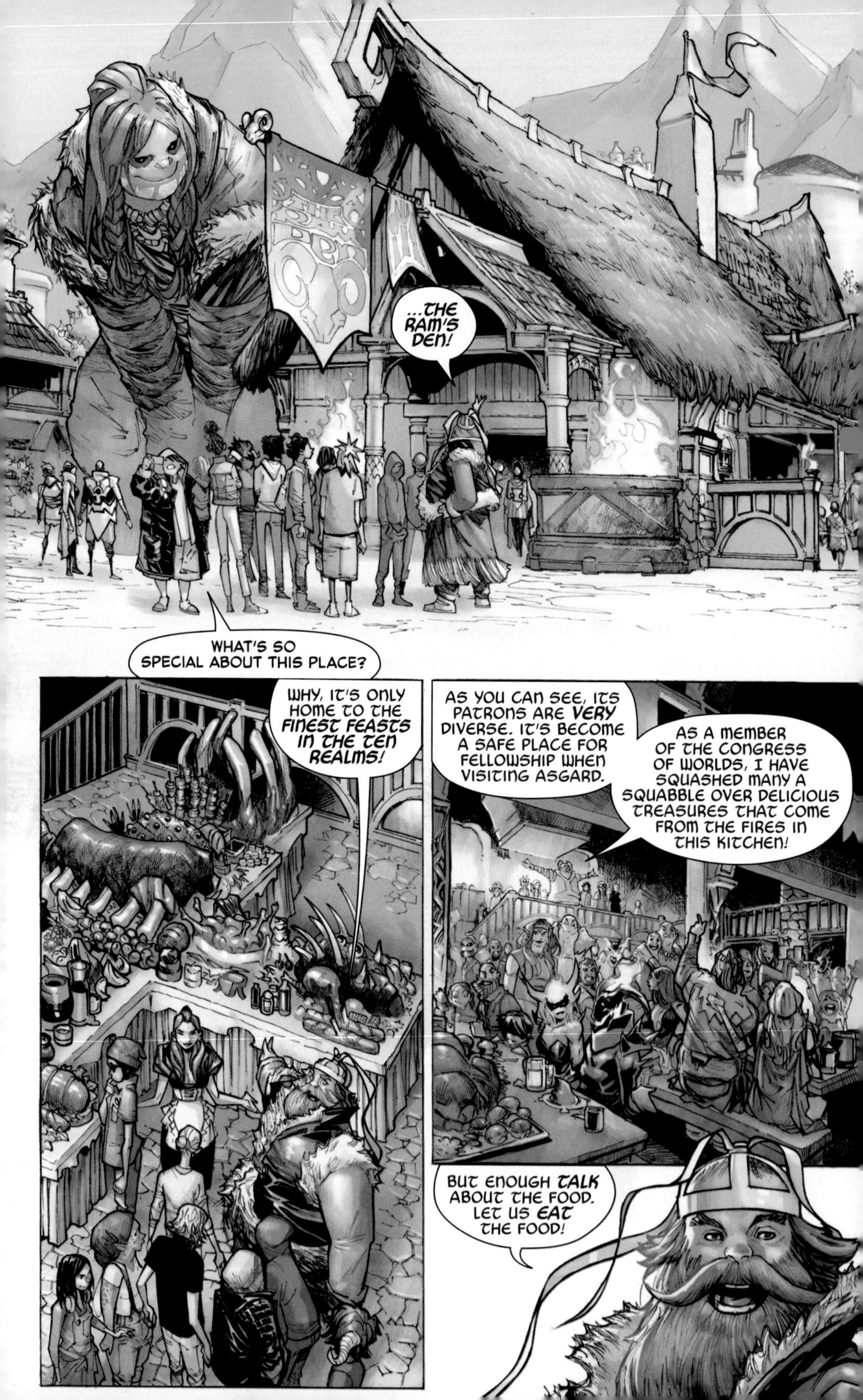
...THE RAM'S DEN!
WHAT'S SO SPECIAL ABOUT THIS PLACE?
WHY, IT'S ONLY HOME TO THE FINEST FEASTS IN THE TEN REALMS!
AS YOU CAN SEE, ITS PATRONS ARE VERY DIVERSE. IT'S BECOME A SAFE PLACE FOR FELLOWSHIP WHEN VISITING ASGARD.
AS A MEMBER OF THE CONGRESS OF WORLDS, I HAVE SQUASHED MANY A SQUABBLE OVER DELICIOUS TREASURES THAT COME FROM THE FIRES IN THIS KITCHEN!
BUT ENOUGH TALK ABOUT THE FOOD. LET US EAT THE FOOD!

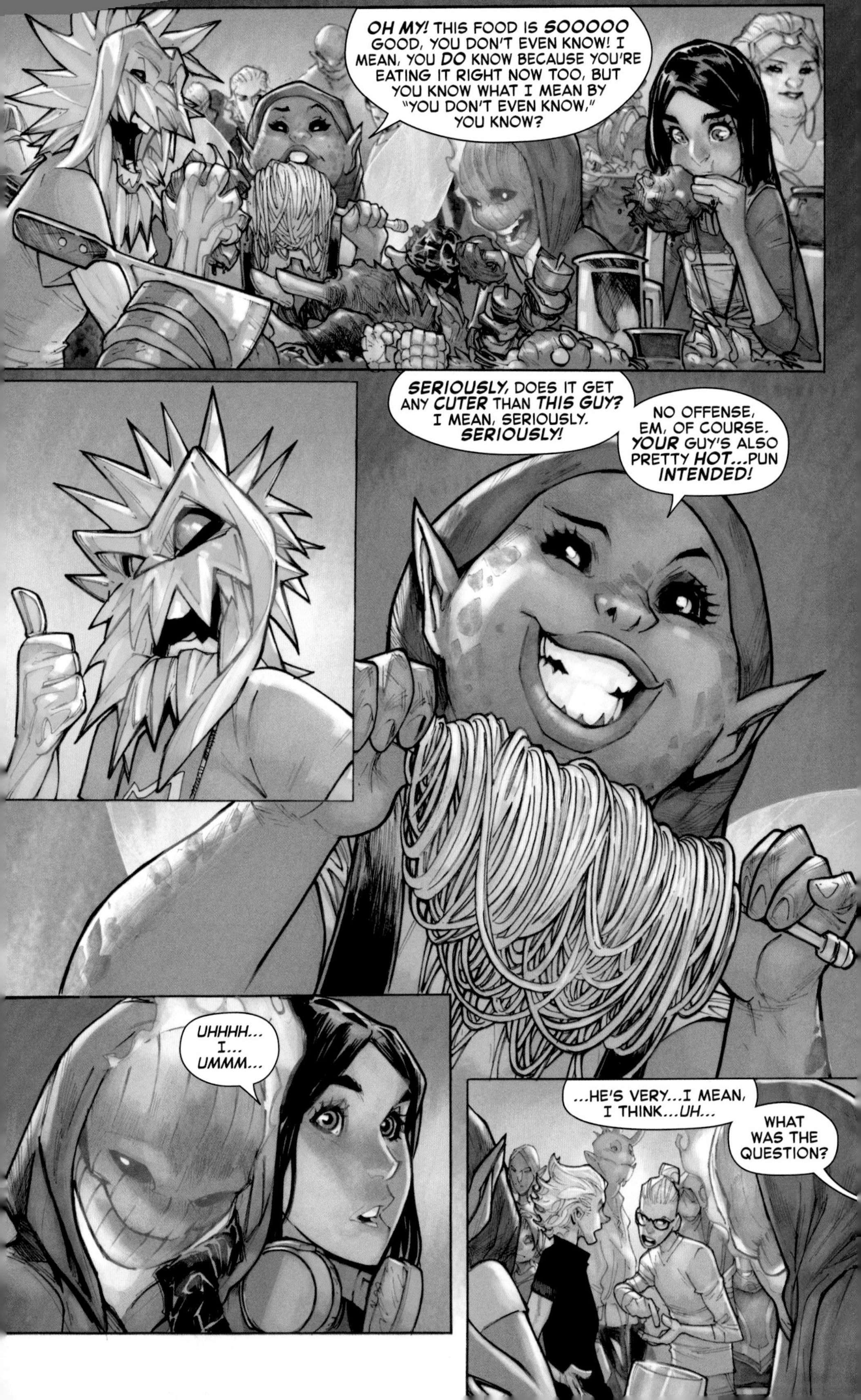

OH MY! THIS FOOD IS SOOOOO GOOD, YOU DON'T EVEN KNOW! I MEAN, YOU DO KNOW BECAUSE YOU'RE EATING IT RIGHT NOW TOO, BUT YOU KNOW WHAT I MEAN BY "YOU DON'T EVEN KNOW," YOU KNOW?
SERIOUSLY, DOES IT GET ANY CUTER THAN THIS GUY? I MEAN, SERIOUSLY. SERIOUSLY!
NO OFFENSE, EM, OF COURSE. YOUR GUY'S ALSO PRETTY HOT...PUN INTENDED!
UHHHH... I... UMMM...
...HE'S VERY...I MEAN, I THINK...UH...
WHAT WAS THE QUESTION?

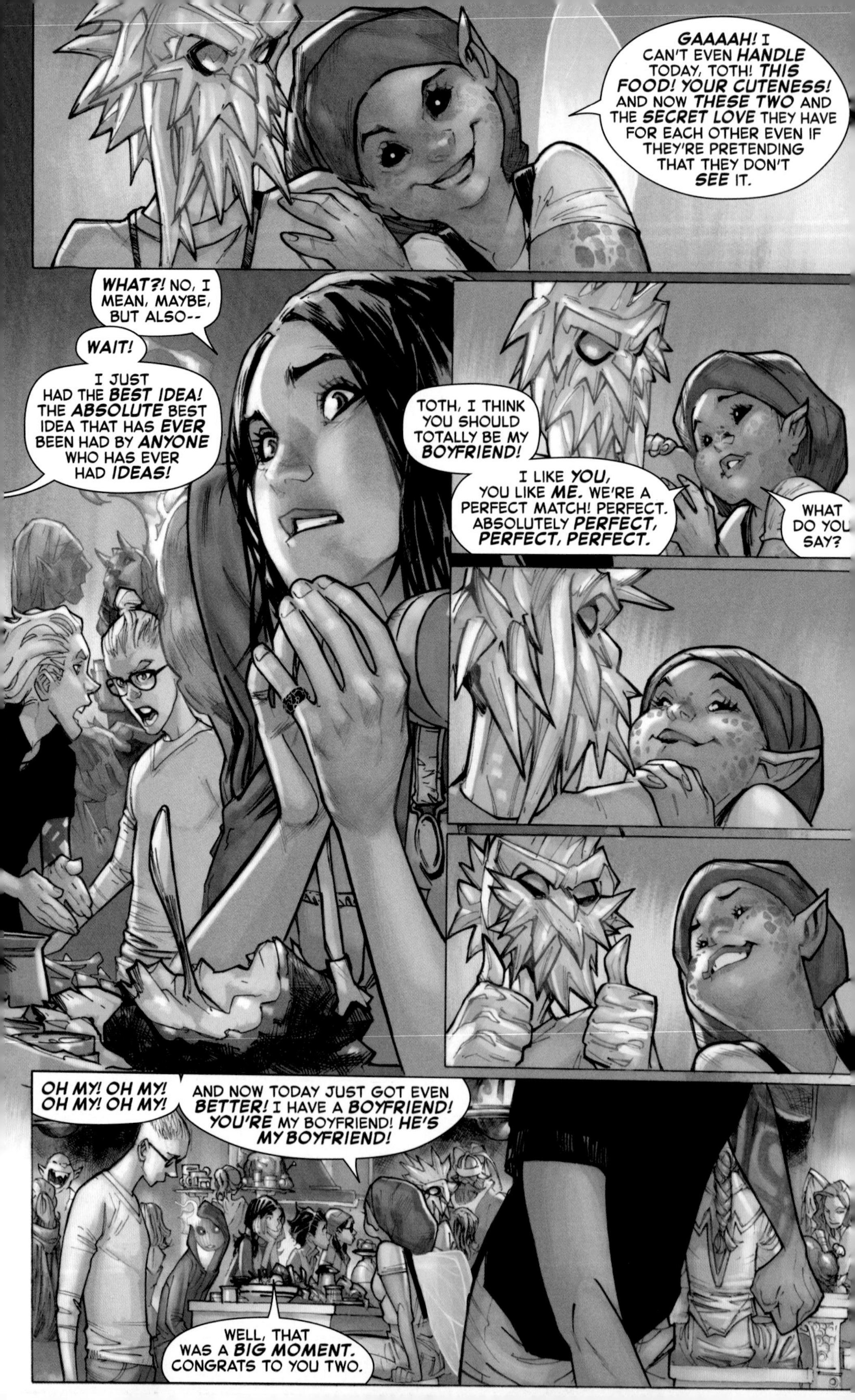

GAAAAH! I CAN'T EVEN HANDLE TODAY, TOTH! THIS FOOD! YOUR CUTENESS! AND NOW THESE TWO AND THE SECRET LOVE THEY HAVE FOR EACH OTHER EVEN IF THEY'RE PRETENDING THAT THEY DON'T SEE IT.
WHAT?! NO, I MEAN, MAYBE, BUT ALSO--
WAIT!
I JUST HAD THE BEST IDEA! THE ABSOLUTE BEST IDEA THAT HAS EVER BEEN HAD BY ANYONE WHO HAS EVER HAD IDEAS!
TOTH, I THINK YOU SHOULD TOTALLY BE MY BOYFRIEND!
I LIKE YOU, YOU LIKE ME. WE'RE A PERFECT MATCH! PERFECT. ABSOLUTELY PERFECT, PERFECT, PERFECT.
WHAT DO YOU SAY?
OH MY! OH MY! OH MY! OH MY!
AND NOW TODAY JUST GOT EVEN BETTER! I HAVE A BOYFRIEND! YOU'RE MY BOYFRIEND! HE'S MY BOYFRIEND!
WELL, THAT WAS A BIG MOMENT. CONGRATS TO YOU TWO.

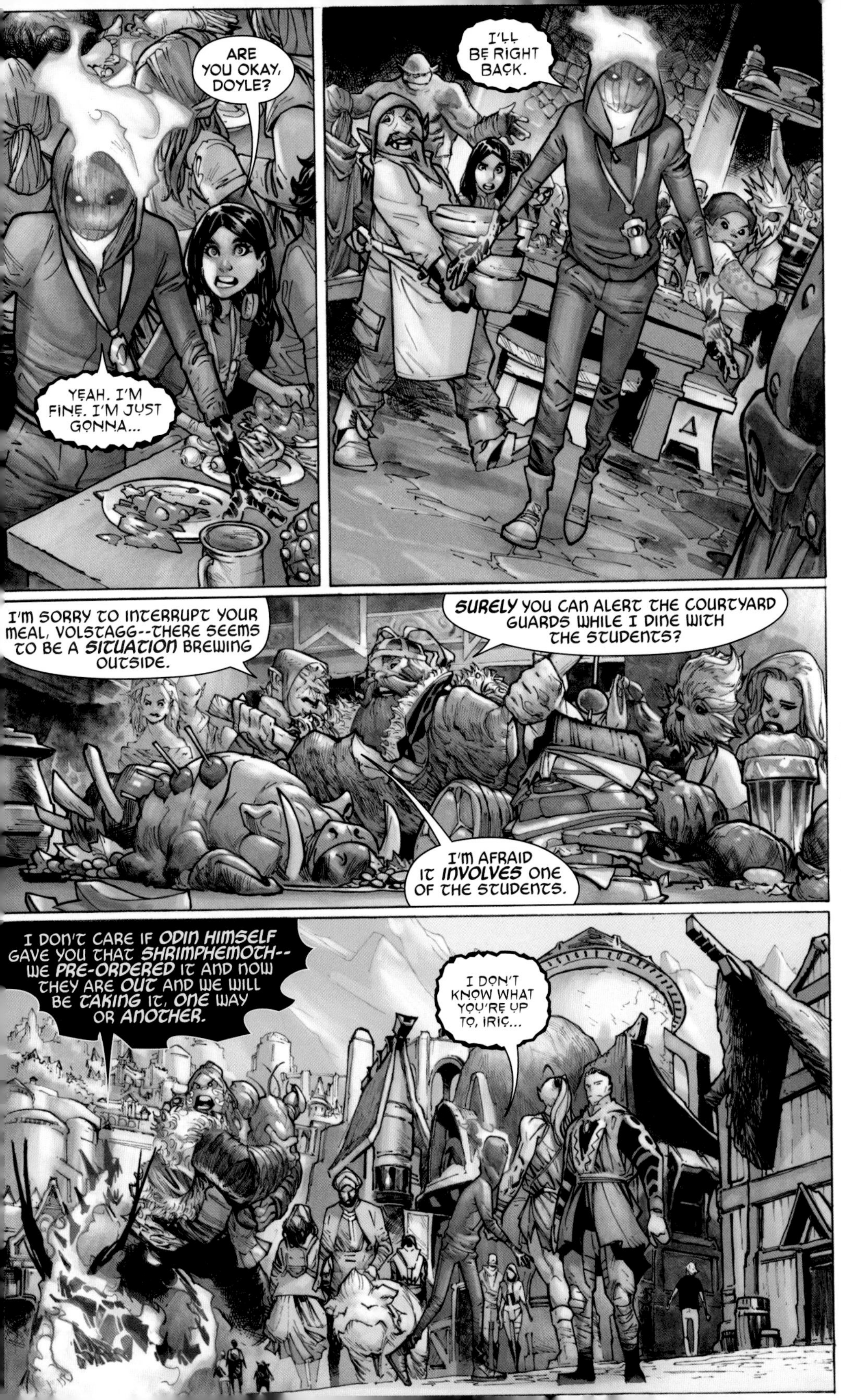

ARE YOU OKAY, DOYLE?
YEAH. I'M FINE. I'M JUST GONNA...
I'LL BE RIGHT BACK.
I'M SORRY TO INTERRUPT YOUR MEAL, VOLSTAGG--THERE SEEMS TO BE A SITUATION BREWING OUTSIDE.
SURELY YOU CAN ALERT THE COURTYARD GUARDS WHILE I DINE WITH THE STUDENTS?
I'M AFRAID IT INVOLVES ONE OF THE STUDENTS.
I DON'T CARE IF ODIN HIMSELF GAVE YOU THAT SHRIMPHEMOTH--WE PRE-ORDERED IT AND NOW THEY ARE OUT AND WE WILL BE TAKING IT, ONE WAY OR ANOTHER.
I DON'T KNOW WHAT YOU'RE UP TO, IRIC...

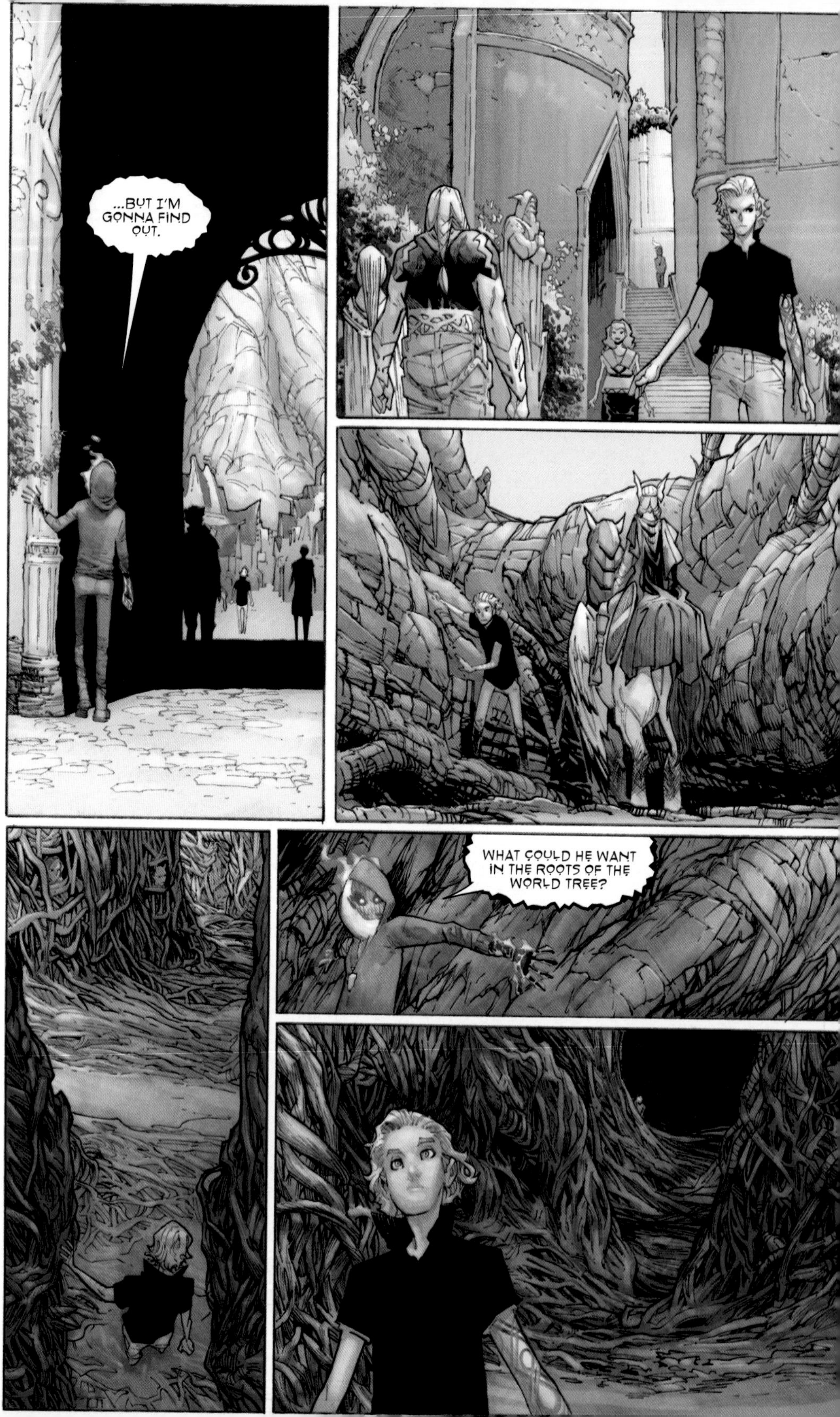
...BUT I'M GONNA FIND OUT.
WHAT COULD HE WANT IN THE ROOTS OF THE WORLD TREE?

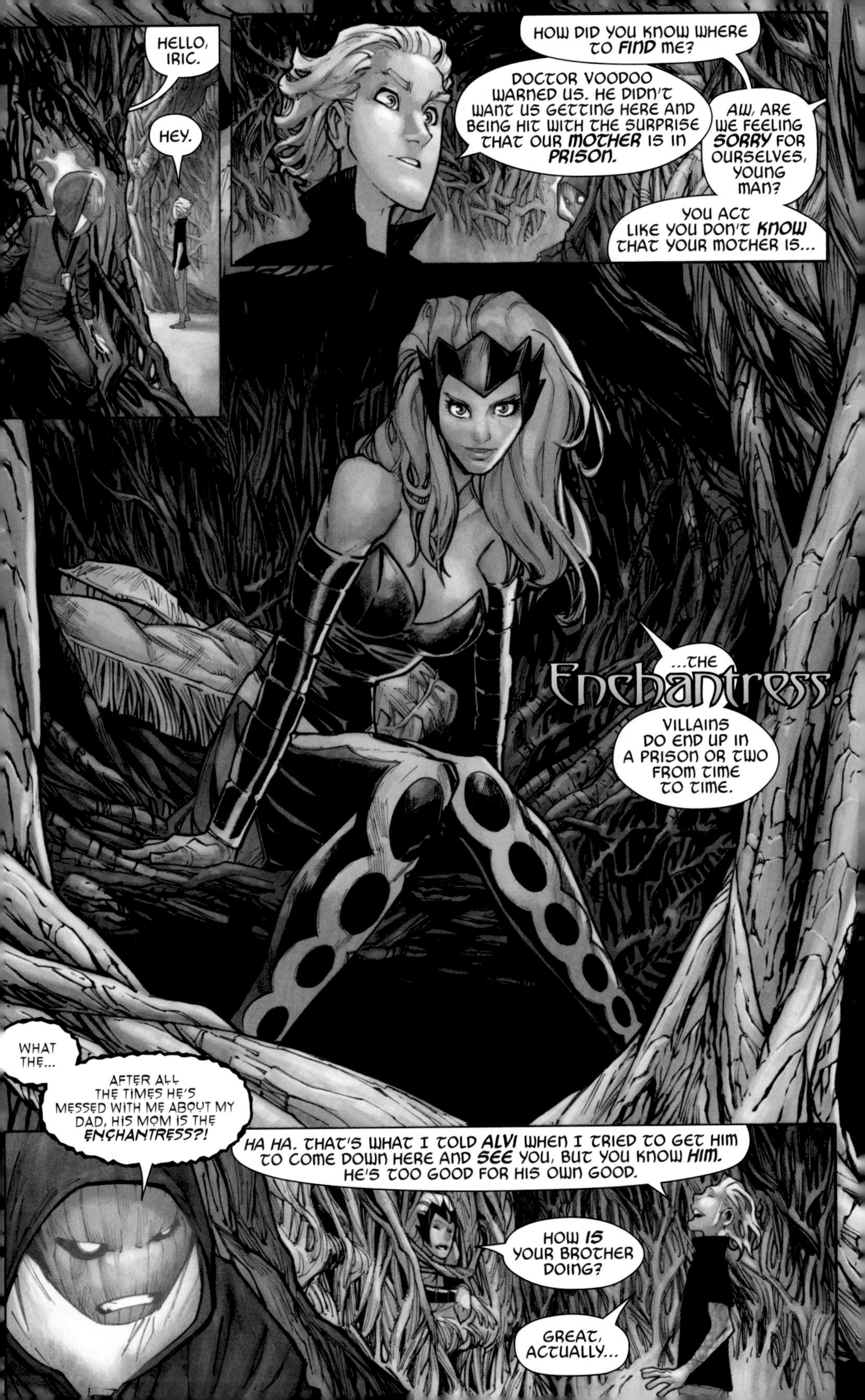
HELLO, IRIC.
HEY.
HOW DID YOU KNOW WHERE TO FIND ME?
DOCTOR VOODOO WARNED US. HE DIDN'T WANT US GETTING HERE AND BEING HIT WITH THE SURPRISE THAT OUR MOTHER IS IN PRISON.
AW, ARE WE FEELING SORRY FOR OURSELVES, YOUNG MAN?
YOU ACT LIKE YOU DON'T KNOW THAT YOUR MOTHER IS...
...THE Enchantress.
VILLAINS DO END UP IN A PRISON OR TWO FROM TIME TO TIME.
WHAT THE...
AFTER ALL THE TIMES HE'S MESSED WITH ME ABOUT MY DAD, HIS MOM IS THE ENCHANTRESS?!
HA HA. THAT'S WHAT I TOLD ALVI WHEN I TRIED TO GET HIM TO COME DOWN HERE AND SEE YOU, BUT YOU KNOW HIM. HE'S TOO GOOD FOR HIS OWN GOOD.
HOW IS YOUR BROTHER DOING?
GREAT, ACTUALLY...

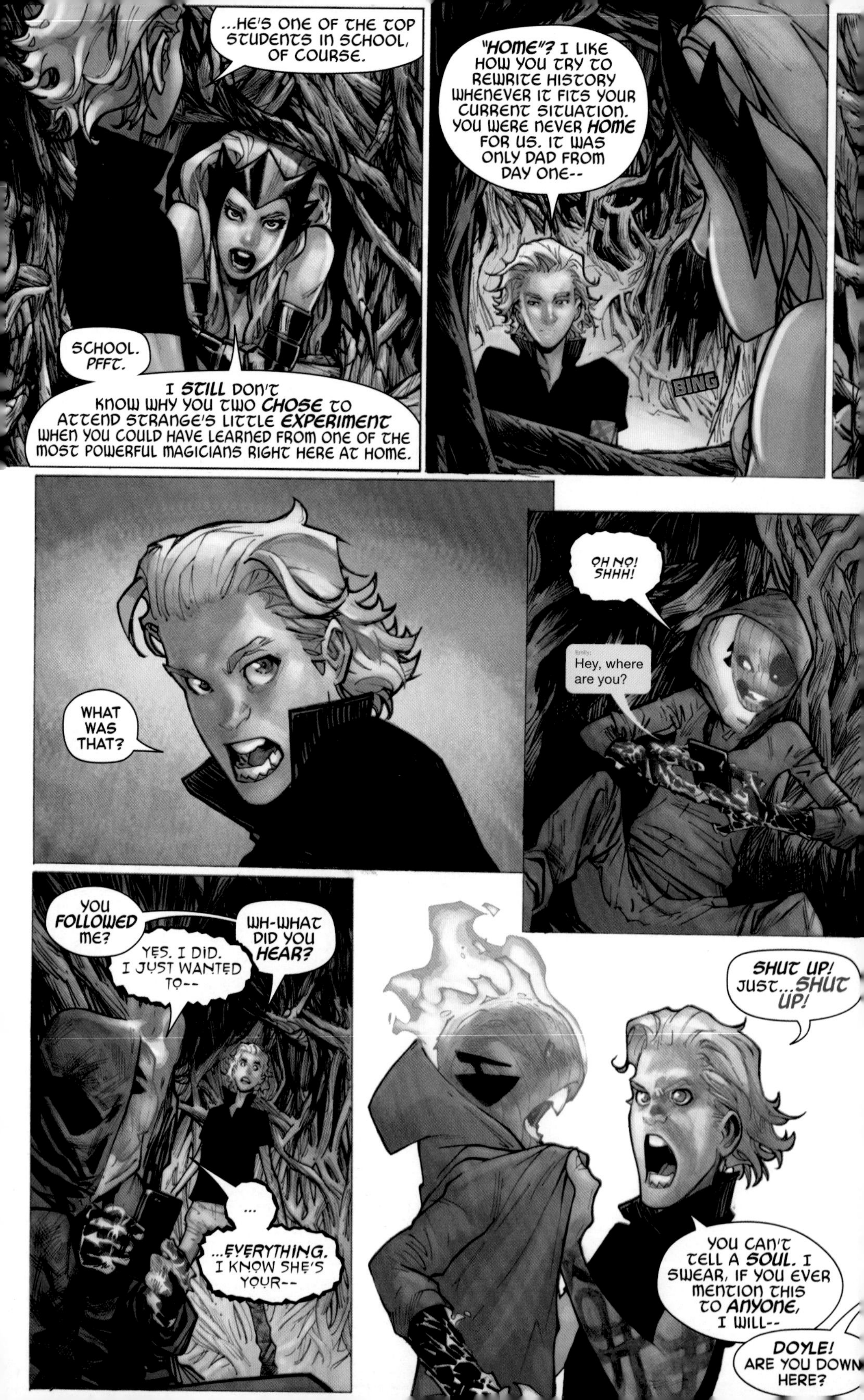

...HE'S ONE OF THE TOP STUDENTS IN SCHOOL, OF COURSE.
SCHOOL. PFFT.
I STILL DON'T KNOW WHY YOU TWO CHOSE TO ATTEND STRANGE'S LITTLE EXPERIMENT WHEN YOU COULD HAVE LEARNED FROM ONE OF THE MOST POWERFUL MAGICIANS RIGHT HERE AT HOME.
"HOME"? I LIKE HOW YOU TRY TO REWRITE HISTORY WHENEVER IT FITS YOUR CURRENT SITUATION. YOU WERE NEVER HOME FOR US. IT WAS ONLY DAD FROM DAY ONE--
BING
WHAT WAS THAT?
OH NO! SHHH!
Emily:
Hey, where are you?
YOU FOLLOWED ME?
WH-WHAT DID YOU HEAR?
YES. I DID. I JUST WANTED TO--
...
...EVERYTHING. I KNOW SHE'S YOUR--
SHUT UP! JUST...SHUT UP!
YOU CAN'T TELL A SOUL. I SWEAR, IF YOU EVER MENTION THIS TO ANYONE, I WILL--
DOYLE! ARE YOU DOWN HERE?

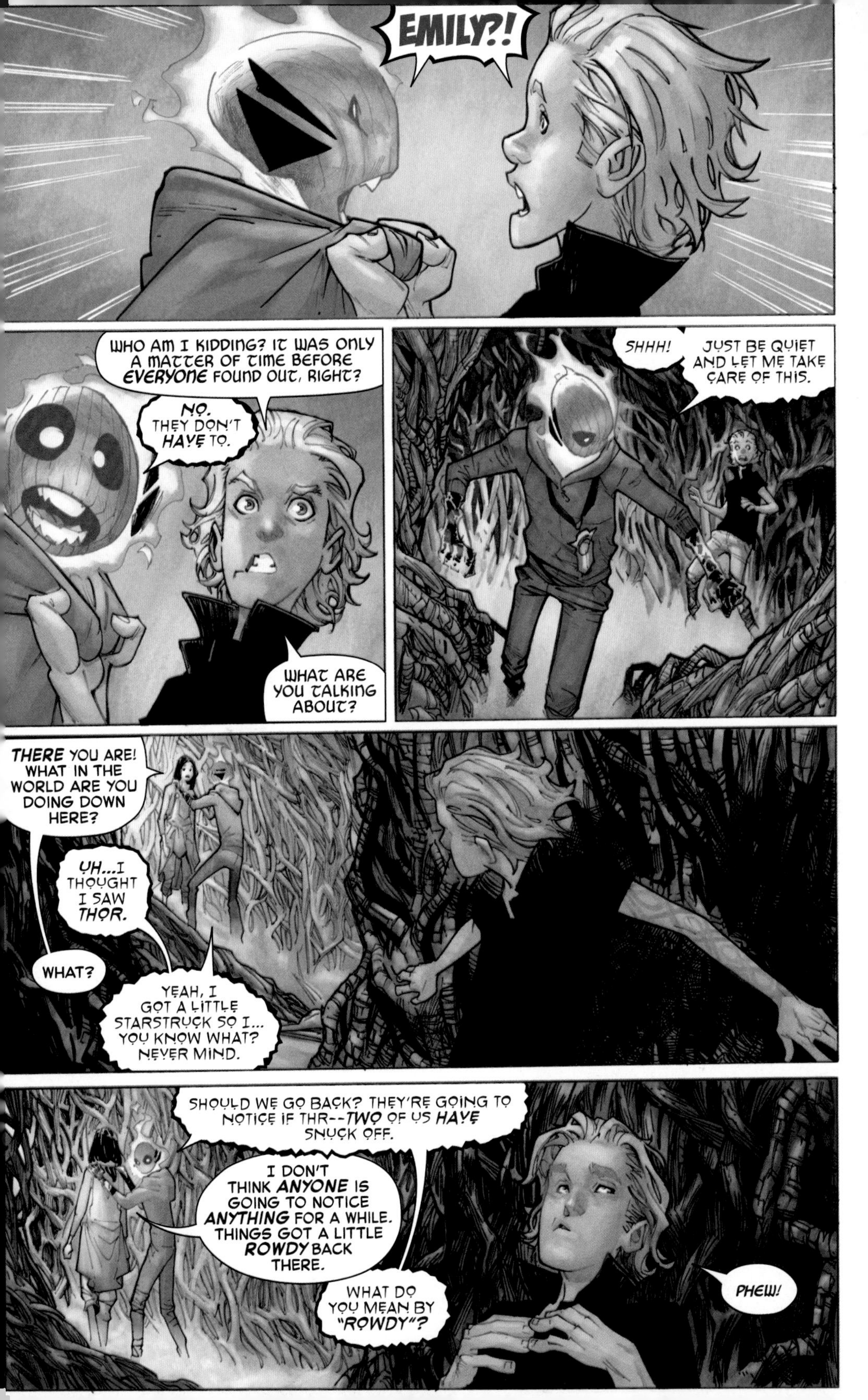
EMILY?!
WHO AM I KIDDING? IT WAS ONLY A MATTER OF TIME BEFORE EVERYONE FOUND OUT, RIGHT?
NO. THEY DON'T HAVE TO.
WHAT ARE YOU TALKING ABOUT?
SHHH!
JUST BE QUIET AND LET ME TAKE CARE OF THIS.
THERE YOU ARE! WHAT IN THE WORLD ARE YOU DOING DOWN HERE?
UH...I THOUGHT I SAW THOR.
WHAT?
YEAH, I GOT A LITTLE STARSTRUCK SO I... YOU KNOW WHAT? NEVER MIND.
SHOULD WE GO BACK? THEY'RE GOING TO NOTICE IF THR--TWO OF US HAVE SNUCK OFF.
I DON'T THINK ANYONE IS GOING TO NOTICE ANYTHING FOR A WHILE. THINGS GOT A LITTLE ROWDY BACK THERE.
WHAT DO YOU MEAN BY "ROWDY"?
PHEW!

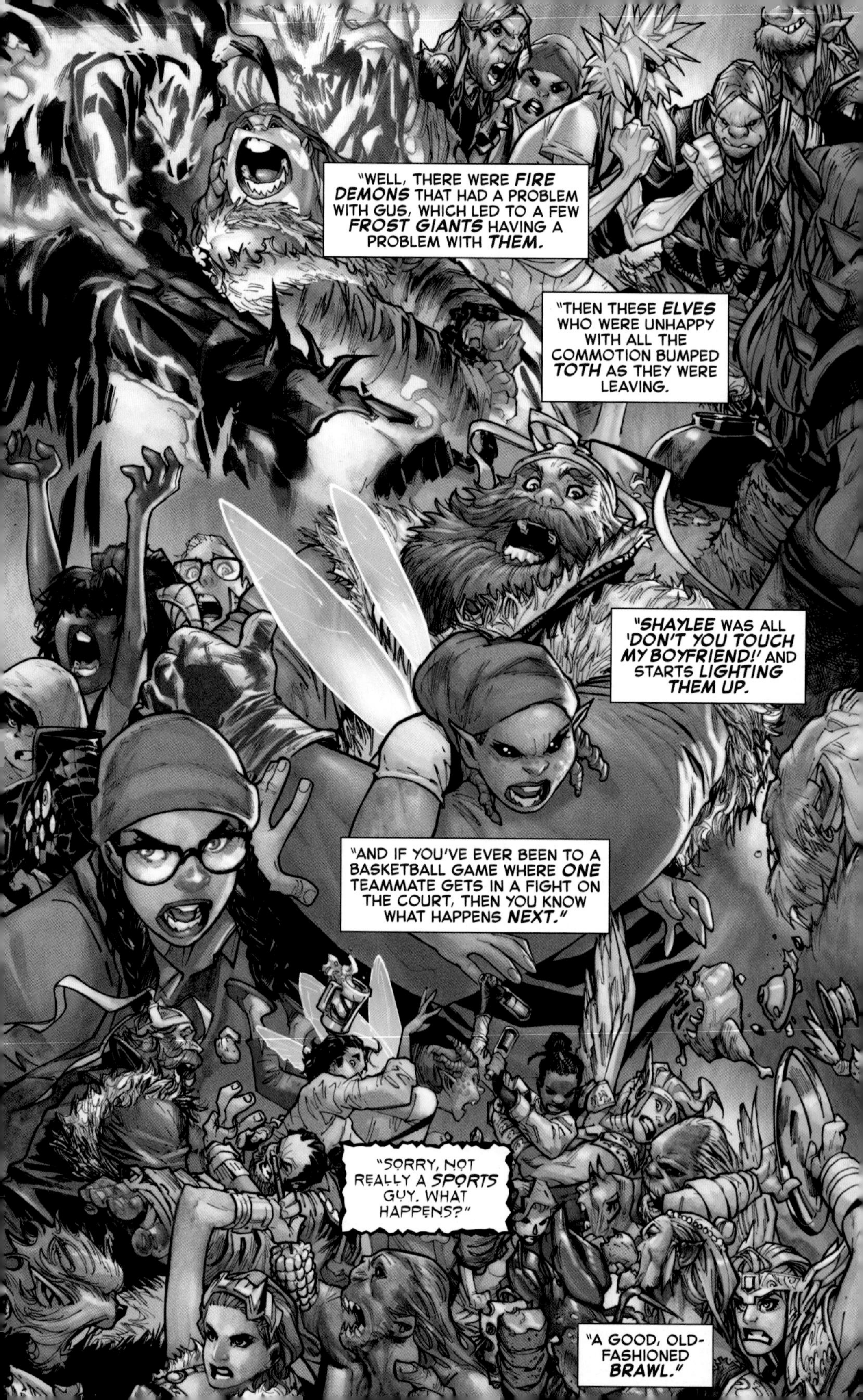
"WELL, THERE WERE FIRE DEMONS THAT HAD A PROBLEM WITH GUS, WHICH LED TO A FEW FROST GIANTS HAVING A PROBLEM WITH THEM.
"THEN THESE ELVES WHO WERE UNHAPPY WITH ALL THE COMMOTION BUMPED TOTH AS THEY WERE LEAVING.
"SHAYLEE WAS ALL 'DON'T YOU TOUCH MY BOYFRIEND!' AND STARTS LIGHTING THEM UP.
"AND IF YOU'VE EVER BEEN TO A BASKETBALL GAME WHERE ONE TEAMMATE GETS IN A FIGHT ON THE COURT, THEN YOU KNOW WHAT HAPPENS NEXT."
"SORRY, NOT REALLY A SPORTS GUY. WHAT HAPPENS?"
"A GOOD, OLD-FASHIONED BRAWL."

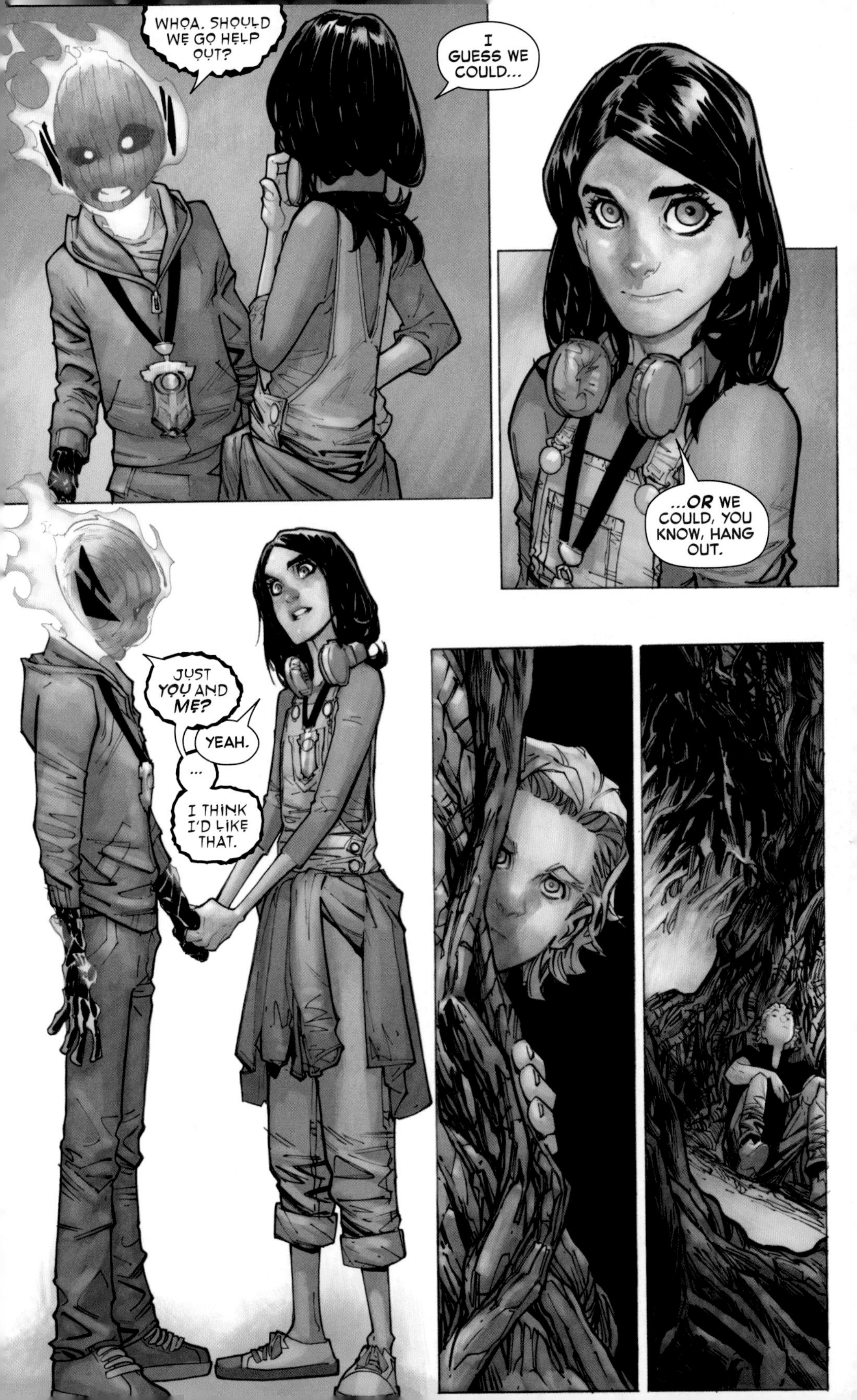
WHOA. SHOULD WE GO HELP OUT?
I GUESS WE COULD...
...OR WE COULD, YOU KNOW, HANG OUT.
JUST YOU AND ME?
YEAH.
...
I THINK I'D LIKE THAT.

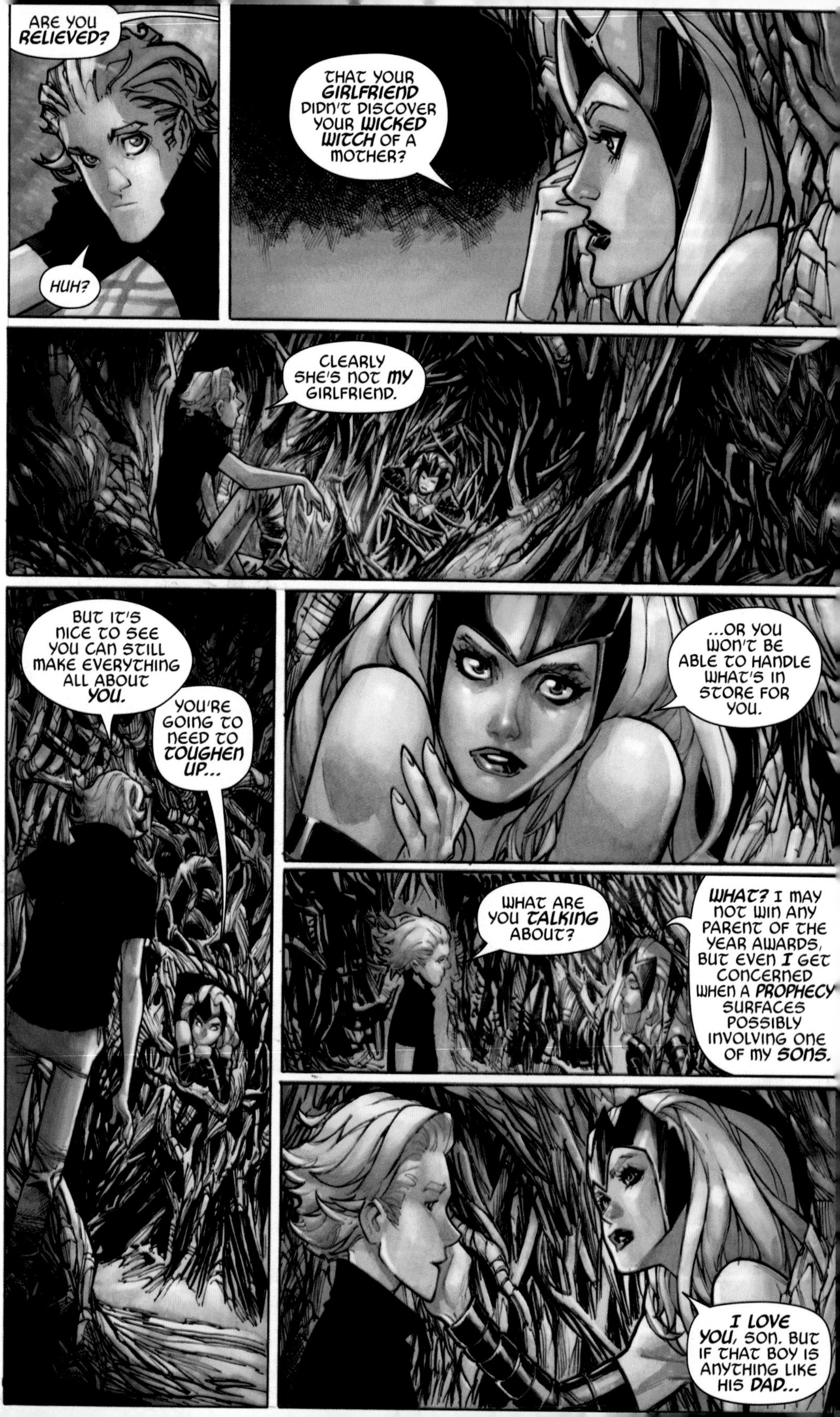

ARE YOU RELIEVED?
HUH?
THAT YOUR GIRLFRIEND DIDN'T DISCOVER YOUR WICKED WITCH OF A MOTHER?
CLEARLY SHE'S NOT MY GIRLFRIEND.
BUT IT'S NICE TO SEE YOU CAN STILL MAKE EVERYTHING ALL ABOUT YOU.
YOU'RE GOING TO NEED TO TOUGHEN UP...
...OR YOU WON'T BE ABLE TO HANDLE WHAT'S IN STORE FOR YOU.
WHAT ARE YOU TALKING ABOUT?
WHAT? I MAY NOT WIN ANY PARENT OF THE YEAR AWARDS, BUT EVEN I GET CONCERNED WHEN A PROPHECY SURFACES POSSIBLY INVOLVING ONE OF MY SONS.
I LOVE YOU, SON. BUT IF THAT BOY IS ANYTHING LIKE HIS DAD...

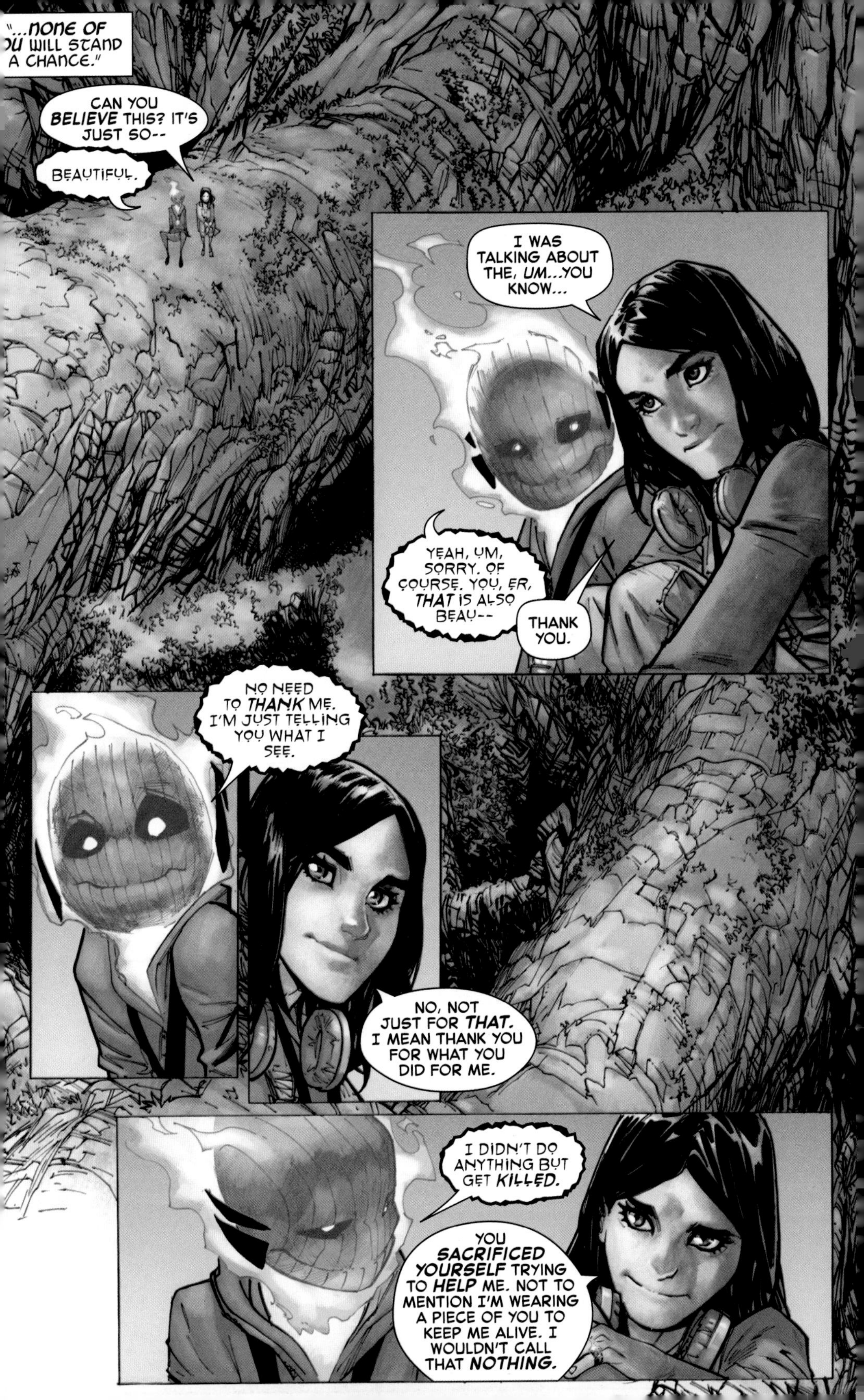
"...NONE OF
OU WILL STAND
A CHANCE."
CAN YOU BELIEVE THIS? IT'S JUST SO--
BEAUTIFUL.
I WAS TALKING ABOUT THE, UM...YOU KNOW...
YEAH, UM, SORRY. OF COURSE. YOU, ER, THAT IS ALSO BEAU--
THANK YOU.
NO NEED TO THANK ME. I'M JUST TELLING YOU WHAT I SEE.
NO, NOT JUST FOR THAT. I MEAN THANK YOU FOR WHAT YOU DID FOR ME.
I DIDN'T DO ANYTHING BUT GET KILLED.
YOU SACRIFICED YOURSELF TRYING TO HELP ME. NOT TO MENTION I'M WEARING A PIECE OF YOU TO KEEP ME ALIVE. I WOULDN'T CALL THAT NOTHING.

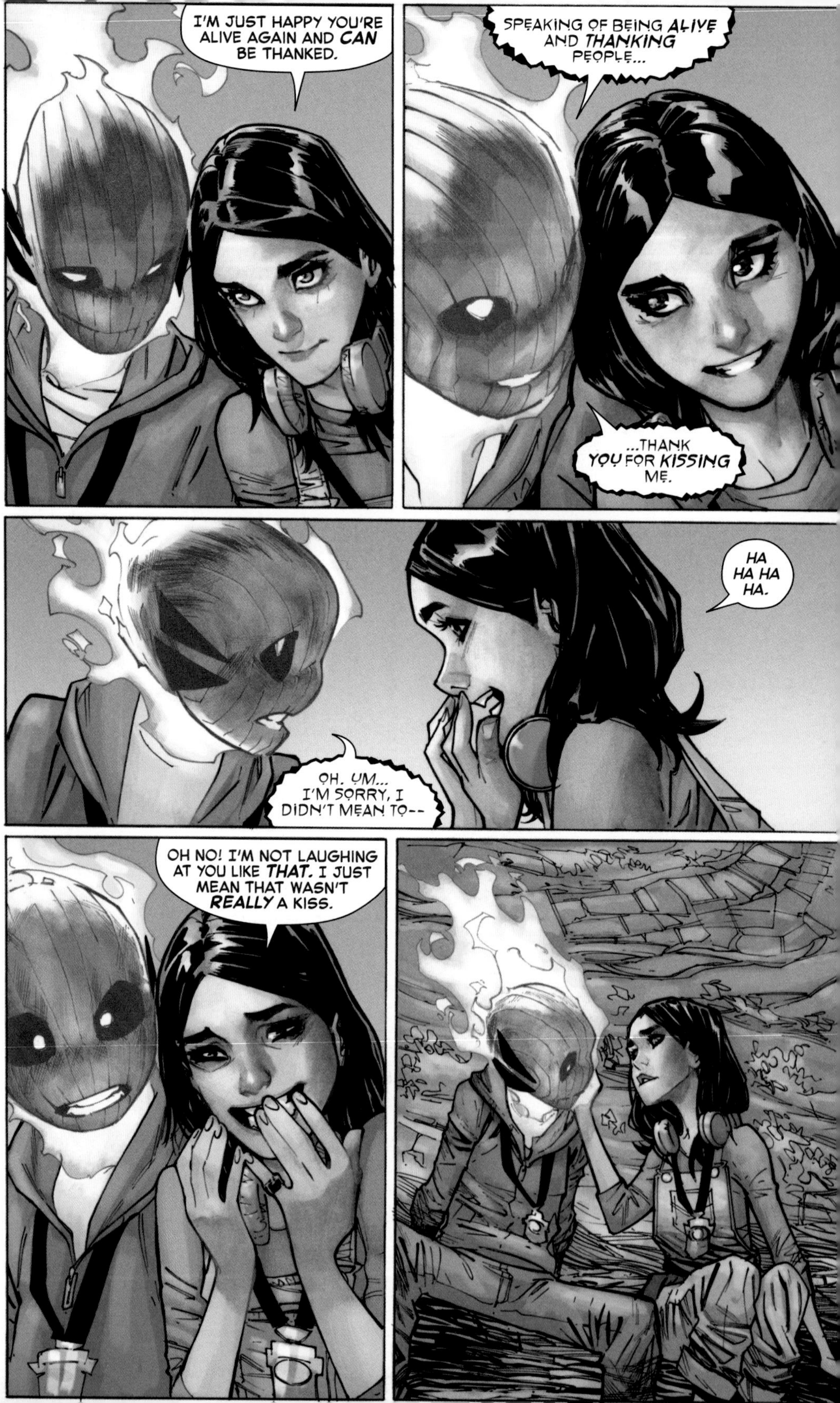
I'M JUST HAPPY YOU'RE ALIVE AGAIN AND CAN BE THANKED.
SPEAKING OF BEING ALIVE AND THANKING PEOPLE...
...THANK YOU FOR KISSING ME.
HA HA HA HA.
OH. UM... I'M SORRY, I DIDN'T MEAN TO--
OH NO! I'M NOT LAUGHING AT YOU LIKE THAT. I JUST MEAN THAT WASN'T REALLY A KISS.

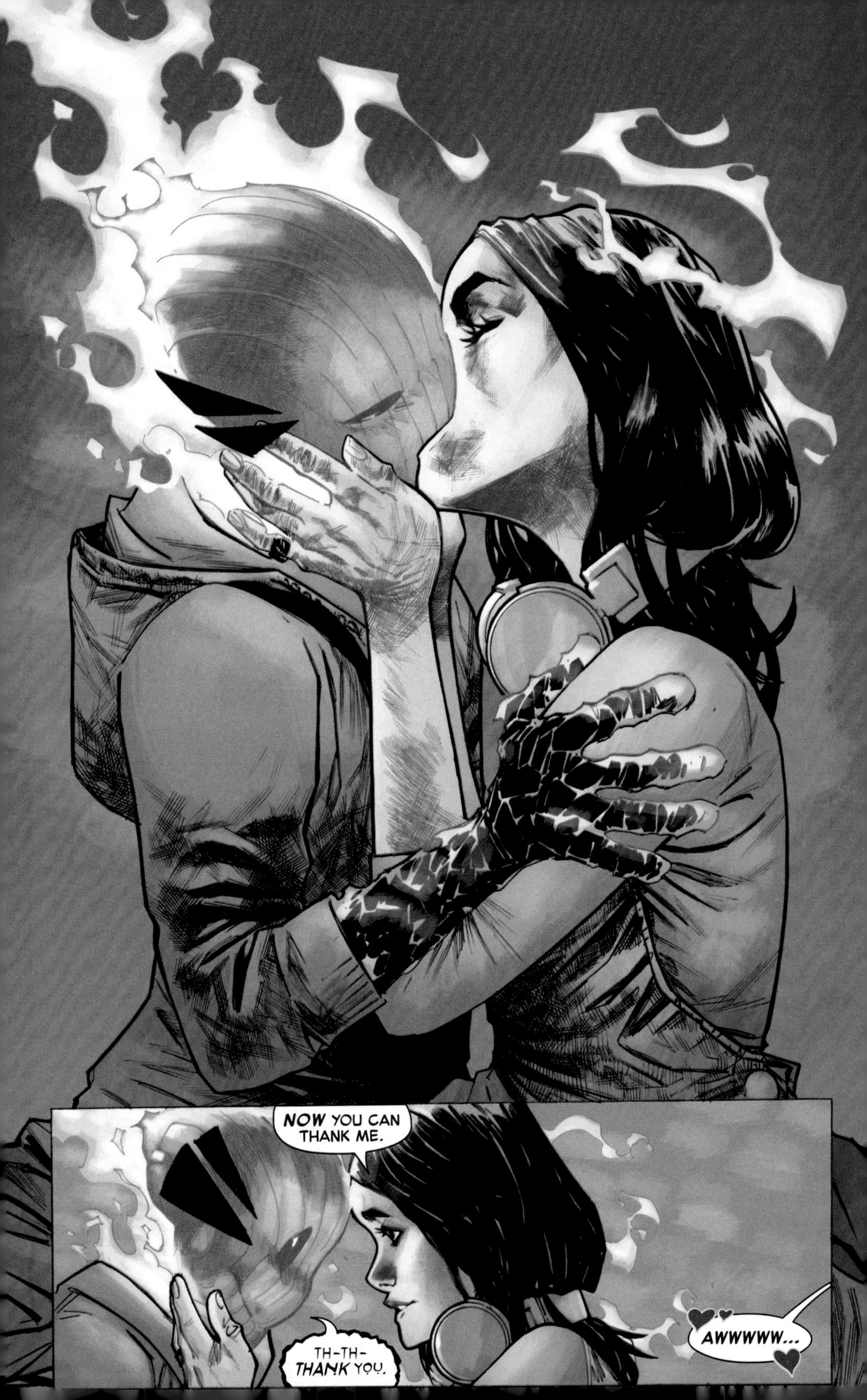
NOW YOU CAN THANK ME.
TH-TH- THANK YOU.
AWWWWW...

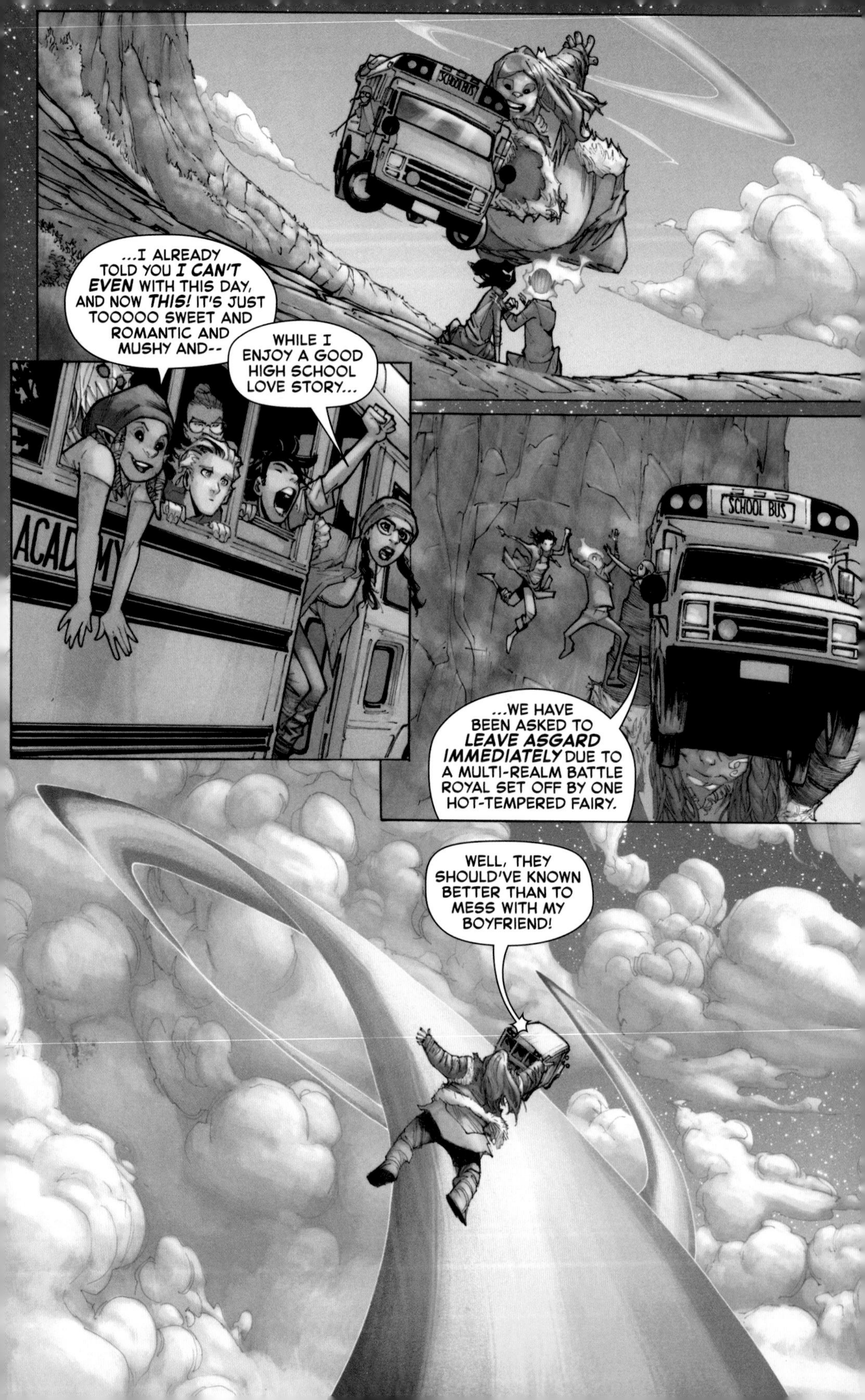
...I ALREADY TOLD YOU I CAN'T EVEN WITH THIS DAY, AND NOW THIS! IT'S JUST TOOOOO SWEET AND ROMANTIC AND MUSHY AND--
WHILE I ENJOY A GOOD HIGH SCHOOL LOVE STORY...
SCHOOL BUS
ACADEMY
...WE HAVE BEEN ASKED TO LEAVE ASGARD IMMEDIATELY DUE TO A MULTI-REALM BATTLE ROYAL SET OFF BY ONE HOT-TEMPERED FAIRY.
WELL, THEY SHOULD'VE KNOWN BETTER THAN TO MESS WITH MY BOYFRIEND!

STRANGE
Academy

REALMIC MAGICKS MIDTERM EXAM

Name: _____Iric_____

D-

SECTION 1 – Multiple choice. Check all that apply.

1. Which of the following are part of the collection of Realms?

- ASGARD ✓
- VANAHEIM
- THUNDERHEIM
- JOTUNHEIM
- CELESTIALLIR
- ALFHEIM
- NIDAVELLIR

- SVARTALFHEIM
- NIFFLEHEIM
- SNIFFLEHEIM
- MUSPELHEIM
- MIDGARD ✓
- HEL
- HEVEN

2. Who learned under the Norn Queen, Karnilla?

- HELA
- ULIK, THE TROLL
- AMORA, THE ENCHANTRESS ✓

- SURTUR
- MANGOG
- BALDER THE BRAVE

IRIC, were you not from Asgard all along? – Prof. Agatha Harkness

---

STRANGE
Academy

REALMIC MAGICKS MIDTERM EXAM

Name: _____Shaylee_____

A+

SECTION 1 – Multiple choice. Check all that apply.

1. Which of the following are part of the collection of Realms?

- ASGARD ✓
- VANAHEIM ✓
- THUNDERHEIM
- JOTUNHEIM ✓

- SVARTALFHEIM ✓
- NIFFLEHEIM ✓
- SNIFFLEHEIM

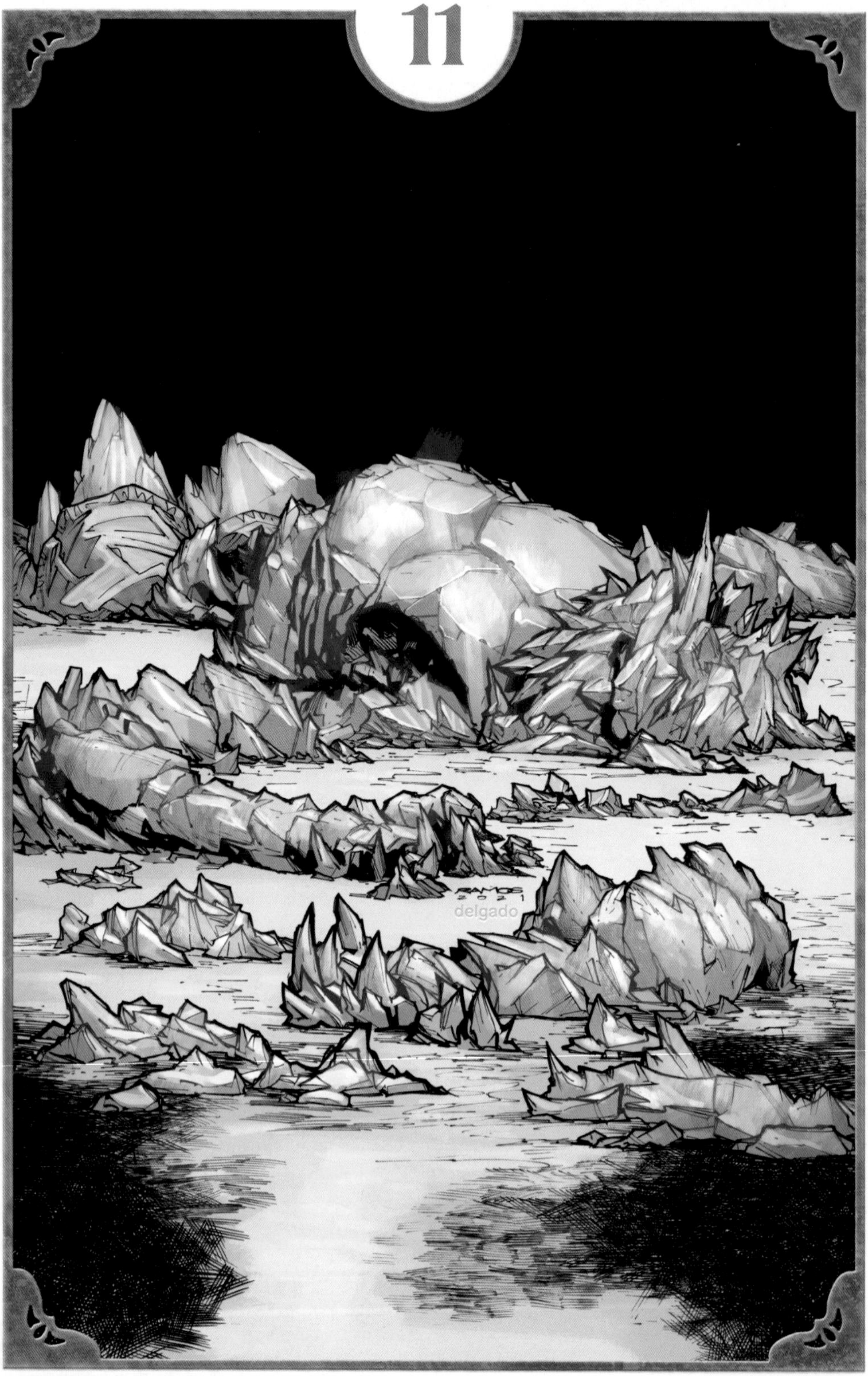
11
RAMOS
2021
delgado

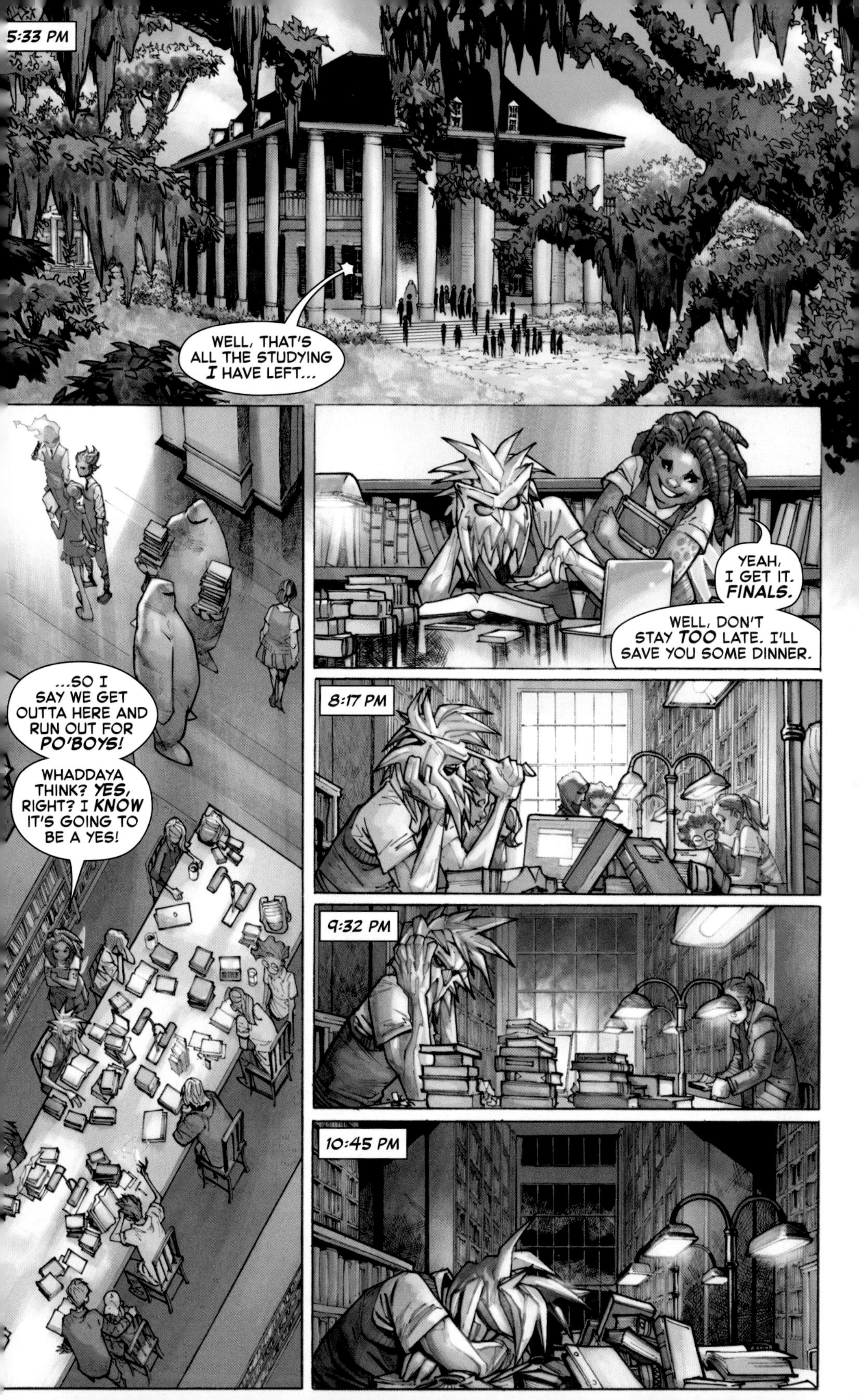
5:33 PM
WELL, THAT'S ALL THE STUDYING I HAVE LEFT...
...SO I SAY WE GET OUTTA HERE AND RUN OUT FOR PO'BOYS!
WHADDAYA THINK? YES, RIGHT? I KNOW IT'S GOING TO BE A YES!
YEAH, I GET IT. FINALS.
WELL, DON'T STAY TOO LATE. I'LL SAVE YOU SOME DINNER.
8:17 PM
9:32 PM
10:45 PM

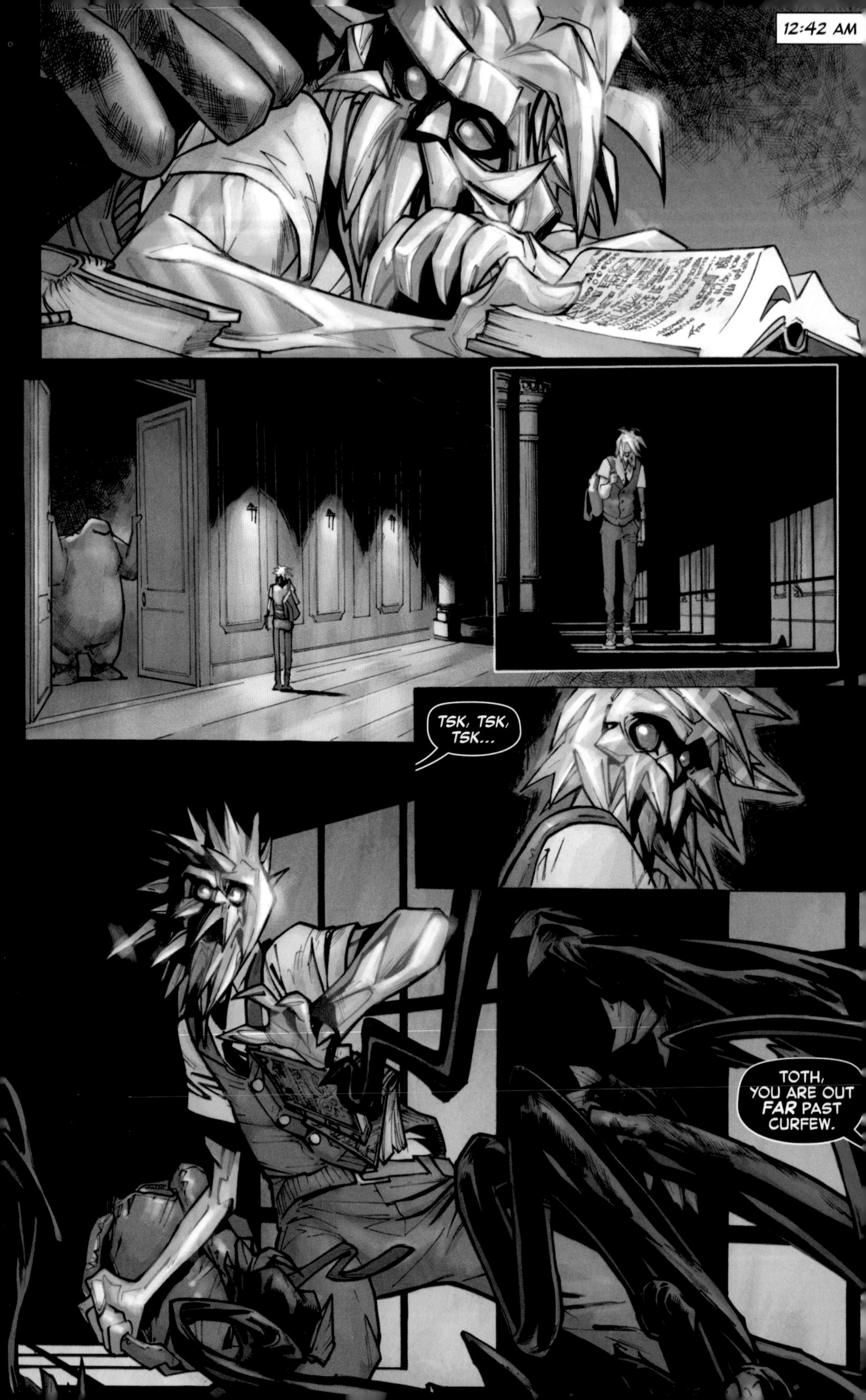
12:42 AM
TSK, TSK, TSK...
TOTH, YOU ARE OUT FAR PAST CURFEW.

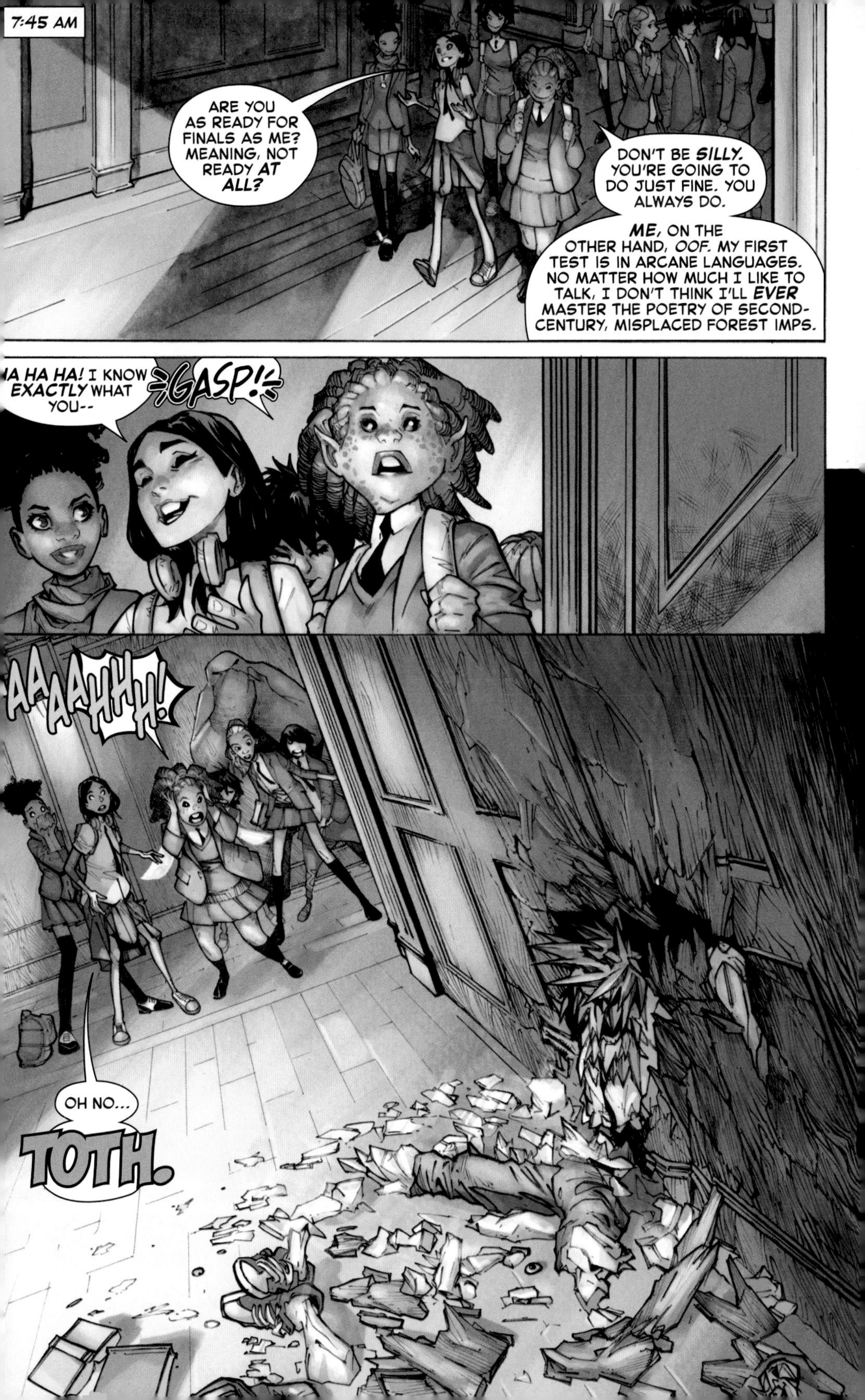
7:45 AM
ARE YOU AS READY FOR FINALS AS ME? MEANING, NOT READY AT ALL?
DON'T BE SILLY. YOU'RE GOING TO DO JUST FINE. YOU ALWAYS DO.
ME, ON THE OTHER HAND, OOF. MY FIRST TEST IS IN ARCANE LANGUAGES. NO MATTER HOW MUCH I LIKE TO TALK, I DON'T THINK I'LL EVER MASTER THE POETRY OF SECOND-CENTURY, MISPLACED FOREST IMPS.
HA HA HA! I KNOW EXACTLY WHAT YOU--
GASP!
AAAAHHH!
OH NO...
TOTH.

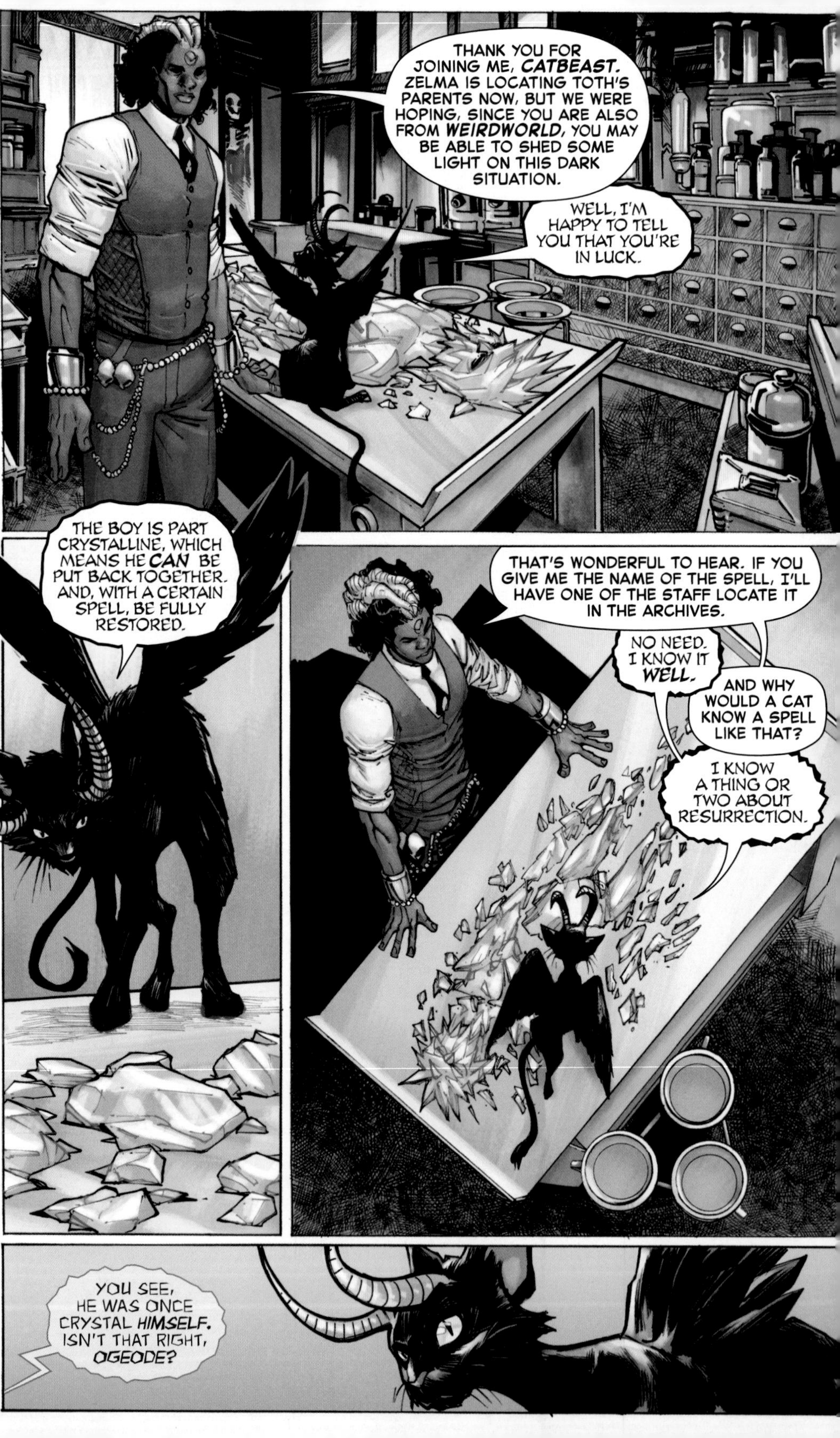
THANK YOU FOR JOINING ME, CATBEAST. ZELMA IS LOCATING TOTH'S PARENTS NOW, BUT WE WERE HOPING, SINCE YOU ARE ALSO FROM WEIRDWORLD, YOU MAY BE ABLE TO SHED SOME LIGHT ON THIS DARK SITUATION.
WELL, I'M HAPPY TO TELL YOU THAT YOU'RE IN LUCK.
THE BOY IS PART CRYSTALLINE, WHICH MEANS HE CAN BE PUT BACK TOGETHER. AND, WITH A CERTAIN SPELL, BE FULLY RESTORED.
THAT'S WONDERFUL TO HEAR. IF YOU GIVE ME THE NAME OF THE SPELL, I'LL HAVE ONE OF THE STAFF LOCATE IT IN THE ARCHIVES.
NO NEED. I KNOW IT WELL.
AND WHY WOULD A CAT KNOW A SPELL LIKE THAT?
I KNOW A THING OR TWO ABOUT RESURRECTION.
YOU SEE, HE WAS ONCE CRYSTAL HIMSELF. ISN'T THAT RIGHT, OGEODE?

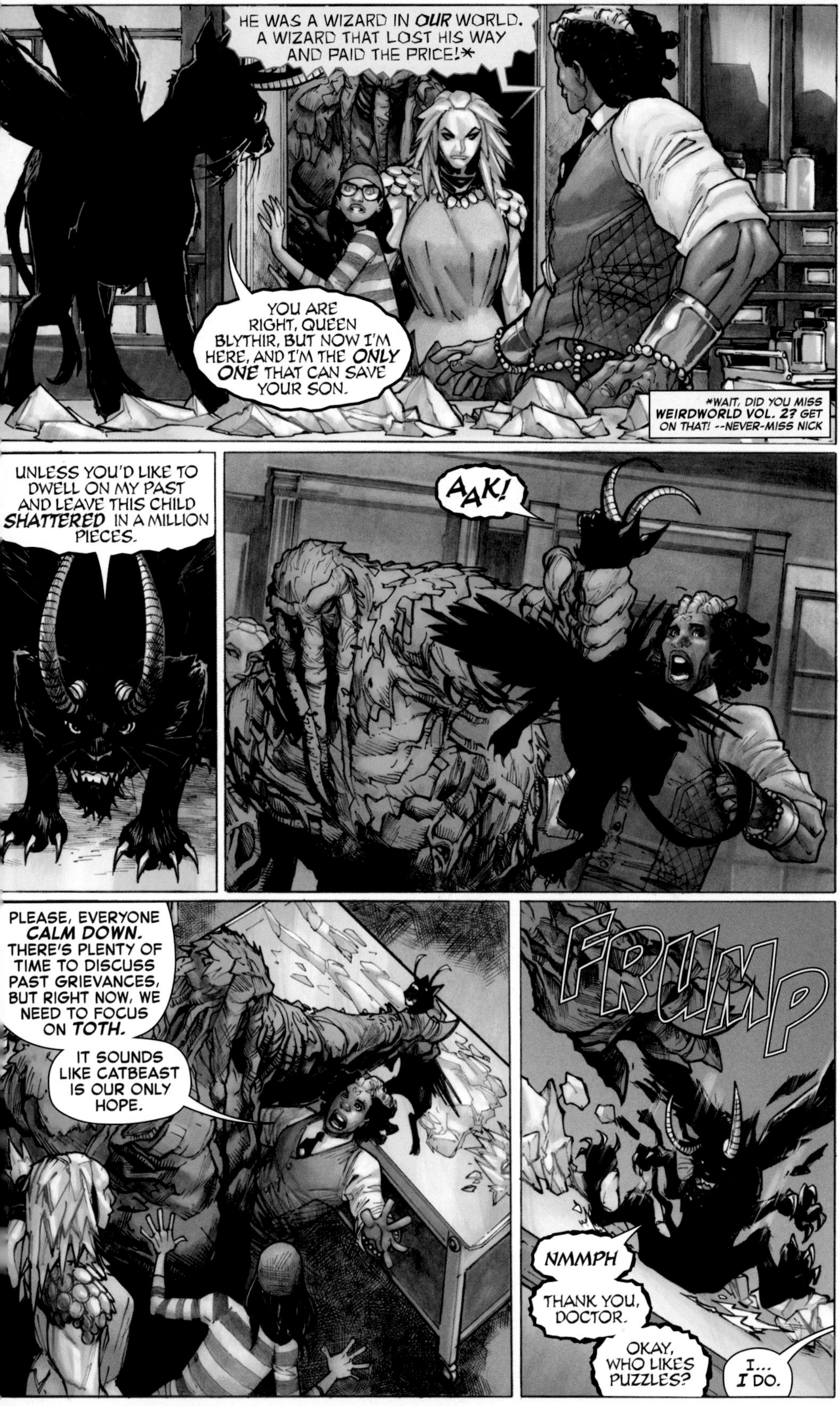
HE WAS A WIZARD IN OUR WORLD. A WIZARD THAT LOST HIS WAY AND PAID THE PRICE!*
YOU ARE RIGHT, QUEEN BLYTHIR, BUT NOW I'M HERE, AND I'M THE ONLY ONE THAT CAN SAVE YOUR SON.
*WAIT, DID YOU MISS WEIRDWORLD VOL. 2? GET ON THAT! --NEVER-MISS NICK
UNLESS YOU'D LIKE TO DWELL ON MY PAST AND LEAVE THIS CHILD SHATTERED IN A MILLION PIECES.
AAK!
PLEASE, EVERYONE CALM DOWN. THERE'S PLENTY OF TIME TO DISCUSS PAST GRIEVANCES, BUT RIGHT NOW, WE NEED TO FOCUS ON TOTH.
IT SOUNDS LIKE CATBEAST IS OUR ONLY HOPE.
FRUMP
NMMPH
THANK YOU, DOCTOR.
OKAY, WHO LIKES PUZZLES?
I... I DO.

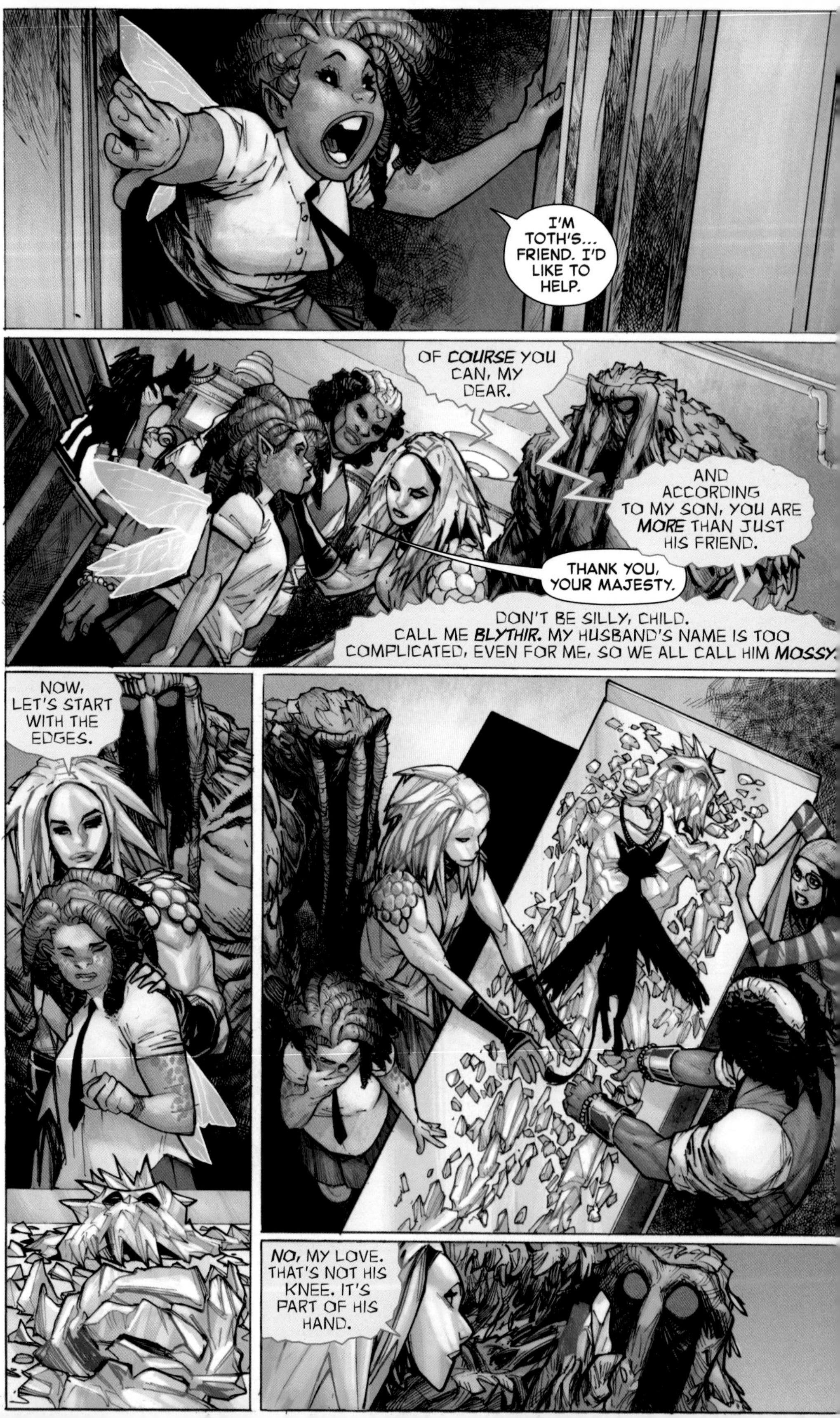
I'M TOTH'S... FRIEND. I'D LIKE TO HELP.
OF COURSE YOU CAN, MY DEAR.
AND ACCORDING TO MY SON, YOU ARE MORE THAN JUST HIS FRIEND.
THANK YOU, YOUR MAJESTY.
DON'T BE SILLY, CHILD. CALL ME BLYTHIR. MY HUSBAND'S NAME IS TOO COMPLICATED, EVEN FOR ME, SO WE ALL CALL HIM MOSSY.
NOW, LET'S START WITH THE EDGES.
NO, MY LOVE. THAT'S NOT HIS KNEE. IT'S PART OF HIS HAND.

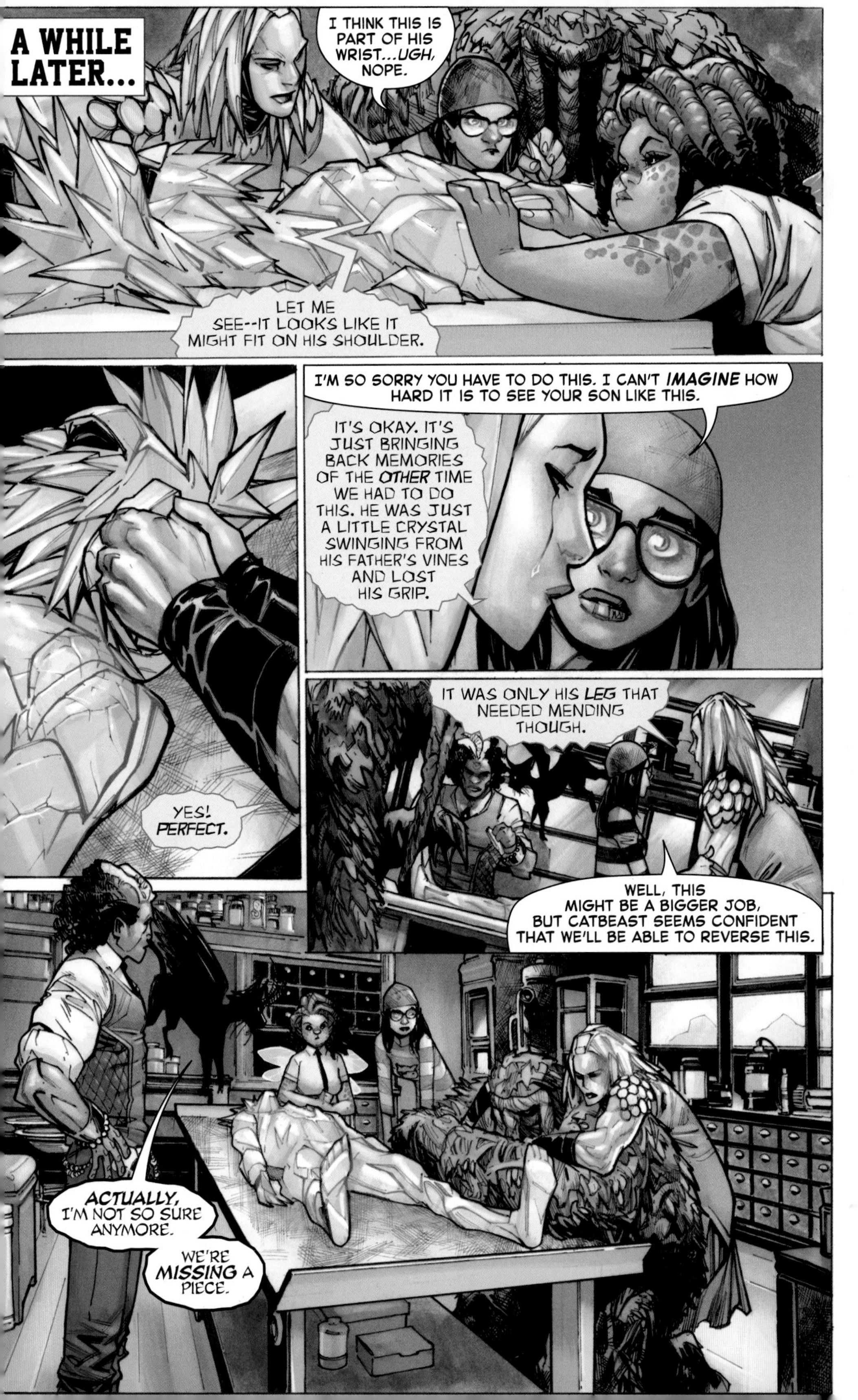
A WHILE LATER...
I THINK THIS IS PART OF HIS WRIST...UGH, NOPE.
LET ME SEE--IT LOOKS LIKE IT MIGHT FIT ON HIS SHOULDER.
YES! PERFECT.
I'M SO SORRY YOU HAVE TO DO THIS. I CAN'T IMAGINE HOW HARD IT IS TO SEE YOUR SON LIKE THIS.
IT'S OKAY. IT'S JUST BRINGING BACK MEMORIES OF THE OTHER TIME WE HAD TO DO THIS. HE WAS JUST A LITTLE CRYSTAL SWINGING FROM HIS FATHER'S VINES AND LOST HIS GRIP.
IT WAS ONLY HIS LEG THAT NEEDED MENDING THOUGH.
WELL, THIS MIGHT BE A BIGGER JOB, BUT CATBEAST SEEMS CONFIDENT THAT WE'LL BE ABLE TO REVERSE THIS.
ACTUALLY, I'M NOT SO SURE ANYMORE.
WE'RE MISSING A PIECE.

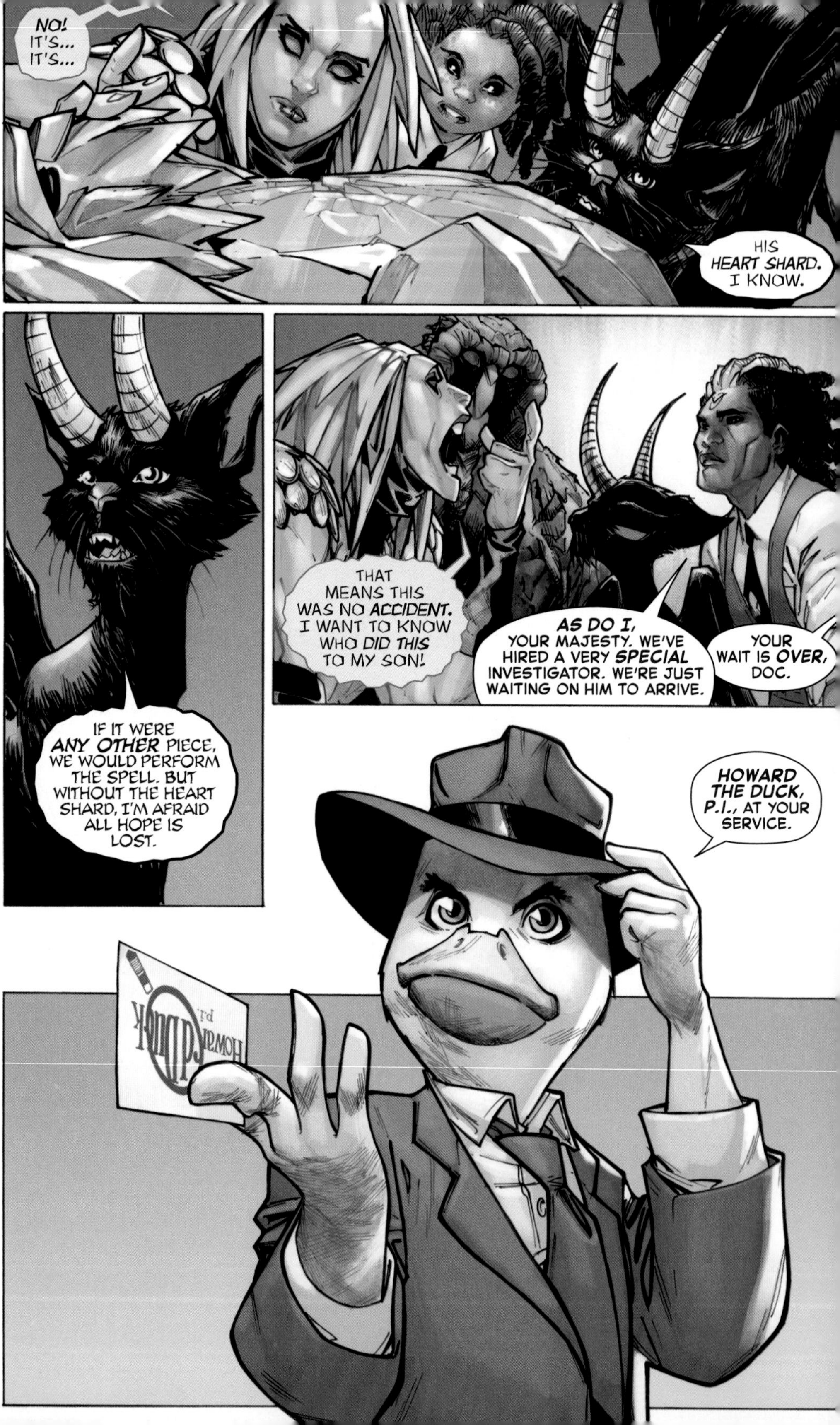
NO! IT'S... IT'S...
HIS HEART SHARD. I KNOW.
IF IT WERE ANY OTHER PIECE, WE WOULD PERFORM THE SPELL. BUT WITHOUT THE HEART SHARD, I'M AFRAID ALL HOPE IS LOST.
THAT MEANS THIS WAS NO ACCIDENT. I WANT TO KNOW WHO DID THIS TO MY SON!
AS DO I, YOUR MAJESTY. WE'VE HIRED A VERY SPECIAL INVESTIGATOR. WE'RE JUST WAITING ON HIM TO ARRIVE.
YOUR WAIT IS OVER, DOC.
HOWARD THE DUCK, P.I., AT YOUR SERVICE.

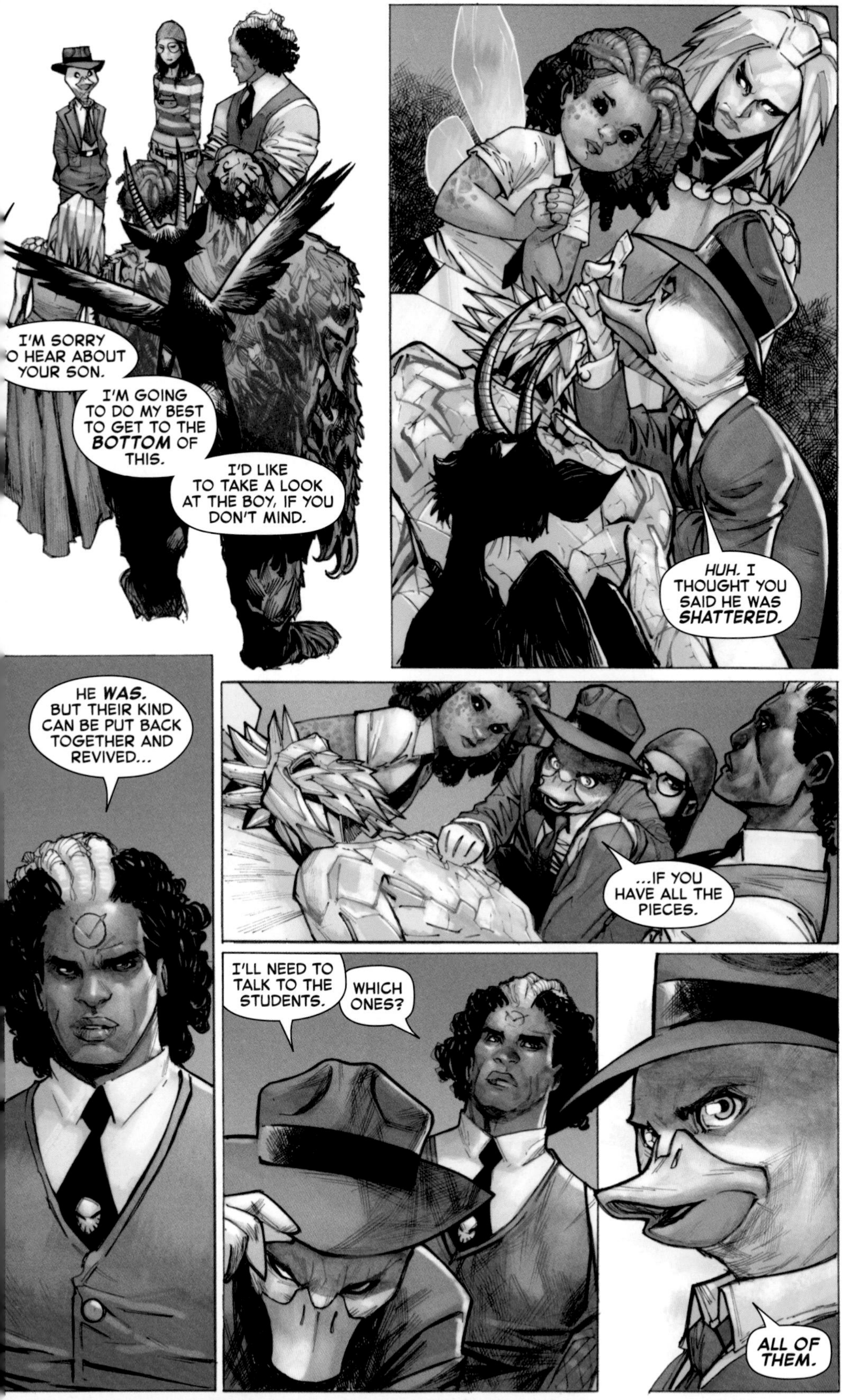
I'M SORRY O HEAR ABOUT YOUR SON.
I'M GOING TO DO MY BEST TO GET TO THE BOTTOM OF THIS.
I'D LIKE TO TAKE A LOOK AT THE BOY, IF YOU DON'T MIND.
HUH. I THOUGHT YOU SAID HE WAS SHATTERED.
HE WAS. BUT THEIR KIND CAN BE PUT BACK TOGETHER AND REVIVED...
...IF YOU HAVE ALL THE PIECES.
I'LL NEED TO TALK TO THE STUDENTS.
WHICH ONES?
ALL OF THEM.

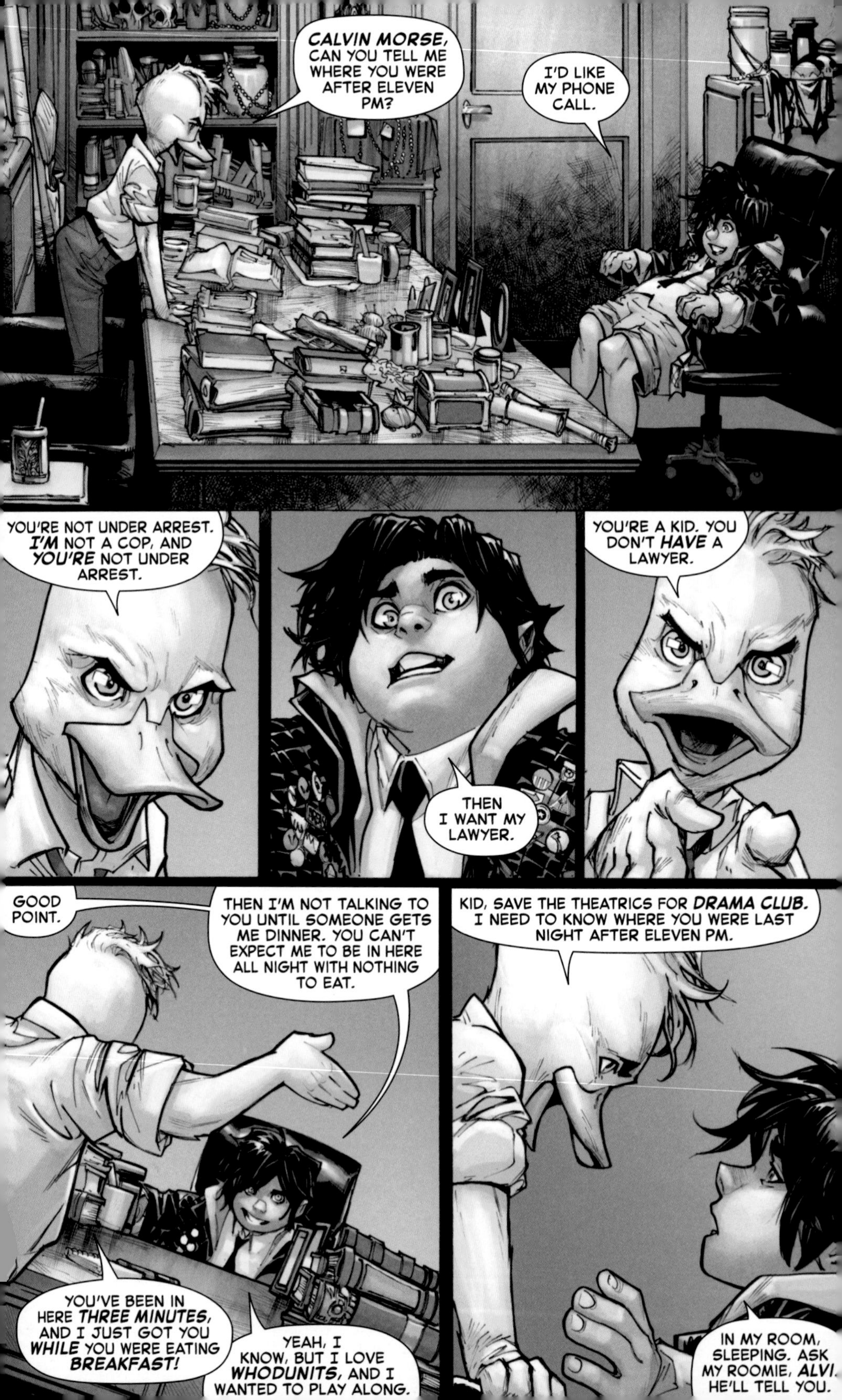

CALVIN MORSE, CAN YOU TELL ME WHERE YOU WERE AFTER ELEVEN PM?
I'D LIKE MY PHONE CALL.
YOU'RE NOT UNDER ARREST. I'M NOT A COP, AND YOU'RE NOT UNDER ARREST.
THEN I WANT MY LAWYER.
YOU'RE A KID. YOU DON'T HAVE A LAWYER.
GOOD POINT.
THEN I'M NOT TALKING TO YOU UNTIL SOMEONE GETS ME DINNER. YOU CAN'T EXPECT ME TO BE IN HERE ALL NIGHT WITH NOTHING TO EAT.
YOU'VE BEEN IN HERE THREE MINUTES, AND I JUST GOT YOU WHILE YOU WERE EATING BREAKFAST!
YEAH, I KNOW, BUT I LOVE WHODUNITS, AND I WANTED TO PLAY ALONG.
KID, SAVE THE THEATRICS FOR DRAMA CLUB. I NEED TO KNOW WHERE YOU WERE LAST NIGHT AFTER ELEVEN PM.
IN MY ROOM, SLEEPING. ASK MY ROOMIE, ALVI. HE'LL TELL YOU.

YES, HE WAS IN OUR ROOM SLEEPING.

GGGGRRRRAAAHHHUUUUU...

"HE WAS THE *ONLY* ONE IN OUR ROOM SLEEPING.

"CAL SNORES LIKE IT'S HIS JOB. LIKE THERE WAS NOTHING ELSE HE WAS PUT ON THE PLANET TO DO.

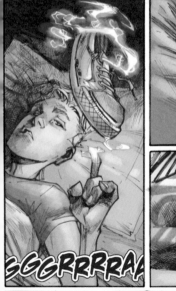

GGGRRRRAA

FRAM

"SO YEAH, *HE* WAS SLEEPING LIKE A BABY."

OR MORE LIKE A BABY *DRAGON.*

THANK YOU, ALVI.

YOU'RE FREE TO GO. WOULD YOU MIND SENDING YOUR BROTHER IN NEXT?

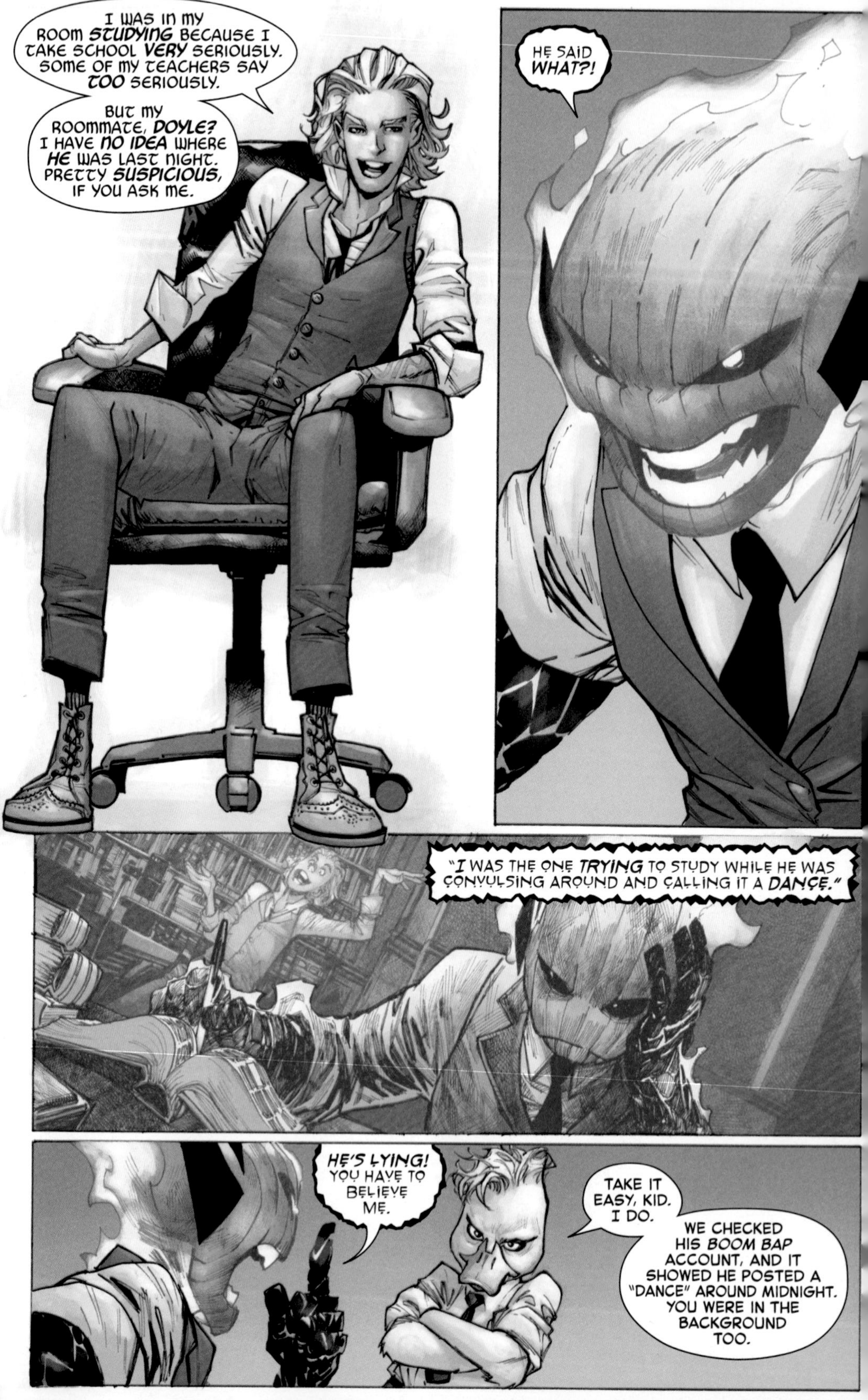
I WAS IN MY ROOM STUDYING BECAUSE I TAKE SCHOOL VERY SERIOUSLY. SOME OF MY TEACHERS SAY TOO SERIOUSLY.
BUT MY ROOMMATE, DOYLE? I HAVE NO IDEA WHERE HE WAS LAST NIGHT. PRETTY SUSPICIOUS, IF YOU ASK ME.
HE SAID WHAT?!
"I WAS THE ONE TRYING TO STUDY WHILE HE WAS CONVULSING AROUND AND CALLING IT A DANCE."
HE'S LYING! YOU HAVE TO BELIEVE ME.
TAKE IT EASY, KID. I DO.
WE CHECKED HIS BOOM BAP ACCOUNT, AND IT SHOWED HE POSTED A "DANCE" AROUND MIDNIGHT. YOU WERE IN THE BACKGROUND TOO.

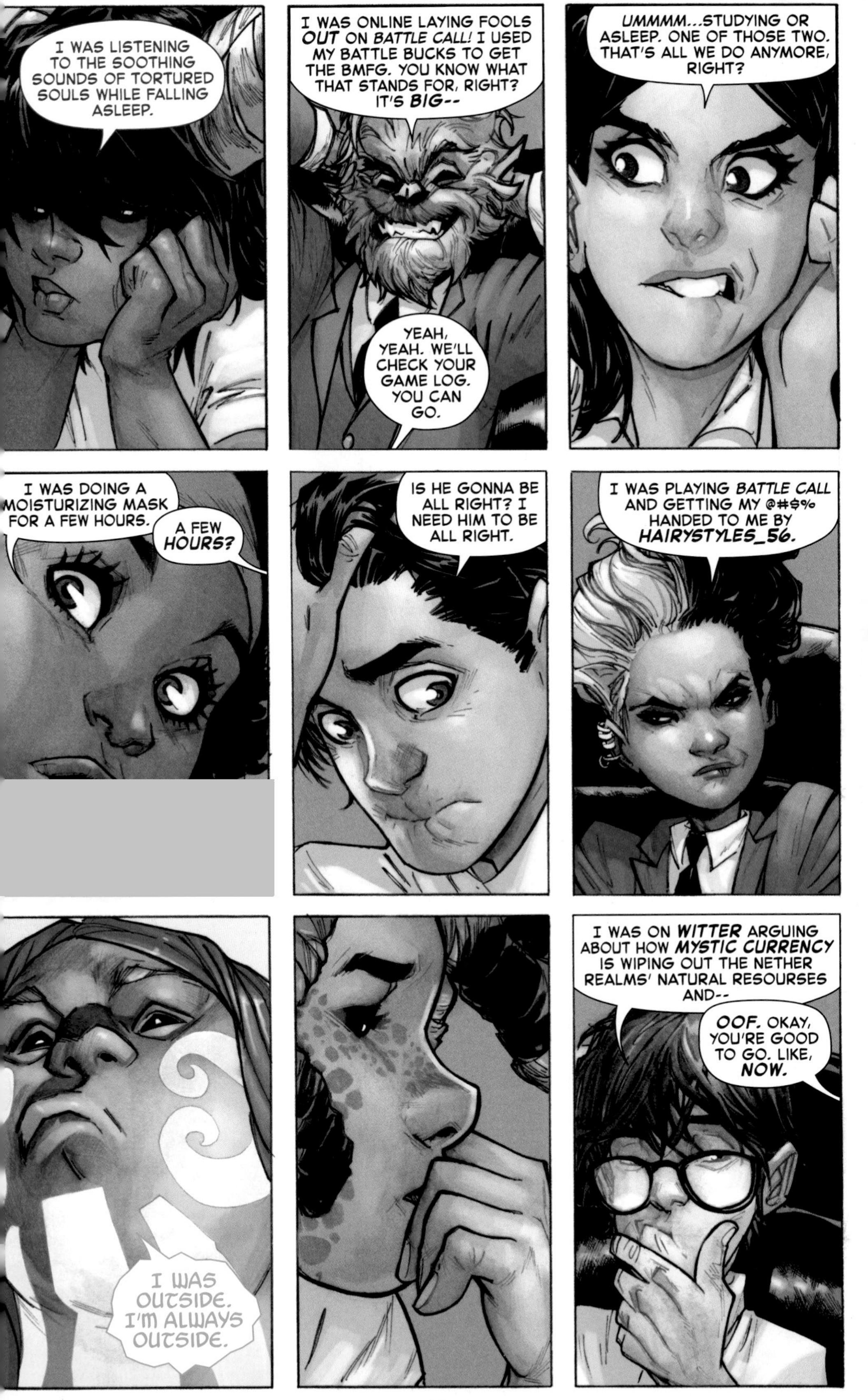
I WAS LISTENING TO THE SOOTHING SOUNDS OF TORTURED SOULS WHILE FALLING ASLEEP.
I WAS ONLINE LAYING FOOLS OUT ON BATTLE CALL! I USED MY BATTLE BUCKS TO GET THE BMFG. YOU KNOW WHAT THAT STANDS FOR, RIGHT? IT'S BIG--
YEAH, YEAH. WE'LL CHECK YOUR GAME LOG. YOU CAN GO.
UMMMM...STUDYING OR ASLEEP. ONE OF THOSE TWO. THAT'S ALL WE DO ANYMORE, RIGHT?
I WAS DOING A MOISTURIZING MASK FOR A FEW HOURS.
A FEW HOURS?
IS HE GONNA BE ALL RIGHT? I NEED HIM TO BE ALL RIGHT.
I WAS PLAYING BATTLE CALL AND GETTING MY @#$% HANDED TO ME BY HAIRYSTYLES_56.
I WAS OUTSIDE. I'M ALWAYS OUTSIDE.
I WAS ON WITTER ARGUING ABOUT HOW MYSTIC CURRENCY IS WIPING OUT THE NETHER REALMS' NATURAL RESOURSES AND--
OOF. OKAY, YOU'RE GOOD TO GO. LIKE, NOW.

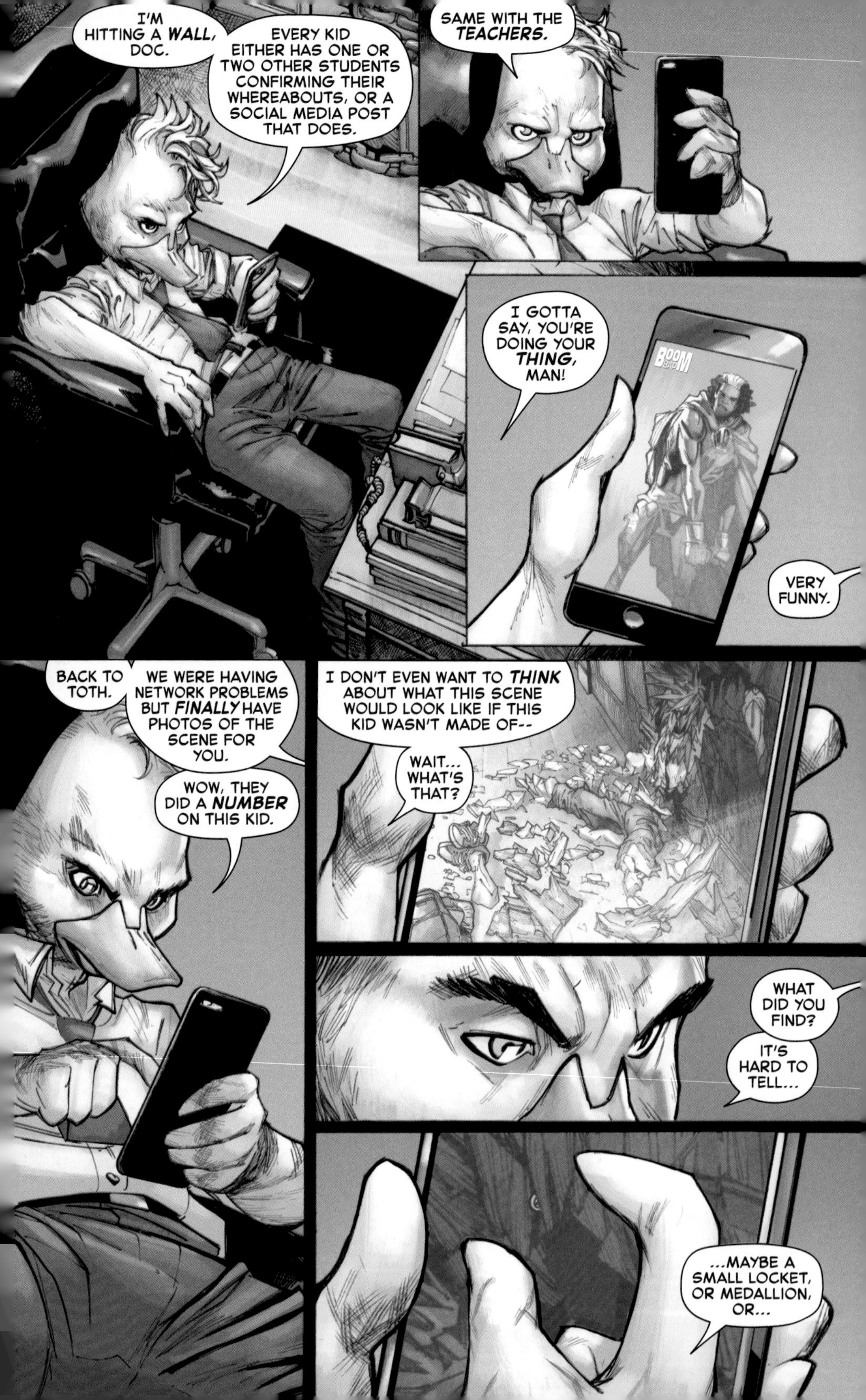
I'M HITTING A WALL, DOC.
EVERY KID EITHER HAS ONE OR TWO OTHER STUDENTS CONFIRMING THEIR WHEREABOUTS, OR A SOCIAL MEDIA POST THAT DOES.
SAME WITH THE TEACHERS.
I GOTTA SAY, YOU'RE DOING YOUR THING, MAN!
BOOM BAP
VERY FUNNY.
BACK TO TOTH.
WE WERE HAVING NETWORK PROBLEMS BUT FINALLY HAVE PHOTOS OF THE SCENE FOR YOU.
WOW, THEY DID A NUMBER ON THIS KID.
I DON'T EVEN WANT TO THINK ABOUT WHAT THIS SCENE WOULD LOOK LIKE IF THIS KID WASN'T MADE OF--
WAIT... WHAT'S THAT?
WHAT DID YOU FIND?
IT'S HARD TO TELL...
...MAYBE A SMALL LOCKET, OR MEDALLION, OR...

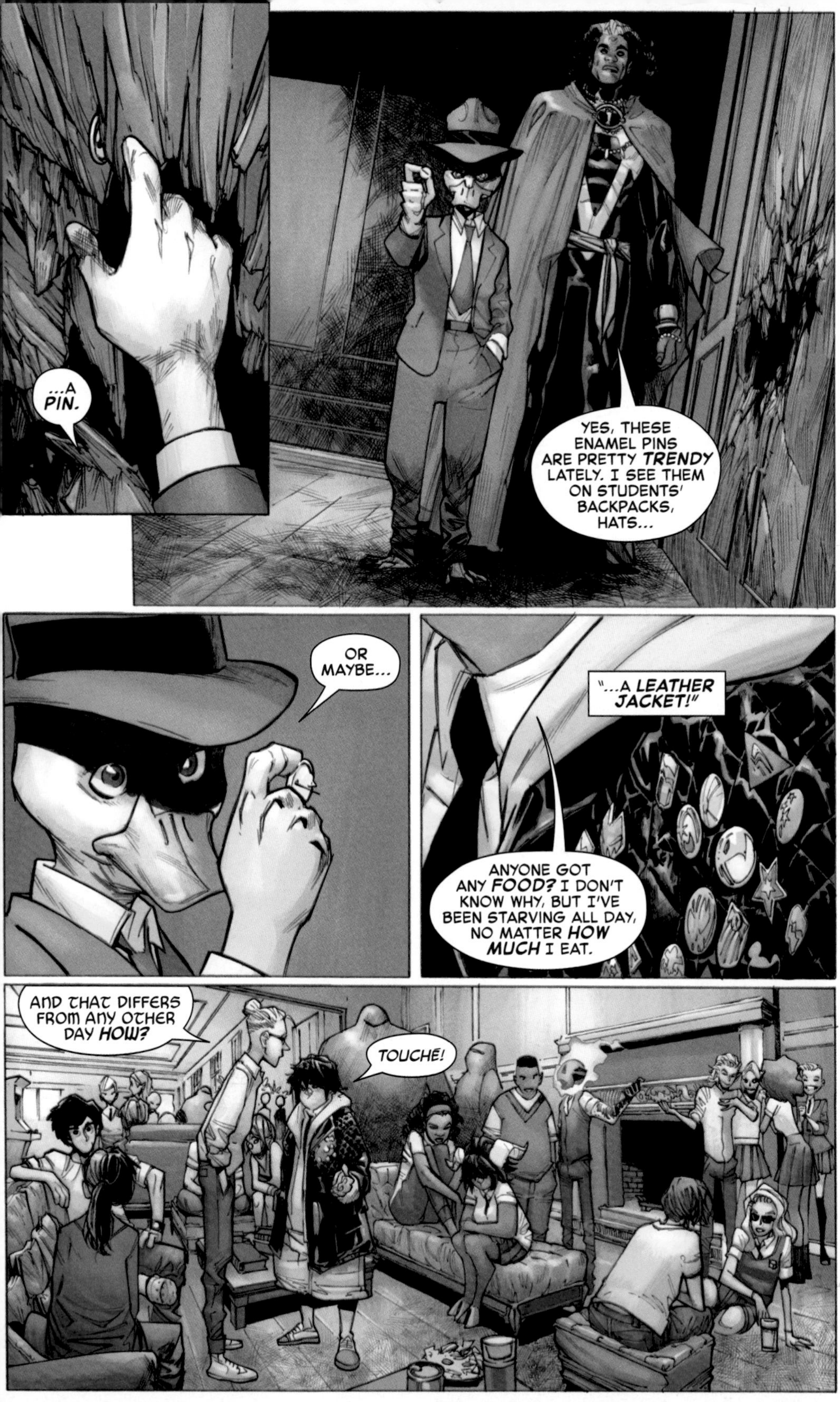
...A PIN.
YES, THESE ENAMEL PINS ARE PRETTY TRENDY LATELY. I SEE THEM ON STUDENTS' BACKPACKS, HATS...
OR MAYBE...
"...A LEATHER JACKET!"
ANYONE GOT ANY FOOD? I DON'T KNOW WHY, BUT I'VE BEEN STARVING ALL DAY, NO MATTER HOW MUCH I EAT.
AND THAT DIFFERS FROM ANY OTHER DAY HOW?
TOUCHÉ!

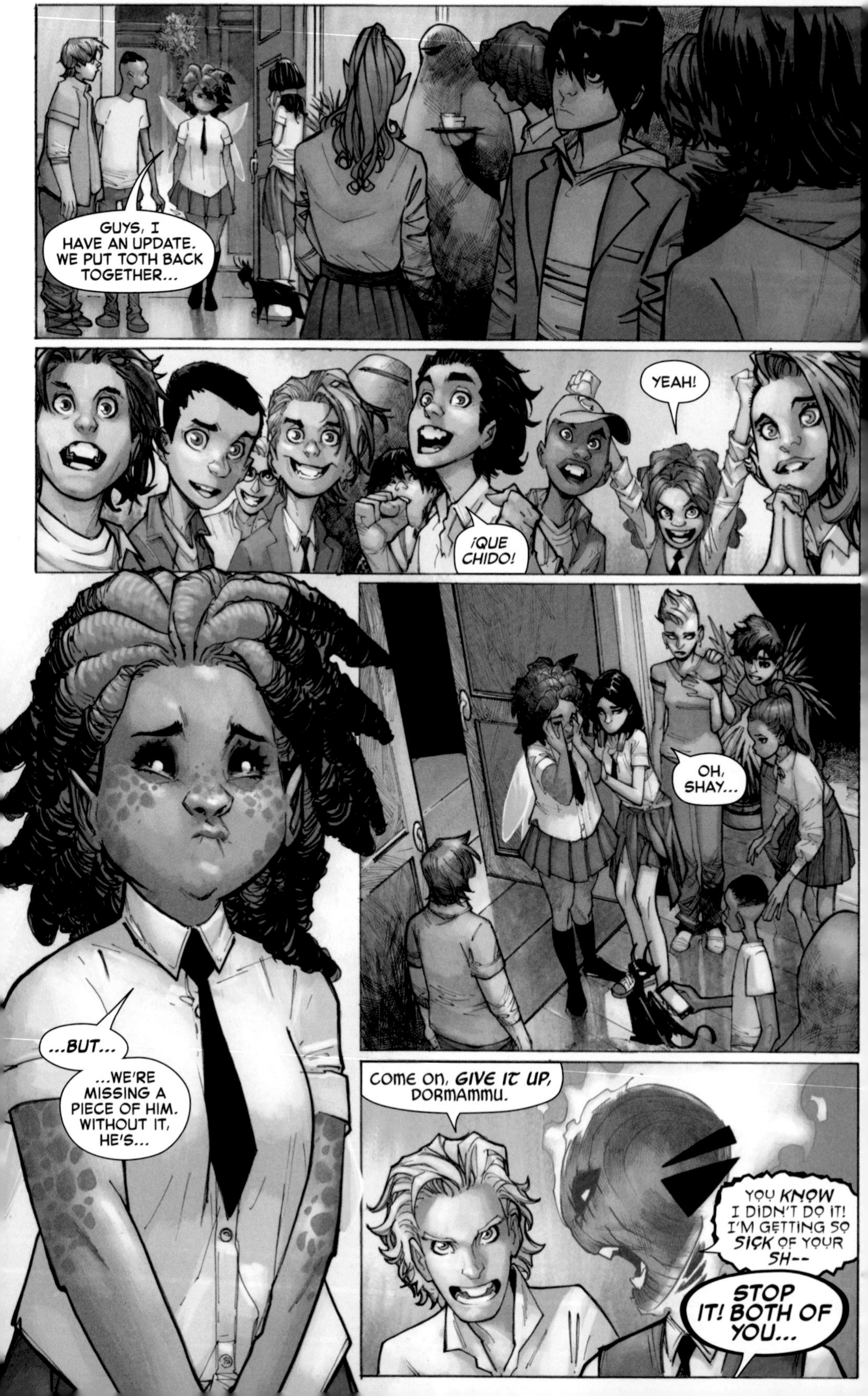
GUYS, I HAVE AN UPDATE. WE PUT TOTH BACK TOGETHER...
YEAH!
¡QUE CHIDO!
OH, SHAY...
...BUT...
...WE'RE MISSING A PIECE OF HIM. WITHOUT IT, HE'S...
COME ON, GIVE IT UP, DORMAMMU.
YOU KNOW I DIDN'T DO IT! I'M GETTING SO SICK OF YOUR SH--
STOP IT! BOTH OF YOU...

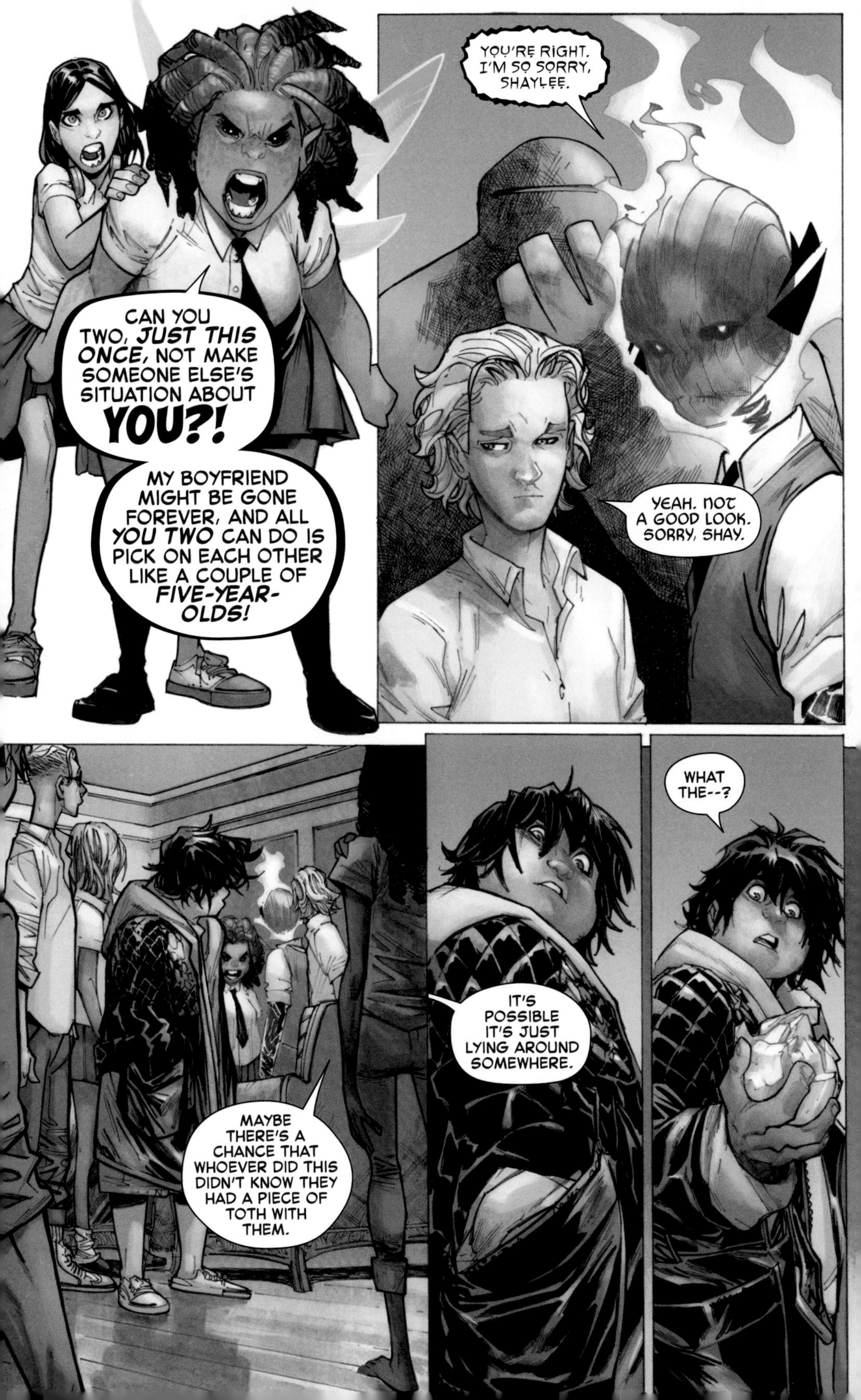
CAN YOU TWO, JUST THIS ONCE, NOT MAKE SOMEONE ELSE'S SITUATION ABOUT YOU?!
MY BOYFRIEND MIGHT BE GONE FOREVER, AND ALL YOU TWO CAN DO IS PICK ON EACH OTHER LIKE A COUPLE OF FIVE-YEAR-OLDS!
YOU'RE RIGHT. I'M SO SORRY, SHAYLEE.
YEAH. NOT A GOOD LOOK. SORRY, SHAY.
MAYBE THERE'S A CHANCE THAT WHOEVER DID THIS DIDN'T KNOW THEY HAD A PIECE OF TOTH WITH THEM.
IT'S POSSIBLE IT'S JUST LYING AROUND SOMEWHERE.
WHAT THE--?

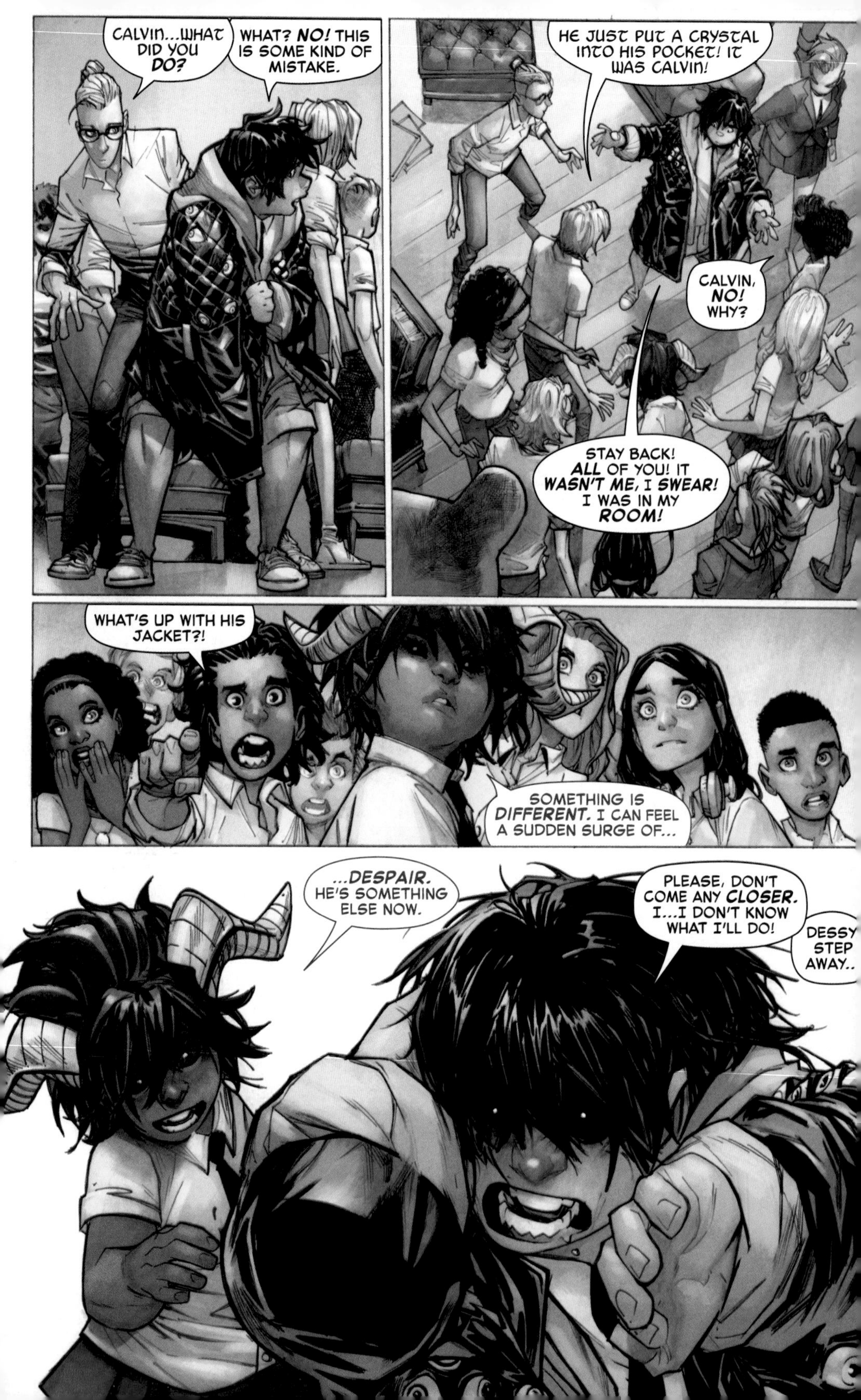

CALVIN...WHAT DID YOU DO?
WHAT? NO! THIS IS SOME KIND OF MISTAKE.
HE JUST PUT A CRYSTAL INTO HIS POCKET! IT WAS CALVIN!
CALVIN, NO! WHY?
STAY BACK! ALL OF YOU! IT WASN'T ME, I SWEAR! I WAS IN MY ROOM!
WHAT'S UP WITH HIS JACKET?!
SOMETHING IS DIFFERENT. I CAN FEEL A SUDDEN SURGE OF...
...DESPAIR. HE'S SOMETHING ELSE NOW.
PLEASE, DON'T COME ANY CLOSER. I...I DON'T KNOW WHAT I'LL DO!
DESSY STEP AWAY..

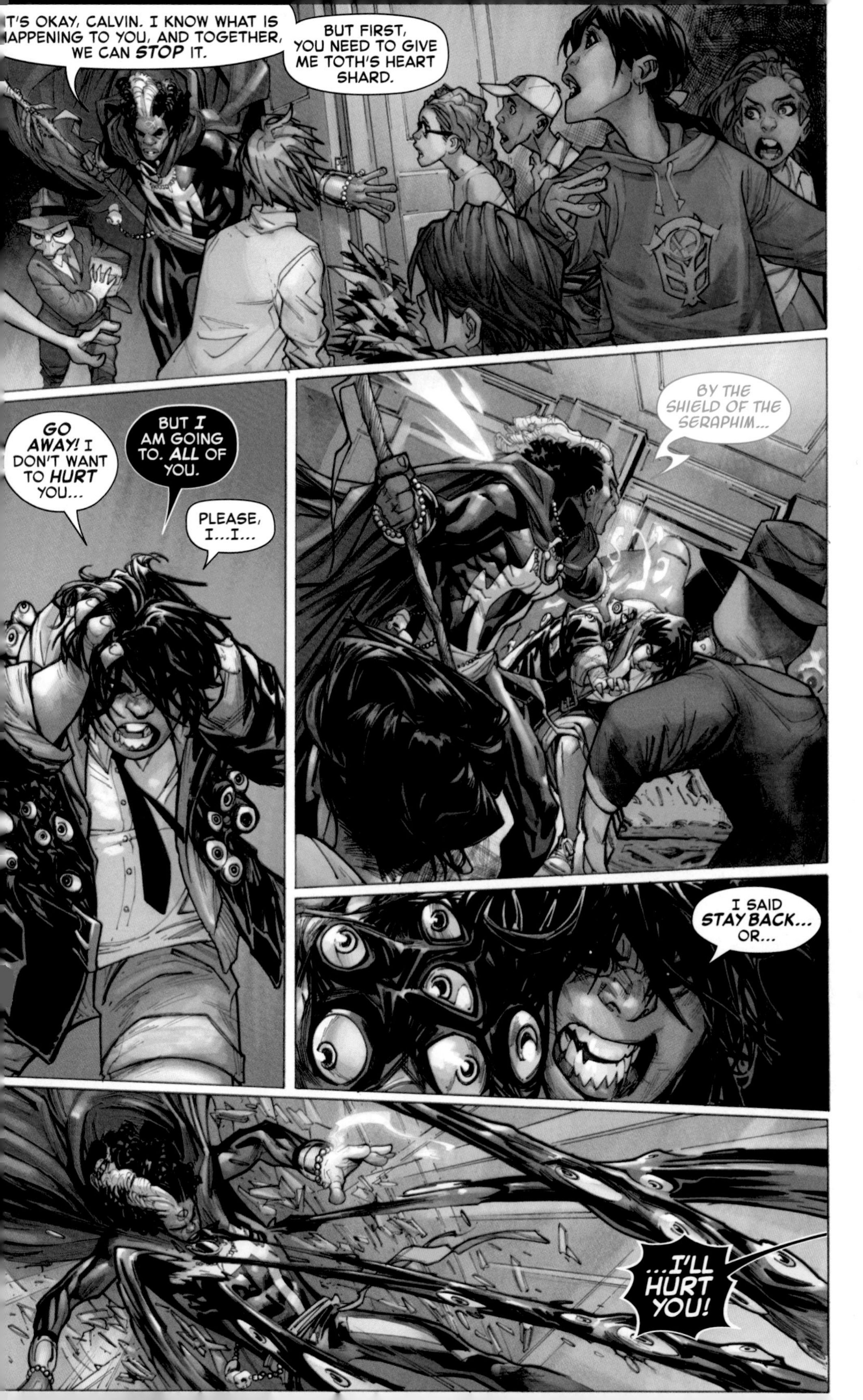

IT'S OKAY, CALVIN. I KNOW WHAT IS HAPPENING TO YOU, AND TOGETHER, WE CAN STOP IT.
BUT FIRST, YOU NEED TO GIVE ME TOTH'S HEART SHARD.
GO AWAY! I DON'T WANT TO HURT YOU...
BUT I AM GOING TO. ALL OF YOU.
PLEASE, I...I...
BY THE SHIELD OF THE SERAPHIM...
I SAID STAY BACK... OR...
...I'LL HURT YOU!

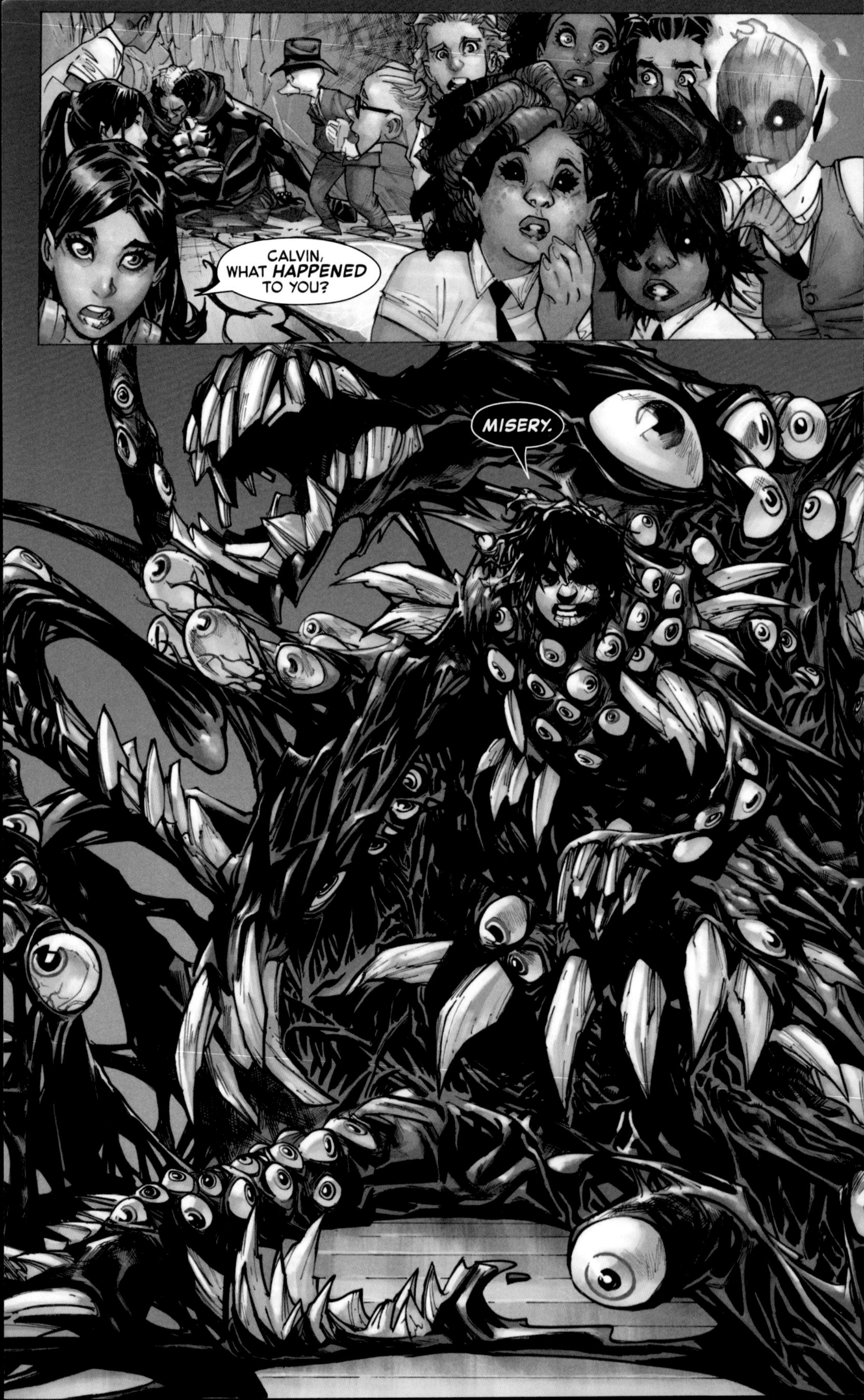
CALVIN, WHAT HAPPENED TO YOU?
MISERY.

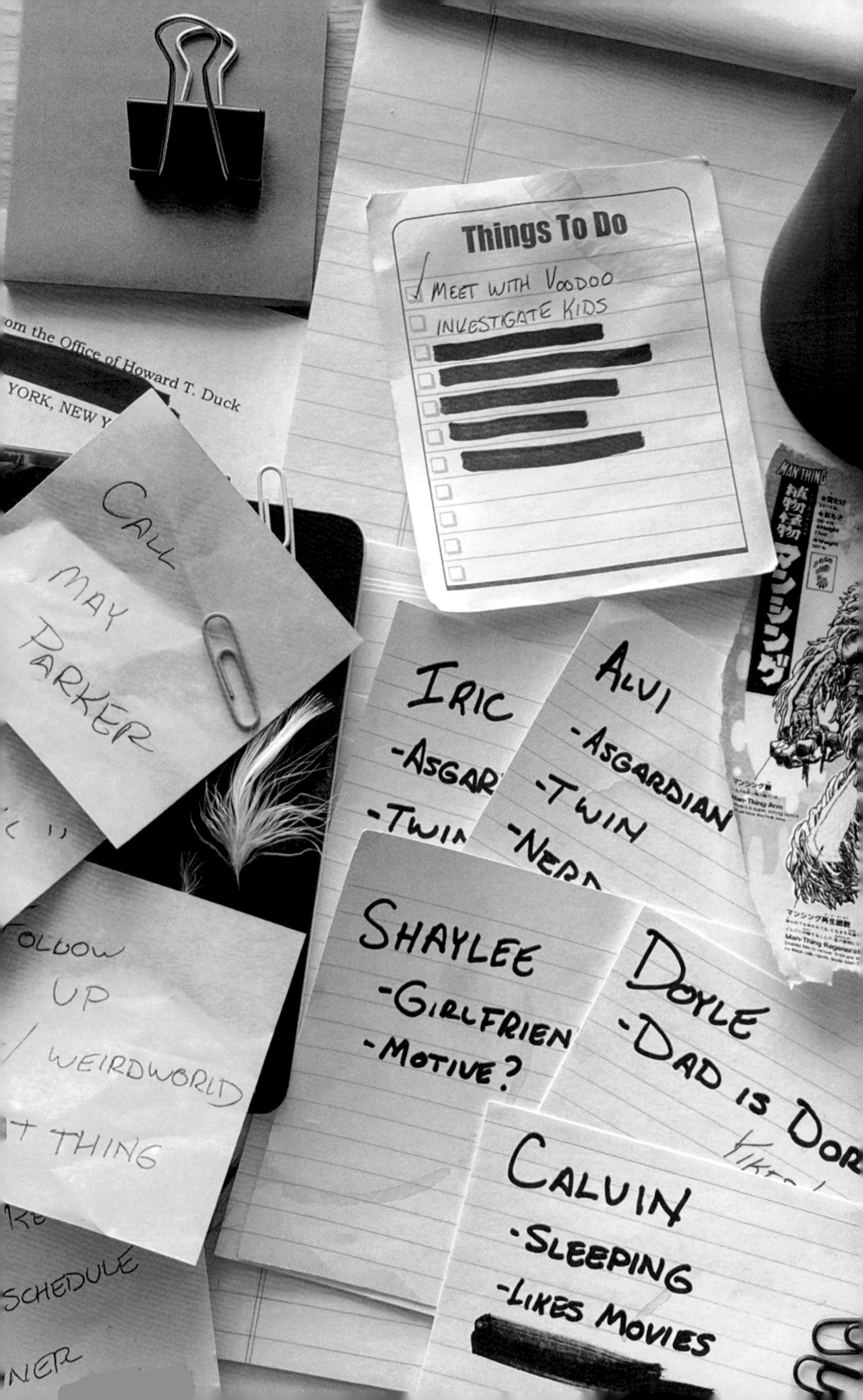

om the Office of Howard T. Duck
YORK, NEW Y
Things To Do
MEET WITH VOODOO
INVESTIGATE KIDS
[redacted]
CALL
MAY
PARKER
FOLLOW
UP
/ WEIRDWORLD
T THING
SCHEDULE
NER
IRIC
-ASGAR
-TWIN
ALVI
-ASGARDIAN
-TWIN
-NER
MAN-THING
植物怪物
マンシング
SHAYLEE
-GIRLFRIEN
-MOTIVE?
DOYLE
-DAD IS DOR
CALVIN
-SLEEPING
-LIKES MOVIES
[redacted]

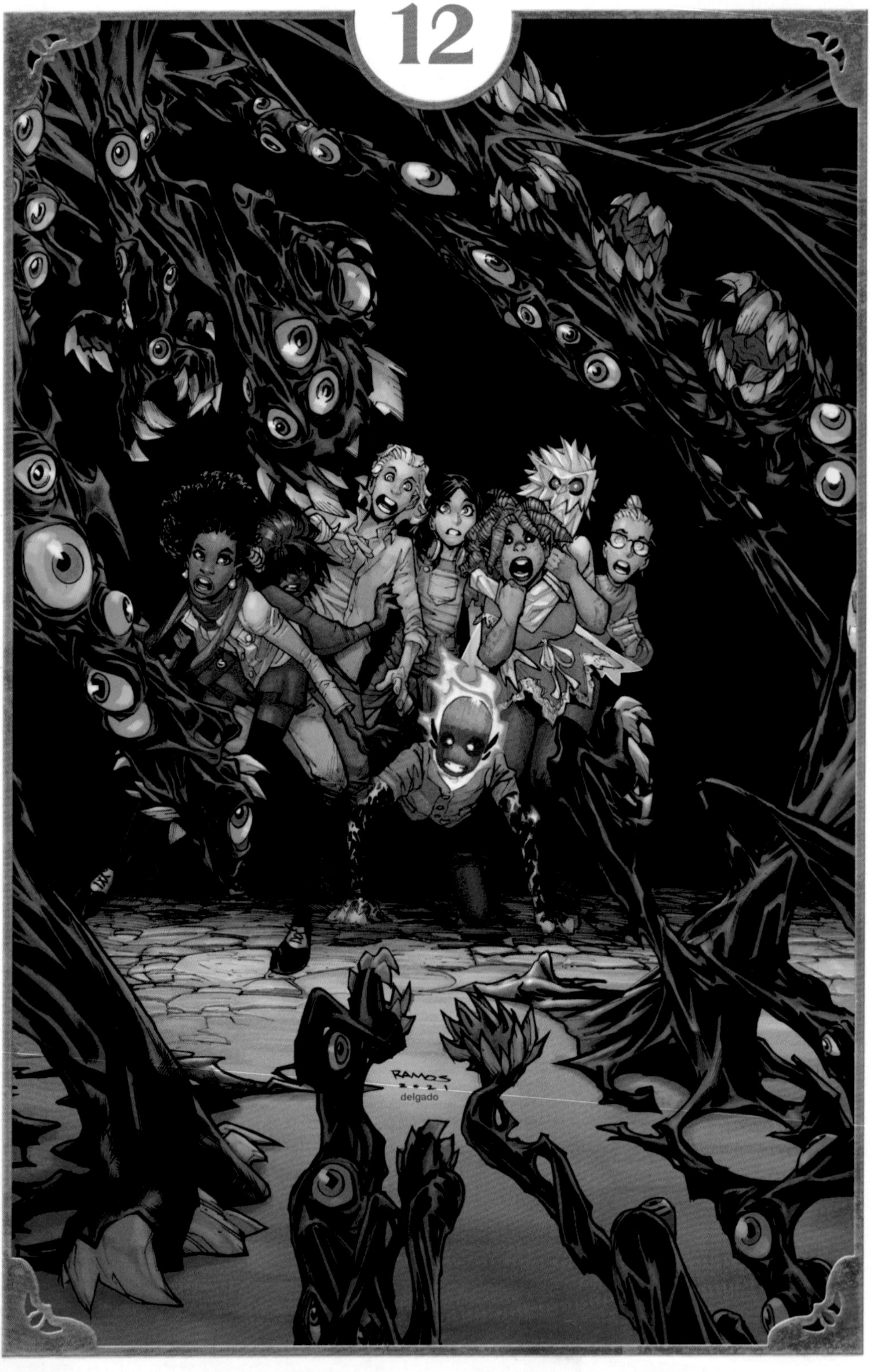
12
RAMOS
2021
delgado

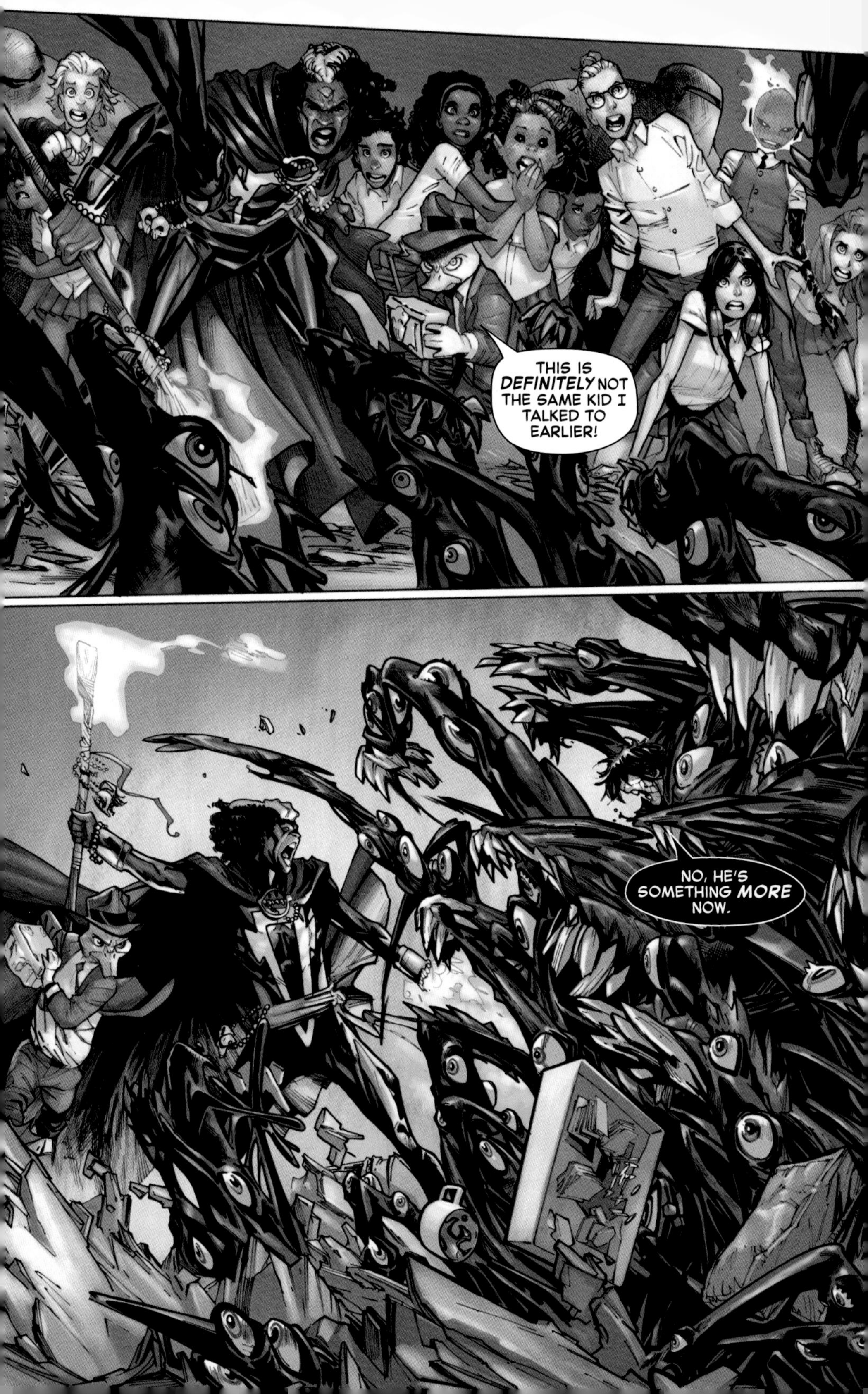
THIS IS DEFINITELY NOT THE SAME KID I TALKED TO EARLIER!
NO, HE'S SOMETHING MORE NOW.

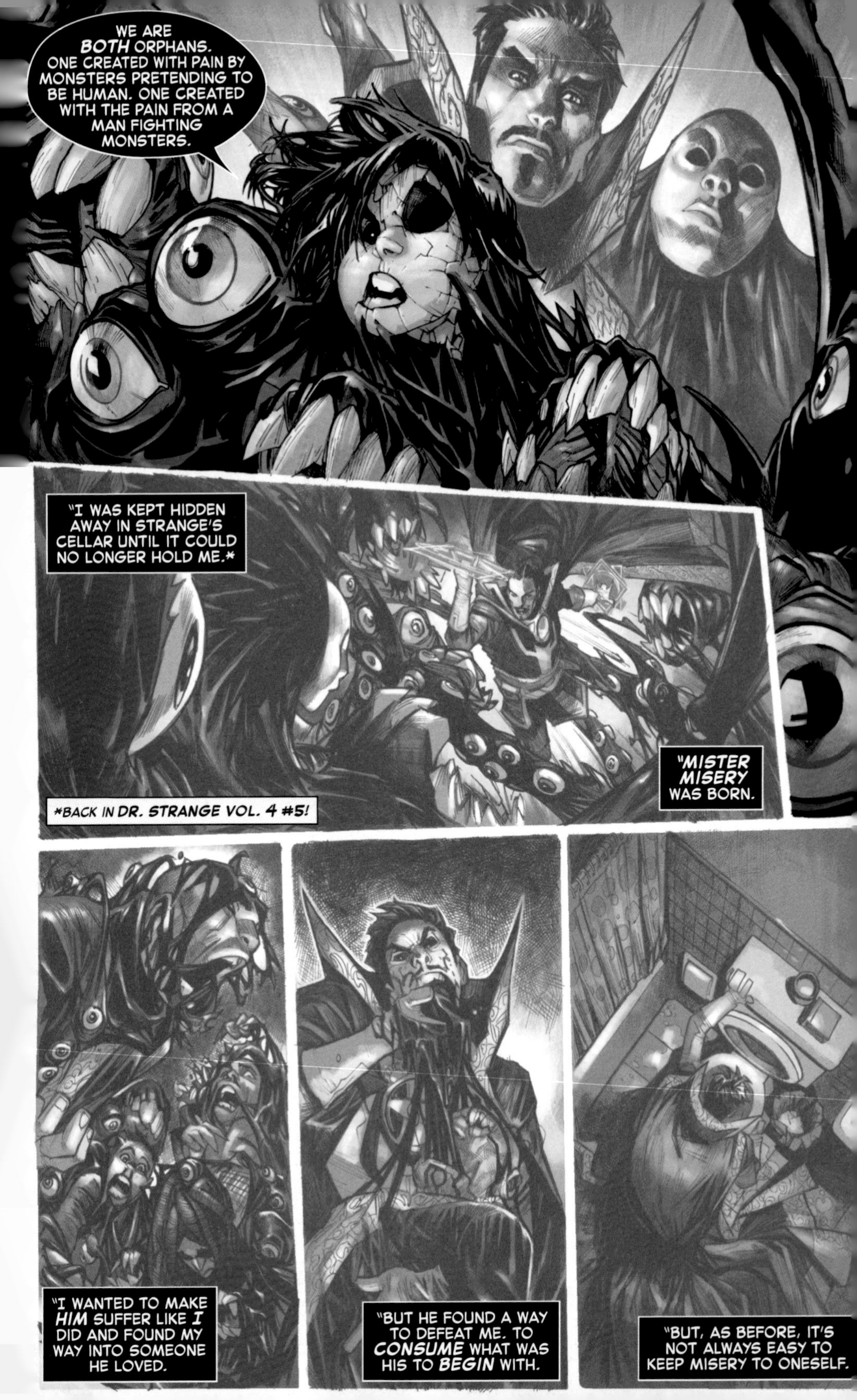
WE ARE BOTH ORPHANS. ONE CREATED WITH PAIN BY MONSTERS PRETENDING TO BE HUMAN. ONE CREATED WITH THE PAIN FROM A MAN FIGHTING MONSTERS.
"I WAS KEPT HIDDEN AWAY IN STRANGE'S CELLAR UNTIL IT COULD NO LONGER HOLD ME.*
"MISTER MISERY WAS BORN.
*BACK IN DR. STRANGE VOL. 4 #5!
"I WANTED TO MAKE HIM SUFFER LIKE I DID AND FOUND MY WAY INTO SOMEONE HE LOVED.
"BUT HE FOUND A WAY TO DEFEAT ME. TO CONSUME WHAT WAS HIS TO BEGIN WITH.
"BUT, AS BEFORE, IT'S NOT ALWAYS EASY TO KEEP MISERY TO ONESELF.

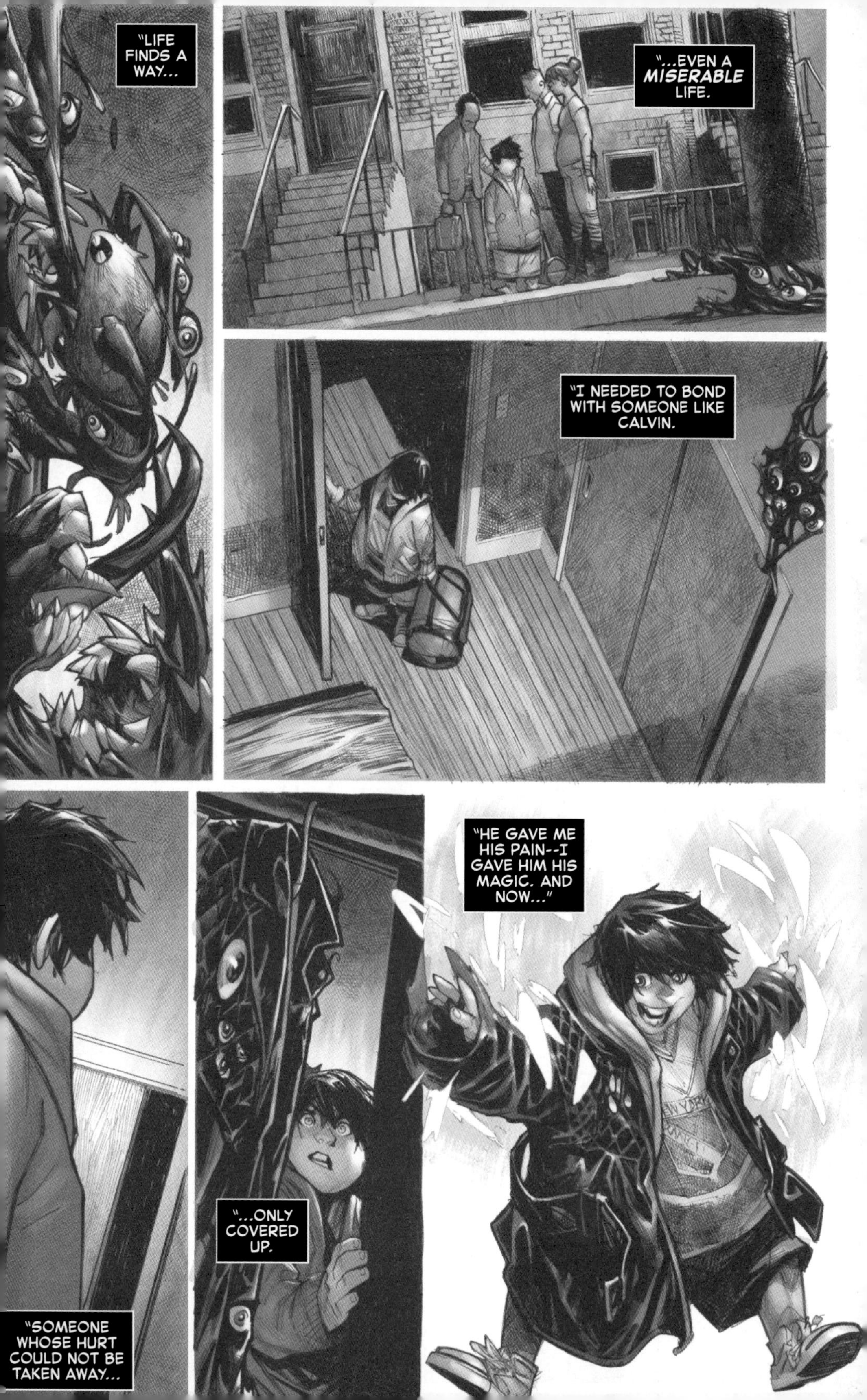
"LIFE FINDS A WAY...
"...EVEN A MISERABLE LIFE.
"I NEEDED TO BOND WITH SOMEONE LIKE CALVIN.
"SOMEONE WHOSE HURT COULD NOT BE TAKEN AWAY...
"...ONLY COVERED UP.
"HE GAVE ME HIS PAIN--I GAVE HIM HIS MAGIC. AND NOW..."

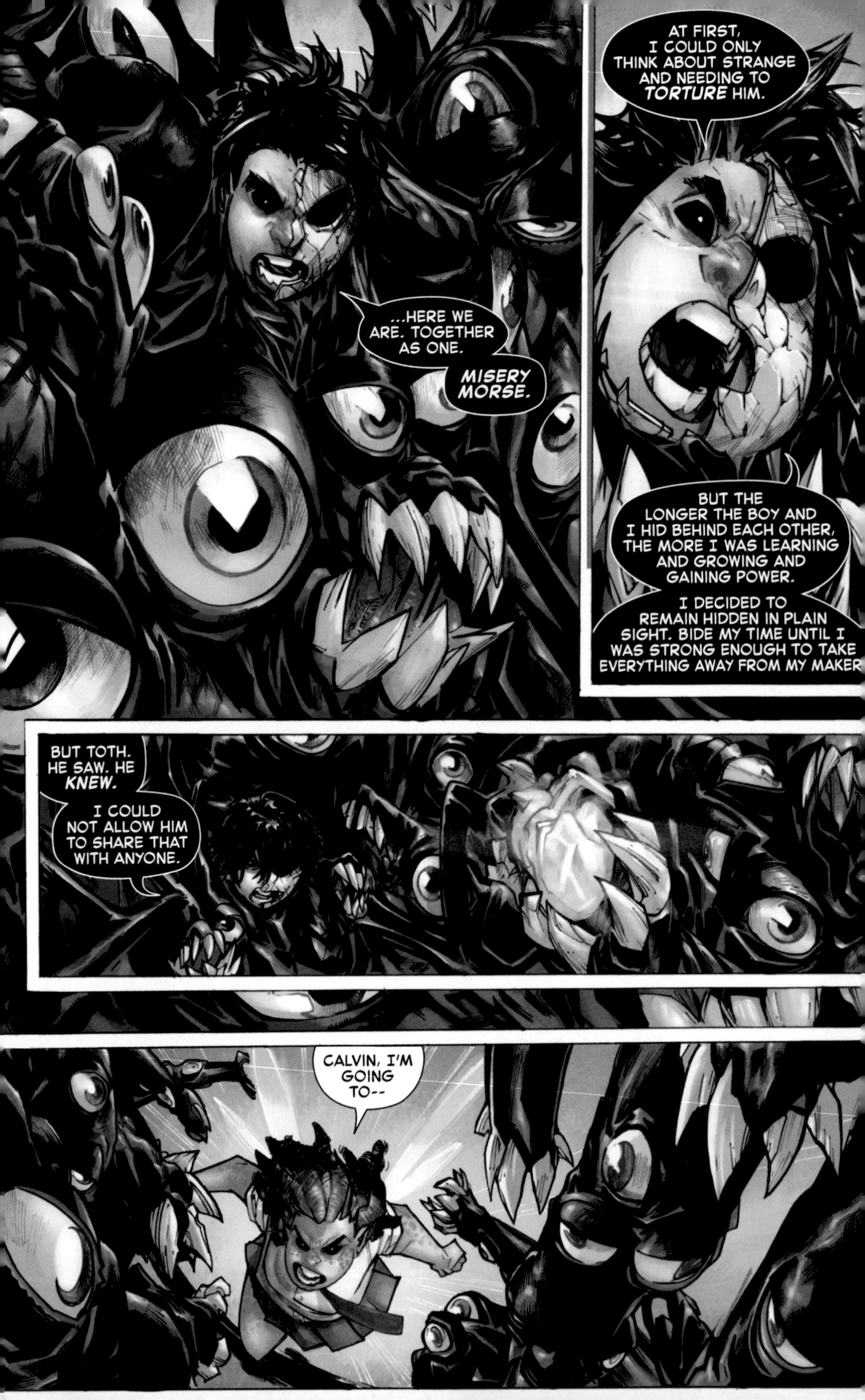
...HERE WE ARE. TOGETHER AS ONE.
MISERY MORSE.
AT FIRST, I COULD ONLY THINK ABOUT STRANGE AND NEEDING TO TORTURE HIM.
BUT THE LONGER THE BOY AND I HID BEHIND EACH OTHER, THE MORE I WAS LEARNING AND GROWING AND GAINING POWER.
I DECIDED TO REMAIN HIDDEN IN PLAIN SIGHT. BIDE MY TIME UNTIL I WAS STRONG ENOUGH TO TAKE EVERYTHING AWAY FROM MY MAKER
BUT TOTH. HE SAW. HE KNEW.
I COULD NOT ALLOW HIM TO SHARE THAT WITH ANYONE.
CALVIN, I'M GOING TO--

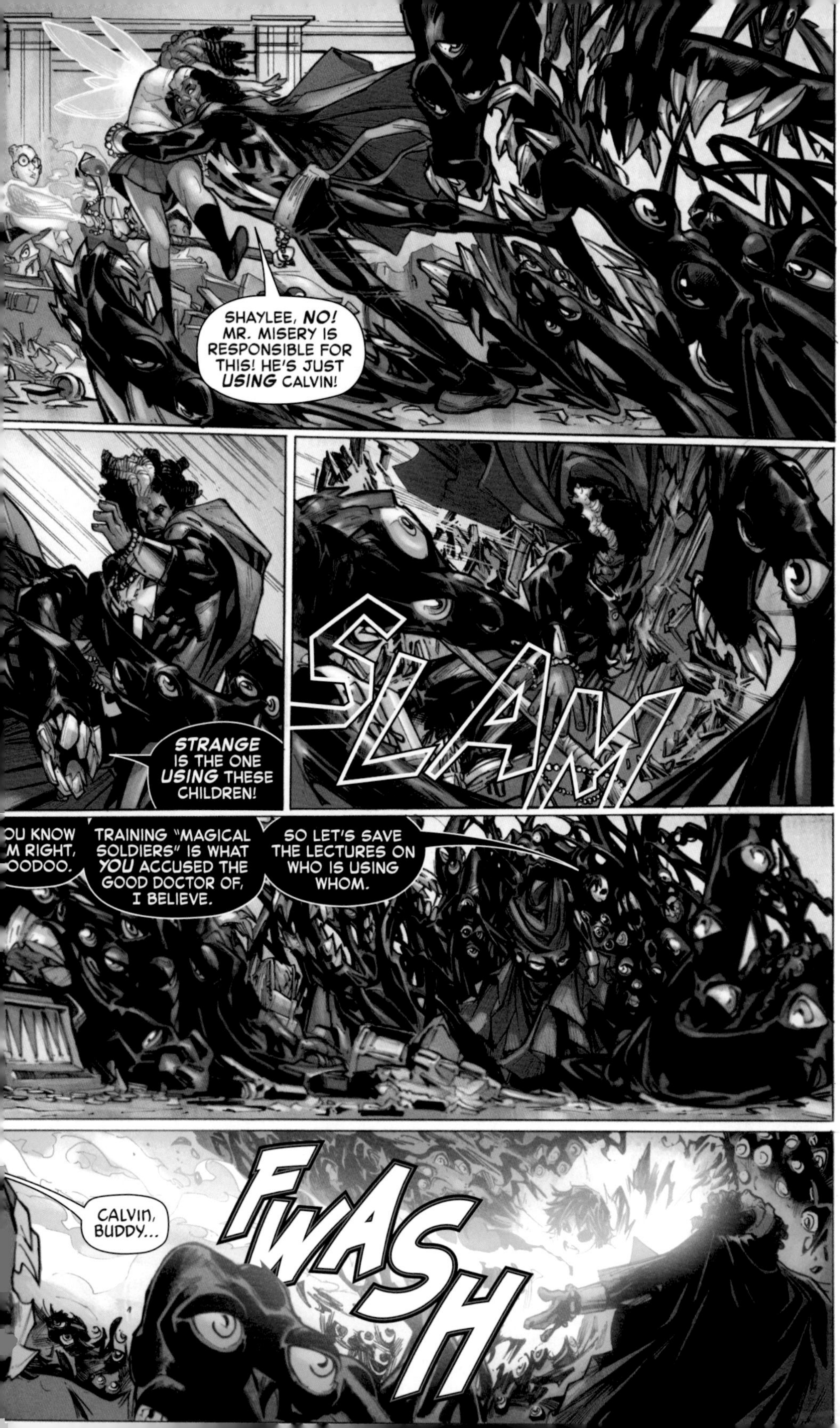
SHAYLEE, NO! MR. MISERY IS RESPONSIBLE FOR THIS! HE'S JUST USING CALVIN!
STRANGE IS THE ONE USING THESE CHILDREN!
SLAM
OU KNOW M RIGHT, OODOO.
TRAINING "MAGICAL SOLDIERS" IS WHAT YOU ACCUSED THE GOOD DOCTOR OF, I BELIEVE.
SO LET'S SAVE THE LECTURES ON WHO IS USING WHOM.
CALVIN, BUDDY...
FWASH

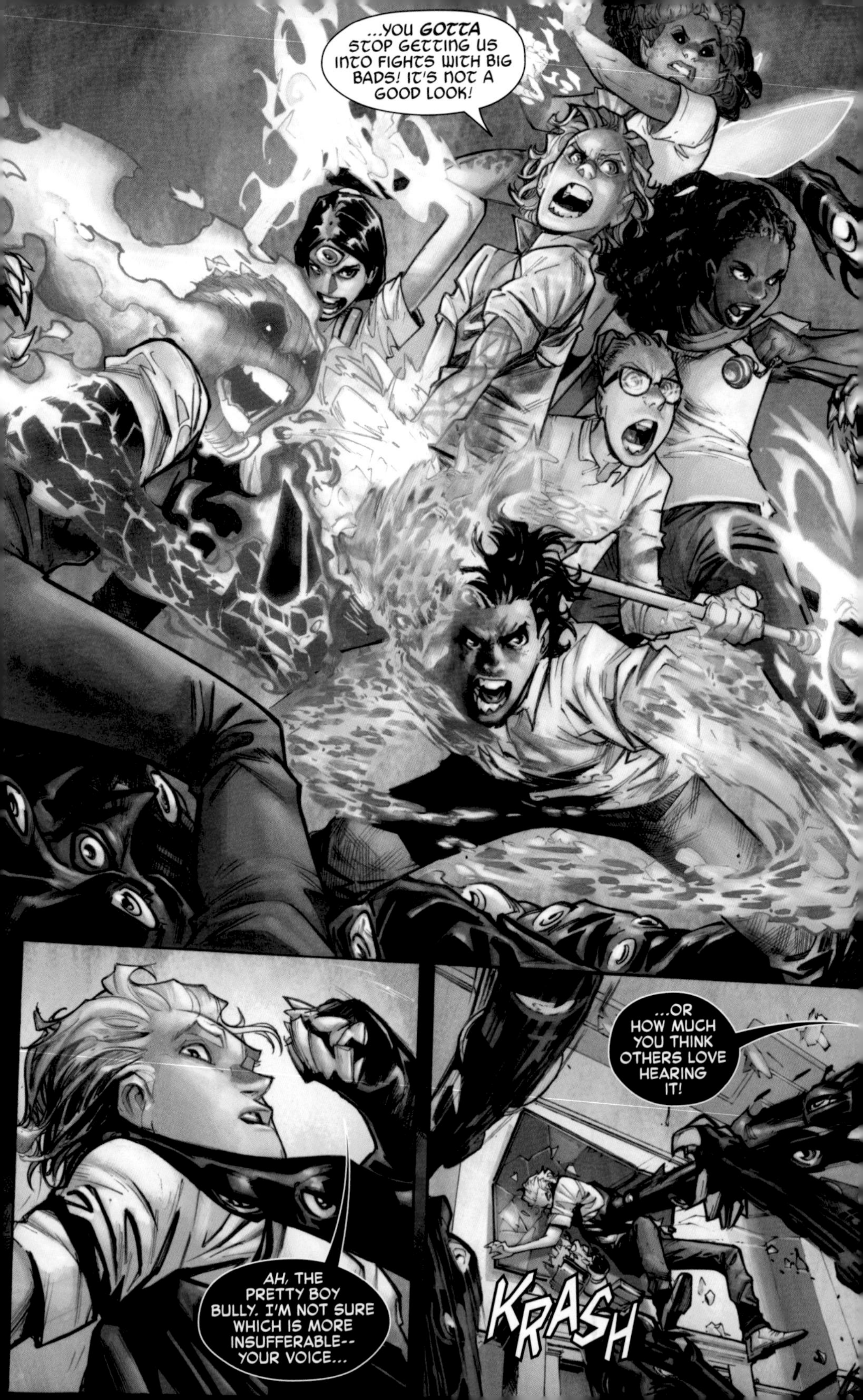
...YOU GOTTA STOP GETTING US INTO FIGHTS WITH BIG BADS! IT'S NOT A GOOD LOOK!
AH, THE PRETTY BOY BULLY. I'M NOT SURE WHICH IS MORE INSUFFERABLE-- YOUR VOICE...
...OR HOW MUCH YOU THINK OTHERS LOVE HEARING IT!
KRASH

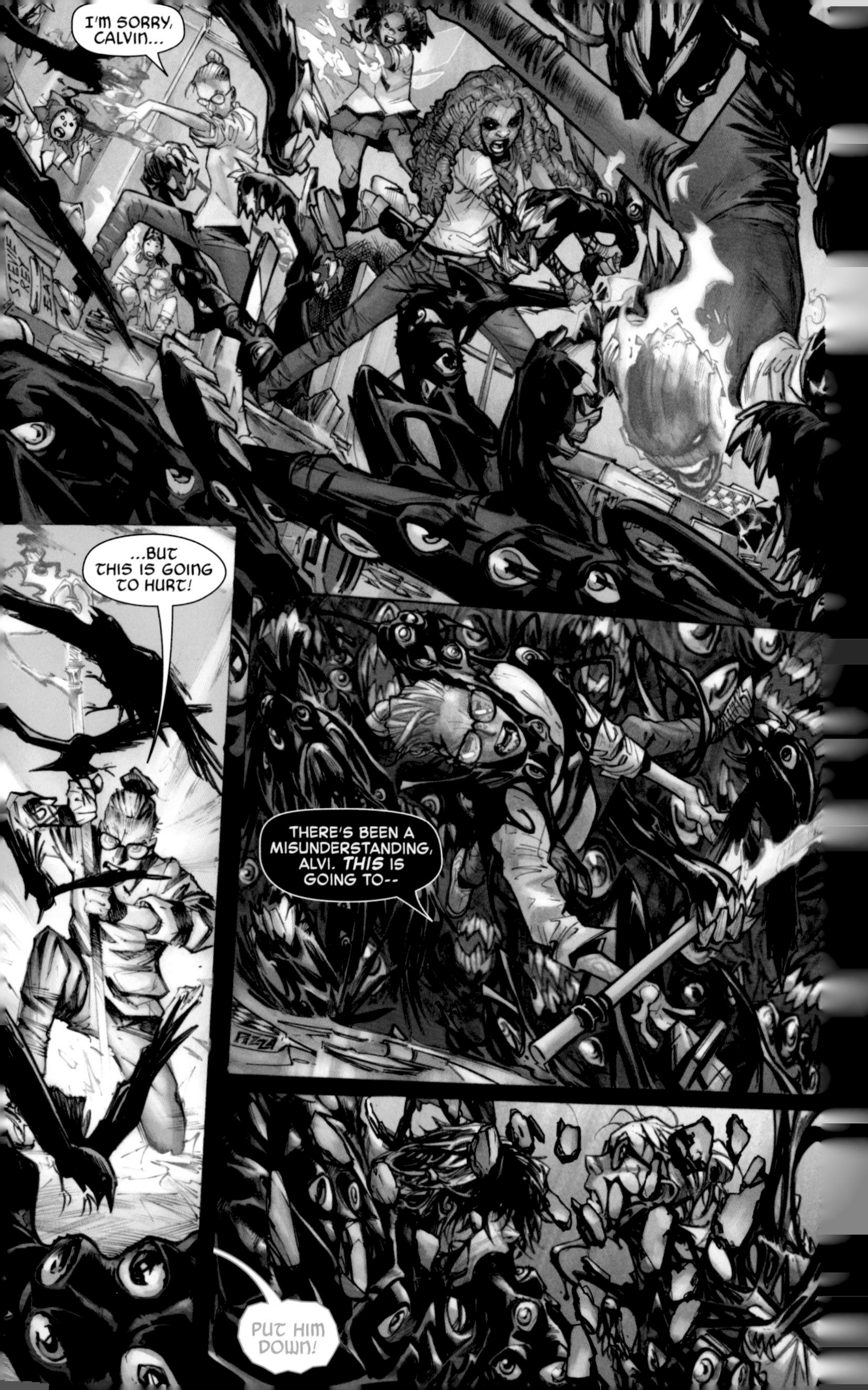
I'M SORRY, CALVIN...
...BUT THIS IS GOING TO HURT!
THERE'S BEEN A MISUNDERSTANDING, ALVI. THIS IS GOING TO--
PUT HIM DOWN!

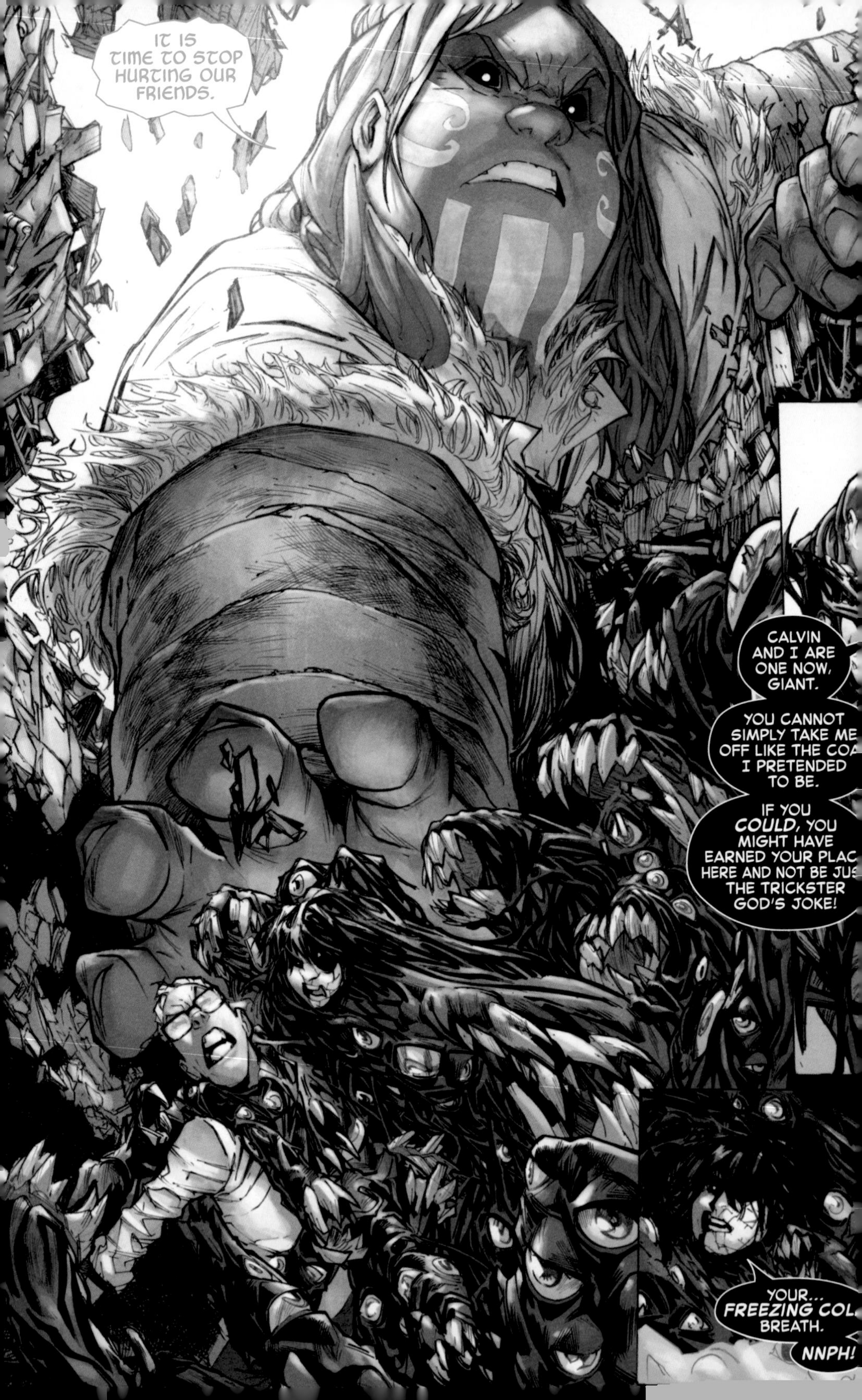
IT IS TIME TO STOP HURTING OUR FRIENDS.
CALVIN AND I ARE ONE NOW, GIANT.
YOU CANNOT SIMPLY TAKE ME OFF LIKE THE COA
I PRETENDED TO BE.
IF YOU COULD, YOU MIGHT HAVE EARNED YOUR PLAC
HERE AND NOT BE JUS
THE TRICKSTER GOD'S JOKE!
YOUR... FREEZING COL
BREATH.
NNPH!

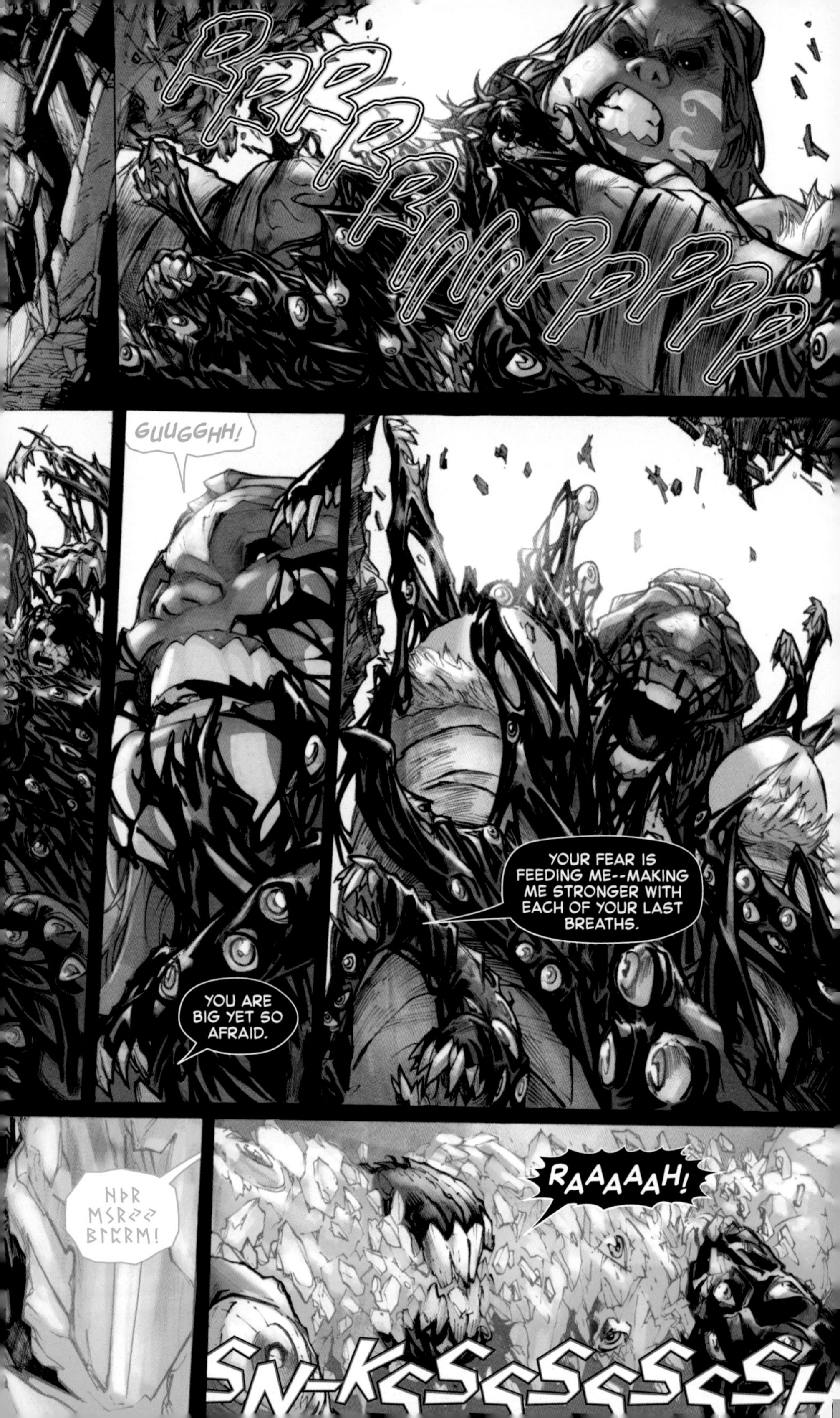
GUUGGHH!
YOU ARE BIG YET SO AFRAID.
YOUR FEAR IS FEEDING ME--MAKING ME STRONGER WITH EACH OF YOUR LAST BREATHS.
RAAAAAH!

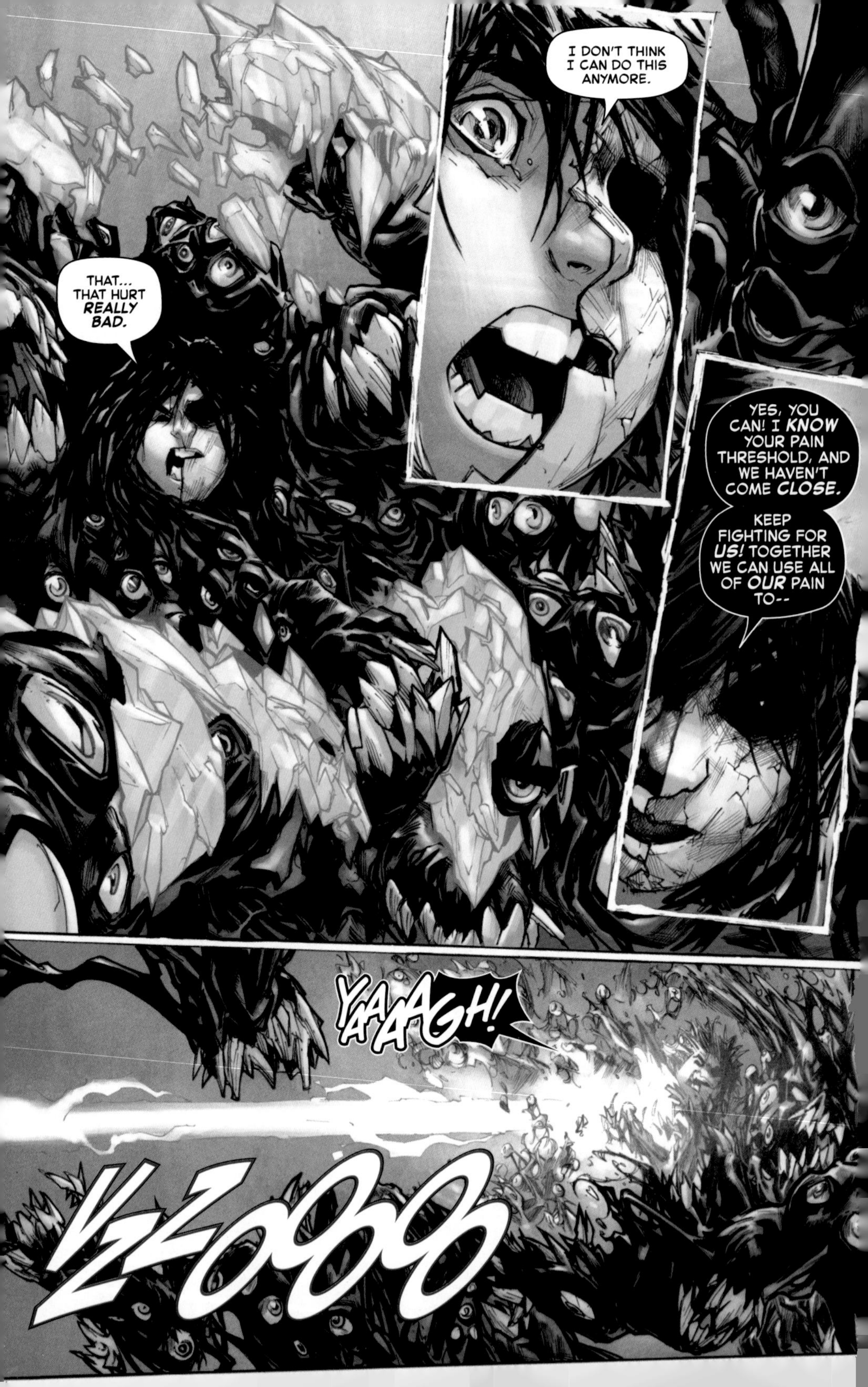
I DON'T THINK I CAN DO THIS ANYMORE.
THAT... THAT HURT *REALLY* *BAD.*
YES, YOU CAN! I *KNOW* YOUR PAIN THRESHOLD, AND WE HAVEN'T COME *CLOSE.*
KEEP FIGHTING FOR *US!* TOGETHER WE CAN USE ALL OF *OUR* PAIN TO--
YAAAAGH!
VZZOOOO

THANK YOU, MINDFUL.

OOF... CAN YOU AND YOUR FRIENDS SURROUND MISERY AND CLOSE IN?

TAKE AS MUCH AS YOU CAN WITHOUT TOUCHING CALVIN.

RRRRAAAAGHHH!

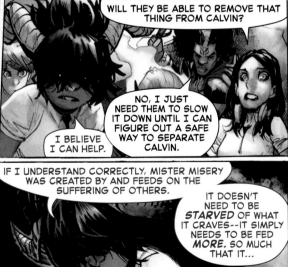

WILL THEY BE ABLE TO REMOVE THAT THING FROM CALVIN?

I BELIEVE I CAN HELP.

NO, I JUST NEED THEM TO SLOW IT DOWN UNTIL I CAN FIGURE OUT A SAFE WAY TO SEPARATE CALVIN.

IF I UNDERSTAND CORRECTLY, MISTER MISERY WAS CREATED BY AND FEEDS ON THE SUFFERING OF OTHERS.

IT DOESN'T NEED TO BE STARVED OF WHAT IT CRAVES--IT SIMPLY NEEDS TO BE FED MORE. SO MUCH THAT IT...

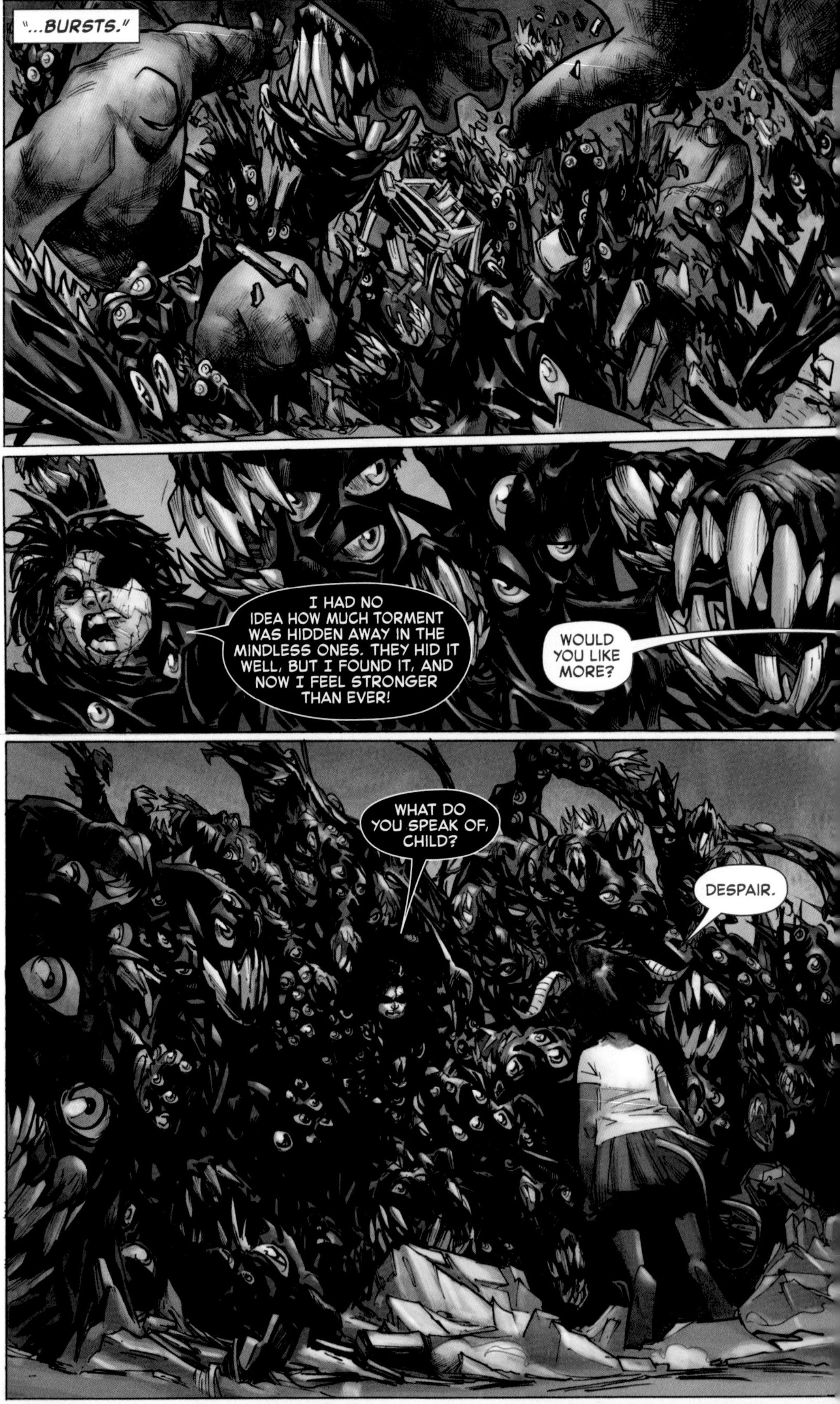
"...BURSTS."
I HAD NO IDEA HOW MUCH TORMENT WAS HIDDEN AWAY IN THE MINDLESS ONES. THEY HID IT WELL, BUT I FOUND IT, AND NOW I FEEL STRONGER THAN EVER!
WOULD YOU LIKE MORE?
WHAT DO YOU SPEAK OF, CHILD?
DESPAIR.

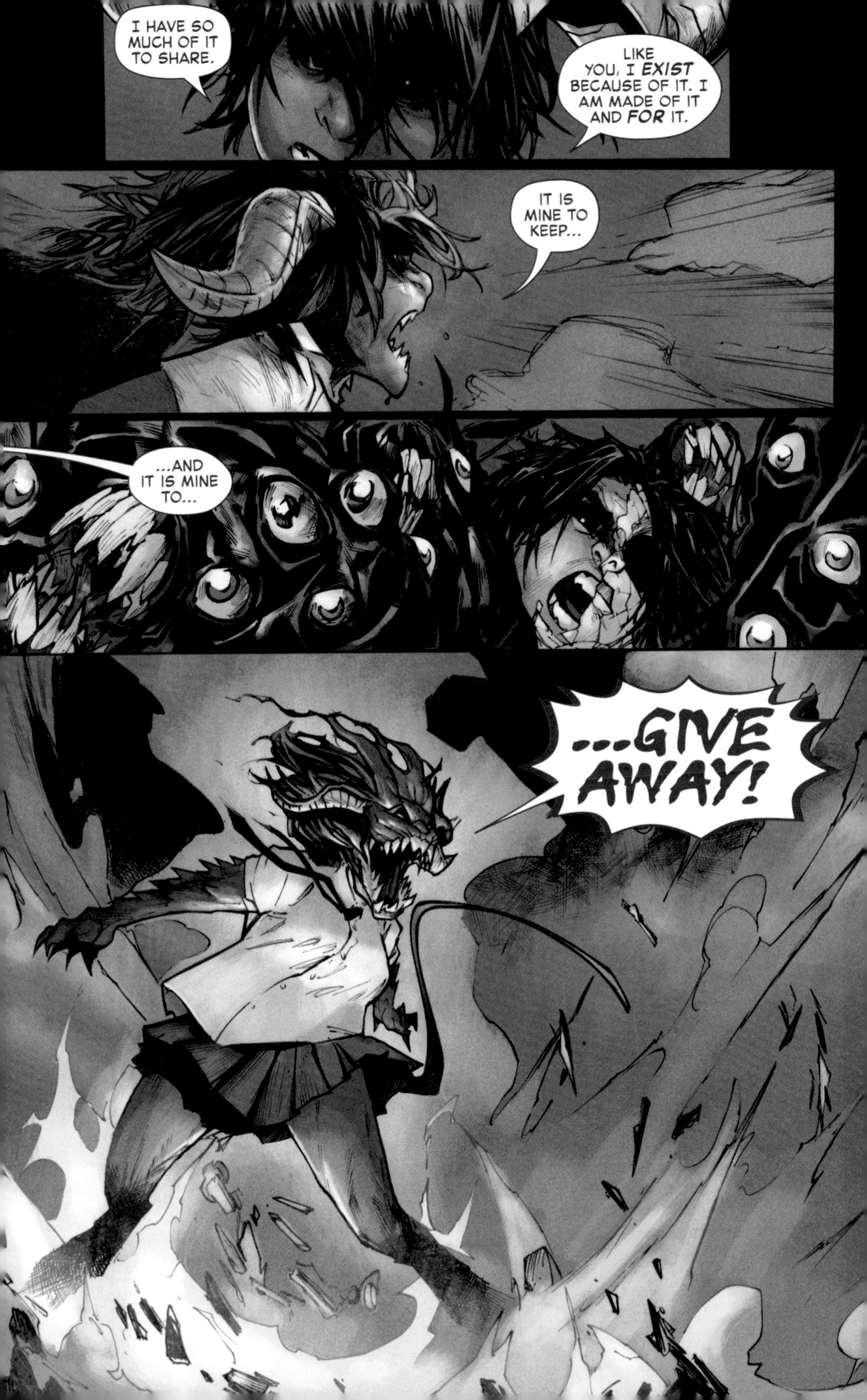
I HAVE SO MUCH OF IT TO SHARE.
LIKE YOU, I EXIST BECAUSE OF IT. I AM MADE OF IT AND FOR IT.
IT IS MINE TO KEEP...
...AND IT IS MINE TO...
...GIVE AWAY!

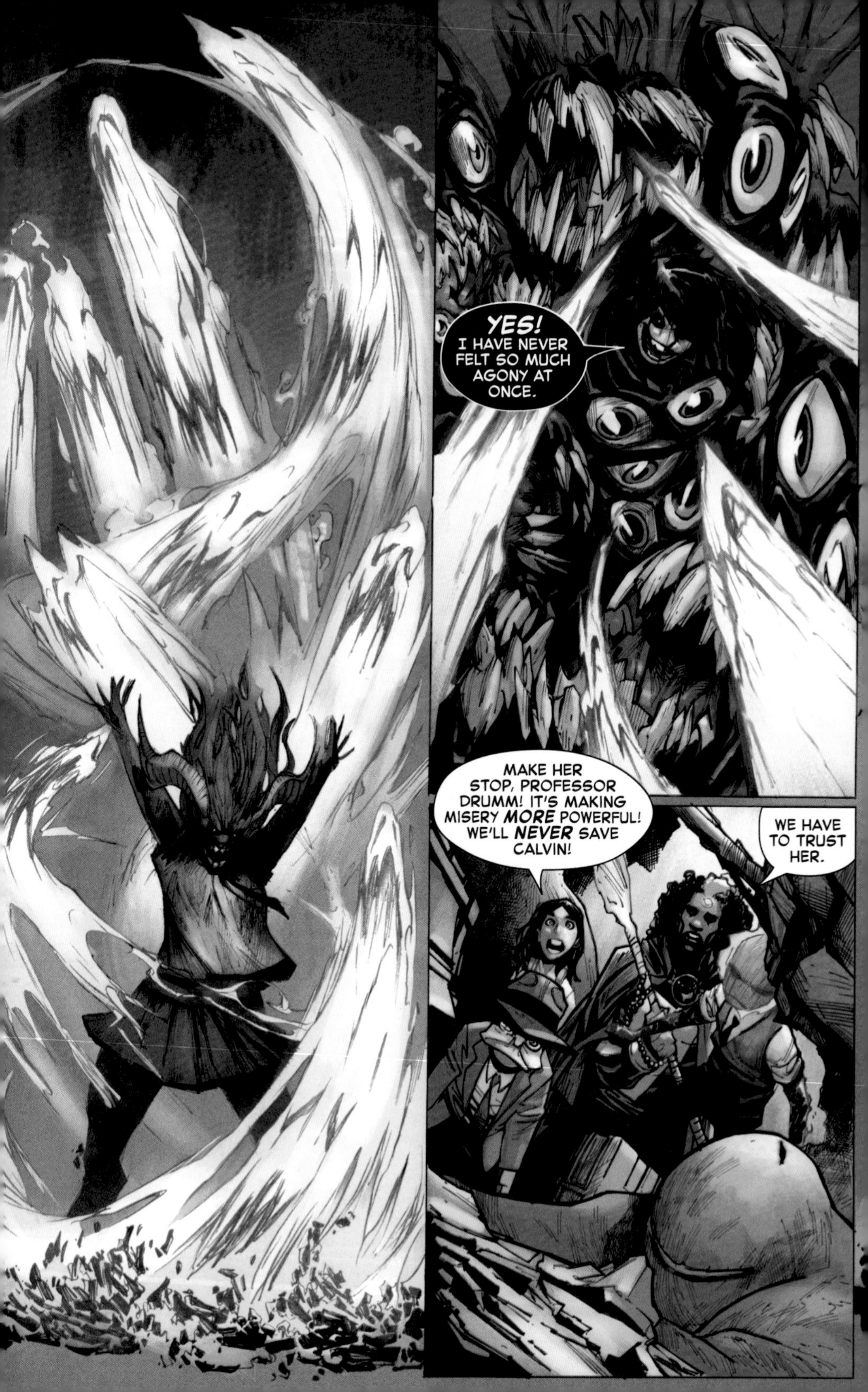
YES! I HAVE NEVER FELT SO MUCH AGONY AT ONCE.
MAKE HER STOP, PROFESSOR DRUMM! IT'S MAKING MISERY MORE POWERFUL! WE'LL NEVER SAVE CALVIN!
WE HAVE TO TRUST HER.

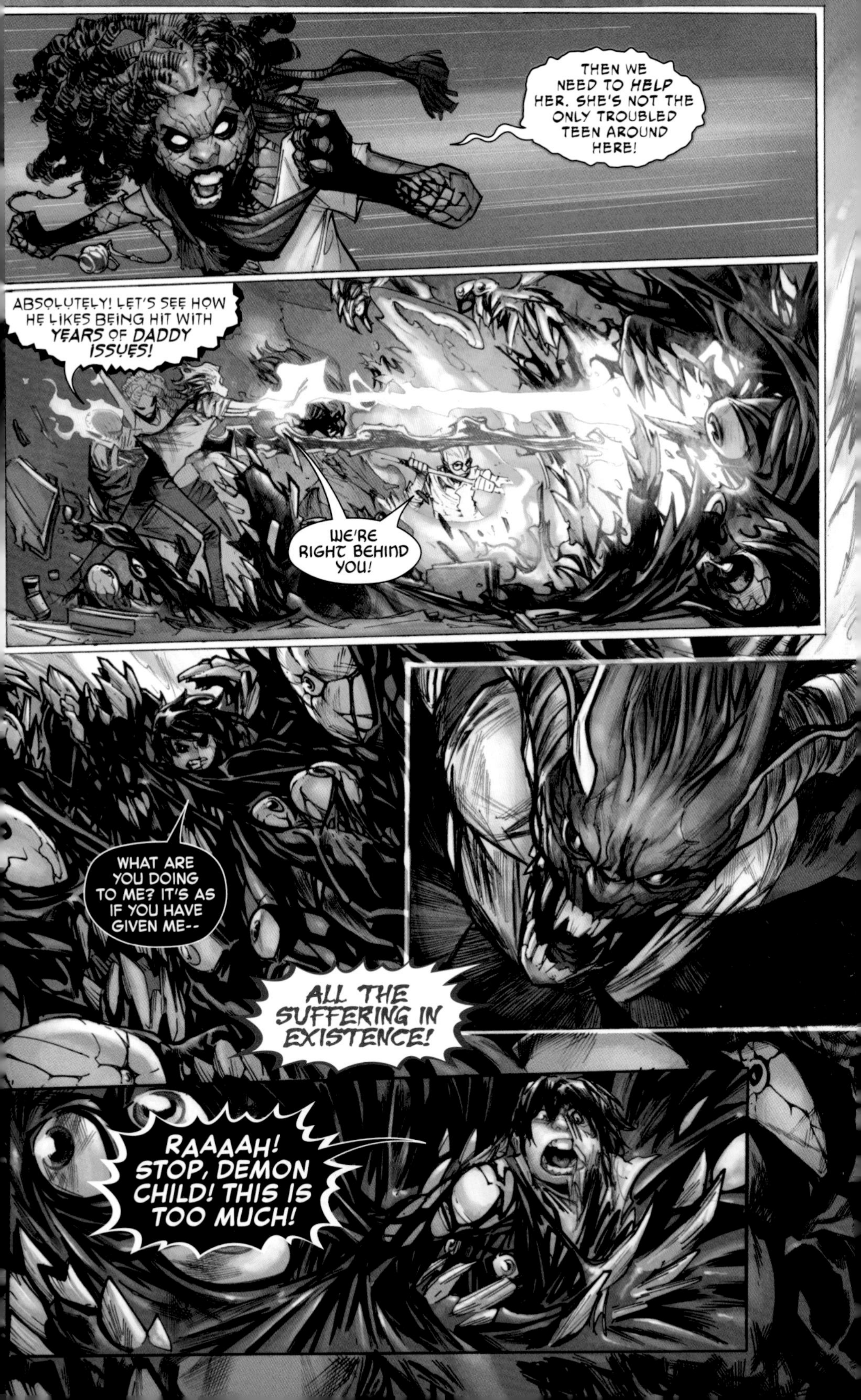
THEN WE NEED TO HELP HER. SHE'S NOT THE ONLY TROUBLED TEEN AROUND HERE!
ABSOLUTELY! LET'S SEE HOW HE LIKES BEING HIT WITH YEARS OF DADDY ISSUES!
WE'RE RIGHT BEHIND YOU!
WHAT ARE YOU DOING TO ME? IT'S AS IF YOU HAVE GIVEN ME--
ALL THE SUFFERING IN EXISTENCE!
RAAAAH! STOP, DEMON CHILD! THIS IS TOO MUCH!

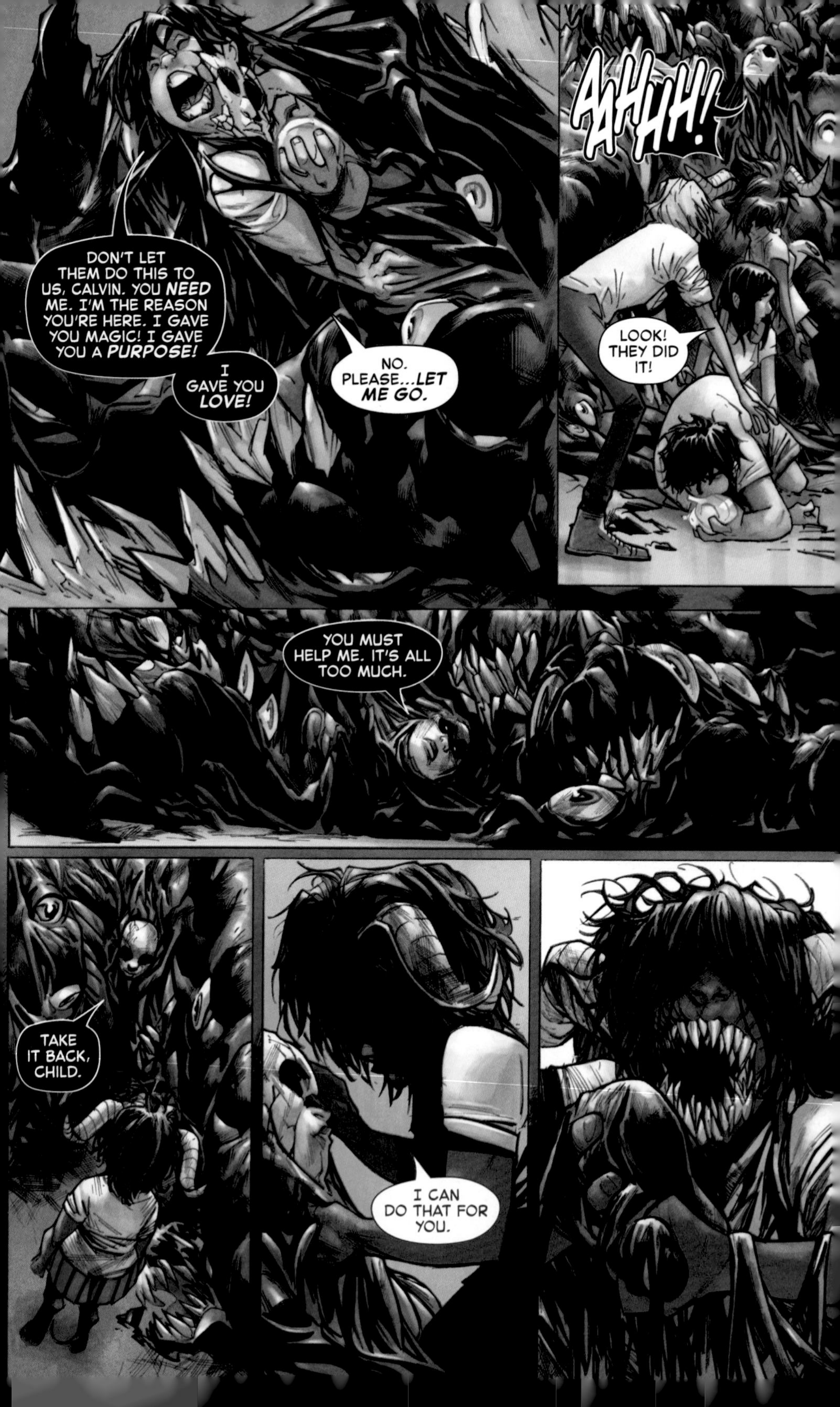
DON'T LET THEM DO THIS TO US, CALVIN. YOU NEED ME. I'M THE REASON YOU'RE HERE. I GAVE YOU MAGIC! I GAVE YOU A PURPOSE!
I GAVE YOU LOVE!
NO. PLEASE...LET ME GO.
AAHHH!
LOOK! THEY DID IT!
YOU MUST HELP ME. IT'S ALL TOO MUCH.
TAKE IT BACK, CHILD.
I CAN DO THAT FOR YOU.

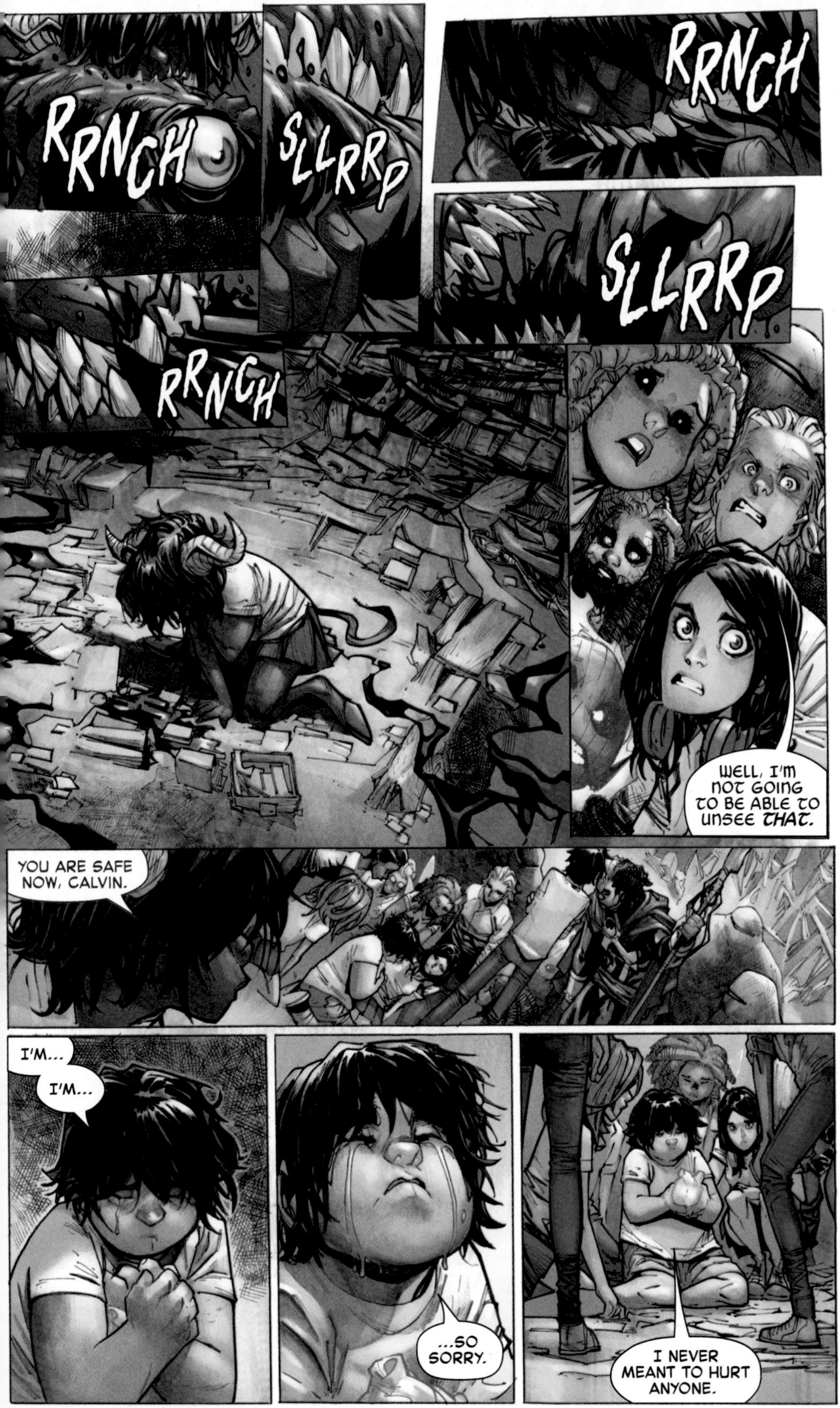
RRNCH
SLLRRP
RRNCH
SLLRRP
RRNCH
WELL, I'M NOT GOING TO BE ABLE TO UNSEE *THAT.*
YOU ARE SAFE NOW, CALVIN.
I'M...
I'M...
...SO SORRY.
I NEVER MEANT TO HURT ANYONE.

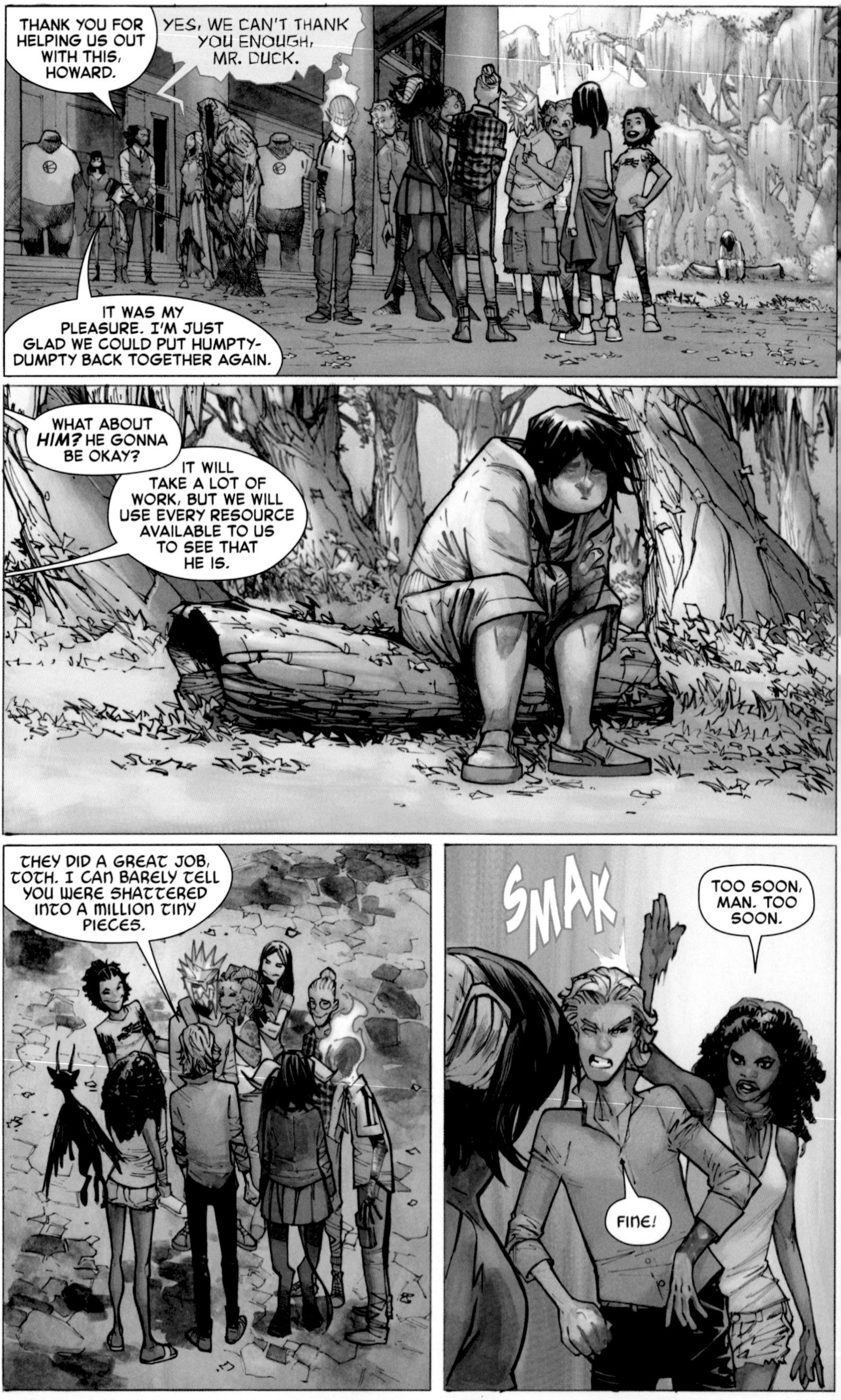
THANK YOU FOR HELPING US OUT WITH THIS, HOWARD.
YES, WE CAN'T THANK YOU ENOUGH, MR. DUCK.
IT WAS MY PLEASURE. I'M JUST GLAD WE COULD PUT HUMPTY-DUMPTY BACK TOGETHER AGAIN.
WHAT ABOUT *HIM?* HE GONNA BE OKAY?
IT WILL TAKE A LOT OF WORK, BUT WE WILL USE EVERY RESOURCE AVAILABLE TO US TO SEE THAT HE IS.
THEY DID A GREAT JOB, TOTH. I CAN BARELY TELL YOU WERE SHATTERED INTO A MILLION TINY PIECES.
SMAK
FINE!
TOO SOON, MAN. TOO SOON.

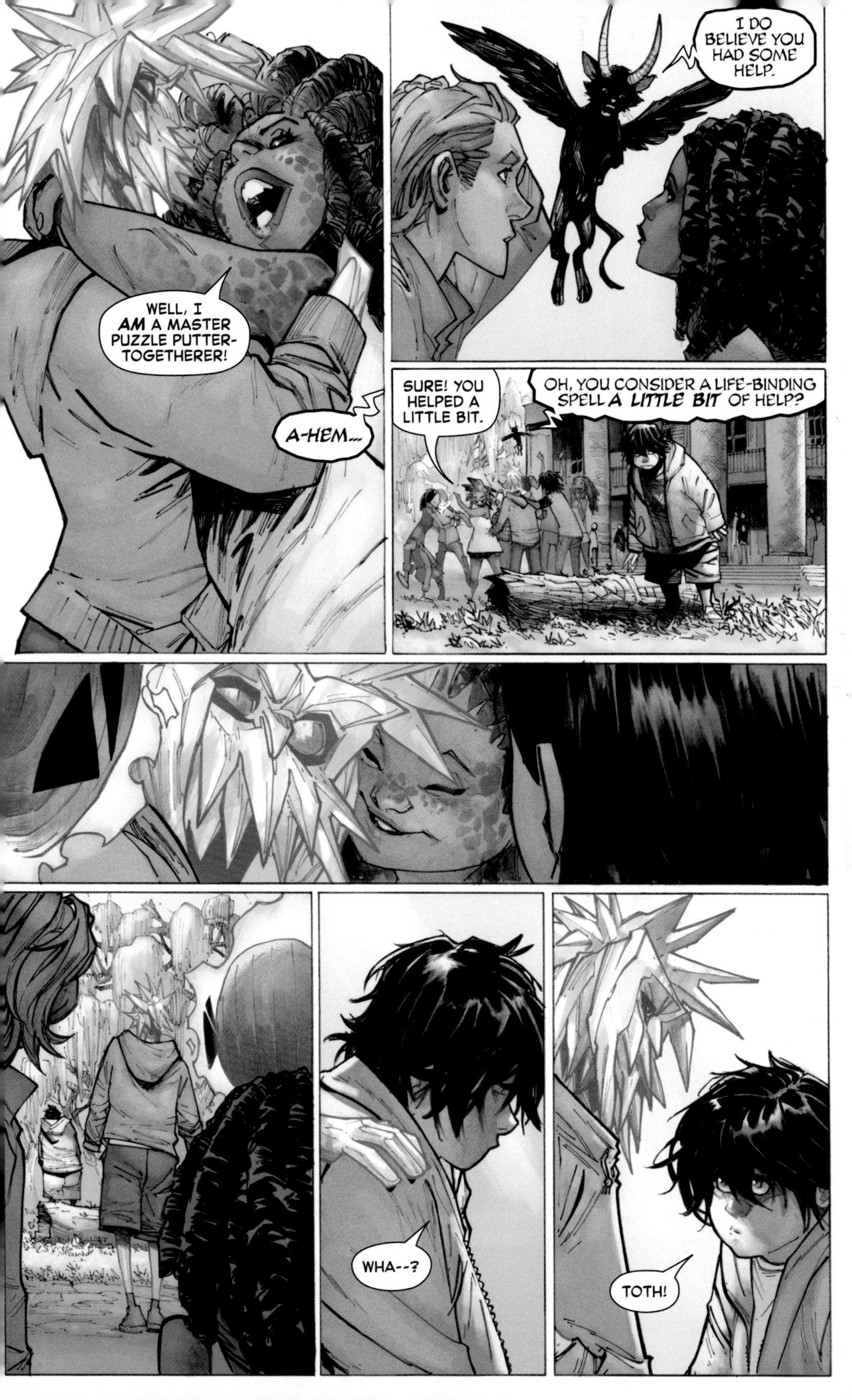
WELL, I AM A MASTER PUZZLE PUTTER-TOGETHERER!
A-HEM...
I DO BELIEVE YOU HAD SOME HELP.
SURE! YOU HELPED A LITTLE BIT.
OH, YOU CONSIDER A LIFE-BINDING SPELL A LITTLE BIT OF HELP?
WHA--?
TOTH!

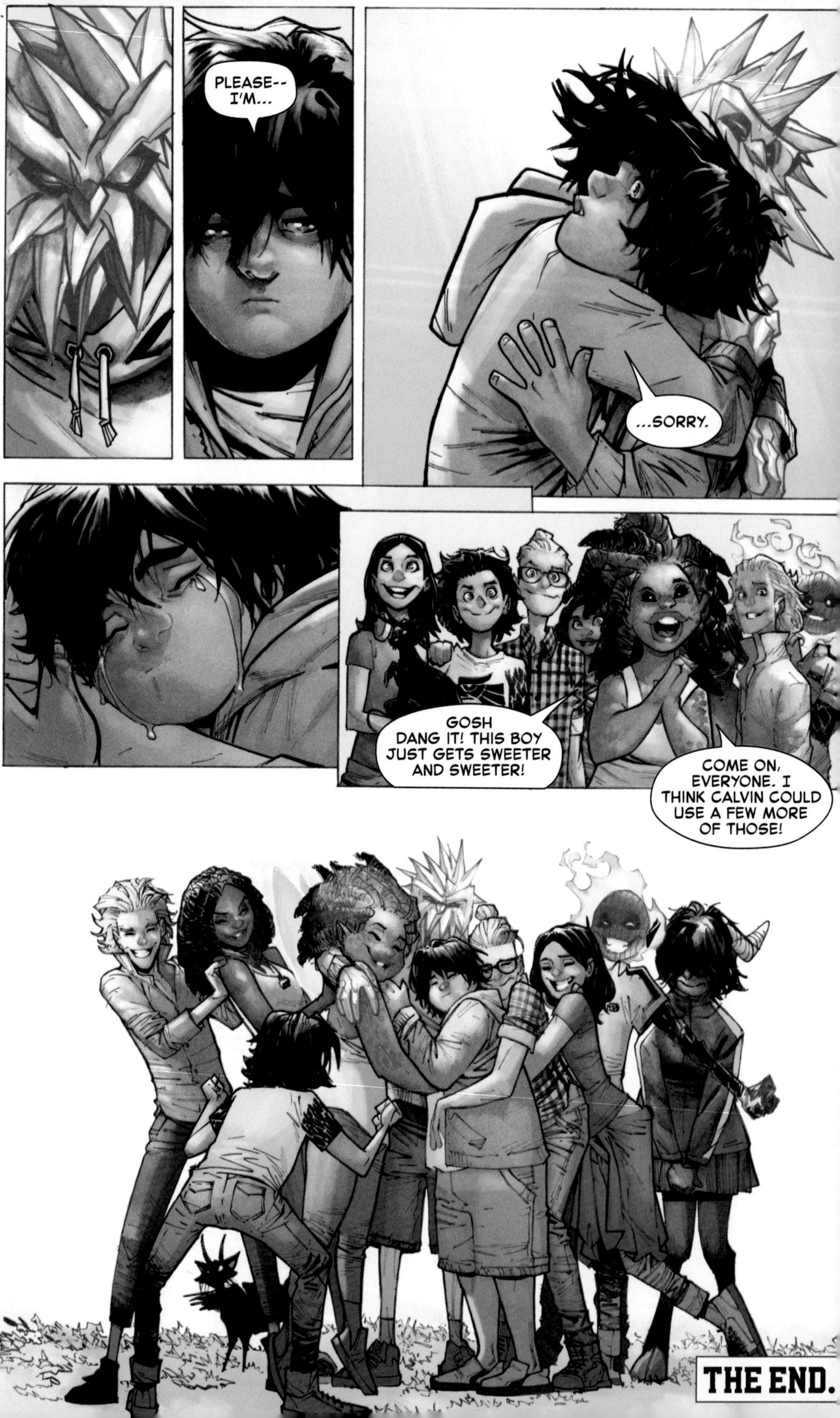
PLEASE-- I'M...
...SORRY.
GOSH DANG IT! THIS BOY JUST GETS SWEETER AND SWEETER!
COME ON, EVERYONE. I THINK CALVIN COULD USE A FEW MORE OF THOSE!
THE END.

ORCHESTRA CONCERT

BEETHOVEN'S TENTH SYMPHONY
(as posthumously divined and transcribed by Prof. Harkness)

Performed by the
SA ORACULAR ORCHESTRA

SOLOISTS
SHAYLEE MOONPEDDLE
(violin, with unicorn-hair bow)

ALVI BRORSON
(weirwood-reed oboe)

GERALDINE O'MALLEY
(harpy-hair harp)

GERMÁN AGUILAR
(bassoon)

*** The SA Jazz Band will perform for a post-concert social and be joined by local spectral guest musicians. ***

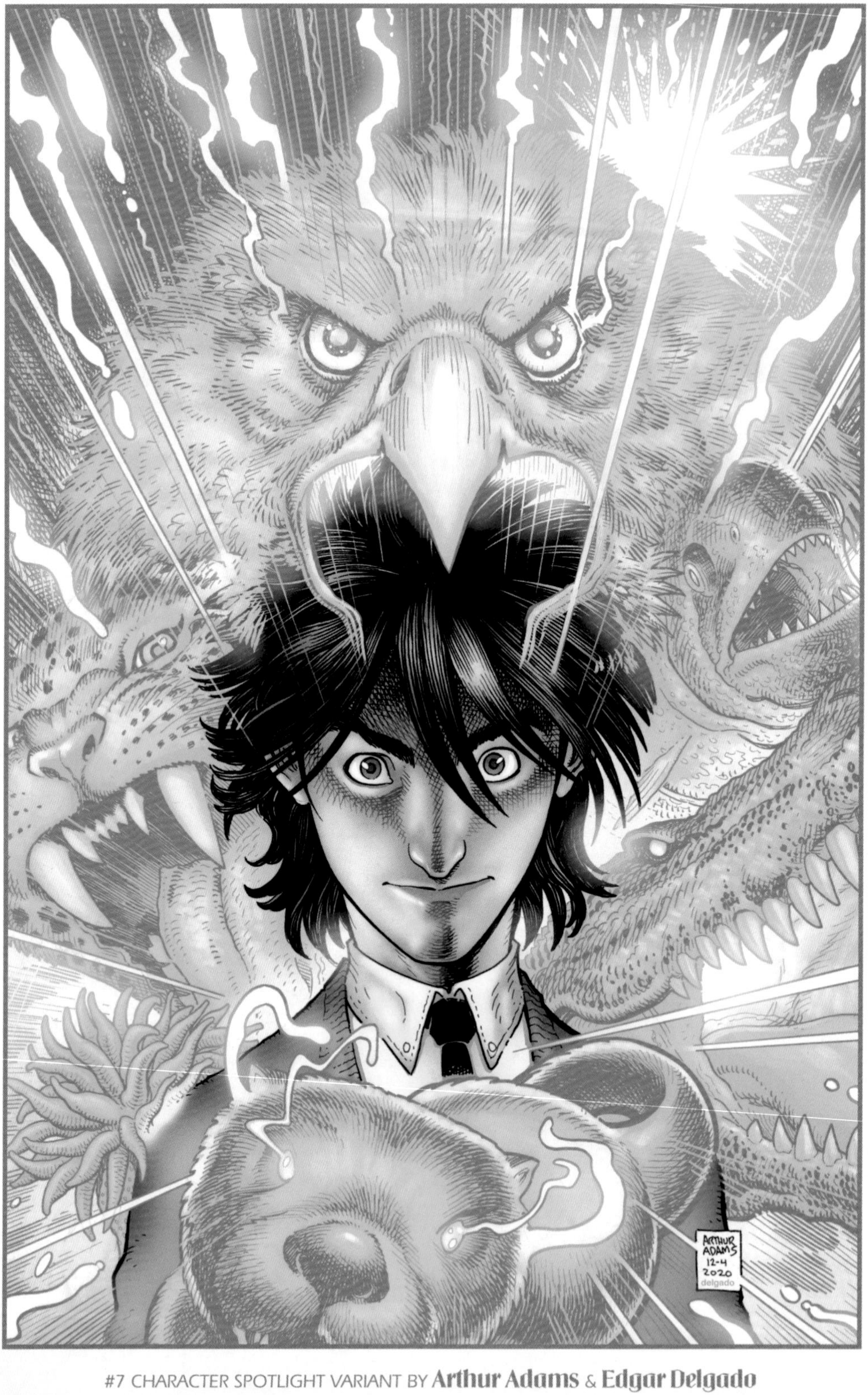
ARTHUR ADAMS 12-4 2020
delgado

#7 CHARACTER SPOTLIGHT VARIANT BY **Arthur Adams** & **Edgar Delgado**

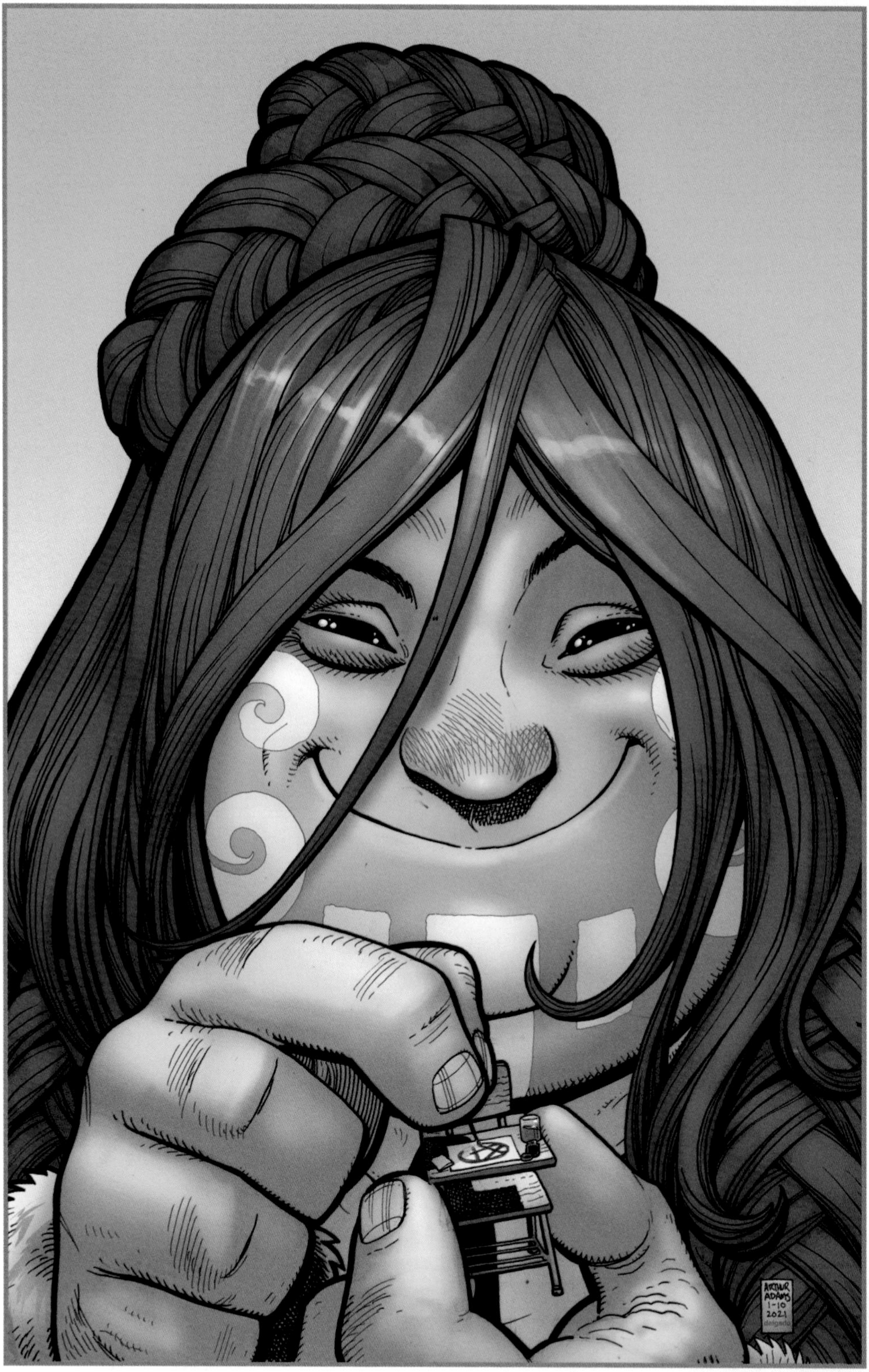
ARTHUR ADAMS
1-10
2021
delgado

#8 CHARACTER SPOTLIGHT VARIANT BY **Arthur Adams** & **Edgar Delgado**

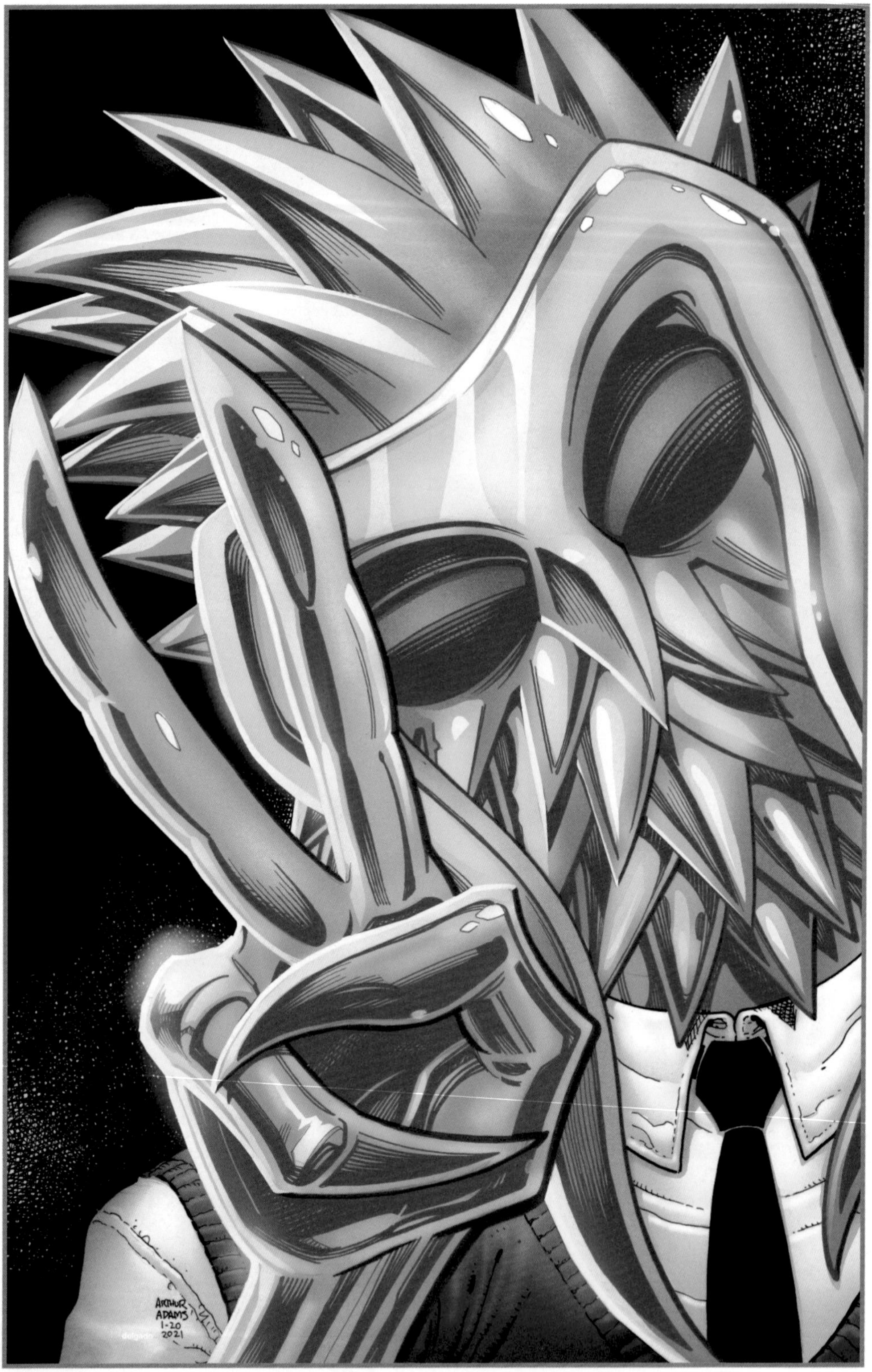
ARTHUR
ADAMS
1-20
2021

#9 CHARACTER SPOTLIGHT VARIANT BY **Arthur Adams** & **Edgar Delgado**

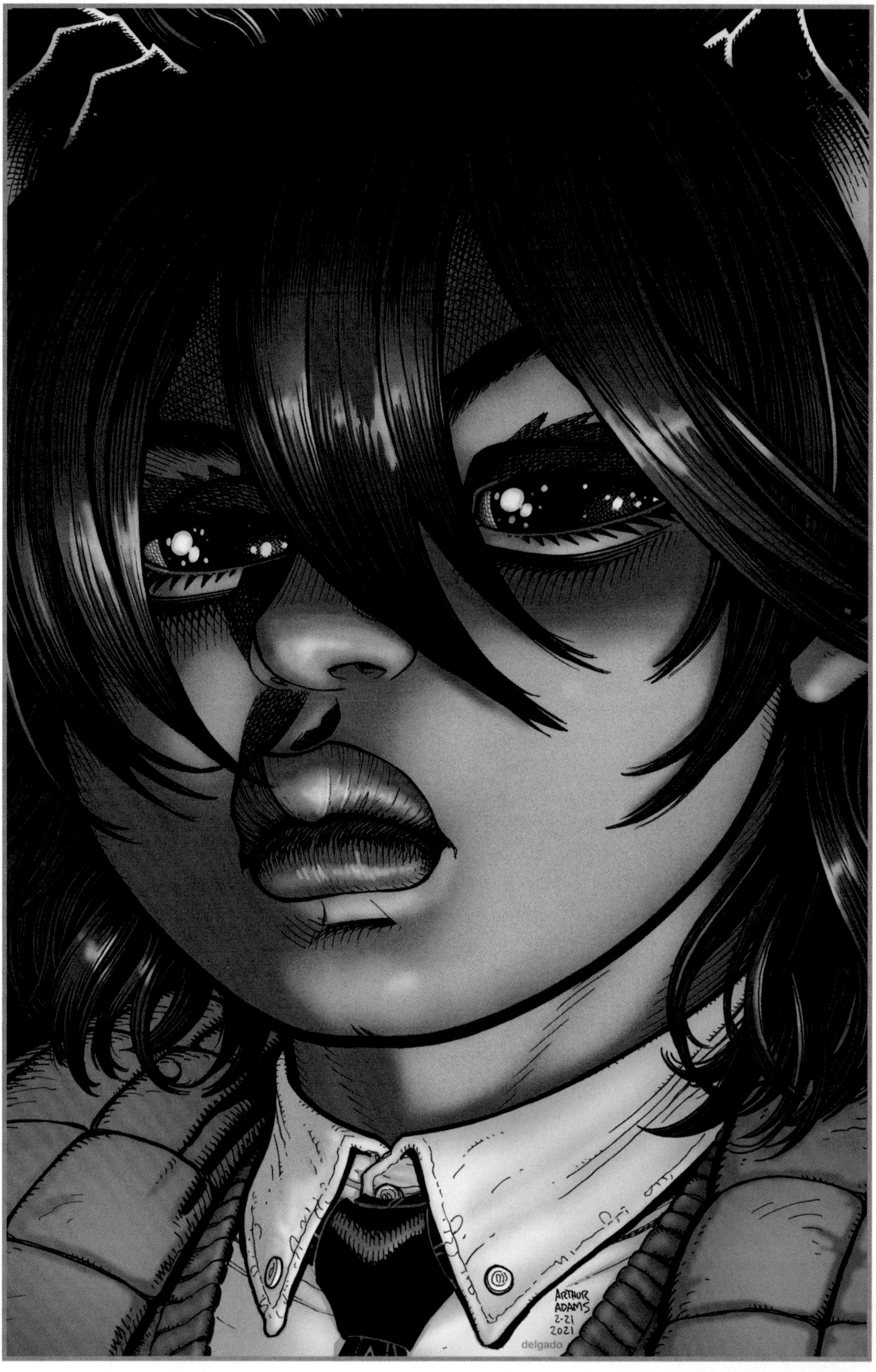
ARTHUR
ADAMS
2-21
2021
delgado

#10 CHARACTER SPOTLIGHT VARIANT BY **Arthur Adams** & **Edgar Delgado**

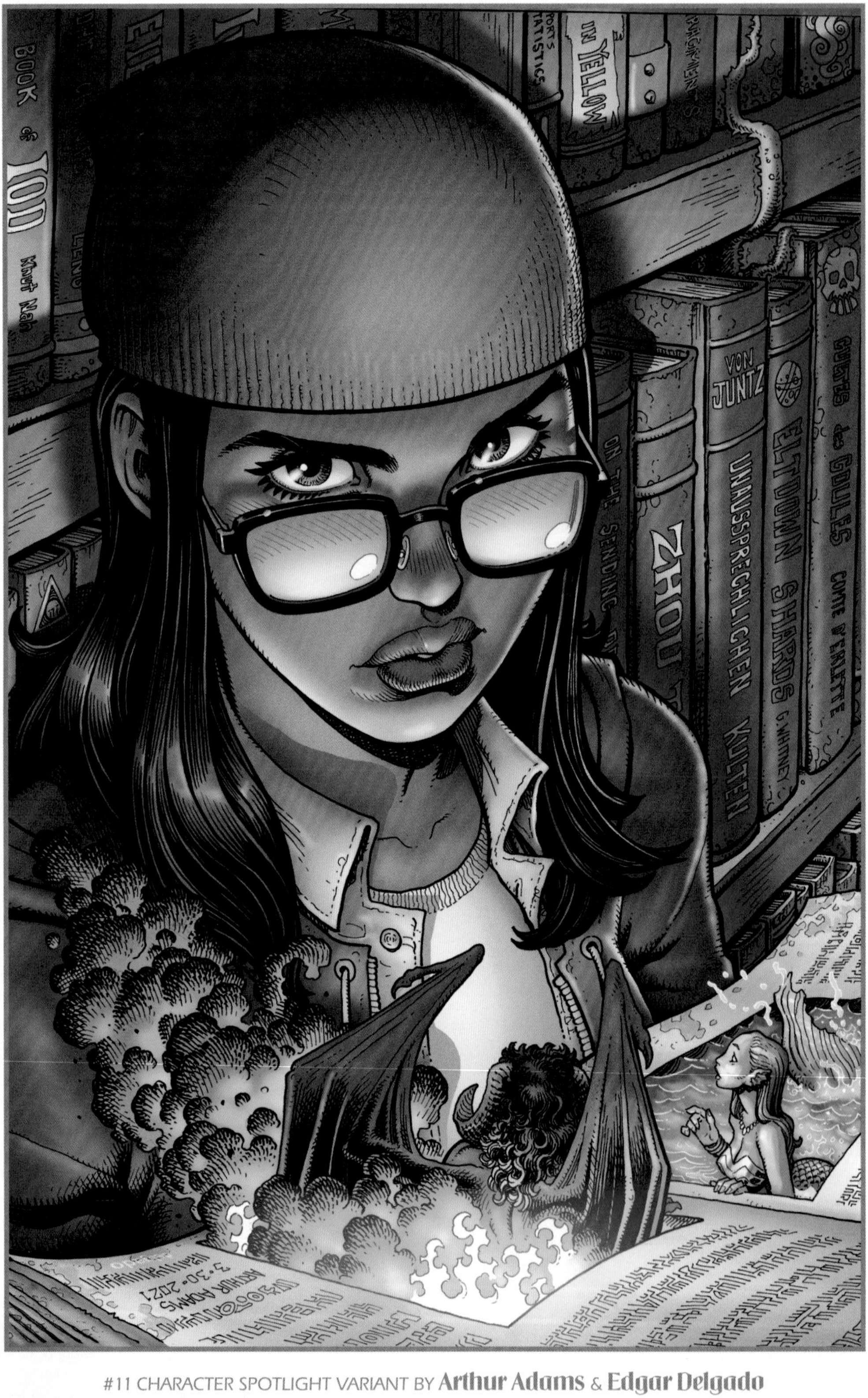
BOOK of IOD
SPORTS STATISTICS
IN YELLOW
VON JUNTZ
UNAUSSPRECHLICHEN KULTEN
ELTDOWN SHARDS
G. WHITNEY
CULTES des GOULES
COMTE d'ERLETTE
ZHOU
ON THE SENDING

#11 CHARACTER SPOTLIGHT VARIANT BY **Arthur Adams** & **Edgar Delgado**

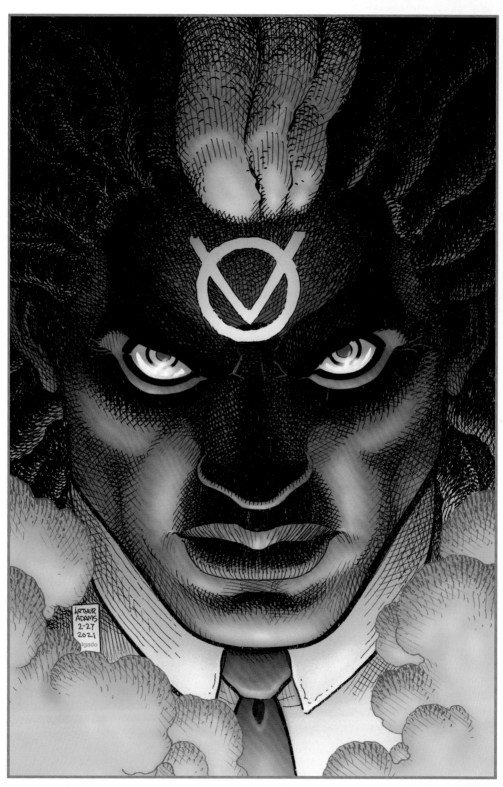

#12 CHARACTER SPOTLIGHT VARIANT BY **Arthur Adams** & **Edgar Delgado**

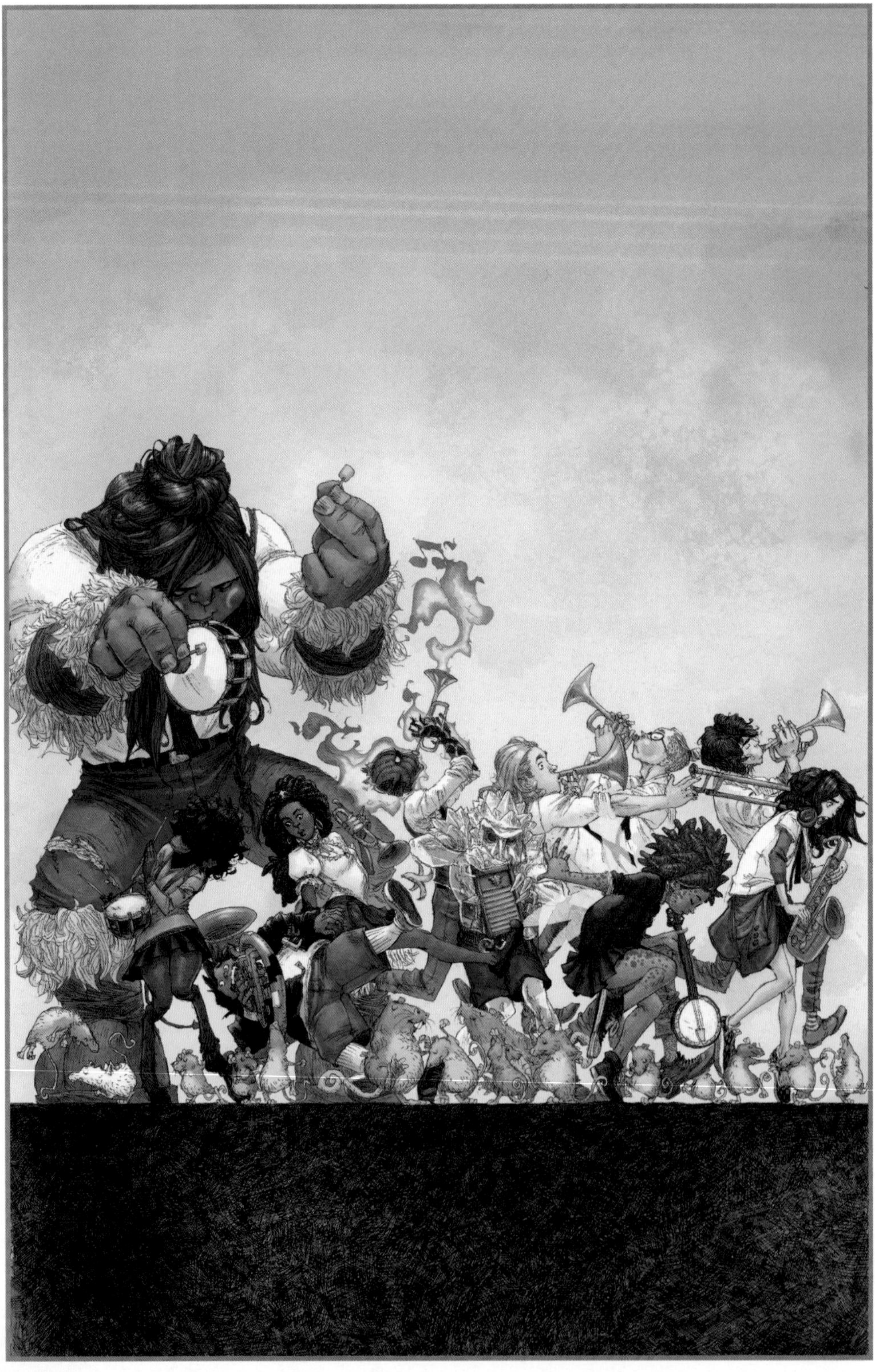

#7 VARIANT BY **Adrian Alphona** & **Dave Stewart**

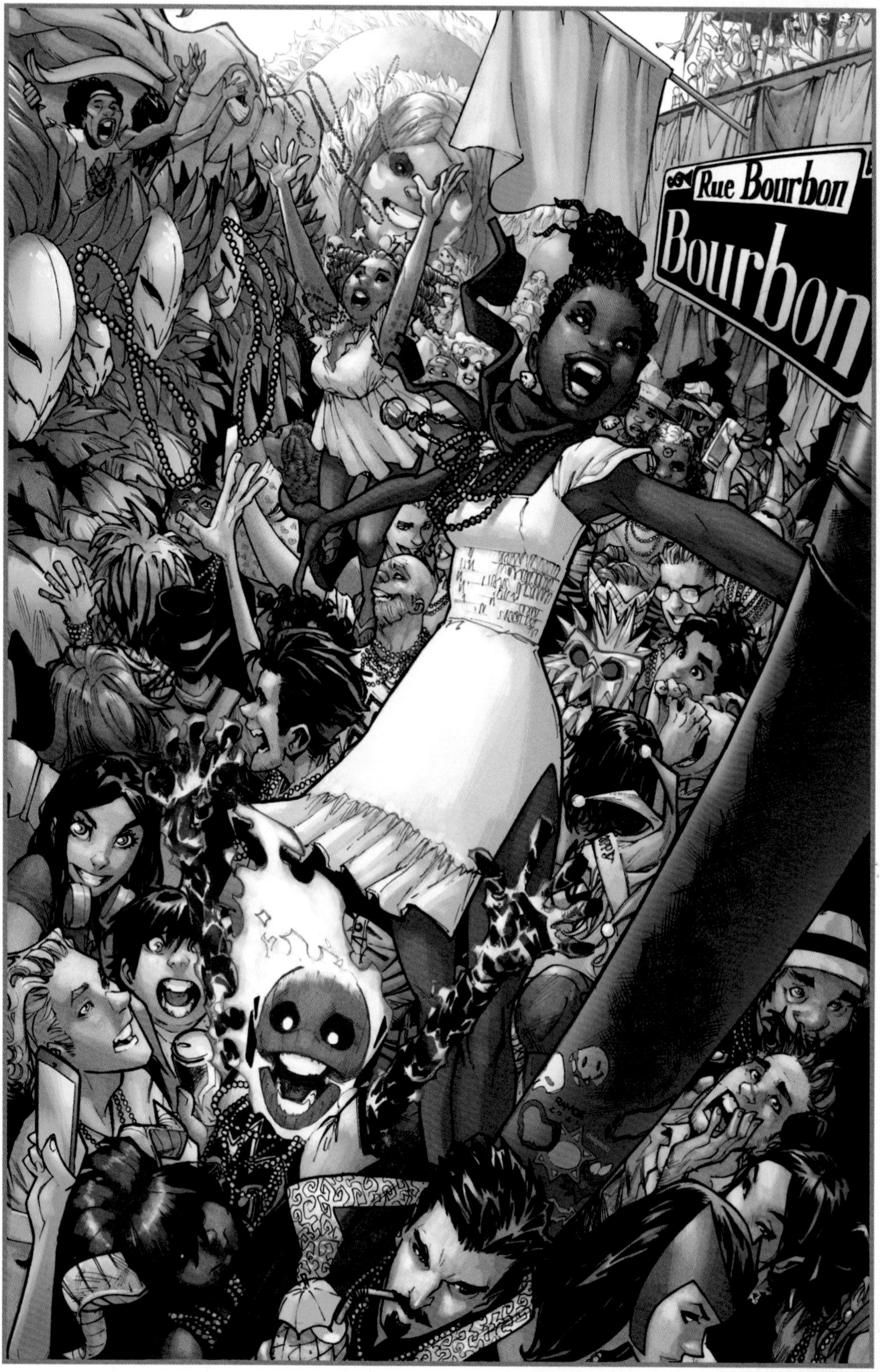
Rue Bourbon
Bourbon

#8 MARDI GRAS VARIANT BY **Humberto Ramos** & **Edgar Delgado**

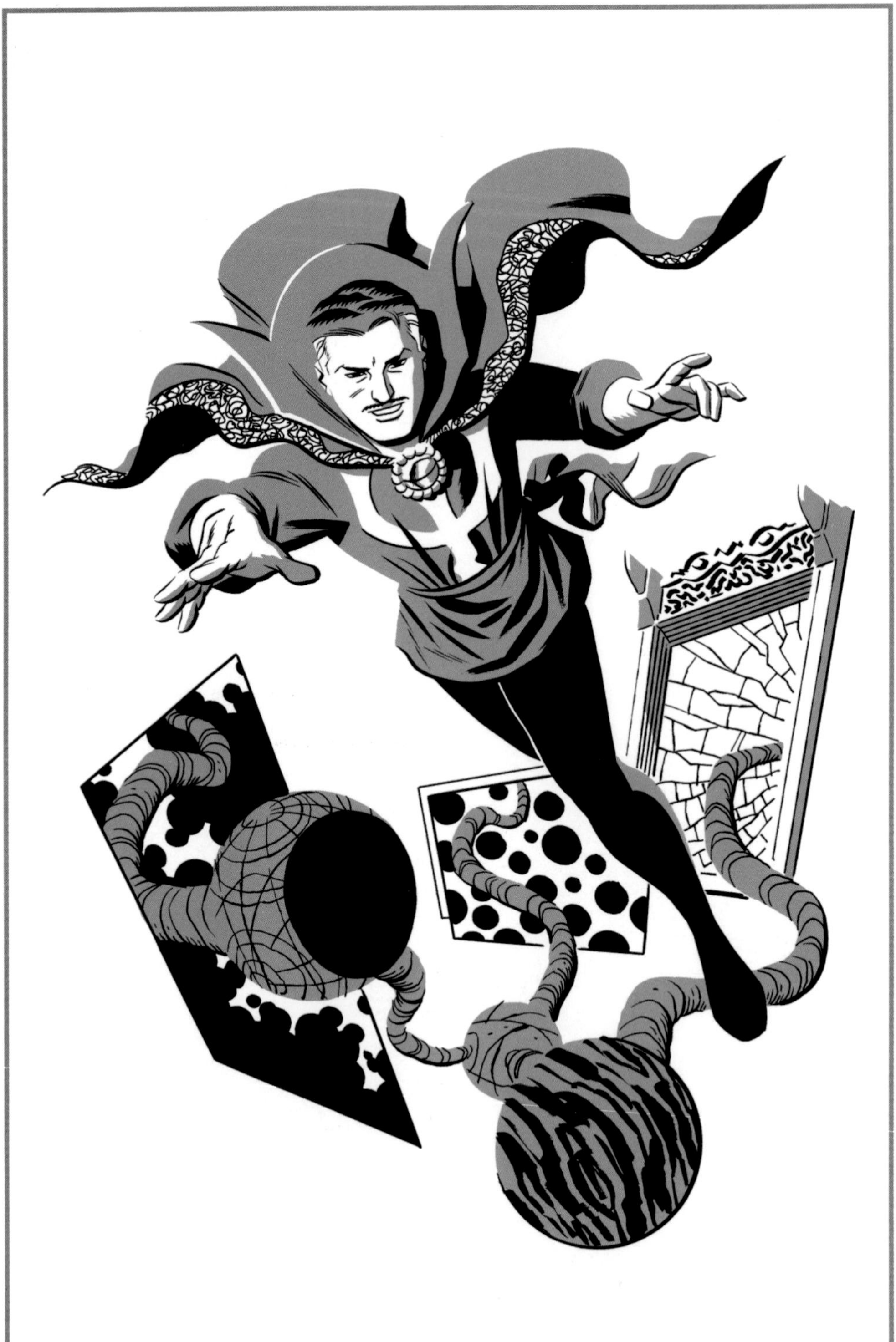

#9 TWO-TONE VARIANT BY **Michael Cho**